MAVISBAI

By

George Donald

CHAPTER ONE

Samuel William Fullerton had been forty-one years of age when his rusting freighter was torpedoed in the unforgiving wintery waters of the Atlantic Ocean and just turned forty-three when for the second time in two years, he had the misfortune to be aboard a targeted ship; on that occasion an oil tanker sailing in convoy in the warmer waters of the Mediterranean.

When in the dark of the starlit night the ship struck a mine in the coastal waters several miles off the island of Malta, Sam had by chance been on deck having a quick and illicit cigarette. Within minutes he found himself thrashing in the rough sea desperately clinging to the side of an upturned, but badly damaged life raft. Disorientated, without a lifejacket and terror-stricken, he had tried to kick the raft away from the dying ship, aware that as she went down she would create a vacuum that would engulf then drag the few survivors and floating debris to the bottom with her. Desperately, he had found himself among other survivors of the blast a short but safe distance before she went down, then listened to the panicked screams of his shipmates about him as they drowned, their lungs filling with the oil that continued to discharge from the bowels of the holed tanker as she settled deeper into the water. His hands numb and to his everlasting shame, he choked back his cries that there was safety on his upturned life raft, suddenly frightened that too many panicked men would fight for a handhold and thus compromise his own safety. As the long minutes passed he watched in dismay as the darkened shape of the convoy sailed away, their Captains too fearful to stop and assist survivors because they did not know it was a mine and suspected a

German submarine was responsible for sinking the tanker and might continue to lurk and seek another target.

Then came the awful quiet and listening in the darkness, heard some of his shipmates calling for help that Sam knew would not come. Some pled for their wives, their sweethearts or their mothers. Still others cursed their God or the sailors in the distant convoy who they believed had abandoned them.

In the moonlight as he drifted closer to some of the men he could see their faces shiny with oil, gasping as they tried to draw air into their damaged lungs then gurgling their last as they slipped beneath the waves.

Even now, thirty-four years after the sinking of the tanker, when he closed his eyes or tried to sleep he could still smell and taste the the oil and hear the dying sailors crying out.

For three, long and parched days he had clung to the damaged raft as it aimlessly floated on the still waters, his body aching, too weak to climb out of the water until at last a Maltese fishing boat crew spotted the wrecked life raft and pulled him from the sea.

The terrifying experience had shaped his life and though it would be the nineteen-seventies before the term Post Traumatic Stress Disorder was recognised and identified, Sam and many others like him lived with their demons for the remainder of their lives.

Unable to explain his wartime experience, his marriage failed. His children and family, incapable of understanding his mood swings, the night-time terrors and eventually, the addiction to alcohol, gradually drifted from his life until at last the seventy-three years old Sam found himself living rough in the derelict sheds and warehouses along the River Clyde where his seagoing career had begun and where once in the heady days of the Empire, he signed onto ships to travel to far-flung lands.

On that dark and dismal evening Sam glanced up at the rain filled clouds and took the route through the twisted remains of the docks cranes and derelict machinery towards the warehouse he knew that would best serve him as shelter for that night.

His collar length grey hair and ragged beard were matted with dirt, his hands and legs covered in festering sores and the clothes he wore, salvaged from dustbins, now ridden with lice. In his hands he carried two plastic bags, one of which contained his worldly possessions; a woollen jumper, a spare pair of baseball shoes two sizes too large and a pair of baggy suit trousers, both gifted earlier that week by the Glasgow charity, the Simon Community. The second, larger plastic bag contained a rolled up sleeping bag that Sam had opportunistically stolen from a fellow down and out who to his misfortune, rolled off it when drunk.

In one pocket of his old and tattered overcoat, he carried a paper bag containing two cold sausage rolls he had recovered from the bin behind the City Bakeries on Paisley Road West while in the other pocket he had a half bottle of Lanliq, the cheap fortifying wine know as 'the Lannie' or 'electric soup' and much favoured by the less affluent drinkers of Glasgow's abandoned society.

Time meant little to Sam and he had no wristwatch, but his inner clock reckoned it was somewhere between seven thirty and eight pm.

Time enough, he grinned to himself, for a bite and a wee swally of the Lannie.

The large metal doors into the warehouse had been padlocked years before by the owners, but the derelict condition of the building left many places where a man could squeeze through the wriggly tin walls into the dark and dismal interior.

Setting his plastic bags down, Sam pulled aside a sheet of tin and pulling the bags in after him, cautiously made his way to where he would intend sleeping for the night.

He had been in the warehouse he reckoned for less than an hour when he thought he heard the sound of a vehicle.

Aware that the Govan polis sometimes patrolled the dock area looking for lead thieves, Sam carefully made his way to the metal wall that faced out into the River Clyde and through a hole in the wriggly tin, peered out with watery eyes into the darkness.

"Aye," he mumbled to himself, "I was right enough, it's a motor."

Though his eyesight was failing, Sam squinted and was sure he could distinguish two separate dark figures that stood beside the car and turning away, rubbed with his knuckles at both eyes. Glancing again through the hole he saw one of the figures drop a white hat to the ground, or so it seemed to him.

Time I tried to get some glasses, he thought and rubbed again at his watery eyes.

Just as he was about to again peer through the hole and though dull of hearing, he thought he heard a woman scream and then a splash and a moment later, the sound of the car being driven off.

Sam reflected on what it was he had seen, but knew whatever it was it had nothing to do with him. Still, his eyes narrowed, it was odd the woman screamed before the splash and he idly wondered…but then his eyes took in the bottle of Lanliq and all thought of the incident left him.

A quick swig, a lick at his lips and the moment passed, then grunting he decided it was really nothing to do with him and turned to sit with his back to the metal wall. With anticipatory delight, he fetched the sausage rolls from the bag and devouring them, took his time savouring the remainder of the cheap wine.

****

The Metrological Office forecast for the September weather of 1977 predicted outbreaks of rain in the early part of that month that threatened to affect most of the northern and western areas of Scotland.

That of course included Glasgow and was proving to be horribly correct.

Staring through the rain lashed windscreen of their three door, blue and white Ford Escort panda car on that evening of Saturday, the ninth day of the month, the two uniformed officers bemoaned their luck to be on late shift while most of the citizens of that great city dressed in their party clothes and geared up to celebrate the start of the weekend in the city centre pubs and clubs.

The driver of the panda that was parked in the the darkness of the lane behind the former Burtons shop at Paisley Road Toll facing the brightly lit Paisley Road West was forty-four-year-old Iain Meikle, a constable with twenty-five years' service and a 'seen it, done it' attitude that frequently irked his Inspector, shift Sergeant and any other bugger who worked with him.

That said though nobody would dispute Iain's beat savvy and encyclopaedic knowledge of the residents of those beats and though he didn't think about it, he was a popular member of his shift. Sighing heavily, he idly picked at the greasy pie and chips from the newspaper wrapping on his lap.

Burping, he reached for the can of Irn-Bru on the dashboard and took a deep swallow.

"Fancy a drink at my place when we knock off?" he turned to his neighbour, thirty-eight-year-old Eric Little who finishing his sausage supper, wound down the passenger window and chucked the crushed newspaper wrapping into the already littered lane.

"No," Little slowly shook his head. "Her indoors expects me back on time. She's got her mother and sister Gemma up for a wee social evening while I'm on the backshift and I've to run them home when I get in after work."

"Well, if there's a sister-in-law to meet, why don't I come back to your place for a drink then?" the divorced Iain grinned teasingly at him before asking, "Is she married?"

Little gave him a sharp look then returning his grin, replied, "No, she's not now, but put it this way, Iain. If I didn't like you, I'd *let* you come back home with me. Her mother has been trying to offload Gemma for the last five years."

"Oh, that bad?" Iain frowned.

"Ugly doesn't do her justice. Put it this way, when Gemma's husband divorced her, he cited waking up next to her each morning was excessive cruelty," Little shuddered then glancing at his wristwatch, scowled and continued, "I thought you told me that Les would meet us here at about nine? It's gone that now by fifteen minutes."

"Maybe she got a call," Iain shrugged, referring to the police parlance for officers attending to a complaint or an incident.

"Can't be that, we would have heard it come over the radio," Little replied.

"What, these bloody things," Iain flicked a finger at the Burndept radio in the top pocket of his tunic. "Before we left the office I tried three of them until I got one that works or is supposed to be bloody working," the disgust in his voice clearly evident.

"It's the batteries. They're all well past their sell by date," Little sighed. "Anyway, I heard we're supposed to be getting new radios soon."

"What, like we're supposed to be getting this magical pay rise too," Iain said then leaning forward to wipe the condensation from the widow, muttered "Where the hell is she?"

Little grinned at him.

"What?" he threw him a dark scowl.

"I'm thinking you've got the hots for our Lesley."

"Course I have," Iain scoffed. "Me and every other red-blooded male in the office. I mean, she's blonde, she's good looking and she's got great tits. Why wouldn't I fancy her?"

"Think you're in with a chance then?"

He turned to stare at Little as though his neighbour had lost his mind. "Look, I'm forty-five on my next birthday. She's what, twenty-six or twenty-seven? She's passed both her exams and looking to be on the next promotion parade while I'm a one-ticket man stuck here at Govan and can barely spell my own name. She drives a year old Mini and has bought her own place over in Langside somewhere. I'm living in a two-bedroom lower cottage flat in Mosspark and drive a banger." He shrugged and with a soft smile, added, "Well, when I say a banger, I really mean a classic car."

"What?" Little turned to stare incredulously at him. "You mean that clapped out old Vauxhall Viva that you polish once a week to try and hide the dents?"

"Aye, you're mocking me now, but that car will be worth a right few bob in a couple of years," Iain sniffed.

"Only if you fill it with petrol," Little retorted.

"Anyway," Iain ignored the jibe and continued, "what I was saying is that Les takes two foreign holidays a year. I'm divorced five years now from a woman that was a real ballbreaker who took and continues to take me for every penny I make and makes it difficult for me to see my boy."

"How old is he now, by the way?" Little quietly asked.

"James? He's fourteen now and the last time I spoke with him he seems to be going through the teenage angst that every adult is an idiot and will never understand him. No," he smiled and slowly shook his head, "That makes him sound like a monster, but the truth is, Eric, we've got a really good relationship and I try to see him at least once a month, but his mother makes it difficult and usually sets the visiting time and date for when she knows I'm on a late shift or night shift; never my day off. If it wasn't for my ex's mother Jill, I wouldn't get to see him at all."

"Your mother-in-law? You still in touch with her?"

"Aye, I am. Jill's the bees-knees and knows fine what her daughter's like."

"Carol still giving you a hard time, then?" Little sympathised.

"Oh, aye, it's an obsession with her, taunting me. Seems to forget it's her that left me and it didn't take her long to find herself another man either or should I say men; usually guys with good paying jobs too as she frequently reminds me when she's on the phone bending my ear about something or other. Likes the good things in life, does my ex, and let's face it, a cop's salary could never keep her in the style she wants, torn faced bitch that she is." he bitterly said. "But in fairness, when we were married she only ever moaned and whined with a day that ended in a Y," and grinned.

"And what about Lesley? Think you might be in with a chance there?"

"What, Les and me? We're that compatible, so we are," he shook his head before adding, "I like Les but let's face it, Eric, she's a pal and that's it. End of story."

They sat for another couple of minutes before Iain decided, "Look, she'll likely be on her way coming to us along Paisley Road West." Starting the engine, he continued, "Let's take a wee turn along the road and we'll try to see if we can find her, eh?"

Turning right from the lane into the main arterial road that travelled west towards Paisley, he drove through along the rain soaked road at a sedate pace until a minute later he heard Little ask, "Who's that?"

They could see a male police officer crossing the road a hundred yards in front of them and walking towards Cornwall Street.

Iain sounded the horn and saw the officer hesitate before turning back towards the car that stopped beside him.

To their surprise it was their shift sergeant, Jimmy Cole, who bent down to stare at them, his nylon raincoat glistening in the rain and drops of water dripping from his peaked cap.

Iain wound down the window and greeted him with, "Hello, Sarge. Didn't expect to see you out in this weather," he struggled to prevent his voice betray the contempt he held for Cole.

"Well, I'm here, aren't I?" Cole growled, "so why don't you get out and let me into the back seat?"

Grunting, Iain opened the door and stepping out into the rain, he turned to push back the drivers seat to permit Cole to climb into the rear of the vehicle. When the sergeants back was turned, Iain made eye contact with Little who tight-lipped, raised his eyebrows.

Returning to his seat Iain closed the door and suspected that the presence of Cole meant something was up for it was well known that the sergeant frequently found excuses not to leave the office unless he was obliged to do so. Even the obligatory checks he was required to make during the shift to ensure his officers were patrolling their beats, when he was supposed to sign the constables' notebooks with the time and location he met with them was falsified, preferring them to leave a line clear and later made the entry in the notebook prior to their end of shift.

Did the officers complain?

No they didn't because it left them free to attend their calls, check their properties and visit their howffs for a cuppa or for those who enjoyed a drink, a pint when it suited them without the worry of Cole shouting for their position.

Removing his sodden cap, Cole said, "Hand me your notebooks and I'll give you a sign while I'm here."

There's a first, thought Little, but did as he was bid as did Iain beside him.

"So, why are you two down here at fourteen beat and not patrolling the Pollokshields? I didn't hear any calls for this area."

Cole didn't miss the brief glance Iain gave his neighbour before he turned in his seat and brittlely replied, "You put Lesley Rudd out on the Toll beat on her own, Sarge. This is Saturday night, for Christ's sake. With the number of busy pubs around here, if something kicks off she's bound to get herself a sore face. The 'Shields is dead at the minute, so me and Eric thought we'd come down to give her a hand if she needs it."

"And does she?" Cole pursed his lips, his voice oozing sarcasm as he handed the notebooks back to Little. "I don't see her sitting here beside me and it seems quiet enough at the minute. Where is she anyway?"

"Don't know," Iain shrugged his shoulders. "We told her we'd be here about nine, but," he glanced at his wristwatch, "it's gone half past now and she hasn't showed."

Cole frowned and asked, "Is she on a call or something?"

"Like I said, we haven't heard anything on our radios, have we Eric?" and watched as Little shook his head. "But saying that, these bloody things are worse than useless. We haven't heard any calls at all."

Cole inhaled as though about to retort, but instead loosened the top button of his raincoat and pulling it back, fetched the radio from the breast pocket of his tunic. Pressing the button, he said, "Sergeant Cole to G Golf control."

His call was answered almost immediately by John 'Hammy' Hammond, the shifts controller who told him to go ahead.

"Hammy, can you give me the current position of G three-five-four, please?"

They listened as Hammond called twice for the position of G three-five-four, Lesley Rudd's shoulder number, but there was no response.

"Sorry, Sarge, nothing heard, over."

"When and what was her last call?"

There was a slight pause while Hammond checked his incident log then replied, "She said she was on her way there just after eight-fifteen, Sarge. Report of a drunk lying in Middlesex Street at the corner of Scotland Street, over."

"Lying in the street in this bloody weather?" Cole muttered, then pressing the button, said, "Did she result the call, over?"

Again a slight pause before Hammond said, "No, we're still waiting for a result, Sarge, over."

"Okay, thanks Hammy, out."

Cole returned his radio to his pocket and with a sigh, said, "Right, let's take a turn past Scotland Street and see if we can find her. If I'm out in this shitty weather, I might as well get her notebook signed too."

Puzzled, Iain turned and asked, "Have you not got the supervisory panda with you, Sarge?"

His face flushed from the body heat of three grown men in the confined space of the small car, Cole shook his head and replied, "No, Inspector Kane is using it tomorrow morning first thing to visit Pitt Street again and left a note it wasn't to be used. Something about an inquiry or some kind of review he is working on for the Divisional Commander. I walked here."

"Oh," was all Iain said and starting the engine, idly wondered who had lit the torch under Cole's arse that so worried him enough to get him away from his desk to walk all the way in the rain from the Orkney Street office.

****

In Orkney Street police office, the dilapidated Victorian office headquarters of 'G' Division whose officers had responsibility for policing the south-west of Glasgow, Constable John Hammond sat at his desk at the control consul in the corner of the uniform bar. He glanced up as the indoor Inspector, Willie McCrae, leaned on top of the stand alone room divider and peering down at the seated Hammond, asked, "What's up, anything doing?"

Hammond removed his headphones and sighing, stared up at McCrae before replying, "That plonker Cole has lost one of his cops, young Lesley Rudd."

Hammond felt safe in making his derisory remark about James Cole, aware that the twenty-eight years old sergeant and university graduate, a product of the police Advanced Promotion Scheme was disliked by the worldly-wise Inspector. McCrae. Whippet thin due to his overindulgence in Scotland's best export, McCrae bore a face with so many broken veins it resembled a roadmap. Shrugging, he shook his head and said, "Anything to suggest the lassie's in any kind of bother?"

"Nope," Hammond shook his head. "The last call Lesley had was to a drunk lying in the street and that was called in and timed at," Hammond glanced down at his incident log, "thirteen minutes past eight. I put the call out to Lesley a couple of minutes later."

McCrae turned to glance at the large clock on the wall above his own desk and muttered, "It's almost half past nine and you've not heard from her since she acknowledged she was attending the call?"

"No, sir, but you know what the bloody radios are like. Half of them aren't working and most of the batteries are duds."

McCrae frowned before a thought occurred and he asked, "What's Cole doing out in the street anyway? He never leaves his bloody office."

"No idea, sir. Popped in here a couple of hours ago to say he was going out to get some notebooks signed when you were on a comfort beak," which was Hammond's subtle way of explaining one of McCrae's frequent absences to the gents lavvy for a nip of whisky.

McCrae, who had less than three months to serve before retirement and resented the idea of anyone or anything fucking it up, stared thoughtfully at Hammond then asked, "Anything else happening in the sub-division? Anything that I should know about?"

Hammond pursed his lips and replied, "The weather's keeping most folks indoor, sir. Couple of the lads attended a domestic over in the wine alley, a ground flat in Kellas Street where the wife apparently chastised her husband with a frying pan to the coupon, but he's not making a complaint. A breach of the peace arrested down in Linthouse, but nothing else of note at the minute. So, apart from that I'm guessing most of the shift are in howffs somewhere having a cuppa."

Or a maybe beer if they've any sense, but kept that thought to himself.

McCrae's eyebrows narrowed. Young Rudd was a nice wee lassie, he thought and for a woman, not a bad polis; sharp and motivated and in the recent past brought in some good captures too, he grudgingly admitted. It wasn't like her to be out of touch on the radio.

"Who's her neighbour this evening?" he asked.

Hammond shook his head and lifting the beat list from his desk, handed it up to McCrae.

"She's on fourteen and fifteen beats on her tod, sir, but Iain and big Eric are neighboured up in the Pollokshields panda, so I'm guessing they'll be keeping an eye on her."

"She's working the Toll beats on her own?" McCrae was surprised, for it was common knowledge the Paisley Road Toll beat with its large number of licensed premises was one of the busiest beats in the sub-division and well before the pubs closed and kicked out their drunks, most supervisory officers routinely deployed extra officers to assist the regular beat men to prepare for the fights and assaults that followed the heavy drinking.

McCrae's lips tightened and inhaling, he snapped and formally instructed Hammond, "Tell Sergeant Cole from me that he is to deploy what officers he has in the adjoining beats and trace Constable Rudd forthwith. It's not like that young lassie to be out of touch," he worriedly shook his head, his concern etched in his face.

"Right away, sir," Hammond acknowledged with a nod and reached for the microphone.

****

The nightshift began to arrive twenty minutes before their shift commenced at eleven that evening and collecting their tunics, caps and equipment from their lockers, assembled in the muster room.

Initially surprised to find none of the late shift were gathering to go off duty, the reason soon became clear.

One of the late shift, Lesley Rudd who was known to them all, was missing.

In low voices, the constables muttered among themselves, opining where Rudd might have got to and though it was jokingly suggested she might be lying pissed in some pub or, as one shift wag suggested, simply forgotten the time while lying in somebody's bed, an undercurrent of uneasiness filled the room.

"It's not like her," a young female constable frowned at her neighbour. "Lesley's like a machine out there. I had to neighbour her last week when she was on overtime and she never stopped; marched me round eleven beat like it was some sort of race. Knackered me before my piece break, so she did," the constable shook her head at the memory.

"Right, listen in," their burly shift Inspector Bob Munroe, his tunic undone and his cap in his hand, stepped out of the sergeant's room with his hands raised to quell the hubbub of noise. "You've all heard that Lesley Rudd hasn't been answering her radio and there is growing concern as to her whereabouts, so with Sergeant Cole her late shift supervisor I'm coordinating a search of fourteen and fifteen beats to find the lassie. Sergeant Smyth is already attending with some of the Pollok late shift and the Duty Superintendent will be arriving shortly to take charge of the search, but before he arrives I want both shifts out there looking for her, okay? Any questions?"

"Do you think something has happened to Lesley, sir?" asked Shona Murtagh, the younger of the two female constables asked.

"The short answer is I hope not," he grimly replied.

"What about outstanding calls, sir? We'll need to get them seen to as well," a stoutly built, middle-aged, grey haired and whiskered constable had his hand raised.

"Aye," Munroe rubbed at his forehead before replying, "good point, Charlie. You take young Harris there," he pointed to the acne faced late shift probationary constable, "and grab the keys to a CID car. Deal with what you can. Prioritise the calls and for God's sake, try not to give anybody the jail because that will only tie you up processing the prisoner, okay?"

"Sir," Charlie acknowledged.

"Will we not need all the vehicles to search for Lesley, sir?" asked another constable.

"No, we'll be conducting our search on foot. Closes, gardens, backcourts, the tenements on on both beats and any buildings that are empty and all the dunnies. One thing. If you are searching the empty buildings, be careful because some of them are like death traps, the state they're in. Any other questions? No? Right then, gather around and I'll designate the areas you've to search."

****

The Traffic car stopped outside the main entrance to Orkney

Street and while the Traffic Sergeant driver remained in the car to monitor the All Stations radio network, the duty Superintendent, Michael Alison, pulled his lanky six foot four inch frame from the front passenger seat. Placing his cap on his head he glanced up at the darkened sky before reaching down into the car and lifting his brown leather gloves and pace stick from the dashboard. Most of Allison's nineteen years of police service had been deskbound and it was unkindly rumoured by his peers that he had never actually ever seen an angry man. Belonging to that small genre of senior officers who believed that appearance instilled confidence in the lower ranks, Alison pulled the hem of his tunic sharply down before glancing up at the dark skies and falling rain then quickly turned and hurriedly strode towards the once ornate but now badly worn front doors. Pushing through the inner doors into the wide entrance, he rapped his knuckles on the public counter of the uniform bar to attract the attention of the bar officer, Colin Watson.

Turning at the sound, Watson paled at the sight of the imposing tall, uniformed man and thought, of all the superintendents to be on duty it had to be that big, humourless bastard Alison. Hurriedly he made his way to unlock the side door that led into the uniform bar and greeted the superintendent with, "Hello, sir."

At his desk, Willie McCrae hastily bundled a handful of strong mints into his mouth before respectfully standing to greet Alison.

"Good evening, Inspector McCrae, what do we have?"

Ignoring the constable, Alison strode past Watson to stand in front of McCrae's desk.

Lifting a sheet of paper from his desk to prompt himself, McCrae responded, "Constable Lesley Rudd, sir. Aged twenty-seven with six years' service, all at the Govan sub-division. Commenced her duties with the rest of her shift at two this afternoon and was assigned foot patrol on fourteen and fifteen beats." He paused then explained, "The beat boundaries are Seaward Street to the east of Paisley Road Toll and Lorne

Street to the west. The River Clyde to the north and the motorway to the south."

"Quite a large area then."

"Yes, sir. The beats encompass both domestic and commercial buildings and there is a large number of licensed premises in the area too."

"When was the last contact with the constable?"

McCrae glanced at his notes and replied, "Constable Rudd was tasked to attend an anonymous call about a drunk lying in the road in Middlesex Street at the junction of Scotland Street, sir. The call is timed at seven minutes past eight and according to my controller," he nodded towards the stand alone room divider where Hammond bent his head to avoid any interest from Alison, "she responded she was en route to the locus."

"Constable," Alison turned and loudly called out to Hammond, "did Rudd acknowledge arriving at the locus?"

Hammond rose to his feet to peer over the top of the divider and shook his head. "No, sir."

To McCrae he said, "Did she have a neighbour?"

McCrae flushed and replied, "Apparently not, sir."

"While I am aware we now serve under the same banner as Strathclyde Police, Mister McCrae, I was under the impression that the city divisions still operate under the former City of Glasgow rules," Alison slowly said, keen to remind McCrae that was not how it was done in Dunbartonshire. "If I recall correctly, all footmen are to be neighboured between the hours of six in the evening to two in the early morning. Why then did this young officer not have a neighbour?"

Behind Alison, Watson decided that it might be an appropriate time to check the prisoners in custody and tiptoed from the bar. At the control room consul, Hammond concentrated on his notes, but was all ears to later relate anything that he might hear.

McCrae swallowed with difficulty and replied, "In the absence of the shift Inspector Kane, Constable Rudd's shift sergeant,

Sergeant Cole, is responsible for assigning duties, Mister Alison. That is a question you might wish to ask him."

"In short, what's been done to find this young woman?"

"Sergeant Cole and his late shift are currently conducting a search of the two beats from the east side that is Seaward Street, westwards. The night shift is currently in the muster room being briefed on their search area by their shift Inspector Munroe. Once they are briefed, they'll be sent out."

"Then when there is any news, that's where I will be," he imperiously replied and was about to turn away when he stopped.

Staring keenly at McCrae, he leaned a further few inches towards the shorter man and theatrically took a sniff.

"If I recall correctly, Inspector McCrae, you have what, two or three months left to serve?"

"Two months, two week and three days, excluding annual leave that I have remaining, sir."

"Then Inspector McCrae," he leaned even closer, his voice no more than a whisper and said, "perhaps you might consider that from this point you refrain from alcohol while on duty and you might leave with your pension, eh?"

Turning away, Alison made his way out of the uniform bar while McCrae, his face pale at the inferred threat, sank back down into his chair and muttered, "Bastard!"

****

Iain Meikle drove slowly along Clifford Street while on foot his neighbour Eric Little and Sergeant Jimmy Cole searched the grassy bank that adjoined the motorway. Even with the rain falling and in the darkness, he had no difficulty distinguishing the two men. While Little used his cheaply made, police issue torch to search the undergrowth, the beam from Cole's lengthy aluminium handled Kel-Lite torch cut a bright ribbon through the darkness.

Iain stopped the panda car twenty yards in front of the two officers and waited for them to catch up.

The passenger door was pulled open by Little who shaking his head to remove the dribbles of water that trickled from his cap's visor, breathlessly said, "Nothing, not a trace and this constant fucking rain doesn't help either."

Iain was about to reply when he saw Cole joining Little at the passenger door and instead asked, "Sarge. I'm not getting anything on my radio and this car's not equipped with AS. Are you hearing anything from Hammy in the control room?"

Cole leaned in the door and said, "Only that she's still not radioed in and the nightshift are out now looking for her too. Right," he pulled back the seat and climbing into the rear, said "there's no point in farting around here. We'd better get back and see what Inspector Munroe has organised. Bloody woman," he angrily shook his head.

Getting into the front seat, Iain sensed that Little was about to retort and subtly laid a restraining hand on his arm, before confirming, "Govan it is."

As he drove he wondered at Cole's insensitivity yet worried that something bad, something really bad, had happened to wee Les.

****

In the sergeants room, Inspector Bob Munroe lifted the phone and acknowledging the call, turned to Superintendent Alison to tell him, "That's the nightshift guys and the dogman finished the sweep from Seaward Street to Cornwall Street on the south side of the Paisley Road West, sir. No trace," he shook his head.

Alison glanced at his watch and yawning, replied, "Well, that's gone four o'clock now, Inspector. I believe it's time to call in resources from the adjoining divisions. We can't let this go on any longer. That young woman must be found." He squinted and staring at Munroe, asked, "Has anyone thought to check her home address?"

Munroe nodded and replied, "Her Mini is still parked in the road outside in Orkney Street, but in the off chance she decided to return home for some reason, I sent the two nightshift CID to check there half an hour ago." He glanced at his wristwatch and added, "I thought I'd have heard from them by now."

Almost on cue, the phone rang and was snatched up by Munroe.

Alison watched as the Inspector listened then saw his face pale, before Munroe said, "Right, Tam, I've got that. Stay there and ensure you get the Scene of Crime people in as soon as possible."

Replacing the handset into its cradle, he turned towards Alison to relate, "That was DS Whelan, sir, one of the two detective officers I sent to Rudd's flat over in Langside. It seems when they got there they found the door forced open and the place ransacked."

****

Jimmy Cole hesitated at the door when he saw the superintendent seated with Bob Munroe in the sergeants room, but nervously stepped in when Munroe said, "This is Sergeant Cole, sir. He's Constable Rudd's supervisor."

Alison acknowledged Cole with a nod then curtly told him, "Take a seat, Sergeant Cole and explain to me why your officer was not out on shift with a neighbour."

Apprehensively, Cole removed his cap and sodden raincoat that he hung on the peg driven into the wall and bought himself a few seconds to collect his thoughts, before replying, "I utilised what resources were available for the shift, sir."

He sat down in the chair facing Alison and continued, "Constable Rudd…Lesley, is a very bright young woman and I believe she would not unnecessarily endanger herself in any situation, but would immediately call for back-up from the two officers I had placed in the panda car as a quick response vehicle."

Alison watched Cole's throat bob up and down and understood his anxiety, for if anything untoward *has* happened to Rudd then it was likely the senior management would seek a scapegoat. Turning to Munroe, with a disarming smile he said, "The sergeant is obviously cold and tired, Inspector. Is there any likelihood we could manage a cup of tea or coffee for him?"

Munroe was long in the tooth and recognised he was being dismissed while Alison wished a private word with Cole and so replied, "I'll see to it, sir." Rising from his chair, he closed the door behind him.

"So, Sergeant Cole," Alison smiled, but his eyes were cold as he stared at the younger officer. "Tell me a little about Constable Rudd."

"Eh, what is it that you want to know, sir?"

Alison shrugged and asked, "Is she competent officer? Has she previously disappeared halfway through her shift? Do you know of any reason why she might have gone missing?"

"No, sir," Cole shook his head. "What I mean is, I've been her shift sergeant for what," his eyes narrowed in thought, "just over five months and I've never known her to be anything but a conscientious officer."

"What about her personal life. Is she married?"

"No, sir, but I don't really know anything about her personal life."

"Boyfriend?"

"Again, sir, I don't know. I, eh…" he paused before continuing. "Off duty, I don't really mix with the shift members, sir."

"Ah," Alison sagely nodded. "I understand from Inspector Munroe that you are an AP promotion candidate. How long have you served in the police?"

"Almost five years, sir."

"And been a sergeant for how long?"

"Just under two years, sir. The last five months here at Govan, to gain supervisory experience."

"And before the police?"

"Bradford University completing my Honours degree in Accounting."

"And then you joined the police."

"Yes, sir," Cole replied, unable to prevent himself from blushing.

"I assume your degree was your stepping stone into the fast-track promotion scheme?"

"Yes, sir," he continued to blush.

"Well, Sergeant Cole," Alison tightly smiled, but his voice dripped with sarcasm when he added, "here's hoping your *accounting* experience will assist you in your future law career."

Before Cole could respond, the door was pushed open by Bob Munroe who carrying a mug of steaming coffee in one hand, handed it to Cole then addressing Alison, said, "I've just been in the control room, sir. Still no trace of our missing constable; however, DS Whelan, one of the two CID officers at Rudd's flat, has called in to say that in light of the break-in he's informed his boss of the circumstances and who's now en route to Govan as we speak."

"Who is in charge of Govan CID?"

"DCI Colin Morton, sir."

"Not a name I'm familiar with," Alison sighed, then asked, "How is the search proceeding?"

Munroe moved to the large map pinned on the wall with broad red coloured lines that indicated the boundaries of the Govan beats. Pointing to fourteen beat, he replied, "The search here is concluded and the guys are now moving in this general area," he swept a hand down towards the area designated as thirteen beat.

Alison arose from his chair and leaning forward to peer at the map, raised his hand and pointing, said, "What's this area here?"

"That's the dockside, sir. It's generally disused these days though we do have the occasional ship tie up alongside because there is still a couple of cranes in operation there. Mostly Polish boats loading up scrap metal. The troops are just winding up the search in that area."

Perhaps it was fate, perhaps just coincidence for at that very moment, when the clock on the wall struck four-seventeen, the telephone on the desk rang.

"Inspector Munroe," he curtly answered, then slowly nodding, replaced the handset and in a quiet voice, said, "Aye, I've got all that."

Alison and Cole saw him swallow before he turned and quietly told them, "They've just found a policewoman's cap on the docks at Mavisbank Quay. It has Lesley Rudd's name and divisional number written in ink in the headband inside it and," he paused, "there's what seems to be blood on it."

CHAPTER TWO

He involuntarily shivered in the first light of the day and wished he'd worn his heavy overcoat instead of the thin navy blue coloured anorak his wife had held ready for him when he'd rushed from the house. Glancing up at the clearing skies, he gave a quiet thanks that at least the bloody rain had stopped then his fingers heavily stained with nicotine, inhaled deeply on his unfiltered cigarette.

Beside him Inspector Bob Munroe and Superintendent Michael Alison stared silently into the still, dark waters below while he watched the two nightshift Scene of Crime officers unhurriedly work their way from the edge of the dockside towards the derelict buildings.

Forty yards away and three feet apart with their heads bowed, a line of ten uniformed officers slowly walked in a line from east to west, searching the ground for anything that might indicate a struggle; any clue as to what might have occurred that could have caused the young woman to go over the edge of the concrete dock into the cold and forbidding waters of the River Clyde.

But, he reminded himself, that's only if she *did* go over the edge.

He turned when Alison asked, "What's your thoughts on this, Mister Morton?"

Colin Morton removed the cigarette from his mouth and with a forefinger, tapped the ash onto the ground and pursed his lips before replying, "Well, sir, according to Bob here," he nodded at Munroe, "Constable Rudd seems to have been well liked by her shift and apparently is a grounded young woman." He involuntarily nodded as he continued, "I knew her to see when she occasionally visited the CID office, but I can't recall ever speaking to her. From what Bob has learned she had no apparent personal or work-related issues that were known to her supervisor and nothing to suggest she has taken off on her own accord." He inhaled and exhaled before continuing, "The presence of the cap and what seems to be blood on it is extremely worrying, though of course I'll need that confirmed by the Forensics. However, at this time and without anything to contradict what we so far know it seems to indicate she met with some violence somewhere here," he waved his hand about him. "Now, the question we have to ask is did she go into the water at this point and if so, did she jump or was she pushed. Another thought is that she might have been abducted."

He sighed and slowly shaking his head, admitted, "Frankly, sir, it's far too early to theorise what happened here; however, with your permission I'd like to call out the Marine Unit and have the crew of *Semper Vigilo* and the divers search this stretch of the water for a body."

Alison stared wordlessly at Morton for a few seconds then turning to Munroe, said, "Perhaps you might make those arrangements, Inspector."

"Sir," Munroe acknowledged with a nod and walked off to use his radio.

"That is obviously your official thoughts, Mister Morton," Alison said, "but you seem to be an officer with a number of years' service under your belt, so what's your personal opinion?"

"My personal opinion," Morton stared down at his feet before slowly raising his head and staring at Alison, "The girl's dead. There seems to be one of two options; either she tripped and injured herself or somebody has cracked her on the head and as a result of either possibility, she's then fell or been thrown into the water."

****

There seemed little point in hanging around Mavisbank Quay so Morton decided that he'd be better placed returning to his office at Govan and setting up an incident room.

Driving his black coloured Austin 1800 through the arched entrance into the rear yard, he was reversing into his designated bay just as DS Tam Whelan and his younger, stick thin neighbour, DC Ian McDonald arrived in the CID car.

Morton liked the tall, forty-eight years old Whelan who was constantly ribbed by his fellow detectives for his bald head and obese stature that likened him to the professional wrestler Shirley Crabtree, who was more commonly known as Big Daddy though to Whelan's relief *he* had avoid being dubbed by that nickname.

"Morning, boss," Whelan nodded to him before asking, "What's the story at the locus?"

"We've found her hat and it's got blood on it, but no trace of the young lassie," he shook his head. "How did you get on at her flat?"

Whelan, his hands dug into his trouser pockets, shrugged and shaking his head, replied, "The door was punted in and the place well and truly turned over." His eyes narrowed as he added, "Funny thing is that there was some good stuff left lying, stuff like a portable cassette player and jewellery in the bedroom that wasn't touched. Makes me think that theft wasn't the reason for the housebreaking."

Morton's eyes narrowed when he asked, "So, Tam, what *do* you think?"

Whelan shrugged and replied, "I think whoever screwed the flat was looking for something," then turning to his neighbour, said, "Ian?"

Taking his cue, McDonald fetched his notebook out of his inner jacket pocket and said, "While Tam was searching through the flat, boss, I dug up the neighbours and asked them if they had heard anything. Lesley's flat…" he blushed, "I mean Constable Rudd's flat is on the first floor so I started with the two ground flat neighbours, but got no reply at the first house and I think they were out. The flat opposite was an old guy, but he was pissed and is half deaf and never heard anything. There was no reply at the other first floor flat and again I think nobody was at home." He glanced at his notes and continued, "The two flats upstairs were occupied by a young couple who were having a party and heard nothing and the remaining flat is occupied by an elderly woman who because of the party next door," he sighed, "wanted me to take a complaint about it. But she said she didn't hear anything either. There is one thing, though." "That is?"

"It might not be much, but one of the lassie's at the party, a Theresa McGregor, said she arrived in the close at fifteen minutes past eight. She's definite about the time because she didn't want to be too early for the party. She hadn't been to her pal's flat before and didn't know where the flat was located in the close, so she checked the doors for her pal's name and is definite that the doors on the ground flat and one up were all closed tight. In short, she is certain that if the door had been kicked in like we found it she says she would definitely have noticed it."

"Any of the other visitors to the party see the same thing?"

"Nobody mentioned it, sir."

"Okay, so you guys found the house screwed at what, three-twenty this morning?"

"That's about right, boss," Whelan confirmed.

"So, that gives us a kind of time frame for when the housebreaking might have occurred." Morton slowly nodded, then asked, "What about the top two flats?"

McDonald shook his head and replied, "The flats in that part of Baker Street have only three storeys, boss; ground, first flight and second flight."

"Right then," Morton rubbed at his forehead. "I know you guys are nightshift but until the rest of the lads arrive, you're it. Tam, Inspector Munroe says that Rudd's car is parked outside in Orkney Street. I'm guessing she won't carry her keys on patrol with her so find her locker, get the keys and search it for anything that might explain her disappearance."

"Boss," Whelan nodded.

"And me, boss?" McDonald asked.

"I'm guessing, Ian, that when you called her Lesley you might have some knowledge of Rudd, so you and I will grab a coffee and you can tell me what you know."

****

The 'G' Divisional Commander, Chief Superintendent Murdo Clarke, arrived at his office to discover Superintendent Michael Alison and the newly appointed Assistant Chief Constable (Personnel) Valerie McIntosh, sitting in the two chairs in front of his desk having helped themselves not only to his coffee, but to his favourite Tunnock teacakes too.

"Good morning, Murdo, and I hope you don't mind," the grey-haired McIntosh turned and smiled as he entered, "but your secretary said we should help ourselves."

Shrugging off his overcoat and hanging it on the hook behind the door, he lifted his tunic from a second hook and slipped it on. Smiling tightly in return, Clarke twirled his RAF style moustache between thumb and forefinger, then asked, "And to what do I owe the pleasure at this time of the morning and you, Michael," he stared curiously at Alison. "Correct me if I'm wrong, but are you not the duty nightshift Super?"

"I am indeed, Murdo, and perhaps I might first explain," Alison said. "I tried to have the control room contact you, but they tell me you have recently moved house and for some reason unknown, didn't have your new number."

Clarke nodded, but didn't miss the fact that Alison was scoring a point with the ACC by inferring Clarke was not keeping his personal details updated with his staff.

"That's right, an oversight by me," he admitted as he sat down at his desk. "So, again," he stared at them in turn, "to what do I owe the pleasure?"

It took Alison a little over five minutes to relate the mysterious circumstances of Constable Rudd's disappearance and the suggestion that she might have met with some violent end.

"My God," his hands flat on his desk, Clarke paled and was genuinely shocked. "Lesley Rudd. She's one of my brightest officers. I've even harboured the idea of recommending her for the Advanced Promotion Scheme." His brow knitted as he asked, "And we have no idea what might have happened to her, none at all?"

"Regretfully, I'm afraid not," Alison shook his head and sipped at his coffee. "Your DCI, Mister Morton, is upstairs setting up an incident room as we speak. The last time I spoke with him, some fifteen minutes ago and just before Valerie arrive," he smiled at McIntosh, "there was no further news about Rudd."

Alison's use of McIntosh's forename reminded Clarke that Alison and the ACC were both former Dunbartonshire Constabulary officers, a fact that instinctively urged him to be cautious.

"And you, Ma'am," he addressed McIntosh. "Are you here to take charge of this inquiry at a senior officer level?"

"Good gracious, no," she seemed perturbed at the thought of being involved in such an incident. "I was at work early when Michael contacted my office to request Constable Rudd's personnel file be sent over so thought I'd deliver it myself, sort of show support for the troops on the ground," she smiled.

Aye, supporting my lads and lassies out in the bloody rain while you're in here eating my fucking chocky biscuits and drinking my coffee, Clarke unkindly thought

"Morton also told me," Alison continued, "that he is standing down the search at the dockside, but will leave two constables on duty there to interview anyone who might be sleeping rough in the abandoned sheds and warehouses. I'm told it's a popular venue for the down and outs and for lead thieves."

"It is," Clarke agreed. "We've had a few cases reported from there. Fagin type scrap merchants sending the younger lads out stealing the lead from the roofs, that sort of thing."

He watched as McIntosh reached down into her large briefcase to extract a brown coloured cardboard folder.

"Here you are, you Rudd's personnel file," she handed it across the desk to him. "I should also mention that the Chief is now aware of the missing officer as regretfully are the media. It seems that the local papers have either used their sources within the Force or their technical people have monitored our radio broadcasts because they're already asking questions of Jimmy Donnelly in the media office. Might I suggest that you contact Chief Inspector Donnelly and come to some agreement about a statement?"

"I'll speak with my DCI and see that gets done, Ma'am. Now, I'd like to get upstairs to meet with Colin Morton, so, unless there's anything else?" he rose to his feet.

Taking the hint, both Alison and McIntosh also rose to their feet, then Alison said, "In that case, Murdo, I'd officially like to hand the missing officer inquiry over to you," he formally nodded at him.

"And when your people are finished with the file," McIntosh nodded to the folder, "please see it's returned to the Personnel Department, Murdo."

Walking them to the door, Clarke sighed with relief when they had gone.

His first port of call was to the uniform bar where he beckoned Inspector Willie McCrae to him. Leading the older man into a corner, his nose twitched at the strong smell of peppermints from McCrae's breath, but decided that rebuking the elderly Inspector was not a priority and instead hissed, "What the fuck's going on, Willie? Why wasn't I contacted right away about this lassie's disappearance and I know," he raised a hand, "I forgot to update my home number, but you could have tried in some way to get a hold of me."

"You're right, we didn't have your home number, sir, and maybe I was a bit lax in that. But for heaven's sake, man, that bugger Alison was all over us like a bad rash," he angrily retorted. "And take it from me, he was more than happy to be here and take charge of the inquiry. It was like he was lording it over us ex-City of Glasgow cops," he growled, "trying to pick fault."

"Aye," Clarke sighed and nodded. "He's got a bee in his bonnet about us, I already know that. Him and that split-arse McIntosh. Now, is there any update from the street?"

"No," McCrae shook his head, "but Colin Morton is upstairs. He's really the man you should speak to."

"Okay." He glanced over McCrae's shoulder and added, "I can see that the day shift is arriving. I assume the nightshift Inspector and his bar staff were out on the search?"

"They were, sir."

"Anything else happened in the Division that I should know about?"

"No," McCrae shook his head. "Thankfully for a Saturday, it's been a quiet night other than the usual domestics and a couple of young women in Pollok lifted for a serious assault, but that's been dealt with."

"You look knackered, Willie."

"Aye," McCrae wearily smiled, "I'm not wanting to wish my life away, but roll on retirement. I'm getting too old for this game, Murdo. Me and my lads stayed on at the bar to cover over, so it's been a long late shift."

"Okay, then. After you pass all the information you can, you and your bar staff get yourselves away home."

"Aye, sir, and thanks."

"For what?"

McCrae pointed to his mouth and his face pale, shrugged and said, "You know, the drink. I swear, Murdo, it won't happen again. Not with the time I've got left."

"Fair enough, Willie, I'll trust you to keep to your word on that issue, then," Clarke nodded and left the bar.

****

With the rest of the late shift, an exhausted Iain Meikle and Eric Little sat quietly in the muster room waiting to be dismissed from duty. Some of the officers had their eyes closed as sleep threatened to overtake them.

At last the nightshift Inspector, Bob Munroe, accompanied by their own sergeant, Jimmy Cole, entered from the sergeant's room then stood at the old wooden lectern, Munroe said, "First, I regret to inform you there's no news about Lesley. As you all know, we have found her cap and though it *is* blood-stained…" he held his hand up to quell the angry muttering and when it ceased, continued, "there is nothing to suggest that she has met with any violence. It might be that she has fallen, become disorientated and…"

"You don't really believe that, Inspector, do you?" interjected an angry Iain.

Munroe stared at the pale faced cop and slowly shook his head. "No, Iain, I don't, but I'm trying to be optimistic, here. DCI Morton is on the case and he's organised an incident room to find Lesley, no matter what the circumstances might be, so for the minute let's try for a half full bottle of milk rather than a half empty one, okay?"

Iain swallowed tightly and slowly nodded.

"Right then," Munroe cast an eye about the dozen seated officers. "You lot are on your chinstraps, so the best thing you can do is get home for some kip."

"Some of us would like to hang on for a bit, Inspector, maybe help out with the search," Eric Little piped up.

Munroe raised both hands as though in surrender and replied, "Much as I understand your concern, Eric," he glanced at the shift, "*all* of your concerns, you all need to get home and get some sleep. The nightshift will be going home too and I'm told that extra resources will be drafted in to continue the street to street search of all the Govan beats. Guys, gals, you've done all that was asked of you and more, so please; let the fresh shifts take over, okay? Thank you."

There was a muttered acceptance and dejectedly first one, then another and finally the rest of the shift got to their feet to change out of their tunics and tiredly make their way home.
****

The Police Marine Underwater Search Unit's vehicle, a large, double wheeled transit van converted to house the numerous items of equipment used by the Unit, was parked close to the abandoned warehouse adjoining the spot where Lesley Rudd's cap had been discovered.

The two uniformed constables instructed to standby the locus, watched curiously as the dive supervisor, a grizzled sergeant in his early fifties, held the yellow coloured connecting line in one hand and sipped from a cup of steaming hot coffee held in the other hand. Close by and sat on a rusting duck bollard, his second diver, a constable wearing an all in one neoprene diving suit that was rolled down to his waist, clutched his coffee mug and said, "It's black as night down there, Martin. The amount of junk and metal that's been tossed into the water is bloody criminal. If Sandy," he nodded to the river below, "gets himself snagged on any of it on he'll cut himself wide open."

"Aye, well that's a risk we'll take if it means we can find that wee lassie," the sergeant sourly replied, his concentration fully on the line in his hand that connected him to his officer below.

Minutes later, a head and masked face appeared above the water line and glancing up, nodded as he raised his gloved hand with something in it.

"He's got something," the sergeant called out.

The constable awkwardly waddled over and lifting a waterproof net bag attached to a nylon rope, threw the bag down into the water to land beside the diver.

They watched as the diver Sandy fumbled with the bag and placed the object into the bag before giving his colleagues the thumbs up.

The constable pulled up the bag, ensuring he kept it free from bumping against the concrete side of the dock and lifting it clear, laid the bag down onto a rubber sheet.

Conscious he still had a man in the water, the sergeant didn't move but called out, "What is it?"

Closely watched by the two G Division constables, the diver opened the bag and with a gloved hand pulled the object free. Staring at it curiously, he called back, "It's a radio. A police radio. A Burndept."

****

Detective Inspector Irene Crichton, a popular woman with jet black hair tied in a tight bun and who usually dressed in unfashionable clothes such as the grey coloured blouse, sensible brown brogues and the mismatched tweed skirt she wore that day and who habitually never wore make-up, was known to be a shrewd individual blessed with a razor sharp mind. Fondly nicknamed Bessie by her colleagues, though never to her face, Irene was always polite and attentive to her colleagues no matter their rank or service. Divorced several years from her former philandering husband, it was rumoured since that time she had sworn off men. It was also quietly speculated that had she spent a little more time with her appearance, Irene might have been considered attractive, despite the fine line of the two-inch scar on the underside of her chin, a graphic reminder of the broken bottle thrust at her face when she was a probationary constable. Knocking on DCI Morton's door and seconds before he could call out, "Come in," she pushed it open.

"That was one of the cops at the locus on the blower to the control room, Colin," she began. "The underwater boys have found a Burndept radio in the River Clyde almost at the spot where her cap was discovered. I checked the sheet downstairs and the number corresponds with the one Rudd signed out when she started her shift yesterday."

In the middle of reading a report, Morton threw down his pen and sitting back in his chair, replied, "But no body?"

"No," she shook her head. "No body."

He rubbed his fingers through his wiry grey hair and exhaled before saying, "Jesus. I'm not sure if this makes me a bad person, Irene, because I don't know whether to be disappointed or relieved."

Staring up at her, he asked, "Any word from the polis boat?"

Semper Vigilo? No, nothing yet. The last I heard was they were following the current's tide flow from when the lassie was last heard of, sometime after eight last night. The crew are trying to work out *if* the body was swept away, what route her body would have taken and where it might come to rest in the river."

"What about, Mister Parsonage? Has he been informed?"

George Parsonage, the Chief Officer of the Glasgow Humane Society, the organisation formed in 1790 that was dedicated to the saving of life and recovery of bodies from the River Clyde, was internationally famous for the 1500 lives he saved during his career, let alone the hundreds of drowned bodies he had recovered. A great friend to the police, Parsonage was always on call at a few minutes' notice.

"Aye, he's been called and is concentrating his search along the east side of the river."

"Well, if anyone can find her…"

He never finished the sentence for the open door was again knocked, but this time by a tall, thin man with a pencil moustache and watery, light blue eyes who wore a grey coloured three-piece suit and a grey coloured Fedora and who softly said, "Not interrupting, am I?"

Morton respectfully got to his feet and smiling, waved him in before replying, "Not at all, sir. Glad to see you," then turning to her, asked, "Any chance of a cuppa for Mister Cruickshank, Irene?"

Before she could respond, Detective Chief Superintendent Alistair 'Patches' Cruickshank, head of the city's south side Divisional CID, raised a hand and said, "Don't bother yourself, Irene. I'll not be here long. I'm only in to find out what's happening about this missing police woman before I meet with the Chief so there's no need for you to leave. Any update?" he addressed his remark to Morton.

Indicating the chair next to Irene, Morton waited till Cruickshank had removed his hat and sat down before resuming his own seat, then asked, "You know about the discovery of her cap in Mavisbank Quay?"

"Aye, I heard. That's the derelict docking bay on the Clyde isn't it?"

"It is," Morton nodded, then added, "Irene has just informed me that Constable Rudd's radio has been discovered by the divers in the water almost adjacent to where her cap was found."

"Oh, that doesn't sound too good," Cruickshank's brow furrowed. "What can you tell me about this young lassie?"

Morton glanced at his notes and replied, "Aged twenty-seven with a few months over six years service and according to her supervisors, a good worker. Single and lives in a flat in Baker Street over in the Langside area. You heard about the flat being broken into?"

Cruickshank nodded and asked, "Any witnesses or a motive? Theft perhaps?"

"No witnesses and we're not certain if anything *has* been stolen, sir, and obviously without Rudd to tell us, we're in the dark. However," he wheezed and reaching for his cigarettes, tapped one out into his hand, "Tam Whelan, my DS, is of the opinion that theft wasn't the motive, that the place has been turned over by someone looking for something. What," he shrugged and then lit up, "we don't know."

Cruickshank fetched an old, worn briar pipe from his jacket pocket and without lighting it began chewing on the stem, then said, "I had a quick word with the Div Comm downstairs. He's called off the physical search, says that he just doesn't have enough resources, particularly as it is still officially a missing person inquiry. He also told me that Rudd was so highly regarded he was considering recommending her for the Advanced Promotion Scheme. Seems to have been a sharp lassie, eh?"

"She's not dead yet, sir," Morton smiled, "or at least there's no evidence of it. As you said, at the minute she's still officially a missing person."

"Aye, of course, you're quite right, Colin. So, how do you propose to deal with the inquiry. You know the bugger will ask," said Cruickshank, referring to the current Chief Constable.

"Well, for the minute I'll try to keep things within my budget and of course I'll have a watching brief. I've set up an incident room in the general office and designated Irene here as the inquiry officer to assess and coordinate all incoming information from whatever source. DS Tam Whelan will be my office manager and is coming off the nightshift with his neighbour. I'll form a second team with another DC and one of the policewomen who is currently acting as an aide to the CID and those four will conduct the inquiries. Without a body," he extended his hands, "I can't justify this as anything other than a missing person enquiry. However," he grimaced, "if as I suspect the lassie does turn up dead, then that will make it a completely new ball game."

Cruickshank did not immediately respond, but slowly nodded and then said, "I agree. There's not much more you can do." His eyes narrowed when he asked, "The blood that was found on the cap. Is it hers?"

"I'm still waiting on the result from the Forensics, but I'm assuming it is because it's on the inside of the hatband."

"Oh dear. Right, well Colin, if there is any hiccup from Forensics please feel free to use my name to shuffle things along."

"Will do, sir, and thanks."

Cruickshank rose to his feet and waving that they remained seated, said, "Here's hoping it is a personal thing that has made her take off and that no harm has come to her."

With a smile and a nod, he left and closed the door behind him.

"Thank God we've got someone like Patches as our boss on the Southside and not that bloody idiot Kerr who's in charge of the CID. Man's a bloody menace," Irene shook her head.

"Aye, couldn't agree more," Morton nodded. "Right, I had a quiet word earlier with young Ian McDonald. Says that Rudd was a decent lassie, apparently didn't mess about and more or less kept herself to herself. You're a woman, Irene. Heard any gossip about her?"

"I did know her to nod to and say hello to if you know what I mean, but she is a bit younger than me, Colin," she grimaced, "so it's not as if we're out at the dancing together. That said, I also heard she recently broke up with her boyfriend. He's in the police somewhere, the city centre I think I heard, but I'm not certain."

"Yeah? Got a name?"

"No, but leave it with me. I'll have a word with the girls on her shift and see if they're any the wiser. You think her disappearance might be linked to her recent relationship?"

"Honestly, Irene, I have no idea and even if I did I'd only be guessing," he shook his head. "That said, it won't do any harm to speak with him if you do get a name. Tell him we're trying to create a profile and treat him as a witness, ask him about her friends and anyone he suspects might mean her harm. Oh, and if he's any idea if she has a bolthole somewhere; some place she likes to go to by herself."

"Sound enough ideas," she agreed, then asked, "Anything else?"

His face twisted when he said, "I know it's going to be a pain in the arse job, but either yourself or one of the guys needs to check through all the cases that Rudd has submitted to the Fiscal in say," his brow furrowed, "the last year. Find out if any of them might have some bearing on her disappearance; maybe someone she's locked up who has a grievance against her."

"I'll get right onto it," she rose from her seat and left the room. She had been gone just a few minutes when his desk phone rung.

"DCI Morton."

"Colin, it's Alistair Cruickshank."

"Hello, boss, what's up?"

"I've just arrived back at Pitt Street and," he audibly sighed, "Mister Kerr would like a word about your missing officer. Can you get yourself up here, say in the next twenty minutes?"

Morton tightly closed his eyes and then opening them, replied, "I'm surprised to hear that the ACC has come in on a Sunday, boss, but of course. Will you be there?"

"Oh, aye, you know how Mister Kerr likes an audience," Cruickshank said, then added with a wry smile, "and particularly if he's talking about his favourite subject. Himself."

"Right then, I'll see you at his office," Morton acknowledged before hanging up.

****

Eric Little decided he was in no hurry to return home and accompanied Iain Meikle back to his cottage flat in Mosspark's Tealing Avenue for what Iain described as a wee aperitif.

"I'll get murdered when I get home," moaned Little, "and particularly if I'm pissed."

"Sheep as a lamb, sheep as a lamb," Iain quietly repeated the old adage and with a shake of his head toasted him with his can of Tennants.

They sat in silence for a moment, broken when Little burped then said, "What about that bastard Cole sending Les out on the Toll beat herself. What the hell was he thinking? Do you think anything will come of it? I man, do you think that the gaffers will do something about him?"

"No, of course they won't," Iain scoffed. "He's an AP man, isn't he? If the Inspector had been on instead of being off for the wedding he was attending, he'd never had let Les or any polis women out on a back shift on her own without a neighbour. Course, Micky Kane is old school even if he is a former Renfrew and Bute man, but county man or not at least he's definitely not like that prat Cole. And you know as well as I do, the bosses will never acknowledge the fact that Cole messed up." He sadly shook his head and continued, "Cole wasn't thinking and that's the problem. He won't take advice from more experienced guys like me and you. Thinks because he's a bloody sergeant that he's supposed to know it all and that's his mistake. If he would only listen now and then…" but he didn't finish. It was pointless going over old ground, repeating the discussion that he and Little had so often argued before. With a sigh, he said, "Look, it's nearly eleven o'clock. About time you were going home and I was in my bed. Do you want me to phone you a taxi? I can bring your car down to the office tonight before the nightshift."

"No," Little shook his head and rose to his feet. "I've only had a couple of cans so I should be okay for the driving. Right," he reached down and lifted his anorak. "I'll be off then. I'll see myself out," and leaving the room, closed the door behind him. Still seated, Iain rolled his head to ease the ache in his neck and loudly burped.

Where the hell are you, Les, he wondered, then getting to his feet made his way through to his bedroom.

CHAPTER THREE

It was the noises that had kept Sam Fullerton awake; the sounds of the vehicles that through the night continued to arrive and depart from the dockside as well as the loud shouts.

Of course he had been at first alarmed and peeking through the gaps in the metal wall saw police officers moving back and forward, talking loudly and pulling the padlocks on the large doors. But then at last when they failed to gain entry to the warehouse and he realised they were not after all looking for him, he settled himself back down into his sleeping bag and tightly closing his eyes, tried to sleep.

Now, with the sun streaming through the hundreds of large and pinprick holes in the metal walls of the warehouse, he pulled the sleeping bag down from his eyes and with a wide yawn, stretched his weary muscles.

He could hear the sound of an engine outside and crouching down again at his spyhole, saw two police officers and a two other men, one of whom was dressed in a diving suit that the diver had pulled down to around his waist, staring down into the water. He noticed the small portable engine by the edge of the dock and pipes running from it, recognising that the pipes were air hoses and concluded there must be a second diver in the water.

What the hell are they after, he wondered, but then remembered the car and the figures from the night before. His brow furrowed as he fought to recall what he had seen, then unconsciously nodding, seemed to remember that he had heard a splash.

A loud splash.

Is that what they're looking for, whatever it was that was thrown into the water?

With a shrug, Sam sat back from the wall and shook his head. It was nothing to do with him. He had decided a long time ago to stay away from the polis just as the polis did their level best to avoid giving the lice ridden Sam the jail, preferring instead to steer him towards the city centre where a number of charities patrolled the lanes and back streets offering overnight shelter for the gentlemen of the road; shelters that in Glasgow parlance were known as 'Models.'

However, Sam neither liked nor trusted the Models, believing them to be dens of iniquities where a man's possessions, few though they might be, would be stolen the minute he shut his eyes. After all, he smiled to himself, wasn't that how he had come by this lovely, warm sleeping bag?

****

Irene Crichton glanced up and smiled when she saw DS Tam Whelan and DC Ian McDonald push open the door of the general office. Both men were dressed in casual shirts and denims with Whelan wearing a dark coloured anorak and McDonald wearing a denim jacket.

"Morning lads," she cheerfully greeted them before adding, "and if I might say, you both look like shit."

"Thanks, Irene," Whelan returned her grin. "It's the lack of sleep that does it. Any update?" he strolled across to his desk and sat down while McDonald stood with his back to the wall and yawned.

"Nothing, I'm afraid. "The Lab haven't yet come back to us with a result of the blood found on her cap, Oh, yes, sorry," she nodded and tapped her hand against her brow as though chastising herself for her poor memory. "Her Burndept radio was discovered by the divers in the water just below where her cap was found."

"Oh, but no body?" McDonald asked.

They both glanced at him, causing him to blush and stammer, "What I mean is, that's good news, isn't it? That there hasn't been a body found?"

Irene sighed and with a soft smile, said, "We know what you mean, Ian. No, Lesley hasn't been found yet so other than the blood on her cap, there's nothing to definitely indicate she's dead."

"But a reasonable suspicion she might be?" Whelan interjected. Her face solemn, Irene nodded.

The door opened to admit an attractive young woman with collar length, curly red hair who wore an almond coloured short sleeved blouse, a pea green knee length pencil skirt and a bright smile who addressing Irene, said, "I hear you're looking for me, Ma'am?"

"Ah, that's right, Janie. Come in and take a seat."

When she was seated at an empty desk, Irene, said, "We're just waiting on Peter Rossi joining us and…"

The door opened to admit a tall, swarthy looking young man with collar length jet black curly hair who wore a herringbone jacket, light coloured plaid shirt and crimson red knotted wool tie.

"I received a phone call to come in to the office, Ma'am," he said, his voice betraying his hesitancy.

"Glad you could join us, Peter," she smiled at him before turning to the others and telling them, "DC Peter Rossi has just been appointed to the Pollok CID from…" her eyes narrowed and she asked, "Where was it again, Peter?"

"E Division. The Shettleston office, Ma'am."

"Right, Shettleston," she repeated and introduced the others by name before continuing, "Now, it was going to be the DCI that briefed you, but he's been called away to Pitt Street by the ACC. So boys and Janie, it's down to me."

"The ACC? You mean Papa Delta? What's he doing in on a Sunday?" Whelan's eyes betrayed his curiosity.

"Good question, Tam, but that's for the DCI to know and if he thinks *you* should know, I'm certain he'll tell you."

The gentle rebuke provoked some smiles from those present, then she continued, "Right, this is about our missing colleague, Lesley Rudd. We five are making up a incident room team because technically, though we suspect some harm might have come to her, she remains a missing person and we cannot justify a budget for a larger team."

Before she could go on, Ian McDonald irately interjected with, "But surely if one of our own goes missing…"

But he got no further when she held up her hand and forcefully said, "Ian! Let me explain before you go off on your high horse!"

She took a deep breath and said, "I realise that the circumstances of Lesley's disappearance seem to indicate that something did happen to her, but until we have conclusive evidence that has occurred, we have to treat her as a missing person. All of us at one time or another have dealt with missing persons; people who for reasons of their own, whether domestic, work related or whatever, decide without rhyme or reason to take off. Now, most MP's as you know return or are found within a forty-eight-hour period; however, here in Strathclyde we average about thirty thousand reports each year of persons gone missing and no," she cast an eye around the room, "before you ask, that's not thirty thousand *different* individuals. Some of these people go missing a couple, three and even four times a year and particularly those with mental health issues and each time they go missing, it's recorded as a separate event, okay? Yes," she nodded, "I realise most do turn up, but there is still a large number who remain unaccounted for and particularly if the MP does not wish to be found. Now, to remind you how we deal with these reports. A form is filled out, the MP's personal details and description submitted to the Police National Computer and if they have not returned within a day or two, we start knocking on doors. Eventually, the file is designated to a particular officer or to a shift and they carry on the inquiry, updating the file as they go on." She smiled when she said, "If like me, you have dealt with some of these long-term MP's you will know how thick their file becomes. The truth of the matter is that we just do not have the resources to continually have officers searching for MP's on a twenty-four hour, seven day week."

She paused for breath and continued again, "Because Lesley *is* a reported MP and primarily because she *is* one of ours, we cannot be seen to favour her inquiry over that of others. Can you imagine the public outcry by the relatives of missing persons if it is disclosed we have spent an inordinate amount of the police budget searching for one of our own when we have so many MP's who continue to remain unaccounted for?"

"So, it's political then?" Whelan, his arms folded, sounded disgusted.

"No, Tam, it's not political," Irene calmly replied. "It's common sense. We rely on the support of the public for solving crime as well as a host of other issues. When we go looking for Lesley, we want people to assist us willingly, not begrudge us any information they might have because they think we're only interested in looking for one of our own rather than every other buggers loved one." She glanced at the others and said, "Does everybody get what I'm saying?"

"Yes, Ma'am," was the quiet response from Janie and Rossi

and a wordless nod from Ian McDonald. Whelan caught Irene's eye and then almost with reluctance, he too nodded.

"Right then, here's what we're going to do. I, among my other duties, will head up the inquiry and you four will make up the inquiry teams; Tam and Ian, you'll remain together while Janie, you will neighbour Peter and introduce him to the Divisional area. Now," she stared down at the paperwork in front of her and glancing at it, said, "A wee update for you. This morning, Lesley's radio was recovered from the water at the docks almost adjacent to where her cap was discovered." She glanced up and continued. "The physical search for her at the dockside has been called off and the underwater lads are standing down too. The polis boat, *Semper Vigilo*, along with Mister Parsonage of the Glasgow Humane Society will continue to search the River Clyde for likely spots where the current routinely deposits floating bodies, so keep your fingers crossed they are *unsuccessful*," she grimly smiled. Turning to Janie and Rossi, she added, "You will not be aware, but Lesley's flat was the subject of a housebreaking and our information is that it occurred sometime between eight-fifteen last night and it's discovery at…" she glanced at Whelan who prompted, said, "Ian and I found the door ajar at twenty minutes past three."

"Well, there you have it and according to Tam and Ian, it looked like the house was turned over and searched rather than anything being stolen."

"Searched, Ma'am, for what?" asked Janie who gently stroked a wisp of hair behind her left ear, a nervous habit she had since childhood.

"We have no idea," she shook her head, "but you knew Lesley didn't you?"

"Aye, well, she was on a different shift, but yes, I knew her to speak with. I neighboured her on a few occasions when she was on overtime from the early shift and my shift were stuck for bodies, but that was several months ago and well before I joined the CID as an aide."

"Can you give us any kind of insight about what kind of young woman she was…" her round face flushed before she corrected herself with, "I mean, she is?"

However, the inference was not lost on the team or Janie, who began, "Like I said, I only knew her slightly and not outwith the job, but she was a pleasant enough woman and a right good looker too. She struck me as being very bright and to be honest, while I was content to meander around our beats together, Lesley was one of those type of cops who fairly pound the beat, you know? Everything at a hundred miles an hour. I can tell you this," she smiled at the memory, a lopsided smile Rossi noticed, "when I finished the shift that day I was ready for my bed. Knackered I was."

"What about her personal life. Did she mention it at all?"

"No," Janie pursed her lips as she shook her head, "but I am aware that she is or rather was going out with a cop from the Central Division. Stewart Street I think he's at. In fact, I heard he *might* be in the CID there."

"Yes, I'd heard she had been seeing a cop. But you said *was* going out. You think the relationship is over, then?"

"That's what I heard, Ma'am, but I can't recall when or who told me."

"Did she mention his name at all?"

"If she did, I'm afraid I can't recall. Like I said, it's been some time since I was on the beat."

"How did she strike you, Janie? What I'm wondering is, is Lesley the sort of young woman you think might just take off like this?"

"Not at all," Janie vigorously shook her head. "She struck me as having her feet firmly planted and if anything, completely job orientated. By that I mean…" she paused. "Well, what I'm trying to say is that as I recall she did nothing but talk about polis work. Not films she'd seen or nights out or anything. In fact," her face twisted as she recalled, "she wasn't an unpleasant person, not at all, but not overfriendly either. I do recall that I thought her to be very ambitious. Kept reminding me she had passed both her exams and was looking for a departmental job to progress her career."

"Yes," Irene nodded, "her personnel file does make comment about her ambition to progress through the ranks. Hardly sounds like the sort of individual to just take off, does she?" She thought for a few seconds then to Whelan and McDonald, said, "I want you guys to return to Lesley's flat. Knock on doors again and try to gain what information you can." She smiled as she added, "You don't need me to tell you what to ask."

To Janie and Rossi, she said, "Lesley's personnel file states her parents died a number of years ago, but she has a sister Alison who lives out in Uddingston. Knowehead Gardens is the address. I'll write out the details for you," she bent over her desk and scribbled onto a slip of paper. "The sister is expecting someone to call so you guys have the difficult task of speaking to her and trying to elicit what information you can and in particular, the name of her former boyfriend and the nature of their relationship," she stared meaningfully at Janie, "and find out if they definitely have broken up and why. Once you have the guys name, phone me here at the office and I'll do a background check on him, okay?"

"Ma'am," Janie acknowledged with a nod.

"Right then, guys," she waved both hands towards them in a sweeping motion and added, "Get to it."
****

Seated in his office, the portly Assistant Chief Constable Martin Kerr's chubby hands lay flat on the large, oak desk as he pondered the interview he intended having with Detective Chief Superintendent Alistair Cruickshank and DCI Colin Morton.

He relished the idea of having both the former City of Glasgow detectives stood in front of him; his little revenge for the way he perceived the Glasgow Force had treated him for few knew that the five feet eight-inch man had once made application to join the Glasgow Force, only to be turned down because of his lack of height. It still rankled and would continue to do so until he finally achieved the position that he really coveted.

The Chief Constable's job.

It amused him that after being turned down by the Glasgow Force he now sat in the city centre at the hub of Scotland's largest Force, though even he had to admit by a circuitous route.

Deflated after his failure to join the Glasgow Force, Kerr had successfully been accepted as a constable by the adjacent Lanarkshire Constabulary where he had gained rapid promotion through the ranks of the CID, though not through his own ability. No, Kerr's promotions had mostly been at the expense of others for his true aptitude was the backstabbing tales he told about his peers and his ingratiating manner towards his senior officers.

Not at all a bright man, Kerr's one strength was that he recognised ability and brightness in others and so as he achieved senior promotions, he surrounded himself with such individuals from whom he would cherry-pick ideas that he passed as his own.

At the time of the dissolution of the City and regional Forces and the formation of Strathclyde Police, the Police Authority responsible for appointing the new Chief Constable, his Deputy and Assistant Chief Constables, were shocked to learn from an anonymous source that Alistair Cruickshank, the main candidate for the position of ACC (Crime) had a severe alcohol dependency. That the story later proved to be false was unfortunate for Cruickshank, for by the time the allegation was proven to be unfounded, Kerr had been appointed to the post. Had they known or even bothered to do a little digging to check the veracity of the story the Police Authority would have been even more shocked to learn the source of their anonymous information was none other than Kerr himself.

While nothing of the lie or who perpetrated could nor ever would be proved, Kerr's deceitful background and previous history of lies about colleagues gave rise to a general suspicion that it was indeed he who had scuppered the career prospects of a good and far more qualified officer. It was therefore no wonder that Kerr was known throughout the Strathclyde Police CID as the Poison Dwarf; more commonly and phonetically shortened to Papa Delta.

Now, as his visitors patiently waited in the outer office with his aide, a uniformed Inspector, Kerr sipped at his coffee until he decided that they had waited long time enough. Running a hand across his thick, gelled hair that continued to retain its strawberry blonde colour thanks to his wife's attention to his weekly shampoo and hair dye, he pressed the button on his intercom and instructed the Inspector to send both men in.

The door was opened by the Inspector, with Cruickshank and Morton closely following behind her.

The Inspector began to announce the two men, "Mister Cruickshank and…" only to be cut short when Kerr loudly barked, "I know who they are you bloody fool, now leave us." Embarrassed though she was, it occurred to Morton for a split second the Inspector was about to angrily retort, but red-faced and tight-lipped she hastily withdrew, though not without slamming the door behind her.

No love lost there, thought Morton who saw that the two wooden chairs in the room had been placed against a far wall and guessed that neither he nor Cruickshank would be invited to sit.

His thoughts proved correct when sitting back in his leather, swivel chair, his hands arched in front of his nose and without the courtesy of greeting the two detectives, Kerr abruptly snapped, "Tell me about this missing policewoman."

Cruickshank turned and nodded to Morton who taking his cue, replied, "Constable Lesley Rudd, sir. Twenty-seven years of age with six years' service. Unmarried and as far as we can ascertain, she lives alone. At the time of her disappearance she was tasked with the Paisley Road Toll beats in the Kinning Park area of Glasgow. She was last heard of just a few minutes after eight on Saturday evening when she acknowledged a call to attend the report of a drunk lying in Middlesex Street near to Scotland Street. The locus is on her beat and is an approximate distance of just about half a mile away from where her blood-stained cap was later discovered in the dockside area of Mavisbank Quay. At that time a physical search of the area proved negative; however, when I dispatched two officers to her home address, they found her flat in Baker Street in Langside had been broken into."

"Anything stolen?"

"We're uncertain, sir," Morton shook his head, "though we did manage to tie the housebreaking down to some time between eight-fifteen on Saturday night and twenty minutes past three this morning." He paused and briefly wondered why Kerr wasn't taking notes. "A subsequent search of the water by police divers found her issued police radio. As we speak, the police launch *Semper Vigilo* and Mister Parsonage of the Glasgow Humane Society continue to search the River Clyde, but nothing found as yet."

Kerr stared at Morton as though trying to see through him, then lazily turned his attention to Cruickshank and asked, "What's your take on this, Detective Chief Superintendent?"

He didn't immediately respond, but then quietly replied, "At this time, sir, everything that can be done is being done. Unfortunately, even though we have blood staining on Rudd's cap, we are unable to ascertain if she has come to harm from another individual. The dock area underfoot is fraught with danger from spilled oil, grease and all manner of other materials and it might be that in the dark she has slipped, injured herself and then fell into the water. We just do not know. However, if indeed she has been the victim of an assault and abducted, DCI Morton has organised an incident room with two teams of paired detectives to make inquiry into her disappearance. At the minute, Constable Rudd is being treated as a missing person for quite frankly, that's all we have."

"And the newspapers? You do realise that once those bastards get the story it will run on all their front pages," he snapped at the two men. "A police officer missing or may be even murdered and they'll say that if we can't find one of our own, how the hell will be able to find any other missing persons?"

"As I said, at this time, sir, with the lack of any concrete evidence there is nothing to indicate she has been assaulted let alone murdered," Cruickshank stared down at him. "As for the newspapers, DCI Morton intends contacting Chief Inspector Donnelly in the Media Office and together they will agree on a press statement. Isn't that so," he turned to him.

First I've heard of it, thought Morton, but dutifully nodded and replied, "Yes, sir."

"What's the chances this woman has just simply taken off somewhere, maybe with a boyfriend?" Kerr leaned forward, his hands flat on his desk.

Cruickshank pursed his lips and slowly replied, "Who knows what goes through the head of a young woman, sir, but if her personnel file is anything to go by and I have no reason to doubt the annual assessment reports, Constable Rudd is a smart and conscientious officer with a bright future in the Force. No," he shook his head, "neither DCI Morton nor I believe, as you so succinctly put it, that she has simply taken off."

"Then what is your *private* assessment of her disappearance and be aware that I will be meeting tomorrow with the Chief Constable and he will undoubtedly have this issue as the first item on his schedule."

"Our private assessment is Constable Rudd is dead."

There we go again, thought the stoic Morton; the boss including me in his own opinion.

Kerr's face twisted as though he were deep in thought, but the truth was he really couldn't give a shit about this stupid woman getting herself bumped off if indeed that is what has happened. Besides, there are too many women in the job anyway, was his own view. However, as the head of the CID he needed something solid, something with which to impress the Chief that he had his finger on the button, that he was leading the charge.

"This incident room you've set up," he addressed Morton. "I assume you are treating this as a major inquiry; a murder inquiry?"

Perhaps if we knew she was actually dead thought Morton, but calmly replied, "No, sir. It remains a missing person inquiry until such times we have evidence to suggest otherwise."

Kerr flushed and his mouth tightened as he realised he had walked straight into that. Taking a slow breath, he sneered, "So how do you propose to fund this incident room if it's not being treated as a major inquiry?"

Morton shrugged and replied, "I'll use what resources I have, sir. I have more than enough willing volunteers who will step forward in the search for one of their own."

Good response, Colin, thought Cruickshank, who smoothly interjected with, "I'm certain if you bring DCI Morton's plans to the attention of the Chief Constable and given his recent speech about the solidarity of the police brotherhood, sir, he must surely agree with the setting up of the incident room to find his missing constable."

"Yes, yes, of course," Kerr nodded, but had no idea to what speech Cruickshank referred. Lifting a sheaf of papers from his desk as though eager to get on with the paperwork, he tightly smiled as he dismissed them with, "I'm certain you gentlemen have more than enough to be going on with. Be sure to keep me apprised of any development."

Taking their leave of Kerr, they walked together through the empty command corridor on the first floor towards the stairs that would take Cruickshank down to the underground car park while Morton visited the Media Department.

"Police brotherhood?" Morton turned towards him. "When and where did the Chief give *that* speech?"

Cruickshank smiled and stifling a laugh, replied, "To the best of my knowledge he didn't, but that wee shite back there would never admit to not knowing. Oh, boy," he reached into his jacket pocket for his pipe, "I'd love to be a fly on the wall tomorrow when he quotes *that* back to the Chief."

****

Promising to make Cruickshank aware of any progress in the inquiry, Colin Morton pushed open the door of the Media Department and walking along the narrow corridor, saw Chief Inspector Jimmy Donnelly, his shirt sleeves rolled back to his bony elbows, sat hunched over a desk chewing the end of a plastic pen as he peered at a sheet of paper in a typewriter and though it was a Sunday, Morton saw at least three other staff members at their desks.

Like most overly tall men, Donnelly was slightly stooped as though used to bending to speak to smaller individuals. With a mop of wiry, unruly grey hair and wire framed NHS glasses, he could easily have been dismissed as a schoolmaster rather than the liaison between Strathclyde Police and the media that he was, but to their cost many reporters and their editors had made that mistake by underestimating the sharp and shrewd Donnelly.

He turned as he heard Morton call his name and and smiling, greeted him with, "Morning, Colin. Coffee or tea?"

"Whisky would be better, but I'll have a coffee for now," Morton grinned at him.

Minutes later with their mugs and cigarettes in their hands, the two men were seated at Donnelly's desk.

"No word of your missing cop yet?"

"Nothing when I left Govan," Morton sighed, "and if there has been any developments, I'm certain Irene Crichton would have tracked me down with the info."

"How is our Bessie these days?"

"Still plugging away. I'm lucky to have her," Morton nodded then sipped at his coffee.

"Bad business about her husband. Heard about it through the usual grapevine. Typist at his office in Maryhill I heard and I also heard he's not the first polis she's run away with."

Again, Morton nodded then with a cautious glance about him to ensure he wouldn't be overheard, quietly replied, "Aye, the bastard left her pretty devastated, Jimmy, but you know what

Irene's like. Jumped right back into it. She doesn't talk much about it, but she's no mug either. I understand she's got a pal that runs a law office and the unofficial word is her lawyer took the cheating bastard for their house in Newlands and goodly bit of his pension and commutation goes to Irene when his thirty years are in. Maybe his typist bird won't be too keen on him now she knows he's going to be scraping by on a lot less than she thinks when he retires. Right, about this press release. I take it that you've had the papers contact you about Lesley Rudd?"

"All the local ones, aye, and by tomorrow if she hasn't turned up, likely we'll have the television crews knocking on our door looking for an update."

Donnelly put his mug down and placing his cigarette on an overflowing ashtray, reached for a pen and a notebook and asked, "Any idea what you want to say?"

"Well, you're the expert, Jimmy, and likely you will have worded more than a few appeals for information about missing persons, so other than providing you with the details, can I leave it with you to type something up?"

Donnelly grinned and nodding, replied, "I wish there were more SIO's like you, Colin, that leaves the press releases to the experts unlike some of these plonkers who think they're God's gift to the news industry. Yeah, I'll get something drafted up by this afternoon and run it by you before I release it to the locals. However as I said, if the lassie isn't found by tomorrow you might find yourself in front of the cameras."

"No," Morton, shook his head, "not me, Jimmy. If it comes to facing cameras, I've appointed Irene as the lead on this. It's politics," he shrugged. "We can't be seen to have a DCI in charge of a missing person inquiry when we don't have DCI's in charge of other such inquiries." He raised a hand to quell Donnelly's protest and continued, "If God forbid, the lassie turns up dead then yes, I take over but for now, it's Irene, okay?"

"So, any information that comes in as a result of the press

release goes to DI Crichton then?"

"That's the way of it. Now," he drained his mug and smacking his lips, asked, "any more of that coffee left?"

****

Janie Wallace elected to drive and opened the conversation with Peter Rossi by asking, "Did you request a transfer to G Division or what?"

"No," he shook his head. "I'd have preferred to remain in the E Division area because that was my parent Division, but the vacancy came up and well, here I am," he stared through the front windscreen as he smiled.

"Do you know the Pollok area at all?"

"Apart from dumping my files and bits and pieces at the office, not really. I've never been there before. It's quite a shabby wee office, I thought. Seems my desk is in the Portacabin through the back. My desk," he repeated and shook his head. "I'll need to do something about that. It's only got three legs and the corner with the missing leg is balanced on a pile of old law books."

"It's likely because you're the new guy, they given you the worst position in the office, but they're not a bad bunch up there. Sometimes my job as a female officer when there are no females on the shift takes me around the Division interviewing women and kids, that sort of thing. Pollok's a bit hectic at times, but you'll probably be used to that if you've worked in Shettleston, eh?"

"Oh, aye," he nodded. "Shettleston can get busy too. So, what's your story? As an aide I take it you're keen to join the CID?"

"That's why I signed up," she smiled as she steered the car on to the M8 motorway. "Don't get me wrong, I liked the uniform side of the job too, but I've always had this hankering to be a detective," she blushed.

He surprised her by agreeing, "Me too. I've got seven years in now and everything I did was to work towards joining the CID."

"So, will you have far to travel to Pollok?"

"No," he shook his head. "I've an upper cottage flat over in Kingsacre Road in Kings Park. Do you know it?"

"I know Kings Park," she replied, concentrating on the road as she manoeuvred around a brace of articulated lorries on the inside lane, "but not that well."

"And you? Where do you live?"

"Oh, I'm living with my boyfriend Paul over in Knightswood," she smiled and briefly turned towards him. "He's a professional footballer, plays for Partick Thistle."

"Oh, the Jags," he pursed his lips. "I'm a Celtic fan myself. What's Paul's surname?"

"Fisher. Paul Fisher. His nickname is Sharkie," she smiled as though it were a little foolish, "and he plays on the left wing."

"Oh, aye," Rossi nodded. "I've seen him play. Isn't he on the shortlist to be called up for the national team?"

"Yes," she smiled happily and a little proudly. "We've had the press at our door looking for a comment, but it's still not been ratified yet."

"Aye, he's a good player right enough," Rossi nodded then asked, "Been together long?"

"Nigh on two years. And you? Married or single?"

"Single and fancy free," he grinned before adding, "Or I am now. I was seeing someone up to a couple of months ago, but it kind of fell through," he shrugged, but didn't explain further.

"Sorry to hear that. Right, can you check the A to Z and give me directions to the house? The book's in the glove box."

He fetched the handbook out and began flipping through the directory until he found Knowehead Gardens.

"Right, let me see," he muttered as he turned to page one-two-four and commenced to give Janie directions. A little over fifteen minutes later they were slowly driving along a quiet road bordered by detached Wimpey houses.

"This is nice," she glanced about her, seeking the number of the house and aware that more than one resident out washing their car or tending their garden gave the CID vehicle a curious glance.

They found the sisters house to be in the cul-de-sac at the end of the road.

Getting out of the vehicle it was clear that the occupants of the house had been expecting them for the door was opened as they strode along the neatly tended path.

Janie stopped, her surprise evident when she saw Ellen McNeill, for though her hair was a little longer and she was not as shapely as Lesley, the casually dressed young woman was an identical twin to her sister. However, feeling a little guilty at what she was thinking, she thought Ellen McNeill to be a frumpier version of the sleek and shapely Lesley.

"Sorry," she blustered, "it's just that I didn't expect…"

Seeing Janie's confusion, Ellen raised her hand and said, "It's fine. We get that a lot," then asked, "Has there been any word yet?"

"No," Janie shook her head, "nothing at the time we left the office."

"Oh," her disappointment was obvious, but then she forced a smile and said, "Please, come in."

Leading them from the front door through the hallway into the front room, Janie introduced them both and turned her head towards the sound of a television blaring from upstairs.

"I've let my daughters watch a video in their room while you're here," Ellen explained then added, "My husband is a manager with JVC so he's got one of the new VHS VCR's home to test run."

Rossi retorted, "Lucky them. I'm still using a black and white tele."

Inviting them to sit in the untidy but comfortable room, Ellen turned when a tall, thin and casually dressed man wearing thick spectacles entered the room behind them.

"This is my husband, Jacob. Jake for short," she introduced him. Nodding, he smiled nervously and asked, "Tea or coffee?"

They both agreed on coffee and with Ellen also seated, Janie asked, "What have you been told, Missus McNeil?"

She took a deep breath and replied, "Ellen, please. A detective Welling I think he said his name was…"

"DS Whelan?"

"That's it. All he said was that Lesley was on duty last night and while she was on shift, she went missing. Oh, and that her cap was found."

Noting that she didn't mention the bloodstaining on the cap, Janie decided there was no need to refer it.

Her lower lip began to tremble and she asked, "Do you think…I mean, is it possible she…" but now biting at her lip, twisted the handkerchief in her hands and her legs began to shake.

"Look," Janie held up her hand and a little more sharply than she intended, said, "we don't know what's happened to Lesley so let's not get ahead of ourselves thinking the worst. The purpose of our visit is to find out if there is any reason that you might know why Lesley would suddenly take off in the middle of her shift. Perhaps something that's been worrying her, something that she might have confided in you?"

Frowning, Ellen inhaled and then exhaling replied, "I can't think of anything and yes, if there was something that is bothering her, Lesley would have shared it with me." She half smiled and continued, "We might look the same, but we have always had different aspirations in life. Even as children I was always the domesticated one, playing with dolls and pretending to keep house while Lesley liked toy soldiers and toy cars, those sort of things. In fact, we were not unlike my own two kids in that we liked different things," she mused.

"Can you think of anywhere she might have gone; anyone she might have trusted enough to visit or seek shelter with?"

Tight-lipped as she concentrated her thoughts, Ellen slowly shook her head and replied, "We lost our parents in our late teens, though of course we have aunties and uncles and cousins, but I can't imagine Lesley contacting any of them before me, if you see what I mean. So no, not unless…" she hesitated, but it wasn't lost on either Rossi or Janie who asked, "What?"

"Well, I know they've broken up, but there's always Fraser Anderson. She might have, I don't know," she held her hands out and shrugged as though doubting herself. "Contacted him? Maybe even went to see him?"

"And who is Fraser Anderson?"

"Lesley and Fraser..." she paused, but this time as though about to disclose a personal detail. "They were together for a long time, nearly three years."

Janie asked again, "And Fraser is?"

"Oh, he's one of you. A policeman, well, he's a *detective* now as he kept reminding us," he pulled a face and it seemed obvious to Janie and Rossi that Anderson was not overly liked."

While Janie asked the questions, Rossi sat quietly, taking notes. "And can you tell me where Fraser works?"

"I think it's in the city entre somewhere. I don't know the name of the office, though."

"Here we are," her husband entered the room carrying a plastic tray with four mugs of coffee, milk and sugar bowl and a plate of biscuits. Ellen rose from her chair to fetch a small table from against the wall that she placed in front of Janie and Rossi. When they had their mugs in their hands, Jake said, "What have I missed?"

"We're just trying to establish where Lesley might have got to," Rossi smiled at him and turning to Janie, his eyebrows raised to indicate she continue.

"When was the last time you heard from Lesley?" she asked Ellen.

"Oh, let me see. Yesterday, about six or just after. She said she was on a break and calling from the office and phoned to ask about a birthday present for our Nicky...Nicola. She's just about to turn six. Fergus is seven," she added with a nervous smile.

"How did she sound?"

"How did…Lesley? How do you mean?"

"Well, did she sound worried, upset, anything like that? That she needed to talk or anything?"

"No, not that I can think of," Ellen's brow knitted as she slowly shook her head. "She just sounded her usual self."

"Now," Janie inhaled, "I don't want to alarm you or anything, but I need to ask. Is there anything you know about anyone who might mean your sister harm? Did she ever speak about being afraid or worried about someone?"

Ellen visibly paled and about to reply, stopped, not trusting herself to speak, but again slowly shook her head.

"Is that what you think," her husband leaned forward from his chair, "that someone might have hurt Lesley?"

"We don't know, but it's a question we have to ask. Is there anyone or anything that you can think of that might have caused Lesley to leave in the middle of her shift?"

Ellen turned to stare at Jake and reached for his hand.

Rossi watched as Jake stepped forward to take his wife's hand, but something about it niggled him, almost like Jake was surprised.

"I've been racking my brains all morning since I got the phone call from your office," Ellen said, "but I can't think of a single reason my sister would do this, just walk off without leaving word. No reason at all," she added in a soft voice as the tears began to trickle down her cheeks.

Janie turned to Rossi who taking his cue, asked, "Tell me about Fraser and her relationship with him. Was it a happy time for her and if it was, do you know why they broke it off?"

Ellen dabbed at her eyes with the handkerchief she held and taking a breath to compose herself, glanced at Jake before she nodded and said, "I really thought they were going to get married and they had talked about getting engaged, but…"

She exhaled as though the memory was hurtful, then continued, "It was Lesley's decision to break it off."

"And do you know why?" he asked.

"Like I told you, I was always the domestic one, the earth mother, as Lesley used to call me," she smiled self-consciously. "She is more driven than me, very career minded. Anyway, I suppose you need to know so the simple truth is that Lesley doesn't want kids and Fraser does. Or that's what she told me," Janie didn't miss the flicker in Ellen's eyes.

"What she told you?" Janie repeated, then asked, "Didn't you believe her?"

There's that glance again to her husband, Rossi saw, then Ellen replied, "Lesley and I shared a lot, but there were some thing she kept to herself." She shrugged and added, "I know she definitely did not want children, but I got the feeling that wasn't the whole story about the breakup."

"And what do you think she held back? Your opinion, I mean?"

"I got the opinion that she didn't fully trust Fraser. He was a bit," she paused, "What is it that you call someone who is a bit full of themselves?"

"You mean you thought he was wide?" Janie smiled.

"That's it," Ellen nodded. "I thought he was too wide."

"Can you recall when they broke off their relationship?"

"Oh, it wasn't that long ago," she turned to Jake as if seeking clarification and asked, "What, about two, maybe three months?"

"No more than three months," he agreed.

"And Fraser. Apart from him being wide, did you like him?"

"Well yes, I suppose he was alright, but…" she turned again to her husband with a glance that indicated she wanted him to respond.

Twisting his mouth, he said, "I thought he was a bit of a blowhard. Anytime we had them over for dinner he would hog the conversation about giving this guy the jail or that guy the jail and it was always about him being a lot smarter than the guys he locked up."

"Oh, he wasn't that bad," Ellen tried to interject, but Jake raised a hand and continued, "That's because he was a bit of a charmer too. Look, I'm not saying I totally disliked Fraser, but he was the sort of a guy that when the women weren't listening, he had a dirty joke to tell and frankly…" he paused and staring at Rossi asked, "that's just not my style." His brow furrowed when he asked, "Will this get back to him?"

"Not from us," Rossi assured him, but thought it wasn't what Jake said, it was what he wasn't telling them and guessed he wasn't being entirely truthful for Rossi got the impression that Jake really did not like Anderson. Not at all.

"Did you see much of Fraser?" Janie asked them both, but it was Jake who replied, "Only when he visited here with Lesley," he glanced at his wife as though for confirmation and added, "The truth is we always thought he wasn't as bright as Lesley, that she could have done a lot better than him. To hear him talk you would think that he was sometimes trying to talk down to Lesley as if to prove that he was..." he paused again and staring at Janie and Rossi in turn, said, "I don't think I'm explaining this properly. What I'm trying to say is that he bragged about being a detective as though her being a uniformed police woman just wasn't up to his level."

"You think," Rossi shrugged, "he was a kind of macho man? Had to be the boss in the relationship?"

"Yes, that's it exactly," Jake nodded, eager to seize upon the explanation.

It was then a thought struck Rossi, one that he couldn't shake for he wondered, was Jake McNeill jealous of Fraser Anderson?

"Can I use your phone?" Janie suddenly got to her feet.

"Oh, it's on the table in the hallway there," Jake pointed to the door.

When she'd left the room, Rossi smiled as though in apology for her absence and asked Ellen, "After they broke up did Lesley meet anyone else?"

"No, not exactly."

"Not exactly?" he repeated, his brow knitting.

"Well, Lesley is a good looking girl …" but then she stopped and blushed, realising that as a mirror image of her sister she was also describing herself. "What I mean is…"

But she got no further for with a grin, Rossi replied, "There's no need to explain." Turning to Jake, he said, "Your wife is an attractive lady and you are a very lucky man."

Smiling, Jake nodded at the compliment though Rossi thought the smile seemed to be a little forced.

He prompted her, "What do you mean, Ellen, when you said not exactly?"

She exhaled through pursed lips and said, "I met Lesley for coffee in the town a couple of weeks ago, just before she was due to go on shift and she told me that there was someone who had taken a shine to her, but that she wasn't really interested. Said that this guy was too pushy and becoming a bit annoying."

Rossi felt himself tense, but remained outwardly calm when he asked, "Did she give you this guy's name or anything about him?"

Ellen didn't immediately respond, but her brow furrowed when she replied, "No, she didn't and when I kidded her on and told her not to be go all mysterious on me she just laughed and said it wasn't going to happen, that she intended dealing with it and like it wasn't worth even talking about."

"It?"

"Well," she shrugged, "I assumed she meant any kind of relationship with this guy."

"I don't want to offend you, but she definitely said it was a man? I mean, it wasn't a woman who had taken a shine to her? These days," he half smiled, "relationships can be…complicated."

Taken aback, Ellen stared at him and frowning, replied, "You know, I don't think she did say it was a man. I suppose I just assumed it was a man." Her brow furrowed as she fought to recall how Lesley had described the person then eyes widening, said, "Lesley told me it was someone. She didn't say a man. I'm sure of that, now. Like I said I supposed I just thought it was a man." Her face reddened when she continued, "I mean, Lesley isn't a queer or anything. She likes men," then waving her hands as though to dismiss smearing her sister's reputation, added, "I mean, she's not…"

Grinning, Rossi held up his hand to stop her and said, "I think I know what you mean, Ellen. Now…"

But he got no further for the door opened to admit Janie who led two small girls into the room.

"Found these two monkeys sitting on the stairs," she smiled as the children run to embrace their mother.

She snatched a glance at Peter Rossi then said, "I also regret having to tell you, Ellen, that Lesley's flat was broken into. We believe it occurred sometime during Saturday evening or the early hours of Sunday morning. We don't yet know if it's related to Lesley's disappearance, but I'm told that there has been quite a lot of stuff thrown around as though the place has been searched. Obviously with Lesley missing, we don't know if anything has been stolen. We wonder if you would be so good at to meet us there at a time convenient to yourself to let you have a look at the place to tell us if anything obvious is missing?"

Clearly shocked, Ellen paled and said, "Her flat was burgled?"

"Ah, yes," Janie didn't explain any more, not wishing to cause further distress.

"Of course, whenever you want," Ellen nodded.

"Good, I'll square it with the boss and get back to you about a time," Janie tightly smiled.

Getting to his feet, Rossi said, "Unless there's anything else you need to ask, Janie, I believe we've enough details to complete the missing person form."

"There is one thing I should warn you about," Janie slowly said. "If Lesley doesn't show up in the next day or two, it's a given that there will be a lot of media attention about a police officer gone missing and more than likely the police will issue a photograph of Lesley to the newspapers and *possibly* the television news programmes." She stared at Ellen and with a soft smile, continued, "As her identical twin, Ellen, you will probably find yourself being badgered by the public thinking that you're Lesley and you might even have the reporters at your door if someone gives them your address. You will need to be ready for that."

"But I can't hide away here in the house," she was aghast, her eyes widening. "Jake's got his work to go to and I've my job and I've the girls to get to school and the shopping and…" she stuttered to a halt as if the enormity of what was happening suddenly hit her and she began to sob.

Sensing their mother's anxiety, the younger of the children began to softly cry and was hugged to Ellen's breast.

"Yes, well," Janie was embarrassed and with a glance at Rossi, added, "I'm sorry if that upsets you, but I felt you had to be prepared," and turned towards the door.

Ellen, holding her daughters by the hand got to her feet and sniffed, "You will let us know as soon as she's found?"

"Of course," Janie nodded goodbye and with Peter was shown to the front door by Jake.

In the hallway Jake turned to ensure the front room door was closed then said in a quiet voice, "If you know Lesley, you know she's not the type to just run off and disappear. You must suspect something has happened to her, don't you?"

He didn't miss the glance Janie gave to Rossi before she replied, "I'd prefer that you don't tell your wife, but we found some bloodstaining on her cap and it was discovered next to the River Clyde. The thinking is that she was down there patrolling and maybe slipped and fell into the water. The boss had the waters at the edge of the dock searched and the divers found her police radio in the water so no, Jake, it isn't looking good." She placed her hand on his arm and softly said, "If you tell Ellen what I've told you it will just unnecessarily worry her. If there *is* to be bad news, better it comes with a full story rather than in bits and pieces, yes?"

He nodded and muttered, "I suppose so, yes."

****

Moments later and seated in the car, Rossi said, "Do you think it was wise, telling her husband about the blood and the radio?"

"Maybe not," she grimly replied, "but what if Lesley turns up dead and they later learn we had that information and didn't disclose it."

"Point taken," he nodded. "I assume you phoned the DI?"

"Yes. She instructed me to mention the housebreaking at Lesley's flat to gauge their reaction, but they seemed pretty surprised, don't you think?"

"They did, yes," he agreed with a nod.

"Well, now the DI's got the name and that he works in the city centre somewhere," Janie replied, "she says she'll contact the personnel office and find out if this guy Fraser Anderson is working out of Stewart Street or is with one of the squads at Pitt Street. In the meantime, we've to head back into the office."

CHAPTER FOUR

Their long hours were beginning to show on the faces of DS Tam Whelan and his neighbour, DC Ian McDonald.

Returning to Govan office with McDonald driving, Whelan sat with his eyes closed and was having an involuntary quick forty winks. Just as McDonald turned the car through the arch into the rear yard of Orkney Street, he nudged his older colleague and said, "Wake up, Tam, we're here."

"Aye, right," Whelan acknowledged him and yawned while he rubbed the sleep from his eyes.

Climbing the wrought iron circular back stairs from the muster room to the CID suite on the upper floor, both men wondered if there had been any developments since they had left to re-interview Lesley Rudd's neighbours and were disappointed that they were returning with no further information.

They were met in the corridor by Irene Crichton who with a sheaf of papers in her hand, beckoned they follow her into the incident room.

In the room they saw a well known face lazily seated at a desk, a mug of coffee in one hand and a Senior Service dangling between the fingers of the other with a fine trail of cigarette ash running down his lapel.

"Tam Whelan," the man grinned at him. "Still hammering the shite out of the Govan neds?"

Whelan smiled and replied, "Not in the recent past, Alex. Not since the rubber heels gave me my last warning."

"Aye, I heard about that," Alex Murray slowly nodded. "Something to do with a wife assault, was it?"

"Guy in Copland Road was using his wife like a punch bag. I took him down to the half landing to explain to him the error of his ways, then had to defend myself when he attacked me," Whelan innocently explained.

"Aye," McDonald grinned, "but it was him that ended up in the casualty, wasn't it big guy?"

"What can I say," Whelan replied to laughter then fetching a crumpled pack of Capstan cigarettes from his jacket pocket and withdrawing one for himself, offered the pack to Irene and McDonald, the latter who refused with, "Too strong for me, Tam, I'll smoke my own."

Drawing deeply on her Capstan and resting her backside against a desk, Irene nodded towards Murray and with a tight smile, said, "Alex here attended at Lesley Rudd's flat. Tell them what you found, Alex."

Murray, a tall, gangly man wearing an old, but sharply ironed brown three-piece suit, highly polished shoes, his thinning Brylcreemed hair combed into a severe left parting with a greying, waxed moustache, stroked his moustache with nicotine stained fingers and smiled. A living legend among the Glasgow CID and even among his peers in the Scene of Crime Department, Murray was born a Glaswegian but served most of his thirty-five years as a SOCO with the Ayrshire

Constabulary. However, after the amalgamation of the city and county police services to the Force that became Strathclyde Police, Murray was to his dismay transferred to the main SOC office at Police Headquarters in Pitt Street. Now approaching his sixty-fifth birthday, he had already decided that by the end of the year he would take his pension and savings then he and his wife would flee the UK for a small two bedroomed flat in the sunnier climate of the Costa Del Sol, a daydream that he never tired of relating.

Drawing a breath, he stubbed the fag end out into a small tea plate that served as an ashtray and was about to begin when the door opened to admit not only DCI Colin Morton, but Janie Wallace who was closely followed by Peter Rossi.

"Ah," Irene held up her hand to stop Murray and said, "You guys are just in time. Alex here has given Rudd's flat the once over and he's got something interesting to report. Alex?" she gave Murray a nod to begin, but was taken aback when fixing his watery blue eyes on the attractive Janie Wallace, he smoothly said in a polite and cultured voice, "We haven't been introduced, my dear. Where have you been all my life?"

"I don't think I was born for the first fifty years," she coolly snapped back to more laughter.

"Aye, very good hen," he grinned at her, then continued, "Right then, before I relate the result of my examination of Constable Rudd's flat, I have to report that the examination of the dock area by my colleagues turned up nothing. Sorry," he shook his head at the DCI, "but I know those guys and I'm certain they did a good job. Now, Constable Rudd's flat. I'm of the opinion that the door was forced open by a rubber key."

"Rubber key?" Janie couldn't help herself and blushed at the knowing stares.

"Aye, the bottom of someone's boot," Murray smiled. "Once the culprit was in I have to agree with Tam Whelan's assessment. It seems to me that whoever broke in to the lassie's flat wasn't there to steal. I say this because there was a lot of relatively valuable stuff left lying or discarded on the floors.

Jewellery, some of it gold, a ring with a diamond that might have fetched a few quid and in a cupboard I also discovered a couple of cameras too; all left lying and ignored. As Tam has opined," he paused, "the way the stuff was strewn about makes me think the culprit was looking for something. Now, I dusted the usual places one might expect to find prints, but all I got was scuff marks that suggests to me the culprit wore gloves." He smiled and reached forward to accept a Capstan from Whelan that he lit from an old, but polished Zippo lighter. Taking a lungful of tobacco, he continued, "For those of you who are perhaps a little short of experience about housebreaking, let me give you some advice."

His face expressionless, Morton silently thought tis was a typical Alex Murray briefing. Why be concise and waste a good story when you can draw it out for half an hour.

"Now," Murray continued as he pointedly stared in turn at McDonald, Janie and Rossi, "your experienced housebreaker will empty his bowels and bladder before he breaks into a property whereas your inexperienced housebreaker, once in the property, will be nervous and anxious. He will find his adrenalin going like a runaway train and he will have the sudden urge either to pee or even have what I like to call, some intestinal hurry."

"What's intestinal hurry?" asked Rossi.

"The urgent compulsion to have a shit," Murray grinned at him. For God's sake, Alex, hurry up, Morton silently prayed, but knew there was no rushing the older, but very professional Murray when he was relating one of his stories.

But he finally gave in to his impatience and asked, "So, Alex, what's this interesting thing you have to report?"

"Well, boss, the first thing I should mention is that Constable Rudd kept a very neat, clean and tidy flat. There was not the usual dust I normally find so while I took a lot of fingerprints that I suspect are hers, I also discovered a lot of the smudges that like I said caused me to suspect the culprit wore gloves. However," he could not but help himself from smiling when he added, "I also found the toilet seat up and it was a plastic toilet seat, too."

"Oh, I see." Surprised but pleased, Morton nodded.

"See what, boss," McDonald turned to stare curiously at Morton, who smiled and replied, "Tell him, Tam."

Whelan exhaled and smiled at McDonald, then as though speaking to a child, said, "Why would a toilet seat be in the up position, son?"

With sudden realisation, McDonald closed his eyes and slowly shaking his head at his own foolishness, replied, "Because it was a man who used the toilet to pee."

"Exactly," Murray interjected and nodded, "and let me ask you this, young Ian. Have you ever tried to fetch your willie out of your trousers and underpants while wearing a pair of gloves?"

McDonald grinned and replied, "No. But I'm guessing that as it was a women's flat the culprit had to lift the toilet seat and when he did, he had taken off his gloves?"

"Spot on, son," Murray grinned at him.

To Morton, he said, "The culprit might have thought he was being clever wearing gloves throughout the flat, but I've lifted what seems to be a perfect index finger print from the right hand underside of the toilet seat, boss, so all I need is a name to compare them to. If you come up with a suspect, the prints will be at the Fingerprints Department just waiting on your suspects name."

"Good man, Alex," Morton smiled at Murray, but then a thought occurred to him and addressing the team, he said, "Under no circumstances, no matter who it might be or what rank they might hold, this information about having a set of prints lifted from Lesley's flat is not to be divulged at this time. Nobody but *nobody* outside this room is to be told unless either the DI or myself clears it. Is that absolutely clear?"

He turned his head and saw each in turn either nod or mumble "Yes, sir."

"Right then. Again, Alex, well done and thank you," which was a polite, though clear dismissal for the SOCO, before turning to

Irene and saying, "Can I have a word, please?"
****

Maybe it was the two fingers of whisky and the beer he had drunk. Maybe it was just the usual poor sleeping pattern from being on the nightshift, but Iain Meikle knew it was neither and finally admitted he couldn't sleep because his mind was in a whirl.

Where the hell are you, Les, he wondered.

Giving in to a full bladder, he grunted and forced himself from the bed then stumbling from the darkened room, made his way to the toilet. As he pee'd, he thought again of Les and his brow furrowed.

Eric Little had almost hit the nail on the head. Yes, he had fancied Lesley Rudd from the minute he saw her. God, who wouldn't? She was stunningly beautiful, but he had never as much as hinted at his attraction for her because after all, what would a young woman with everything going for her ever see in the likes of a deadbeat like him. But then that attraction faded for he had come to realise that rather than being sexually attracted to her, he liked Les both as a friend and a colleague. Besides, he grinned at his foolishness, apart from that time on holiday he hadn't been near a woman since the divorce and as there was currently no woman in his life, didn't see himself having one in the near future.

Yawning, he flushed the toilet and run his hands under the tap, wiping them on the towel hanging behind the door and idly noted it needed washed.

Making his way through to the kitchen he set the kettle to boil then running a hand through his thick mop of hair, slumped down into a chair. Sunday night was the fifth of the seven late shifts that finished on Tuesday, then court duties aside, he normally slept for the whole of Wednesday morning, completed his domestic chores during the remainder of the day and had Thursday to himself before commencing the early shift on Friday. He didn't want to wish his life of the next five years away away, but God; sometimes he ached for retirement.

The whistle of the kettle disturbed his thoughts and he rose from the chair to brew a pot of tea. Much as he enjoyed coffee, Iain was convinced the caffeine was ruining his bladder and was unsuccessfully trying to wean himself off it or at least cut down on his intake.

Settled back into the chair with his mug, he thought again of the discussion with Eric Little. They had both agreed that if the Inspector, Mickey Kane, had been on duty he would never had let Les out on her own, no matter how capable an officer she is. He smiled and recalled the time some months previously when she had argued with both him and Eric when they had teased her that policewomen needed a male cop with them on the beat to protect them.

"Aye, like we're all shrinking violets…I don't think!" she had furiously responded, then burst into a wide grin when she realised he and Eric were winding her up.

That was the thing about Les, he sighed; she was *not* a shrinking violet and quite prepared to hitch up her skirt, draw her handbag sized wooden baton and get stuck in when there was any kind of melee. He smiled when he recalled an incident some months before when a fight had erupted at a well known, but troublesome hostelry on the corner of Rathlin Street at Govan Road.

It was when he, Eric Little and Inspector Kane were trying to remove both the bruised and bloodied protagonists and drawing their batons, were laying about them at the rest of the pub's rough clientele who pulling, punching and kicking at the three officers, tried to rescue the prisoners. Suddenly and to the surprise of the crowd, a stunning looking, blonde haired bombshell appeared from the doorway behind them then with her handbag sized baton in one hand and her cap in the other, laid about their heads and shoulders. So surprised were the crowd they peeled away like a rotten banana skin, their faces registering their shock as Les effed and blinded at them, all the while using her baton and kicking at them too while she cleared a path for her colleagues and their prisoners.

Aye, he continued to smile, she was a game lassie…he stopped and his face contorted, suddenly aware he was already thinking of her in the past tense.

It never for one moment occurred to Iain that Les had simply walked off and disappeared from her shift. He gave some thought at what was wee being bandied among his colleagues, that she had probably slipped on the dock and struck her head on the concrete ground then rolled towards the edge of the dock before plummeting down into the water. However, the more he thought about it the less likely it seemed to him that someone as smart and as bright as Les would be so foolish to walk on the oil and grease coated ground so close to the edge of the dock and particularly on such a wet and windy night.

His brow furrowed as he considered the other and to his mind, more plausible explanation; that she had been assaulted and thrown or forced into the water. Yes, a chill run down his spine as he unconsciously nodded. That seemed to him to be more likely what had happened.

She had been attacked…but by who?

Obviously it must have been a ned, maybe someone who had been thieving around the dock area, but then biting at his lower lip, he wondered; what was there to steal from the docks now that they were mostly derelict?

He couldn't imagine that what lead remained on the roofs would be of any interest and thought it highly improbable that even a desperate ned would be on the warehouse roofs in such wet weather and on a Saturday night?

No, it had to be something else.

Though he could not know it, he mirrored the thoughts of DCI Colin Morton who suspected that if indeed Les had been assaulted, it was likely by someone she had dealings with; some ned with a grievance.

Aye, he angrily nodded, that was it. Some bastard who had it in for her probably followed her when she was out walking the beat and took advantage of the lonely and desolate dock area to attack her.

But that again provoked the previous thought.

What the hell was she doing down in the dock area?

His eyes began to close and at last realised he was ready for sleep.

With that thought in mind, he rose from the chair and made his way through to the bedroom.

****

With his worldly possessions carried in his two plastic bag, Sam Fullerton shuffled along Cadogan Street towards the Anderston bus station where he knew there was always some good pickings in the bins there and was unmindful to the curious stares and glances of the occasional passer-by.

Though many ignored the old man, some stepped aside or stared with silent compassion while still others gawked with hostile eyes at his appearance. Though he heard, Sam did not react when he heard one fashionably dressed young woman even loudly commenting to her sniggering companion that, "People like him shouldn't be allowed out in public."

Yet none of those who passed him by would ever give thought as to what caused a man like Sam to be so pitiful, never consider that this survivor of two wartime sunk ships, this man who in his younger years survived the cold waters of the Atlantic and the burning sea of the Mediterranean, might be suffering from a mental illness.

It was unfortunate too that because of the life he had fallen into, Sam had no access to a radio or television and the only newspapers he came across were those that had been discarded and were usually at least one day out of date. Even then he paid sparse attention to the written content, for the newspaper itself was more valuable to him as an insulating material rather than a source of world or local events; wrapping them around his body beneath the overcoat he so treasured or scrunching them into tight wads to be consumed on the small fires he lit to reheat the food he found in waste bins.

Head down and blissfully unaware that he might have information the police could consider vital to the inquiry, Sam continued towards the bus station and so did not see the young woman who stood in the shadow of the lane.

Aged just twenty-nine years, the slightly built Elsie McClure had been on the smack for nigh on six years and prostituting herself for the last four years. Her heroin habit had cost her everything. Her marriage, her two weans to the social and her mother who overcome by grief that her only daughter had fallen into this kind of life, suffered a stroke from which she never recovered.

That Elsie was still alive was testament to her frequent spells in hospital where counsellors and former drug abusers worked hard to persuade the unfortunate men and women like Elsie to quit the habit that most had come to accept would finally kill them.

Shivering in the shadow of the tall buildings on either side, the stick-thin, dyed blonde short-haired Elsie wore nothing beneath her long sleeved, grey coloured hooded top nor knickers beneath her red coloured, leather mini skirt. Her outfit was completed by knee length, once white coloured schoolgirl socks and grimy training shoes.

Well, she *had* worn a pair of knickers when she started out earlier that morning from the squat she shared in Maryhill with three other junkies, but her last punter just fifteen minutes before had not only refused to pay her the twenty quid for the knee-trembler, but then laughed when he slapped her to the ground and ignoring Elsie's curses, torn then stolen her knickers and brandished them like a trophy as he run off.

Not that Elsie was unused to such treatment, for in the four years she had been prostituting herself in the streets and lanes in the Anderston area known locally as 'The Drag', she had suffered an endless number of humiliations as well as countless beatings by men who considered her nothing more than a dirty whore; a quick shag who was lost to thought minutes after they finished using her.

Now shaken, but more with anger than hurt, she sniffed and wiping her running nose on her sleeve, then tightly wrapped her arms about her while she wondered if she should move to another street nearby, somewhere she might have a better opportunity to earn enough money for a hit. However, the problem was that just like Elsie, other girls had their own corners where they offered their bodies and to encroach upon another prossies territory was inviting some form of retribution that usually took the form of a good kicking.

Not that Elsie was afraid of a good square go with some of the prossies, but feeling as she was right now with the sweats and her bowels about to erupt, the last thing she needed was physical confrontation.

Frowning, she thought again about the punter who had ripped her off. A weedy teenage *bastard* who had still been wearing his Saturday night party clothes and who obviously had just finished at an all night bash somewhere. Probably bet his fucking mates he would get his Nat King before he went home, she thought.

Fucking men! She hated them all! All of them!

Her rage knew no bounds and tight-lipped, her brow creased, for that's when she saw the shuffling figure of Sam approach. Searching the ground around her, her eyes shone when she saw the empty, discarded wine bottle and impulsively reached down to lift it by the neck.

CHAPTER FIVE

Now seated in his office across the desk from Colin Morton, Irene Crichton sighed and said, "Young Janie and the new lad, Peter Rossi, told me they've been out to see the sister. Apparently she has no idea where Lesley is, but did say that a couple of weeks ago Lesley told her that," she waved his forefingers in the air as quotation marks, "some individual had an interest in Lesley, but that she wasn't interested. Tomorrow I intend having them look into that."

"Sorry," Morton shook his head as though confused, "what do you mean by some individual? Was it a man or a woman?"

"That's what the sister wasn't sure about," she shrugged. "She *assumed* it was a man but when Rossi asked her if it *was* a man, she didn't know."

"You don't know or think Lesley is queer, do you?"

"I don't know her other than to see," Irene shrugged, "but there's nothing to say she wasn't into women. However, she didn't strike me as the type if there is such a thing as the type," Irene pursed her lips. "But these days," she followed it with a sigh.

"How did Tam and his neighbour get on at the lassies address?"

"Being Sunday, they got most people at home and knocked on doors in the closes on either side as well, but nobody had anything new to tell us," she replied before asking, "How did you get on with Papa Delta?"

"All that wee bugger is interested in is the bloody budget and how much money we'll spend on finding the lassie. That and if she's found alive, take the credit or if something goes apeshit, look for some bugger to hang out to dry," then made Irene laugh when he related Alistair Cruickshank's lie to the unpopular ACC about the 'police brotherhood.'

"Any word back from the polis launch or George Parsonage?"

"Nothing yet, Irene, but to be honest, I think you'll agree it's just a matter of time before the poor wee lassie surfaces somewhere in the Clyde." He shrugged then added, "George Parsonage won't give up though, that's not his style, but much as I don't want to I think about it at the minute we'll need to consider pulling the plug on using the police launch." Before she could protest, he continued, "You know as well as I do, we'd need a reason for its extended use and if the word got out that we're spending all that money searching for one missing person on the presumption she *is* in the Clyde…" he didn't finish, aware there was no further need to explain.

Then he asked her, "Do *you* think she fell in? Slipped and banged her head?"

"No, not at all. I think somebody done for her, but until we recover her body and find out exactly what shape she's in and particularly after the length of time she's been in the water, we won't know. I suppose it all depends on how long it takes for us to find her body. It bloody frustrates me that we're treating her like any other missing person when we both know…"

She didn't finish, but stared at him and saw she was wasting her breath, for Morton felt exactly as she did. Softly inhaling then blowing out through pursed lips, she said, "So, digressing. How did you get on with Jimmy Donnelly in the Media Office?"

"Fine and oh, before I forget, Jimmy sends his regards. Anyway, he says he's going to make up a press release for us. Do you have Rudd's personnel photograph?"

"It's in the file."

"Have one of the team run it up to Jimmy. He'll make copies for the newspapers."

"They'll just love this story," she sighed.

"Aye, perhaps, but they'll be doing us a big favour if they get the request for information out there. Now, the lassie's recent cases. Do any of them stick out with somebody who might have a grievance against her?"

"Eh, not so much the cases to the PF; however, I searched her locker and lifted out a couple of her recent notebooks. Quite an organised young woman is our Lesley and kept clear and neat handwritten notes too," she slowly nodded. "One thing stood out. She's got a bee in her bonnet about Charlie Gallagher."

His eyes narrowed as he repeated, "Charlie Gallagher? *Our* Charlie Gallagher from Linthouse?"

"Aye, that Charlie Gallagher and she also has a note of his address in Burghead Drive. According to what I read in a folder she kept in her locker, she sent an intelligence report to Headquarters about him."

"Well, that's a bit of a turn-up," he was clearly surprised, then asked, "What do you mean a bee in her bonnet? Gallagher's a top player, a Z Index target for the Serious Crime Squad and the Drug Squad too. What's Rudd's interest in him?"

"Not quite sure," she shook her head. "I was going to phone the Criminal Intelligence at Pitt Street, but on hindsight I'm thinking of taking a wee turn up there to see what kind of reporting she was firing into them. Oh, and I've not told the rest of the team about this. I was thinking of keeping it to myself, for the time being."

"Yeah, probably wise," he muttered in response. "I'm worried we could end up going off on a tangent with this if after all it should turn out the lassie has slipped, dunted her head and fell into the water."

She stared keenly at him and said, "But clearly you don't think so?"

He shook his head before replying, "No, I don't. From what you've told me and the little we know about her, Lesley Rudd seems to be a sharp young woman, so my gut tells me she's dead," he sighed, then quickly added, "But that's something else we'll keep to ourselves for the time being."

"Charlie Gallagher," he mused before asking, "From what you've read in her notebooks, what's your opinion? Why is she so interested in him?"

"Well, it seems to have started about three weeks ago when she arrested Gallagher's lemon curd."

He grinned and said, "The fair maiden Paula Menzies."

"Well, that's one way of describing the torn faced bitch," she dryly replied. "Anyway, I looked out the case and it seems that Paula was caught shoplifting at the new Cooperative Hypermarket superstore in Morrison Street beneath the Kingston Bridge. Tried on an expensive ladies' woollen jacket then kept it on under her anorak and tried to walk out. Kicked up a bit of a fuss when the security got a hold of her and was also charged with assaulting two of them." She smiled and added, "Paula raked her nails down the guy's cheek and butted the female security lassie and burst her nose, though luckily for the lassie, it wasn't broken. According to the copy report I got out of the registry, when Lesley and her neighbour Iain Meikle got there, they had to handcuff Paula who also had her nose burst and had bled all over the woollen jacket she had stolen." Irene smirked when she added, "And she was and I quote, threatening to kill any bastard that touched her, unquote."

"Has the case been tried yet?"

"No, I checked," Irene shook her head. "Trial is set for December at the Sheriff Court."

"The Sheriff Court?" his face expressed his surprise. "For shoplifting and two minor assaults?"

"You're forgetting, Colin, this is Paula Menzies we're talking about here. It's her previous convictions that's taking her to the Sheriff. I mean, she's the most prolific shoplifter I've ever dealt with and though I'm only guessing here, she must have accrued what, thirty of forty odd convictions? And don't forget, that's only the times she has been caught."

She frowned and then continued, "The curious thing is though that it was Lesley who reported Paula to the PF and when I read the case, it read fine till I got to the antecedent history."

"What do you mean?"

"Well," her eyes narrowed and she leaned forward as though to emphasis the story, "she lists Paula's previous convictions like you would expect, but there was a couple of throwaway remarks that puzzled me. For one she commented that Paula had a difficult upbringing and no moral guidance in her youth that led her to a life of crime and…"

"That's a kind of odd statement to make," Morton grinned, then rubbed a weary hand across his face for the early rise was now taking its toll.

"Aye, quite the literary woman was our Lesley, but it was the second thing she wrote that stuck with me. She said that if the court were to consider a suspended sentence, Paula would willingly admit the crimes and not only apologise but make restitution to the two security officers that she had injured."

Morton stared narrow eyed at Irene and slowly said, "I see what you're getting at. You think she was trying to do a favour for Paula and in turn…"

"Paula would return the favour, yes."

"And this favour might be?"

"I'm only guessing here," she twisted her mouth, "but I think she was in the process of trying to sign Paula on as a tout."

"And of course as Charlie Gallagher's bird, Paula is in a unique position to provide information about him," Morton nodded.

"That's what I'm thinking," she agreed.

"Okay," he slowly nodded, "and that explains why Rudd has such an interest in our Charlie. But why would Paula take such a risk to inform on him? I mean, he's a vicious bastard and would easily rip her face or any other part of her that took his pleasure if she thought she was grassing on him. Or worse," he added with a frown.

"Well, whatever the reason it seems to me that Lesley thought she was in with a chance of signing Paula on. Anyway, I discovered a wee notation in Lesley's notebook for that day with a question mark against Gallagher's name and apparently she sent an Intel report to Pitt Street the same day, so first thing tomorrow morning that's where I intend starting my inquiry by having a look at that Intel report."

"Okay, then," he nodded his head in dismissal. "Let me know how you get on."

****

The blow to his head had brought Sam Fullerton to his hands and knees and dazed, he turned to stare up at the young woman, the bottle still held in her hand.

"Oh, shit!" he heard her mutter and saw her raising her free hand to her mouth and her eyes widen as though shocked at what she had done before she dropped the bottle and run off. He could feel a trickle of blood at the back of his neck and realised that the blow had broken the skin. Still dazed, he shakily tried to rise to his feet.

Seconds later, a voice beside him said, "You all right there, mister?" and turning his head he saw the legs of a woman standing next to him.

"Aye, fine," he mumbled. "I think I fell."

"Oh, right, as long as you're fine then," the woman warily replied and staring sympathetically at him, seemed content that she had done her civic duty before walking off.

He managed to drag himself and his two plastic bags to the wall of the building and slumped against it. Why the lassie had belted him with the bottle he didn't have a clue, but Sam was no stranger to abuse and casual violence. Too often at night he was the victim of drunks or bored youths with nothing to do other than heckle or tease the old man. In recent years he had learned when it got dark to keep away from people and stay in the shadows. But it was still light and shaking his head, wondered again why he had been struck. She hadn't tried to steal his bags, the thought causing him to possessively drew them closer to him. With his free hand he tentatively felt the back of his head and stared in resigned acceptance at the crimson staining on his fingers. It didn't feel too bad and taking a breath, decided that he would forego the bus station and just make his way back to his favourite doss at Mavisbank Quay. A little shakily, he got to his feet then lifting the plastic bags, stumbled as he retraced his steps along Cadogan Street.

****

Showered and shaved, Iain Meikle dressed and readied himself to commence his shift at five o'clock.

Though the late shift normally commenced at two pm, the Divisional Commander Murdo Clarke was acutely conscious that in response to the disappearance of Lesley Rudd his officers had worked well beyond their normal shift hours. In an unprecedented order he instructed that the early shift remain on overtime duty till five and the late shift to take an extra three hours, telling his sub-Divisional Chief Inspector, "To hell with the budget, Archie! One of my officers is missing and *that* is my priority, so any bugger from Pitt Street that wants to complain about the overtime bill, patch the call through to me." Now stood in his front room with the ironing board set up, Iain had just finished and was clearing the board and iron away when he realised it was almost three o'clock. Making his way into the kitchen, he turned on the radio and filling the kettle, yawned as he stood to listen to the Radio Clyde news headlines. To his surprise, the lead story was that Marc Bolan, the lead signer with the rock band T. Rex had been killed in a road traffic accident.

"Pity," he murmured and shook his head. "I liked that guy." As he listened he frowned for there had been no mention of the missing police woman, Lesley Rudd.

Has she turned up or has she been found…he hesitated to even consider that she was dead and had to resist the urge to phone the control room at Orkney Street and ask.

So wrapped up in his thoughts was he, the sudden whistle from the boiled kettle startled him and smiling at his nervousness, he poured the water into the teapot and lit the oven to heat in preparation for making his evening meal.

Juts under an hour later he changed into his uniform trousers and shirt and once again in the kitchen, prepared himself sandwiches for his shift break.

****

Stood at the dining table in the front room of his second floor flat and wearing just a pair of football short, the shaven headed, six feet two inch, heavyset Charlie Gallagher was indeed an imposing sight. Weighing in at a little over nineteen stone, he peered in turn at the both the six by four inch photographs held in each tattooed hand. From the kitchen he could hear his partner Paula Menzies singing off tune to the The Emotions number one hit, *'Best Of My Love'* that was playing loudly on the radio.

"First time I've ever done business like this," Gallagher muttered and now just a few months after his forty-fourth birthday, was too vain to admit that he needed glasses as he peered through slanted eyes at the photos.

The scrawny Liverpudlian courier wearing the Everton football top stood nervously in front of him staring at the numerous tattoos that adorned Gallagher's arms, torso and neck before replying, "Billy says to tell you that if you're happy with the product, he's willing to take the hit for the delivery. No charge," he beamed as though Gallagher was being done a huge favour. "Oh, and I've to tell you, lad, that Billy says the smack is a pure belter."

Gallagher didn't respond, but stared again at the colour photograph of the cellophane wrapped bars of heroin then turned to gaze at the second photograph that showed one of the bars neatly sliced open to expose the brown sand like material inside.

"I wouldn't be paying for the delivery anyway," Gallagher finally growled. "It's your responsibility to deliver and no way am I paying up front for anything till it's in my hands.|

"Yeah, of course, big lad," the courier vigorously nodded. "Now, about delivery. Billy says I'm to square it with you when and where and of course, the cash."

Gallagher looked at him as though he were mad and said, "I'll want to test the purity first."

"Right, yeah. I've brought a sample with me."

"What? You've brought smack into my fucking home?" Gallagher took a menacing step towards him.

"No, well, yeah, but it's banked, big lad," the courier hastily replied, his eyes betraying his fear. "If I can just use your loo…"

"No fucking way are you shitting out smack in my toilet and I'm not testing it here anyway," Gallagher snarled. "I'll give you an address a couple of streets away and you take it there." Staring hard at the smaller man, he continued, "You wait while he tests it and if it's the right purity, then my man will phone me and if it's the proper gear, I'll phone Billy and *we* work out a deal, savvy?"

"Yeah, of course, big lad," the courier held up both hands, "but will you want me to come back here to see you?" he asked, his throat as dry as a Cockney's patter.

"No. If it's a goer, you can get your arse back down the road. I'll do everything by phone from now on."

Gallagher moved to the fireplace and lifted a pen and scrap of paper from the mantelpiece and wrote down an address.

"The guy's name is Tonto, but the name on the door of the ground flat is Carson. If you're walking it will take you less than ten minutes to get there," and gave the courier directions to Morefield Road.

Nodding eagerly the courier was about to leave when Gallagher, holding up the photograph of the bars of heroin, said, "One more thing, Scouse. I'll be taking your boss's word that he delivers to me what's in these photos. If he tries to do me over," he bared his teeth, "I'll be looking for you as well as him and believe me, I *will* find you. Am I clear?"

"Fucking crystal, big lad," the courier quickly nodded.

****

DI Irene Crichton had the team in front of her when she sighed and said, "I realise that it's been a long day and though we haven't located Lesley Rudd, the boss and I are grateful for what you guys did today." Turning to Tam Whelan and Ian McDonald, she smiled and added, "Particularly you two. I can see you're both like half shut knives and as Scarlett O'Hara said, 'tomorrow is another day,' so get yourselves home and I'll see you in the morning."

While the three men collected their coats, Janie Wallace stepped towards Irene and hesitantly asked, "What's your gut feeling, Ma'am? Are we going to find Lesley alive?"

She stared at the young woman before slowly shaking her head and replying, "I think we both realise that it's unlikely, Janie. From the little I know about Lesley it strikes me she's not just simply walked off from her beat duties." She slowly inhaled before exhaling and added, "I think it's just a matter of time and we'll probably find her in the water somewhere."

Janie's brow creased before she asked, "I suppose the question now is, did she fall or was she pushed?"

Irene gently placed a hand on Janie's arm and softly replied, "And that's why we are going to do our damnedest to find out, isn't it?"

"Yes, Ma'am," Janie tightly smiled as she nodded. Turning away she saw Peter Rossi stood at the door holding her jacket. "Thought I'd walk you out," he smiled at her.

Making their way to the broad stairs that carried them down to the front entrance, he said, "What were you and the DI talking about?"

She shrugged and replied, "Just wondered what she thought about Lesley being alive or what."

"And what did she say?"

"She doesn't think so," Janie shrugged. "Said that Lesley isn't the type of cop to just wander off."

"So," he puffed, "she thinks this is going to look a like a search for a body?"

"Seems that way," she nodded.

At the front entrance, Rossi nodded and said, "I'm parked over there. The red coloured Aston Martin."

"Oooh, get you, James Bond," she teased him with a smile. "An Aston Martin. And on a cop's wage too."

He blushed and replied, "It's not a new one, it's seven years old. A present from my nonna when I graduated that I got just before I joined the polis," he stopped and smiled at the curious expression on her face. "My nonna is my grandmother."

"So, you come from money, then?" she grinned at him.

"No, not really. When my nonna died the business went to my parents, but she left some money aside to get me through Uni and for a gift when I completed my degree."

"So, what's the business?"

"Hey," he held his hands wide and grinned, "we're Italian. It's a chippy on the Great Western Road, what else would it be?"

"Aye, right, it might have been ice-cream."

"Oh, we do that too," he continued to grin before asking, "So, what you up to? Straight home for your dinner?"

"Yes, that and a hot bath," she sighed. "With some luck Paul might have rustled up the grub, but knowing him," she shook her head. "Let's just say he came from a doting mother to live with me so I'm still training him in the art of domesticity." She peered curiously at him then asked, "And what about you? No live-in girlfriend?"

"Naw, not at the minute," he breezily replied, then smiled as his brow creased. "I was seeing a girl for about seven months, but she got a bit too intense for me. If I was late home after work she'd tell me that she was worried about me, that something might have happened to me. Of course I believed her and thought it was concern for me, but then the questioning became a bit intense. I have to admit that I didn't at first pick up on it when she began to question where I'd been, who I'd seen or met then one day I found her sitting in her car watching my house."

"Watching your house? What do you mean?"

He inhaled as though the story was difficult, but then continued, "It was early morning and I'd nipped out to a local shop for milk and was on my way back. I hadn't thought to open the curtains so I'm guessing Linda…" he paused and said, "That was her name, Linda. Anyway, she must have thought I was still in the house and she was sat outside."

"I'm guessing where this is going. She thought you were *inside* with someone else?"

"That's the sum of it. I thought maybe she had forgotten her key or something and when I knocked on her window she almost wet herself. Next thing I know she's out the car and accusing me of all sorts of things, mostly cheating on her."

"And where you cheating on her?" Janie asked with a sly smile.

"No, of course not!" his nostrils flared and she was taken aback by his sudden anger.

"Calm down, Peter, I was joking," she forced a smile.

He shook his head and exhaled. "Sorry, but cheating is just not my style. Call me old fashioned or maybe it was the way I was raised," he shrugged.

"So, that ended it?"

"Well, she was making quite a scene in the street and I persuaded her to come into the house though it wasn't too difficult because really, she didn't believe me and wanted to see for herself. Next thing I know she's crying and telling me she's sorry, that her previous boyfriends had all cheated on her then dumped her…"

"Wait, I'm sensing a pattern here," Janie frowned.

"Yeah, call me dim-witted, but it was about then I then realised why she kept getting dumped. Unfortunately, it took me seven months to cotton on to that."

"I get the feeling you felt she might have been watching you for a while before you found her in her car?"

Peter nodded and said, "I did ask her and believe it or not, she admitted she didn't trust me, that I was," he waved his fingers in the air like quotation marks, "too good looking to be with one woman."

And you are good looking, Janie suddenly realised, then feeling her face redden, quickly said, "I take it that's when the relationship ended?"

"Well, not that day," he admitted with a shrug. "I suggested I take her to dinner on my next day off and we went to a small Greek restaurant in Sauchiehall Street." He slowly shook his head at the memory as he said, "It was a nice wee place in a basement near to the Charing Cross end of the Street. Anyway," he blew through pursed lips, "halfway through the dinner she very loudly and to my complete embarrassment, accused me of making eyes at the waitress."

"Oh," she grimaced. "What happened then?"

"I realised then she had problems I couldn't deal with and to my everlasting shame, I paid the bill then said cheerio and left her sitting at the table, but the worst thing was I didn't get my sweet."

Janie stared at him then burst out laughing before asking with a grin, "And you haven't heard from her since?"

"Oh, I heard from her, yes," he nodded. "Half a dozen abusive phone calls on my answer machine and then started phoning the office trying to speak to me. I was still in uniform at that time and it caused me a bit of bother with my Inspector who told me to get the situation sorted out or the rubber heels might have to get involved."

She was appalled when she asked, "What! He threatened you with the Discipline Department?"

"Let's just say he wasn't the most understanding of guys."

"But you eventually got it resolved?"

"Oh, aye, but it took a couple of months of harassing phone calls and threats until I spoke to a Federation representative who got one of the Fed lawyers to send her a letter telling her that if she continued to harass me, she'd be charged with a breach of the peace."

"And you haven't heard from her since?"

"No," he wryly smiled, "but it took a wee while for me to stop looking over my shoulder."

"Oh. Peter," she laid her hand on his chest, "maybe you should find yourself a nice Italian girl. At least then you won't have to worry about being harassed."

"A nice Italian girl? Really? Don't kid yourself, Janie. If you mess with or upset those nice Italian girls you need to learn to breathe through a pillow," he joked and then with a wave made his way across the road to his car, calling out over his shoulder, "See you in the morning, neighbour."

Janie made her way to her Ford Fiesta and getting in, turned on the radio before starting the engine. Driving home through the light traffic to her mid-terraced house in Knighthood's Fulton Street, her thoughts strayed to Peter Rossi and she unaccountably blushed. Yes, there was no denying he was a right good looker, but get a grip, girl, she shook her head as though to clear it. You've got yourself a good bloke and forced herself to think about Paul. Younger than Janie by two years, the twenty-seven-year-old was six feet two inches tall with curly blonde hair and what the sports writers considered to be really swift for a tall winger, yet she knew from the newspapers that after the number of goals he had scored in this and the preceding season he was one of the most sought after players in the Scottish Football League and there had even been talk about some of the English clubs showing interest.

Yet though they had been a couple for nigh on two years, Janie sometimes wondered if she was enough for Paul for whenever they attended functions or even visited the city for a night out, he was besieged by adoring female fans, many of who were not beyond shouldering their way past Janie to embrace him. She thought of the last few months together, of her tolerance of his mood swings and nights out with the boys when on a number of occasions, he failed to return home till the early hours.

Of course she took it all with resigned stoicism for she was confident that though Paul undoubtedly enjoyed the attention he *was* being faithful and she would not become the sort of woman Peter Rossi had described just fifteen minutes before. Arriving home, she began to sigh, but it turned into a wide yawn for she had not realised how tired she really was.

Switching off the engine, she turned to glance at the house and her eyes narrowed in surprise. Though it wasn't yet night-time, she could see the front room curtains were closed as were the upstairs window curtains.

She knew that Partick had played yesterday's match at home against Hearts and the game resulted in a draw with Paul scoring the equaliser, but had assumed he would be exhausted and spend Sunday relaxing at home in front of the tele.

Where the hell is he, she wondered.

Opening the front door, she called out, "Paul?"

It was an eerie silence that greeted her, but she saw the front room light was switched on. She realised then he did not expect her to be home till after dark and before leaving the house he had closed the curtains and switched on the light to give the appearance to passers-by that someone was home.

In the kitchen when she opened the curtains she saw a note on the small table that read:

'Sorry, just had a phone call from Archie White, the club doctor. I took a knock yesterday, nothing serious though, but Archie has heard there might be an English scout arriving on

Monday to watch me in training and asked me to come in to Fir Park for some last minute physio and to discuss some extra exercise. Don't wait up. Paul - X.'

Crumpling the note, she realised that she should not be suspicious, but the unsettling thought persisted and though she understood what the possibility of an English scout would mean to Paul, why would the club doctor want him in for physio on a Sunday evening?

She sighed for she was not naive and angrily assumed that the last minute physio he had written was more likely to be a piss-up with his teammates.

****

The Scouse courier glanced again at the handwritten note and licking his dry lips, ignored the three youths stood at the corner who huddled together and smoking, were also watching him through slitted eyes.

Last fucking thing I need is getting done over with Billy Madison's gear up my back shaft, the weedy man thought and hurried on without making eye contact for to do so was akin to inviting the youths to challenge him to what these Scotch bastards called a square go.

With relief, he saw the street sign that identified Morefield Road and hurried into the close, first ensuring the three youths had not followed him.

He found the door with the peeling yellow coloured paint and the strip of paper tacked to it with the handwritten name, 'CARSON.' With his ear pressed against the door and listening intently he could hear the sound of someone inside who sounded as though they were coughing their lungs out.

Nervously, his stomach churning, he pounded a fist against the door and inwardly prayed the DS were not inside waiting for some mug like him to come calling and the local drug squad turning him over.

Almost a minute passed and he was about to knock again when the door with a shrill squeak was pulled open six inches.

The gaunt figure with the pale, face and sunken eyes that stared at him asked, "What?"

"I'm looking for Tonto. Your fella, big Charlie sent me."

"Yes, I'm Tonto. I received a call," the man replied in a polite and curiously cultured voice then with a rasping cough that shook his body, pulled the door open wide.

Stepping into a dingy and foul smelling hallway, the courier almost gagged, but taking a breath through his mouth, said, "I need to use your loo to get the gear."

"In there," Tonto nodded to the door along the hallway and added, "When you've shit the gear, please wash the bag first then come into the kitchen."

Like I'm not going to wash the fucking bag, the courier thought, but instead said, "Right oh, mucker. Give me five minutes."

A little over four minutes later with the small, cellophane bag of heroin in his hand, the courier pushed open the kitchen door to see Tonto bent over a wooden table that in a complete contradiction to the state of the room, was neatly laid out with a set of scales, a small petri dish, a polished dessert spoon with a bent handle, nail scissors, lit candle, rubber tube and a syringe with a hypodermic needle. A small bag of baking powder, notebook and a sharpened pencil lay next to the petri dish.

"May I have the sample, please," Tonto held his hand out for the bag then using the scissors, nipped the top of the bag open. "What's the strength?" he asked, using the sleeve of his stained sweatshirt to wipe at his running nose before being overtaken by another coughing fit.

The courier waited till he calmed, then replied, "I'm told it's purity is about ninety-five percent."

Tonto stared at him in amazement. "You're kidding, right?"

"No, lad," the courier vigorously shook his head. "That's what me Guv'nor told me. According to our Billy, this stuff comes straight from the Smoke down south. You can guess where they get it," he toothlessly grinned.

As though in disbelief, Tonto stared at the courier then slowly shaking his head, make a notation on the pad with the pencil. Carefully he used the spoon to measure out some of the heroin onto the scales and did the same with the baking powder. Once he was satisfied, he poured the mixture onto the petri dish that he held above the lit candle and peering intently at it, used the spoon to stir it. As the courier continued to watch, Tonto poured the mixture onto the spoon that he now held over the candle. When the mixture began to bubble and turned to liquid, he cautiously poured the mixture into the syringe and then attached the hypodermic needle.

Watching him, the courier said, "You seem to know what you're doing there, lad."

Without turning and in the same polite voice, Tonto replied, "I had almost completed my Chemistry degree at Glasgow University when, how should I put it, I fell under the spell of the Golden Brown. So yes, you could say I've had a lot of practise during the recent years."

Using the rubber band, he sat on the chair and wound it about his arm, using his teeth to draw it tight. Tapping his arm to draw the vein, he licked at his lips before injecting himself. After a few seconds, Tonto gave a long sigh and turning to the courier with glazed eyes, said, "Good stuff, this. You want some?"

"No, lad," he waved his hands. "Tempted though I am I'm only here to deliver the sample and I've to get back down to the 'Pool tonight. You'll remember to phone big Charlie, won't you, lad?"

"Yes of course, I'll remember," Tonto replied, then mumbling incoherently, his head flopped back and he closed his eyes as the heroin coursed through his veins.

****

The underground Finnieston Tunnel had been constructed then opened in 1895 to permit pedestrian and horse drawn carts and carriages to travel beneath the River Clyde from both its

Rotunda entrances on Tunnel Street on the north side of the river to Plantation Place on the south side.

Though the tunnel had for some years been declared unsafe for public use, it was a regular route for Sam Fullerton with Plantation Place conveniently located next to Mavisbank Quay where he almost nightly found shelter in the derelict warehouses. That and the use of the dank and waterlogged tunnel kept him safe from the predatory youths and drunks whom he frequently encountered when using the roads to or on the bridges across the Clyde.

Still dazed from the unprovoked attack upon him and though he didn't know he was also suffering from a mild concussion, the old man staggered into the dimly lit Rotunda and slowly worked his way around the barriers that were erected to keep out a curious public.

It took him almost fifty minutes to feel his way along the sodden and flaking tiled walls of the dark and gloomy tunnel until at last he reached the worn and moss covered stairs that led upwards into the Rotunda's exit.

Still clutching his plastic bags, he saw his way lit by a clear moon and though he had fallen several times, gasped with relief that he was now in Mavisbank Quay.

Making his way along the dock area, he stopped and gently touching at his aching head, felt the crusty scab of dried blood. God, he thought, I'm so thirsty.

Staggering on he could hear the gentle slap of the river as the tide turned and the waters beat against the piers.

He was no more than forty yards from where the hole in the metal wall was located that would permit him entry to the warehouse when his legs gave way and with a weary sigh, he tumbled to the ground as darkness overcame him.

CHAPTER SIX

The late shift officers who arrived at Orkney Street quickly learned that no, nothing had been heard from or about Lesley Rudd and so it was with disappointment they took their seats in the muster room to await their briefing.

Sitting on one of the unforgiving plastic and tubular chairs beside Eric Little, Iain Meikle crossed one leg over the other and with notebook in his hand, widely yawned.

"Last night too much for you, old timer. Think you'll cope?" said a voice behind and turning, saw it was Ian Harris who was grinning at him, the skinny and acne plagued teenager and the youngest of the shifts three probationary constables. A likeable young man, Harris had joined the shift from his first training stint at the Police College and already made his mark as the shift comedian.

Returning his grin, Iain replied, "Oh, I think I'll cope, sonny, and if I recall correctly, I was coping when you were hanging off your mammy's teat." His brow creased as though in thought before he loudly added, "Tell me, Ian, is your mammy still wearing the pink see-through nightie's these days?"

Both Harris's eyes and mouth widely opened, but he was too slow with a response and his face reddened when the shift erupted in laughter.

"Aye, very good," the nineteen-year-old joined in the laughter.

"Right, bit of order, please," called out Inspector Micky Kane who entered the room with a thick file under one arm that he then placed down onto the four-foot wooden podium. In his wake came Sergeant Jimmy Cole who stood silently and to one side behind Kane.

When silence fell, Kane stared grim faced at the shift and then said, "I hope that after Mister Clarke authorised your extra three hours in your beds you are all raring to go. Now, to business," he shuffled some papers on the podium as though wasting time before delivering bad news. Clearing his throat, he begun, "Likely you will all now be aware that there is no update on our Lesley. I've spoken with the DCI who informs me that the polis launch has been stood down, but Mister

Parsonage whom I'm certain needs no introduction to you all, will continue at daylight to search the river." He paused for breath and then as though reluctant to continue, said, "I am also to inform you that at this time, Lesley's disappearance will be treated as a missing person inquiry…" then immediately raised his hand to quell the murmur of discontent that sped around the room.

"Listen…listen!" he slapped a hand heavily down onto the podium, then waited till the room was silent. "We all know about the blood-stained cap, but there is no evidence, *nothing*," he emphasised, "to suggest Lesley was the victim of any assault." He paused yet again and added, "The CID's hypothesis is that she fell, banged her head and went over into the water."

"So, the bloody CID are accepting she's dead!" Eric Little was outraged.

"No, Eric," Kane calmly shook his head. "The CID, just like us, don't have a clue what happened to Lesley, but they've got a team working on it to find out out. Remember," he stared with beady eyes around the shift, "she's a police officer like us, regardless of what department she is in so we're *all* doing what we can to find her and yes, that includes the CID."

He paused again and said, "Sergeant Cole will read out the beats for tonight, but Iain," he singled him out, "you're not being assigned a beat. I want you to conduct a kind of roving search. I know the area around the docks has been thoroughly searched, but you're an old sweat and the senior man on the shift so if anyone knows that area well, it's you and I want you to check all the nooks and crannies again. If it means knocking on doors of anyone you know…" he stared meaningfully at him and left the rest unsaid, but the inference was clear. Iain Meikle had carte blanche to take any of the local neds he suspected might have some information about what happened to Lesley Rudd into a dark corner and by persuasion or otherwise, find out what he could.

"Sir," he nodded in acknowledgement.

Kane stood to one side as Cole stepped up to the podium with the duty roster and clearing his throat, read out the beat duties. Silence greeted Cole as the officers stared at him for most if not all the shift knew of his bad decision to permit Lesley Rudd to work the beats alone on a busy Saturday night; a decision that some like Iain and Little believed might, even unintentionally, been contributory to Lesley's disappearance.

"Right, to your duties, dismissed," he called out, but none of those present caught his eye and it was not lost on Kane who tapping Cole on the shoulder, quietly said, "A wee word please, Jimmy."

In the Inspector's room, Kane removed his cap and laying it down onto the desk, indicated Cole close the door and then take a seat while he continued to stand.

It was obvious to the burly Inspector that Cole was nervous.

"I'll not beat about the bush, Jimmy," Kane began, his arms folded and his back resting against the wall as he stared down at Cole, "but that was a bad decision you made last night, putting young Lesley out alone on a Saturday night onto the busiest beats in the sub-Division. What the *hell* possessed you to do that?"

Kane saw Cole's throat tighten before he replied, "I thought that she would have the back-up of the Pollokshields panda, Inspector. I had Meikle and Little manning the car and…"

"And let's say they two got involved with an incident that resulted in an arrest. Who were her back-up then?" he shook his head. "My God, you've been here in Govan long enough to know the unwritten rule, Jimmy. Six pm to two am, the cops on the beat always have a neighbour and particularly the women. I know there's this thing going on about equality, but a young lassie out on her own in the dark in an area with a high incidence of drunken violence? Call me old fashioned," he shook his head, "but it's just not on."

"Am I in trouble about this, Inspector?"

Kane stared curiously at him before quietly replying, "Whether or not you're in trouble is nothing compared to what might have happened to Lesley Rudd, is it Sergeant Cole! Your career might take a dent," he hissed, "but *she* might have lost her bloody life!"

Cole said nothing, but lowered his head and quickly realised his question was completely the wrong thing to ask.

"You do realise the shift blame you for whatever has happened to her, don't you?" Kane continued.

Cole's head snapped up and he was about to retort, but Kane raised a hand and barked, "And before you again try to justify your decision, in future you will not assign beat duties to my officers without running it past me first."

Cole swallowed and asked, "Are you going to have me transferred to another shift?"

"That's not a decision I can make," Kane quietly replied, "that will be down to the sub-Divisional Chief Inspector, but as long as you continue as a supervisor with *my* shift, you will not put any of my cops at risk again. Is that understood?"

"Yes, sir."

Kane turned away and staring down at his desk, abruptly said, "I assume you will have some paperwork to be getting on with, Sergeant."

The dismissal was clear. Cole stood up from the chair and left the room, closing the door behind him.

****

It was almost eight o'clock that evening when the phone rang in Charlie Gallagher's flat. The big man laid the chunky glass with the remaining two fingers of vodka down onto the carpet at his feet, before using the remote control to turn down the sound on the television, then hauled himself up from his favourite armchair. Lifting the phone from the small side table, he said, "Hello."

"It's Tonto. Can you speak?"

Gallagher glanced at the sleeping Paula Menzies lying stretched out on her back on the three seater couch, her ankles demurely crossed and knees slightly apart, one arm thrown backwards and the other resting on her stomach. Staring at her tight, sleeveless white tee-shirt and the bottle green coloured mini-skirt that rode up her thighs and exposed her pink knickers, he felt himself become aroused as he told Tonto, "Go ahead."

"The guy you sent round with the sample. It's shit hot stuff." That was all Gallagher needed to hear, so with a soft smile, he replied, "Keep what's left for yourself as payment," then abruptly ended the call.

From behind the carriage clock on the mantelpiece, he fetched a small notebook and flicking through the pages, found the number he needed then dialled in the sure knowledge that the man he was phoning would be awaiting his call.

"Hello?" said the brusque voice.

"It's me. How's it hanging?"

"As stiff as usual," Billy Madison replied in a gruff, Glasgow accent, for though he had lived for almost twenty years in Liverpool, Madison like Gallagher was a native of Govan, though had fled the city all those years before after slashing a rival gang member and escape being murdered.

"Your man phoned you?" Gallagher asked.

"He did. He's on his way back now after dropping my wee present off. What's the score?"

"I've had a positive feedback from my man, so if what you're offering is pukka like in the photos, we're on."

"Oh, it's kosher right enough," Madison enthusiastically agreed, before asking, "All we need now is to agree a delivery date and payment."

"What's your best price?"

"Depends on how many bars you want to take?"

"I can shift, say," Gallaher did a quick mental calculation then rubbing at his forehead with a meaty hand, said, "forty bars."

"If you can move fifty, I can give you a discount," Madison teased.

Gallagher's eyes narrowed and he grinned for that was exactly the deal he was looking for. "Okay then I'll consider fifty, but it depends of course what kind of discount we're talking about, here."

There was a slight pause as Madison quickly did his own mental calculation, before he replied, "I'm usually looking for around twelve hundred a bar, but the purity of this product kicks it up to thirteen hundred because of the number of times it can be cut. For you though, old pal, I can knock a bar down to say, eleven-seventy-five."

Gallagher was not and never had been Madison's old pal, but for a discount he was willing to play along and so replied, "Make it eleven-fifty a bar and you've got a deal."

"Done," Madison was pleased, but frowned when Gallagher reminded him, "No funny stuff. You know I don't take kindly to being fucked over."

"Stand on me, big man. What you saw in the photos and had tested is what you'll get."

"Aye, well see I do and give me a bell when you've organised the delivery."

"While you're on, Charlie…" but got no further when Gallagher snapped.

"Why don't you give out my fucking address too, you idiot!"

"Sorry," the chastened Madison apologised. "Okay then, I'll give you a bell before the delivery is due at finalise arrangements for the handover. Now, about payment?"

"Same as before. I'll have a man waiting with a bag of cash to meet your man. When they're together and I'm satisfied the delivery to the destination has been made and the stuff is pukka, my man will hand the bag over for your man to count the cash, unless you trust me to be on the nose with it? That okay with you?"

"I trust the money will be as agreed," Madison loudly sighed, but inwardly thought if it isn't there would be consequences for the big bastard. "Okay then, sound big man. I'll be in touch."

Gallagher replaced the phone in the cradle and smiled, satisfied that he had completed a very profitable deal. If the stuff was as good as Madison said it is, then he would be able to have his team adulterate it far more times than normal and he'd make a real tidy profit distributing it to the dealers throughout the city and beyond. Might even consider shifting some of it to those toffee-nosed wankers in Edinburgh, he mused.

Returning to his armchair, he bent down to lift the chunky glass and smacking at his lips, finished the vodka in a swallow.

Turning to ensure Menzies was still asleep, he turned the television off and tiptoed towards the couch. Stood over her, he stared lustfully down at the busty redhead and watched her breasts rise and fall as she breathed.

He briefly considered running his hand up and along her bare legs to her crotch, but grinned and decided instead he'd first shower then call her through to the bedroom for some fun and games.

Gently closing the door behind him, he would have been surprised and suspiciously angry had he known that Paula Menzies was not sleeping, but had heard every word of his side of the conversation with Billy Madison.

****

Deciding to go to bed and have an early night, Janie Wallace glanced at the digital alarm clock and saw it was now half past nine, yet her boyfriend Paul had still not returned home.

And he's supposed to have a training session tomorrow morning with an English scout watching him, her eyes narrowed.

She lay on her back in the almost total darkness with just a dagger of moonlight on the far wall from a crack in the drawn curtains. Staring at the ceiling she guessed that Paul had gone on from his physio, if his note was true, to meet with some of his teammates and likely either to a club or back to one of the houses for a drink.

"Bastard!" she murmured, then raised her hand to her mouth, suddenly shocked at her expletive. It wasn't like her to be so suspicious, yet she just couldn't shake the feeling that he had lied, that there was no phone call from the physio.

She didn't know how long she lay awake, but exhaustion finally overtook her and she drifted back to sleep.
****

Stood with his back to the police box at Paisley Road Toll, Iain Meikle glanced at his wristwatch and was disappointed. It was almost ten-thirty and for a Sunday night the pubs and the general area seemed to be unusually quiet, but then from further down the uncommonly quiet road he heard the sound of the engine before he saw them; old Wally and his equally aging neighbour, Paddy McGurk, more commonly known as Paddy the Mouth due to him having teeth like tombstones.

He was aware from his time working the beat that Wally and Paddy usually worked through the week nights, but sometimes in the summer months did an occasional weekend overtime shift.

The two City of Glasgow Council employees were slowly moving east in Paisley Road West and abreast of Portman Street, pulling their small hand barrow with the mounted engine and using the attached hoses to clean the pavements and streets of dirt accumulated during the week.

With a smile, he began to stroll towards the two men who seeing him approach, waved in greeting.

"Not seen you for a while, Iain," the short, but heavy built and whiskered Wally gasped at him.

Iain knew that Wally was in the first stage of emphysema and Paddy struggled with a bad leg, but to the credit of their manager at the Glasgow Council's local Cleansing Department in Helen Street, he continued to employ both men in the street cleaning duty rather than retire them too early with a smaller pension.

"Aye," Paddy reached to turn off the petrol engine, "where have you been hiding, big man?"

As short as Wally was, Paddy was as tall and lean, though limped badly from the break in his left leg that had never fully healed.

"Here and there and lately working up in the Pollokshields beats," Iain smiled at them. "How are things with you guys?"

"Oh, the boss did his best by us, son, but it looks like we're finally for the scrapyard," Wally sighed. "The council are cutting back on the cost of employing us old guys across the city that are left hosing down the pavements and the boss says that likely by the end of the year, we'll be gone."

"Sorry to hear that," Iain shook his head.

"Time was there used to be full teams washing down all the main roads and streets in Glasgow," said a wistful Wally. "But with all the cuts and councillors needing their jolly's travelling abroad on expenses to see other how councils spend *their* public money," he bitterly shook his head and to the smiles of the other two, grinned when he added, "It's all going down the drain…if you pardon the pun."

"Ach, well, we've had a good innings," Paddy cheerfully interrupted, then added, "Time for a break, wee man?"

"I think so," Wally winked at Iain then from the bin in the small hand barrow that carried the portable engine, fetched out a large newspaper wrapped, steaming parcel.

It was a common practise that on route to the Toll from their depot in Helen Street, the two men usually dropped into the chippy located in the row of shops at Cessnock where the owner, grateful to them for hosing down the front window and pavement in front of his shop, always repaid their good turn with a parcel of fish and chips.

Moving into the shelter of a nearby close, Iain and the two older men shared the portions.

"Is the wee lassie not on duty tonight, then?" Paddy asked as he wolfed down his chips.

Iain, choking down a mouthful of battered fish, tensed then asked, "Are you talking about Lesley? Blonde haired girl?"

"Aye, Lesley she said her name was," Paddy turned to nod at Wally as though seeking confirmation. "Had a poke of chips with us last night. Is she not on this beat with you tonight, Iain?

A real looker, so she is," he nodded as he grinned. "You'd be doing yourself a favour nipping a nice lassie like that."

"When did you see her? Last night, you said it was?" he glanced keenly at them in turn.

"Eh, aye, last night. Just about, where was it again, Wally?" Wally blew through pursed lips and shaking his head, replied, "Every night's the same these days to an old duffer like me, but aye, it was definitely last night we saw her. Eh, just about Lorne Street it was. Isn't that right, Paddy?"

"Lorne Street. That's right," he agreed.

"Was she on her own?"

"Aye, she was. Well, I think so," he frowned. "I mean I didn't see anyone else with her. Why?" Wally sensed something was amiss. "Is she all right?"

He sighed and disclosed, "It will be all over the papers in the morning. Lesley went missing last night. We don't know where she is and we think something has happened to her. Something bad."

If Iain Meikle had told the old men that the world was about to end at that very minute, they could not have been more shocked.

Wally turned to Paddy and said, "I told you I thought something was up, didn't I?"

"What do you mean?" Iain interjected.

"Look, it might be nothing, Iain, but the wee lassie seemed…I don't know how to describe it, kind of distracted. Paddy here was giving her a line of patter you know? Said to her if he was thirty years younger he'd be chasing after her, that kind of thing, you know?"

"Aye, but I didn't mean anything by it," Paddy hastily interrupted. "It was just banter. I mean, for God's sake, I'm old enough to be…"

"It's okay, Paddy," Iain smiled reassuringly at him and laid his hand on the older man's arm. "I'm sure she would probably have taken it as a compliment. Les wasn't daft, okay?"

"But that's the thing, Iain," Wally's eyes narrowed. "She

smiled at Paddy's patter, but her mind was elsewhere. Am I making any kind of sense here?"

"Her mind was elsewhere," Iain slowly repeated. "Did you get the impression she was thinking about something or someone else?

"Well, she never said anything but aye, she definitely had her mind on something else."

"And don't forget, she looked at her watch a couple of times too," Paddy reminded Wally, "like she was in a hurry to get away."

"Oh, and what time was this about then? When you met her, I mean," Iain asked.

Wally made a face and grimacing, replied, "We can only guess, Iain, because I don't have a watch and neither does Paddy, but if we met the lassie at Lorne Street and we knock off at one in the morning, then I'm guessing it must have been what…" he turned towards Paddy, "some time between half seven and eight? That sound about right?"

Paddy nodded in agreement.

"Did you see where she went when she left you guys?" he turned from one to the other.

It was Paddy who raised an arm and said, "I think she headed into Cornwall Street, but I'm not certain. Is that important?"

Iain thought, if Lesley was seen by the two old fellas at the latest, eight o'clock, that gave her a full hour before she was due to meet with him and Eric Little in the lane at Paisley Road Toll. Cornwall Street would lead her into Scotland Street and a couple of minutes' walk would take her to Middlesex Street. The call about the drunk in Middlesex Street was broadcast to her about ten past eight, so by that time she would have left Wally and Paddy if she went to the call and dealt with it and that might take no more than twenty minutes.

But she never resulted the call about the drunk, he mused. Even if she had dealt with the drunk or he'd gone before she arrived there, it would take her but a few minutes to walk from Middlesex Street to the Paisley Toll Lane, but she would still have plenty of time on her hands before meeting us. Why then did she decide to take a wander down to the Mavisbank Quay dockside and particularly if it was teeming with rain at the time?

Maybe she was just killing time before meeting Eric and me, he wondered, yet he could not think of a reason why Les would not patrol the busy Paisley Road West on a Saturday night.

His brow furrowed as he also wondered; what was it that that Les had on her mind that caused Wally and Paddy to notice how distracted she was? And glancing at her watch. Probably reminding herself she had me and Eric to meet, he guessed.

"Iain?"

He smiled and said, "Sorry, Wally, I was a million miles away, there. I was trying to think why Lesley would have walked over to Mavisbank Quay if she didn't have a call to attend to there. I mean, the place is deserted and on a Saturday night too, considering how busy Paisley Road West is with the the number of people hanging around or moving between the pubs. Aye," he slowly nodded, "funny that because I'd have thought she would be more likely to have a wander up and down the road here."

"Aye, I suppose so," Wally sighed, then crumpling his chip paper into a ball, carried it and Paddy's paper to a waste bin on a nearby lamppost.

"Did you guys see anyone hanging about last night when you were moving along towards the Toll?" he asked.

Wally pursed his lips and shaking his head, glanced at Paddy before he replied, "No more than the usual bampots, bevvied up and having a laugh at us. Couple of kids down Cessnock way gave us a bit of abuse," then he cracked a smile before adding, "but Paddy gave them a right good soaking with the hose, so that settled their hash. Pair of arses they were," was his throwaway comment.

"Right then," Iain crumpled up his chip paper and stepped across the pavement to place it into the waste bin and said,

"Thanks for the fish and chips, guys. I'll mosey along and let you get on with your job."

Waving cheerio to the two older men, he glanced up at the dark cloudy sky and the light fall of rain then decided to take a walk down to Mavisbank Quay.

****

Seated at his desk in the sergeants room, Jimmy Cole's face was still burning with rage and embarrassment; that the Inspector, that *bastard* Kane, spoke to him like that!

Well, as an Advanced Promotion candidate he was almost guaranteed a speedy promoted career and come the day he would be promoted to Inspector and then Chief Inspector, he prayed that Micky Kane would still be in the job for he would make sure he let the bastard know who was the boss, then!

Just you wait, Kane, his fists clenched he slowly nodded as he imagined how he would in some way exact his revenge on the sanctimonious shit!

He startled when the door was knocked and Ian Harris, the probationary constable stuck his head in to politely ask, "You wanted to see me about a report I did, Sarge?"

Cole couldn't do anything about Kane, but this prat was available and so replied, "Get your arse in here."

Drawing the typed report from a bundle on his desk, he threw it to Harris and sneered, "What kind of fucking school did you go to, a spastic one?"

****

Making his way through the rear courts of the old Victorian tenements towards Govan Road and in the quiet of the night, Iain Meikle could hear the distant sound of traffic travelling on the Paisley Road West and more pronounced, the roar of bus diesel engines. He stopped and smiled for his ear also caught the sound of shouting coming from an open rear window in one of the tenements. The bawling and shouting that was liberally sprinkled with expletives had all the hallmarks of a domestic argument and likely Eric Little and his neighbour, young Shona Murtagh, would be getting the call some time soon. Normally,

Iain would have headed in the direction of the racket, but the Inspector had instructed he was to remain free from beat duties to search again the area for any sign of Lesley's…

He stopped, appalled that he was about to consider the word body.

Shaking his head at his own insensitivity, he stumbled on through the rutted and torn ground and exited onto Govan Road before making his way towards Mavisbank Quay.

At the boundary wall, he used the pedestrian stairs that took him down to the dockside and fetched his torch from his coat pocket. Switching it on, he mouthed an expletive for again he'd forgotten to renew the batteries and sighed at the weak and fading light, then switched it off to conserve what energy was left in it.

Before he continued, he stood and mouth slightly open, listened in the darkness for any sound that indicated anyone who might be in the dock area for if there was any person or persons about, there was little doubt they would be up to no good.

Taking a deep breath and as satisfied as he could be the place was empty he began to make his way towards the derelict warehouses, preferring to use the moonlight rather than his torch that he knew would would be a dead giveaway to anyone watching for the police.

Conscious of the CID's opinion that Lesley might have slipped on the treacherous dockside, Iain stayed well back from the water's edge as he made his way along the dock.

His eyes now adjusted to the darkness he stopped when he saw the shape lying on the ground fifty feet in front of him.

Glancing about him, he couldn't hear or see anyone else and quickly made his way to the shape, switching on his torch and playing it over the area saw it to be the body of a man.

Bending over the man he gagged at the strong smell, a combination of body odour and alcohol and realised it was old Sam, the homeless man who was forever being moved on by the police or complained about by the local shopkeepers.

Removing his leather glove, he went down onto one knee and

with two fingers, felt on Sam's neck and felt the slight throb of a pulse, inwardly sighing with relief there was no need for mouth to mouth resuscitation.

"Sam! Sam, can you hear me?" he loudly asked. Playing the beam on the old man's face and head, his eyes narrowed when he saw what looked like a wound on the back of Sam's scalp. "Sam, what happened to you, pal? Did you fall over? Did someone hurt you?"

Sam, his eyes still closed, shivered and moaned.

Wrestling off his light raincoat, Iain used it to cover Sam's body and gasped as the smell of faeces hit him. Breathing through his mouth he realised the old man must have shit himself. Yanking his radio from his pocket, he requested the controller, 'Hammy' Hammond to summon an ambulance.

"Right away, Iain, where are you exactly?"

Relating his location, Iain asked that the CID also attend the locus, that it looked like Sam had either fallen and hurt himself or perhaps been the victim of an assault.

His mind focused on the search for his friend, Iain thought this was too coincidental, Les going missing almost at the same spot where he had discovered Sam.

Within minutes Hammond responded that an ambulance was en route, the CID were being informed and that Inspector Kane was also making his way to Iain's location.

He had done as much as he could for the old man, but continued to ask him what had happened, though assessed that Sam was to dazed to tell him much.

But then to Iain's surprise and before he passed out, the old man stuttered, "I didn't do anything to her. I mean, I didn't hurt her."

My God, Iain stared disbelievingly down at him.

Was it possible that old Sam was talking about Les and what did he mean, he didn't hurt her?

It was simply an unfortunate quirk of fate that he found Sam Fullerton almost at the same location where Lesley Rudd had disappeared. Iain, eager for any clue that might have indicated the whereabouts or what happened to Lesley Rudd, could not have known at that time the confused and concussed Sam Fullerton was referring to someone else; a gaunt and scantily dressed young woman who earlier that day and for a reason unknown to the old man had struck him on the head with a bottle.

CHAPTER SEVEN

The ambulance arrived with it's klaxon blaring just as Inspector Micky Kane stepped from the supervisory panda to ask, "What's the score, Iain?"
Quickly, he reported his discovery of Sam Fullerton and almost with a heavy heart related Sam's statement before the old man passed out.
"Not old Sam," Kane's shocked response to Sam's comment was almost as doubtful as was Iain's. "I can't see how that old guy would have overcome a healthy and smart lassie like Lesley," Kane's eyes narrowed as he rubbed with a gloved hand at his chin. Taking a deep breath, he continued, "Right, Iain, you travel with the ambulance to the casualty and if Sam regains consciousness, see if you can get anymore out of him."
"What about the CID? I asked them to attend here."
"Don't worry about them, I'll hang around till they show up and give them the story."
"Sir," he acknowledged with a nod and grabbing Sam's two plastic bags, climbed into the rear of the ambulance.
A minute later with the blue lights and klaxon activated, the ambulance raced through the night towards the casualty department of the Southern General Hospital in Govan.
In the rear of the vehicle, the ambulance man leaned across the unconscious Sam to fit an oxygen mask to his face and grimacing, said, "You've not done us any favour, pal. There's some bloody stink off this old guy. Me and Jimmy up front will

get hell from the casualty staff for bringing him in, I can tell you."

Fuming at the tactless comment, Iain was about to remind the ambulance man that old Sam deserved the same treatment, kindness and consideration as any other emergency patient, but wisely kept his cool and instead choked back his cutting retort to ask, "That bump on his head. How serious do you think it is?"

Using a medical wet wipe, Iain watched as the ambulance man carefully wiped the dried blood from the wound and shrugging, replied, "It doesn't look too deep, but of course I can't say what kind of internal damage he's maybe suffered to his noggin. The doctor will likely have him X-rayed and no doubt they'll keep him overnight for observation, but probably in an isolation ward," he joked, thinking he was being funny, but his one-man audience wasn't laughing and embarrassed, he looked away when Iain stared hard at him. "I'm guessing you know him?"

"Aye," Iain nodded. "Sam's hung about the Toll area for a number of years now. He's never caused any bother, but because of the state of him the locals and the shopkeepers give him a bit of a rough time and there's always complaints to us that we should move him on. The thing is, where do you move a guy like him on to?"

The ambulance man leaned over Sam and sniffed. "I think he's had a right bevy too, by the smell of his breath. That won't help if they have to give him medication."

"At least he's unconscious. If he was awake, he'd be fighting to get out of the ambulance," Iain snorted. "Sam doesn't like hospitals or anything to do with authority."

"Has he a family?"

"Can't say," Iain shook his head. "I've spoken with him on plenty of occasions, but he never discloses anything about himself. Tight as a drum, the old bugger."

The ambulance man smiled and said, "It sounds to me that you like the old guy."

"I don't *dislike* him," he relaxed and agreed with a smile, "and he's cost me a few quid over the years in cups of soup or the occasional bag of chips, but he's always been very polite and respectful any time I've had to deal with him. He's a lot easier to handle than some finely dressed folk I've had to deal with." His brow furrowed and continuing to smile, he added, "Yeah, I suppose I've always thought of him as just being a harmless old man who decided to opt out of society."

But then he remembered what Sam and said and he frowned.

"Here we go," the ambulance man stood up as the vehicle reversed into the casualty department bay. The door opened a moment later and Iain stood to one side while the two crew carried the still unconscious Sam through the double doors and into the ward.

Placing the stretcher onto a trolley and closely followed by Iain, they wheeled Sam into a cubicle then in a flash were gone before the nursing staff had time to question them.

The curtain was pulled back by a male Staff nurse who officiously asked, "Right, what do we have here?"

Iain inwardly groaned. Of all people to be on duty it had to be Joe Prescott. Aged fifty, the balding and portly Prescott on account of the thick lensed glasses he wore was nicknamed Joe Ninety after a popular children's TV puppet programme where the hero is a nine-year-old child. However, Prescott's nickname was not just because of the glasses, but more due to his childish behaviour when supervising the nursing team in his department.

As one of his colleagues previously confided to Iain, "Joe is a delegator, not a doer" which was the auxiliary nurse's polite way of explaining Prescott was a lazy bastard.

Turning to Iain, he made a face and asked, "What the fuck are you doing bringing someone like this into my ward?"

Working hard at keeping his cool and aware of the attention Prescott's outburst attracted from his fellow nurses, he replied, "Perhaps you never noticed, but Mister Fullerton is not only injured after some sort of blow to the head, but he is also unconscious, so where the *fuck* do you expect me to take him?" Prescott's face turned pale and he retorted, "I don't care for that sort of language in my department, Constable!"

"Then don't use it to me!" Iain snarled in return.

"Let me get you a cup of tea, Iain," a middle aged enrolled nurse took his arm as he allowed himself to be gently led him from the cubicle to the small, almost cupboard like room used by the casualty staff as their refreshment room.

When the door was firmly closed and now out of earshot of Prescott, Iain relaxed and removing his cap, turned to the nurse and slowly exhaled before telling her, "Thanks, May, but that bugger gets right on my tits."

"Aye," she grinned good-naturedly and slapping at her chest, laughed, "well mine are bigger and he gets on them too. Tea?"

"Please," he replied, but had no sooner sat down on one of the plastic chairs when the door was opened by a red-faced Prescott who said, "So, that's why you brought that old tramp here. Just to get a cuppa and a chocolate biscuit?"

Before Iain could respond, May burst in, "He's having one of my teabags, Joe, not one from the kitty *and* need I remind you that the chocolate biscuits are provided by the beat cops from the Plantation area who get them for us from the security guys at the Gray Dunn's factory."

Prescott was about to angrily respond, but took a breath and instead said, "The doctor is admitting your patient for X-raying and observation, Constable, so I see no reason for you to hang around my casualty ward."

Knowing it would annoy the older man, Iain smiled and calmly replied, "*Your* patient is of interest in an ongoing inquiry, Staff Nurse, so I'm to remain here with him till the arrival of the CID. Anything else?"

Tight-lipped, Prescott glowered then leaving, banged the door behind him.

"Is that right?" May asked as she carefully poured boiling water into a mug. "Old Sam is to be interviewed by the detectives?"

"Aye, they want a quick word about his injury," he carefully replied, for much as he liked the popular middle-aged nurse, he knew May to be an awful gossip. As it was he was saved from any further questioning by May when the door opened and to his surprise, admitted Irene Crichton.

Nodding a greeting to May, Irene said, "Heard you might have something for us, Iain? Something about old Sam Fullerton." He didn't expect the Detective Inspector herself to attend and replied, "You took me aback there, Irene. Are you still on duty?"

She smiled and with her hand, pointed to her hair tied back into a fierce ponytail then at the old grey sweater and charcoal coloured jogging trousers she wore and said, "I was at home preparing to have a nice glass of chardonnay with my supper when I got the phone call about Sam. As I'm the SIO in the inquiry, I stood down the late shift guys and hotfooted it down here myself. Now, what have you got for me?"

He nodded that they return to the corridor where satisfied he wouldn't be overheard, Iain quietly related the circumstances of his finding Sam and what seemed like an admission from the old man.

"Has he said anything else?" Irene asked.

Iain shook his head before replying, "Sam was unconscious during the trip here in the ambulance and he's being treated for his head wound as we speak, so I haven't had the opportunity to learn anything more."

"I'm right in thinking he's the old jakey with the white hair and beard that hangs about the Toll?" she asked.

"That's him," Iain confirmed. "He's never any bother and even when he's got a drink in him, he's usually compliable."

Her face contorted when she muttered, "The late shift that attended the dockside told me when they phoned that they didn't find anything there that indicated why he was attacked, but come the morning I'm going to organise another search of the area and this time even if some of the warehouse are padlocked, we'll be going into them too."

She frowned before continuing, "I find it odd that old Sam would have a go at Lesley or any polis for that matter. That and by all account she's a fit lassie, so I can't really see her being unable to handle herself with old Sam, can you?"

"No," he replied with another shake of his head. "definitely not. That's why I find it strange, what Sam said." He paused then continued, "As long as I've known him, he's always carried what few possessions he has around with him, so I looked in the two plastic bags I found lying beside him and," he shook his head, "there was nothing that I could see belonged to Lesley."

"And no offence, Iain but you're definite that's what the old guy said?"

"One hundred per cent," he nodded.

"Well," Irene sighed, "I suppose we'll just need to wait now until he regains consciousness to find out more. Now, where can I get a decent cup of coffee round here?"

****

Janie Wallace awoke to the sound of a diesel engine in the street and guessing it to be a taxi, heard the slamming of two doors before the vehicle moved off.

The other side of the bed was empty and turning her head, she glanced at the digital clock to see it was almost midnight.

Where the hell are you, Paul, she wondered?

****

In the early hours of that Monday morning, Charlie Gallagher rolled off the naked Paula Menzies and grunting, pulled the quilt cover across his body before telling her, "Right, doll, wake me when breakfast is ready."

Turning onto his side with his back to her, he was asleep within minutes.

She nervously waited till she heard him snore and certain he was asleep, quietly slid from the bed then bending to collect her clothes from the floor, carried them with her through to the bathroom where she sat numbly on the toilet seat.

Sex with Charlie had quickly become a routine for him with no pleasure for her. Yeah, it had been exciting in the beginning, six long months before when Charlie had seen the thirty-three-year-old Paula dancing provocatively in the Sauchiehall Street night club and insisted in buying her a drink; a drink that quickly turned into an invitation to accompany him back to his place and within an hour of their arriving at his flat, to his bed. Of course she had known who he was for after all, who didn't know Charlie Gallagher, the man you went to see if you needed something done or someone hurt or in particular, drugs.

She shivered in the chill of the night and gently touched at her swollen eye.

She was trapped like some animal in a gilded cage but as her old Ma used to say, you made your bed now fucking lie in it. Placing the bundle of clothing onto the lip of the bath, she arose from the toilet seat then putting on her robe from the hook behind the door, turned to stare at herself in the mirror above the wash hand basin.

Paula was acutely aware of her sexual attraction to men and that first night with Charlie had been for a laugh, a dare from her pal to see if she could pull the well-known gangster. She definitely hadn't intended coming over to Govan to live with him; however, within a week of meeting him it just sort of happened. Him suggesting that it wasn't worth her while continuing to rent her one-bedroom flat in Springburn when she could save her money by moving in with him. He would take care of her, take care of all the bills and more, he had promised her. All she had to do was look after the flat and see to his needs, no matter what they were.

"Besides," he had told her, "you said your wee sister is looking for her own place. Why not turn your flat over to her?"

She hadn't given his proposal as much consideration as she should have, but the temptation to get Cathy out from under their father's control was tempting and so she had quickly agreed.

She sighed and shook her head.

She couldn't fool herself any longer, that what was happening to her was because she was just getting Cathy to safety. No, it was her own stupid fault that she had been seduced by his money and his notoriety. Hanging on to his arm while punters at the clubs opened doors for him, guys getting out of his way or eager to speak to him or to buy him drink, all so they could say they knew or had been seen with Charlie Gallagher. It had excited her that people would see her as his girlfriend.

What a *fucking* mistake that was, she sighed.

It had seemed so simple at first, for Paula wasn't a stranger to men nor their desires and from the outset willingly put up with Charlie's weird urges and his one-sided sexual fulfilment.

But as the months went on and particularly after…

She shuddered at the memory and though she bit at her lower lip, was unable to prevent the tears flowing.

With a sob, her hands reaching across to clutch the rim of the sink, her body shook as she wept.

Raising her head, she took a deep breath and stared at her reflection in the mirror above the sink then gritting her teeth thought of the police woman, the young blonde woman called Constable Rudd.

Charlie had warned her to knock off from the shoplifting, but in the huge and busy Hypermarket store it had seemed so easy.

Or it did until she was caught nicking the fancy woollen jacket and handed over to the two cops. She had set out to con the polis lassie, but when she got back to the flat made a huge error telling Charlie about what happened and laughing about it, thinking he would see the funny side of it too. It was when she had told him of her promise to the policewoman that she would do her best to stay out of bother, that she would give they two security wankers at the Coop some money to compensate them after scratching the guy's face and butting the woman she had sensed a change in his mood.

Gazing in the mirror at the fading bruise on her eye she recalled how quickly she'd realised that Charlie didn't see it like that, her speaking to the polis even though she had lied to them. He had taken her by the throat and snarled that he just didn't trust her to keep her mouth shut and didn't trust her to keep shtum about what he did, about his business.

His backhanded slap had taken her by surprise and knocked her to the floor with him stood over her, his face contorted with such rage he had her so badly frightened she had almost wet herself.

So angry was he that for one awful moment lying on the floor, she curled up into a ball and had thought he was going to beat her.

But then the questions had begun.

"Who was this polis woman? What was her name? Where did she work out of? What questions had she asked you? What did you tell her? Did she ask about me? What does she look like? What did she tell you about contacting her again?"

She had no choice but to tell him and each time Paula had been slow to answer or had told him she didn't know or wasn't sure, he had bent down and cuffed her on the head, but hitting her had aroused him too and…closing her eyes she swallowed with shame at the memory of him dragging her by the hair through to the bedroom, then what he did to her and made her do.

It wasn't sex, she had come to realise; it was rape, his way of punishing her.

And through it all, the pain and indignation of his assault upon her body, she had come to recognise that perhaps deep within her she wanted the young police woman to jail the bastard!

She inhaled deeply and continuing to gaze at her reflection, tossed her head and watched her curly red locks fall naturally about her shoulders.

She knew now that his rough sex was just the start of it, that he was getting bored with her and she meant nothing to him, nothing at all. Even as recently as last week she had seen him chatting up a blonde in the Sauchiehall Street nightclub and knew her days as his live-in girlfriend were numbered and soon it would be back to the flat with…

She stopped and swallowed, the saliva tasting like bile when she remembered that Cathy was no longer there, in the flat. Her shoulders sagged when she thought about it, what she intended doing and was relieved he didn't know about Cathy, for if he did her plan might not work. Paula, a fighter all her life, knew her own limits and months before would not have dared walk out or grass on Charlie Gallagher. But when her darling, baby sister had become hooked on his vile drugs, her game plan changed.

Well, she continued to stare at her reflection, she would make her plan work, though conscious she would need to be very careful, to look out for herself for if he ever suspected…and she shivered.

She thought again of the bit of conversation she overheard about Charlie taking forty or fifty bars; heroin she guessed. That and when she'd opened the flats front door to that Scouse guy, she didn't need to be a genius to work out that Charlie had made a deal and probably with somebody from Liverpool. All she needed now was the time and place of the delivery and then, she again touched lightly at her eye and grimacing, thought, we'll see who's doing the fucking.

****

They had left the small and cramped staff refreshment room, preferring to give the nurses their own place back and made their way along the corridor to the waiting room beside the public entrance. Now seated on uncomfortable chairs and each holding a white plastic cup of barely palatable coffee, Irene said, "You're well past your finishing time, Iain. Are you sure you don't want me to phone for a car to take you back to the office, let you get home? There's really no point on hanging on while I'm here."

He smiled and shaking his head, replied, "Old Sam is a right nuisance Irene, but he's not a bad guy and besides, I'd like to see this through, find out if what he said has any bearing on Lesley's disappearance." Toasting her with his cup, he grinned and added, "And if nothing else I'm a gentleman so I'll keep you company till we find out what's happening, eh?"

She had smiled and sipped at her coffee then shaking her head as if at her own forgetfulness, asked, "You and Lesley, you were neighbours now and then, yes?"

"Occasionally, yes," he agreed, "but only when the sergeant got the beats mixed up."

She didn't fail to detect the trace of bitterness in his voice and quietly said, "You'll be referring to Jimmy Cole?"

"Aye, the guy's a right wanker, Irene. Honestly. If that's the breed of new bosses then the polis and the public in general are in real trouble," he shook his head.

She didn't want to get into a whining debate about Cole who was fast becoming known throughout the Govan office as an incompetent supervisor, so instead said, "I'm wondering about one day not too long ago when you neighboured Lesley. The day you gave a shoplifter the jail from the Hypermarket. A woman called…"

He quickly turned towards her and grinning, interrupted with, "Paula Menzies, you mean. That bugger Charlie Gallagher's girlfriend?"

"Aye, you recall the arrest?" her interest quickened.

"Oh, aye, who could forget *that* particular woman. A right good looker and that's part of her problem," he nodded.

"What do you mean," her brow furrowed.

"Well, think of it like this. Most of the security staff in these big shops these days are guys, yeah?"

She slowly nodded in agreement.

"Guys being guys," he spread his hands wide and smiled, "are more likely to spot and keep and eye on a good looking bird than a dumpy wee housewife wearing a headscarf and specs. Now, if Paula had any sense when she's out blagging at the shops, she should be more concerned with dressing down than looking like she's stepped off a Vogue shoot. A lot of these security guys like being seen swaggering about and hoping to catch the eye of the good looking dolly birds, to engage them in conversation perhaps and play the macho man; so it stands to reason that they're bound to notice a good looking woman like Paula and they don't need to be The Sweeney off the tele because they're bound to catch her when's she's lifting stock."

"So, by your reasoning, if Paula and I are in the Hypermarket shoplifting, she'll get caught because she's a young, good looking woman while a dumpy old bird like me will get away with it?"

"Now you're putting words in my mouth," he laughed and shaking his head, added, "I think it would be an even match, Irene. I mean, how anyone could think of you as a dumpy old bird. You completely undersell yourself and…" he stopped and glancing away, forced himself to take a swig of coffee to hide his embarrassment, then nearly choked when it went down the wrong way.

But the comment had been made and he could not know that Irene was secretly delighted at the compliment.

"Tell me," she pretended not to be amused as he coughed and spluttered, "did Lesley take an interest in Menzies? I mean, did she try to sign her on as a tout or anything like that?"

He cleared his throat and laying the coffee cup down onto the floor, frowned before answering, "I remember when we arrived back at Govan, the Inspector was busy at the charge bar with a drunk driver giving him the breath test and you know how long that can take, particularly if the suspect is being stroppy. I went to the uniform bar to fill in the crime report for the shoplifting and the assaults and left Les with Menzies so I was away, what," his brow wrinkled, "fifteen minutes or so? Anyway, when I got back the drunk driver was in the wee room where the breath machine is and we took Menzies to the charge bar. Les was doing the report case so she charged her and I corroborated." He exhaled before shaking his head and adding, "But she didn't say anything about trying to sign her on as a tout, no. Mind you, if that was her intention she did the right thing, didn't she? I mean, the less people that know a ned is a tout, the safer it is for the ned."

"One other thing," Irene said. "In the time that you neighboured Lesley, did she ever mention anything about a..." she stopped, then choosing her words carefully, continued, "about anyone pestering her? I mean, romantically?"

"You mean a guy taking an interest in her?" He shrugged and said, "Les is a good looking young lassie, Irene and to be honest, I'm pretty sure there was a number of guys would like to have nipped her, but I'm guessing you're asking about someone in particular? Well, as far as I know," he shook his head, "nobody that I can think of and she definitely didn't mention anybody. Well, not since she broke up with her boyfriend. He's a cop or rather, he's in the CID over in Stewart Street."

"I know about him," she muttered, then asked, "What about a woman? I mean, another woman taking an interest in Lesley?"

He stared curiously at her and fighting the urge to smirk, replied, "I'm not daft, I'm sure she must have attracted the attention of both men and some women, but again no. Besides, Les wasn't a lassie who talked much about herself," yet inwardly thought, just how much did I *really* know about her?

It was then that their attention was taken by the young and very tired looking Indian doctor who left the cubicle and approached them to ask, "Sir, Madam, you are the police who came here with Mister Fullerton, yes?"

Irene nodded to confirm they were indeed.

The doctor wearily drew up a chair and sitting opposite, in a quiet almost resigned voice told them that it was unlikely that Sam would regain consciousness. In perfect though slightly accented English he explained his assessment was based on a combination of issues that included Sam's undoubted elderly age, the blow to the back of his head, his apparent underlying medical conditions of which there were many and no doubt brought on by his lifestyle of poor diet, his recorded alcoholism and general disdain for life. In short, he added, it meant it was almost a given that Mister Fullerton would soon succumb.

However, the doctor had taken the precaution of contacting the duty Neuro consultant and expected him to arrive shortly.

"After the consultant examines Mister Fullerton," he fought a yawn, "we will be better placed to confirm my initial diagnosis, but I believe I am correct in my assessment. I am so very sorry," he glanced at them in turn.

Almost in disbelief, they both stared at the doctor.

Irene was the first to speak when she asked, "Is there a likelihood he might regain consciousness, Doctor? We're keen to know how he came by his injury and have other questions we would like to put to him."

"I do not know the answer to your question, Madam, but if you have details of his family, I would suggest you make provision to have them attend here as soon as possible. In the meantime," he rose from his chair, "if you wish to sit with him, I see no reason why you cannot."

Irene turned to Iain who said, "As far as I'm aware, doctor, we don't know anything about Mister Fullerton, not even his true age. No date of birth," he shook his head, "no previous address and certainly nothing about any family. In fact, all we do know about Sam is that he arrived about four, maybe five years ago and was living rough in the Kinning Park area of the city."

"Fingerprints," Irene interrupted, then herself getting to her feet, quickly continued, "If you've no objection, Doctor, I'll arrange for a scene of crime officer to attend here as soon as possible and take Mister Fullerton's fingerprints. If we can get those and run them through the system and only if he's known to us previously, we might be able to fully identify him and perhaps even have time to contact a relative."

The doctor shook his head and replied, "I have no objection, Madam, but if you do this thing then I would urge you to be very quick."

That said, he turned and left them alone.

"Right," she briskly said, "you nip into the cubicle and sit with him while I find a phone to contact Pitt Street and get some poor bugger out of his bed."

****

May, the helpful nurse, suggested Irene Crichton use the desk phone at the Nurses Station to make her call.

After explaining her request, to Irene's surprise the Duty Inspector at the Pitt Street control room told her that she was in luck, the on-call scene of crime officer, the SOCO, had been called out earlier to a violent incident in the north side of the city and was almost finished processing the locus.

"If you can tell him to call down here at the Southern General casualty, I'll be grateful and I have one more request of you."

"Okay, shoot," the Inspector replied.

"Can you have someone from the Fingerprint Department called out, too. Once the SOCO has the prints, I'd like to know if our man is on file…" she stopped and brow knitted, cursed herself for not previously thinking of it, before continuing, "In fact, can you do a speculative check on the PNC for me? Check to see if a Samuel Fullerton," she spelled Fullerton, "is on record at all. If he's got a criminal conviction, then it's likely his prints will be recorded and we might get some background on him. Family members, that sort of thing."

"How urgent is this, Irene?"

"Well, according to the doctor here, old Sam is teetering on the edge and we're keen to contact a family member before he dies."

"Oh, that serious is it?" the Inspector muttered before telling her, "I'm at a screen now, let me log in. Right, I'm in. I take it you don't have an age?"

She glanced at the nurse May who watched her and pursing her lips, said, "We're guessing his date of birth is between nineteen hundred and say, nineteen-fifteen."

She saw May nod in agreement before continuing, "Again we're guessing, but reckon him to be about five feet ten to six feet tall."

"Any distinctive tattoos, birthmarks or scars?"

"Give me a minute," she replied and repeated the question to May who held up a hand and dashed off to the cubicle. She returned less than two minutes later to tell her, "Sam has an old, faded six-inch abdominal scar on the right side, presumably after an appendix operation and a three-inch tattoo of an anchor on his left forearm."

"Did you hear that?" she asked the Inspector.

"Got that, give me a minute," he drawled then said, "The PNC is showing eighteen Samuel Fullerton's, but I've narrowed them down to…no, wait, one fits your description. Samuel William Fullerton, born in Glasgow in nineteen oh four. Several convictions for drunkenness and one for theft and another for serious assault, both in the nineteen thirties. He got the jail for the serious assault, nine months. However, to be honest, Irene, it was so long ago I'll be surprised if his record still exists."

"Was he fingerprinted?"

"Aye, and there *is* a Scottish Criminal Records Office number," that he dictated, "but there's a real chance if it does still exist, it will be archived. However," she could almost hear the smirk in his voice, "that's a problem for the Fingerprint Department. Now, anything else I can do for you?"

"No, that's grand for now," she thanked him and ended the call, a little elated that she had so easily identified Sam Fullerton's details. All they had to do now was find a family member. However, when both she and May turned and the saw the young Indian doctor walk towards them, his face grave, they instinctively knew they were too late.

"I am so sorry, Madam," said the doctor. "Mister Fullerton died just a minute ago."

CHAPTER EIGHT

Irene Crichton was uncertain whether or not to contact DCI Colin Morton and inform him of the demise of Sam Fullerton nor whether his injury had been the result of an assault or a simple fall, but with a shrug, made her decision.

Tired and disappointed and even though Iain Meikle had been sitting with him at his demise, the old man had died without having spoken anything further.

She explained to Iain, "Given his age and general state of his health, the smell of alcohol on his breath, the condition of the dockside," she stared pointedly at him, "and you know better than anyone how treacherous it is underfoot when it's been raining, as well as the absence of anything to suggest that he had been struck on the head…" she paused before continuing, "That all said, I'll meet with Colin Morton in the morning and as I said earlier, I'm going to arrange for a better, daylight search of the area and the locked warehouses too regarding Lesley's inquiry, so it won't do any harm to include old Sam's fall."

If indeed it was a fall, thought Iain, but said nothing other than slowly nodding.

"Anyway," she sighed, "there will be need to be a post mortem so maybe that will firm up what happened to the poor old bugger. As well as that I'll cancel the SOCO's visit too. There's no need for him to come tonight when the fingerprinting can be done at tomorrow's PM."

It took a bit of persuasion, but Iain finally convinced her that while he could lie late in the morning, she as both the SIO in Lesley's missing person would also need to be in early to the office to inform the DCI of the circumstances of both old Sam's statement and his death.

"Besides, I'll need to hang on here to collect details for the Sudden Death Report from the staff about his admission and treatment and to take possession of his belongings too."

Assuring her that yes, he'd arrange his own transport back to Orkney Street, she reminded him that she'd confirm his application for his overtime spent at the casualty ward then bid him good night and tiredly left the waiting room.

Rubbing wearily at his brow, Iain yawned and getting to his feet, saw on the large waiting room clock it was now almost one am.

Making his way to the staff refreshment room, he knocked on the door and entering, saw Joe Prescott, May and a second nurse having a break. In the corner, the Indian doctor was pouring himself a cup of coffee.

"Yes?" Prescott snapped.

"Just need the usual details of the treatment, time of death and the possessions of Mister Fullerton," Iain politely replied.

Turning to May, Prescott sharply instructed her, "See to your pal and give him the details he needs then get that smelly old guy out of my ward and down to the mortuary."

Pale faced, Iain was about to angrily respond, but to the surprise of both him and the two nurses, it was the young Indian doctor who turning towards Joe Ninety, calmly and in an even voice said, "Staff Nurse Prescott, I insist you refrain from such language about any of our patients. We are here at the disposal of those who seek our help. It belittles your good self and that of your staff to be so judgemental about an uncle of Mister Fullerton's age. Neither you nor I know what brought that old man to lead the life that he did. We can only thank our God that we do not live as did he and I now expect you to make your apology to your staff and also to this police officer."

Wide-eyed and red-faced, Prescott stared angrily at the younger man who met his stare until finally Prescott hissed, "I apologise."

"Then the matter is ended," the young doctor said and turned back to finish making his coffee.

With a tight-lipped beckoning nod to Iain, the auxiliary nurse May rose from her seat and led him from the corridor to the cubicle where the body of Sam Fullerton reposed under a white sheet.

Iain's nose twitched at the strong, lemon scented smell in the cubicle and realised that something had used an aerosol can to spray the room.

"The mortuary team will collect him within the next hour," she quietly informed him before adding, "Try not to take any notice of that idiot, Prescott. He's not worth bothering about or getting upset over."

Iain shook his head and sighing, replied, "He gives the caring profession a bad name. I'm pleased that young doctor had the sense to take him down a peg."

"Aye, Doctor Pradesh might seem like he's a quiet young lad, but he's nobody's fool. I'm of the opinion that come the morning before he finishes his shift, he'll be having a word with the Matron."

In a tired voice Iain said, "Right then, May, down to business." Fetching his notebook from his tunic pocket, he continued, "Just the usual details, hen. Time of admittance, time of death, who pronounced life extinct and what treatment old Sam got."

"Oh, right," she reached for a clipboard and donning her spectacles, provided the details. When she had finished she asked, "Did you trace any relatives?"

"Not at the minute, but there will be a PM in the morning so we'll get Sam fingerprinted and try to find someone who can both positively identify him and maybe arrange for some sort of funeral. It would be a shame if the council end up putting him in a paupers grave."

"Aye, it would," she agreed, then said, "He's wearing a wedding band."

"Oh, I didn't notice. Can you take if off his finger? I'll put it with his property."

He watched as May wrestled with the wedding ring before applying a salve as a lubricant, but her ring did not budge. "Sorry, but it's just not coming off."

"No bother. I'll mention it on the report that he's wearing it." She smiled and stroked a wisp of hair from Sam's brow before saying, "I think he thought that I was someone he knew."

Iain's brow furrowed and he asked, "What, you mean he regained consciousness? Did he say something to you?"

"Aye, just before he died," she nodded, then turning to Iain, added with a soft smile, "Well, not anything that really made sense, if you know what I mean. Opened his eyes and told me I should have stayed back from the edge, that the water is too deep or something like that."

He felt his stomach tense as he quietly asked, "Did he say anything else? Anything at all?"

She inhaled, suddenly aware that Iain was intensely interested, that it might be important to the policeman, then slowly exhaled as though trying to recall before replying, "I couldn't make out much of what he was mumbling. Said something about a white hat on the ground, the splash and a woman screaming. No, I've got that wrong," she involuntarily raised a hand to her lower lip as her eyes narrowed in thought. "It was a white hat on the ground, then a woman screaming and *then* a splash. At least, I *think* that's what he said. Why, is it important?"

"Did anyone else hear what he said?"

"Well, Joe Ninety was in the cubicle too, but as usual," her voice was full of disdain, "he was busy filling out a chart rather than getting his hands dirty, so I don't suppose he paid much attention. Wait! I think Ajish bent over him too, but again I don't know if he told him anything either."

"Ajish?"

"Doctor Pradesh."

"Oh, right. Can you ask the doc to come in here a minute, please?"

"Wouldn't you rather speak with him in the refreshment room?"

Iain's eyes narrowed as he recalled reading an article in an issue of the monthly Police Federation magazine about cognitive interview techniques and replied, "No, if he's in here in the cubicle *with* Sam, it might help jog his memory."

"Oh, okay then, I'll fetch him," she nodded though slightly confused at his reasoning, but went anyway and returned a moment later with the equally puzzled young doctor.

Explaining that it was important and an ongoing inquiry, Iain asked Pradesh if he had heard Sam say anything before the old man died.

Stroking at his chin, Pradesh's face twisted when he replied with a smile, "I bent over the uncle when I saw his lips moving and believed he was trying to say something, but to be frank, Constable, it made no sense. No sense at all," he shook his head.

"But he did say something?" Iain asked, his voice flat and level as he tried to hide the excitement that coursed through his body.

"I do not know if it is significant," Pradesh held up both hands as though in apology, "but he said he saw him and her, that is the words he used; him and her. When I asked who him and her were, he didn't say, but he did say something about the hat that fell on to the ground and I *think* he said something about a splash, or at least that is what the word sounded like. That was as far as I can recall, Constable. I'm sorry, but there was no more," Pradesh shook his head before adding, "You must understand, the old uncle was very confused. Is that of any help to you?"

"Doctor," Iain, his notebook in his hand, grinned when he said, "you cannot believe how very helpful that is."

He was about to turn away when the doctor's eyes narrowed and he said, "A vehicle. The uncle said something about a vehicle."

"A vehicle?" he pressed the doctor.

"Well, pardon me, correctly what he said was a car…no," the doctor shook his head and held up his hands in apology. "Sorry, I am wrong again. He did not use the word *car*, he used the word what you here in Glasgow call a car; a motor. That is why I said vehicle. Is that of any use to you?"

"Yes, doctor, it just might be," Iain thoughtfully nodded.
****

Janie Wallace reached a hand behind her to touch her partner Paul, only to find he wasn't in bed. Dazed from sleep, she felt for the pull switch on the bedside lamp and blinking when the light lit up the room, saw the time on the clock to be almost six am. Turning, she frowned when she saw that his side of the bed was indeed empty and no indentation on the pillow meant he hadn't yet been to bed.

Now awake, she yawned as her bladder reminded her she needed to pee and getting up from the bed, shivered in the cold before grabbing her dressing gown and staggering sleepily towards the bathroom in the hallway.

Glancing downstairs, she could see the ground floor was in darkness and wondered where he might be at this time of the morning.

After washing her hands, she carefully made her way down the stairs to check he hadn't passed out on the couch, but it was as she thought; Paul had not returned home.

Where the hell can he have got to she wondered and as there seemed little point in going back to bed decided as she was up anyway, she'd have a cuppa.

It was when the kettle was boiling she thought she heard the sound of his car and made her way to the front room to glance out into the street, but saw to her disappointment it was a neighbour across the road backing into his driveway as he returned home after finishing nightshift.

Cupping her hands around the mug, she sat at the small kitchen table and wondered about Paul.

The interest he was receiving from the English First Division teams was exciting for him and it was only last week he had suggested that if as seemed likely he did make the move to England, Janie would go with him. Yet she had to admit the thought of giving up her job and moving to England was more than a little daunting for her and when she pointed out she had a career with the police, her comment ended with them both disagreeing; he that his career would provide them with a very affluent lifestyle and that really, her career would only last until such time she got pregnant.

Infuriated at his offhand dismissal of her professional ambitions, the disagreement had turned into a full-blown quarrel with heated words from both. She closed her eyes when she recalled that she had angrily reminded Paul that it was her salary that was paying the mortgage as well as the groceries and the utility bills while he spent most of his money on his fancy car and nights out.

He had stormed from the house and was gone for two days before he arrived home with a large bunch of flowers and a contrite apology.

But the issue had not been resolved and no agreement reached about the probable move to England.

Her brow furrowed when she recalled that was the first time she had admitted to herself that perhaps their relationship was not meant to be. In fact, she shivered in the coolness of the kitchen, though she hated to admit it she excused his behaviour far too often.

Glancing down, Janie realising the tea in her mug had grown cold and with a sigh decided that maybe a bath would cheer her up.

****

After a sleepless night, Irene Crichton arrived at Orkney Street office a little after seven-thirty that morning to find the night shift preparing their notes for handover to the dayshift.

"Glad you're arrived early," the young female detective told her. "I was just about to leave you this," and handed her a sheet of paper with a scribbled note from Iain Meikle.

Her eyes opened wide when she read the note, but before she could question the detective, the younger woman said, "Iain dropped that with us before he went home. Says to tell you that he'll come in early and give you the full story and do the witnesses statements when he gets here." Grinning, the detective yawned before asking, "I take it, Ma'am, that what he's found out is useful regarding Lesley Rudd?"

"More than useful," Irene nodded, her eyes narrowing as she muttered, "If this doctor and the nurse heard correctly, I think we're looking at a murder."

****

Iain Meikle too had a sleepless night, for his mind was in whirl. That said though, he startled wide awake when the alarm sounded at eight o'clock, then rubbing tiredly at his eyes, swung his legs from bed and headed for the bathroom.

As he shaved he thought again of the previous hours. Excited though he had been when he interviewed Doctor Pradesh and the nurse, May Johnson, his excitement had diminished and self-doubt set in, wondering if he was making too much of what the two staff heard old Sam say. Did they really hear the old man mutter that he had witnessed Les being murdered? His uncertainty had continued in the darkness as he tried to sleep. Was it that he was looking for some excuse for Les's disappearance, that perhaps in his confused state Sam had spoken of another time and another incident and had not after all seen anything?

He stared in the mirror at his reflection and shaking his head decided that all he could do was report what he had learned. It was up to the DCI and Irene Crichton to decide if the two statements he submitted were of any interest in the inquiry. Towelling his face dry, he headed for the bedroom to get dressed.

****

In the bedroom of their three bedroom, mid-terraced house in Langton Road in the Wavertree area of Liverpool, William 'Billy' Madison, now fifty-one years of age and suffering from a vodka induced hangover, woke with a start causing his wife Sheila to mumble, "For fuck's sake, our Billy. What's wrong now?"

Gently lowering his shaven, aching head back down onto the pillow, Madison stared at the ceiling and exhaled through pursed lips before replying, "Just another bad dream again, love. Me getting the nick."

Sheila, his wife of eighteen years, turned towards him and rubbing the sleep from her eyes, said, "Then don't get caught. For Christ's sake, I keep telling you, you're taking too many chances these days." She sighed and continued, "This is about that Glasgow fella, the one that wants the fifty kilos, isn't it?" He nodded as she asked, "Just how well do you know him and more to the point, how much can you trust him?"

"Well, I knew him when I run around Glasgow with the Barlanark team," he shrugged, "but never really had any dealings with him until a few years ago when a couple of times I helped him get some gear."

"Any problems at that time?" she asked, stifling a yawn.

"Naw," he puckered his lips and shook his head. "The first deal went through sweet enough and I let him have some gear a couple more times, but that's not what's worrying me," he frowned.

"What is it then that *is* worrying you," she exhaled and propping herself up on one elbow, pretended interest, because she had been through this with him more than a few times. In fact, every time he intended sending gear north to Glasgow or to one of the Scotch places up there, he worried himself sick and all because of that time the Glasgow Drug Squad had captured one of Billy's couriers who turned Queens Evidence and given up Billy's name as the supplier of the seized heroin. She frowned as she remembered the only thing that saved him from going down for ten years was the skill of his Queens Counsel who was already into Billy for a large sum for the coke that Madison provided for him. Well, that and the heavy backhander to the corrupt Judge.

But since then he had got it into his head that any agreement with the Glasgow dealers was dodgy, that the Drug Squad in Glasgow were too good to fuck about with.

And now this.

"If you've got a bad feeling, lad," she sighed and rubbed at an itch on her fanny, "why not just cancel the whole thing? I mean, it's not worth you losing sleep over it, is it? You can shift the gear to somebody else, can't you? What about that black fella, the Paki guy over in Sheffield? You've done business with him before and he's never given you any shit, has he?"

"It's not about shifting the gear, Sheila, it's about reputation, isn't it? If word gets out that I've backed off after giving my word…" he shook his head.

It was the same old argument, she realised with a sigh. He wanted her to try to persuade him not to go through with it in the sure knowledge his mind wouldn't be changed.

"Look," she tried one more time. "Like I said, if you've got a bad feeling about it, why not let one of your team take charge of the delivery arrangements. Yes," she nodded, "you organise the time and date and place for the handover, but choose somebody to take the blame if the delivery goes tits up. Then you're in the clear and you've got somebody to blame for fucking it up, haven't you?"

"Yeah," he grinned, his eyes narrowing. "I do like that idea." He lay for a moment considering her suggestion then said, "Doughnut. I'll let Doughnut handle the delivery. It's about time that fat git did something to earn his wages anyway."

With a wide grin, he turned to stare at his blonde wife and turning suddenly towards her, pulled at her top and leered, "Get your knickers off, girl, I'm in the mood for love."

****

On her way to the office that Monday morning, Janie Wallace was in a foul mood.

Paul had still not arrived home and leaving her departure for work for as long as she dared finally realised that there was little point in remaining any longer.

Nor did she leave a note. No, she'd have it out with him when she returned home that evening.

Physio indeed, she fumed.

Arriving in Orkney Street, she found a parking space directly opposite the front entrance to the office and sat for a few moments to compose herself for she was determined not to take her personal life to work with her.

Locking the car, she crossed the road and mounting to steps to the front door smiled at the middle-aged uniformed constable who courteously held the door open for her, greeting him with, "Morning, George."

Head down, the cop hardly glanced at her before responding with a muttered, "Hi, Janie."

Making her way up the broad stairs to the CID general office, she pushed open the door to see that already there were a number of detectives had arrived.

It puzzled her that though some were obviously sharing a story in the newspapers they held, they all stopped talking and turned away, busying themselves with paperwork at their desks.

"Morning," she cheerfully called out, yet remained mystified when a couple of her colleagues returned her greeting while others turned away.

Turning, she bumped into Peter Rossi and was in the act of apologising when he abruptly said, "Can I have a quiet word?"

He didn't wait for a response, but turned on his heel and made his way to the adjoining narrow room used to store files.

Baffled, she followed him into the room and saw him stood there, his face solemn and holding a copy of that morning's issue of the 'Glasgow News.'

"Okay," she smiled at him, her face betraying her curiosity. "What's going on?"

"I take it you've not read this mornings edition?" he asked in a flat voice and held up the newspaper.

Her eyes narrowed as she asked, "Is this about Lesley? Has she been found?"

He slowly shook his head as he sighed and nodding to a chair by the desk, replied, "I think you should sit down, Janie. Here," he laid the newspaper onto the desk.

He opened the newspaper at page three and sitting herself down, felt the colour drain from her face.

The clear and sharp photograph took up almost half of the page and was of a pretty, blonde girl with a toothy grin who seemed to be either a teenager or in her early twenties and was being ushered into a black Hackney cab. The photographer had captured the instant the girl's miniskirt rode up her thigh to expose her underwear and her blouse seemed to be in disarray too, suggesting the girl was drunk. The man assisting the girl into the taxi held up one hand to shield his face from the flash of the camera while the other hand solicitously helped the girl into the cab.

However, Janie saw there was no need for the man to hide his face, for the headline said it all: SHARKIE SCORES AGAIN.

"I'm sorry," Rossi said, "but I thought you should read this before you heard it being bandied about."

"Yes," she replied, her voice a mere whisper as she continued to stare at the photograph. If he had asked how she was, how she felt, she could not have truthfully answered for all she could feel was a sense of detachment from what she was reading; like a numbness.

The door opened to admit Irene Crichton who seeing Janie sat at the desk with the newspaper opened at the photograph, sighed, "Oh, I see you've read it, hen."

Turning to Rossi, she said, "Can you give us a wee minute?"

"Yes, of course Ma'am," he nodded and left the room.

Irene drew up the only other chair in the room and seating herself, said, "Men are all bastards, Janie, but it still doesn't make you feel any better knowing that. Look, if you want to take some time off, a day or two…"

She raised her head and swallowing with difficulty, stared at the DI before replying, "I'd rather not, if you don't mind, Ma'am." Then, with a soft, sad smile, asked, "I suppose I'm the talk of the steamie?"

"Probably," Irene tactfully replied, "but could it be a mistake? Maybe Paul was taking her home because she was, or I should say looks like she's steaming drunk. Maybe it's a pal's girlfriend or…"

"I think we both know she's with him," Janie interrupted and exhaled slowly.

"Okay," Irene agreed, "but don't think you've done anything wrong, Janie. You're the victim here, not him," she nodded to the photograph.

Janie sighed then said, "I can't explain it, but I think I already knew it was over anyway. Too many late nights getting home and," she made quotation marks with her forefingers, "too many evening appointments with the club Physio and his agent."

"How will you deal with it?"

"It would be unfair to dump him without an explanation so we'll probably talk when I get home this evening," she tactfully replied, but inside her anger knew no bounds. What she really wanted was to rake her nails across his face and batter the shite out of him!

"Maybe give some thought to giving him a second chance?"

"No," Janie vigorously shook her head. "I can forgive most things, Ma'am, but not betrayal."

"For what it's worth and though I'm not in a relationship, I've been where you are now and I totally agree," Irene sighed as though with regret. "Right," she slapped a hand down onto the table, "you're going to have some awkward moments today with your colleagues who will be embarrassed for you, but keep your head up and I'll share with you what my old dad used to tell me when I started in the polis," she slowly got to her feet.

"What was that, Ma'am?"

"It's Latin and sounds something like Illegitimi non carborundum, that loosely translated means don't let the bastards grind you down."

Seeing Janie smile, Irene added, "I'm going into a meeting with the DCI and Iain Meikle, one of the cops on Lesley Rudd's shift. In the meantime, Janie, keep your chin up. Go out there and round up the others and tell them to grab a coffee and I'll brief them when I'm done."

****

Getting out of bed, Charlie Gallagher made his way to the bathroom where after making his toilet, he showered and changed into a clean, red coloured tracksuit.

In the kitchen he saw Paula Menzies wearing her dressing gown and stood by the open window, her right hand cradling her left elbow while she held a cigarette and blew the smoke out through the window.

"I'm heading down to the gym for a workout. Be back in a couple of hours," he called to her before grabbing his sports bag and turning towards the front door.

Grunting, she privately believed that the fat fuck did nothing at the gym other than chew the fat with his cronies while they stood around the chocolate bar machine, but common sense dictated she kept this opinion to herself. It just wasn't worth getting a belting for opening her mouth.

Hearing the front door slam close, she hurried through to the front room and stood behind the curtain, peeked out and down to the roadway below.

Moments later, she saw Gallagher squeeze his bulk into the driving seat of his black coloured Ford Capri then with a roar, drive off.

Satisfied that he was gone, she licked nervously at her lips and lifting the phone, dialled the number she had been given.

****

DCI Colin Morton sipped at his coffee as DI Irene Crichton and Constable Iain Meikle, sitting opposite, stared at him.

"Right," Morton began. "The death of Samuel Fullerton. What's the story?"

Briefly but concisely, Irene related the discovery of the old man by Iain, of his conveyance to the casualty department at the Southern General Hospital where he succumbed to what the treating doctor surmised was a combination of his age, a blow to the head, ongoing medical afflictions and general fatigue to his body brought about by his lifestyle.

"However," she added, "the post mortem will likely confirm the doctor's prognosis."

"So, let me be clear. What you're telling me is that there is nothing at this time to suggest he was the victim of an assault?"

"Not that we can determine, no," Irene shook her head before continuing, "Not that Sam had anything of value to steal, but when Iain found him he still had his possessions and of course it was the dockside that you know yourself, Colin, is a death-trap in the rain. Slippery with grease and oil and there's every indication Sam had a wee swally in him, too. Not the best combination for walking there at night."

"Why was he there, then?"

Iain interjected and said, "Sam used to kip down that way, sir. He'd find shelter where he could and it's quiet too, away from the hustle and bustle of the pubs and the bampots that hang around."

Irene spoke again to intimate, "I've arranged for a PM to take place today, Colin. I've still to firm up on the time, but like I said we'll be able to determine then if there was anything amiss about old Sam's death."

Morton slowly nodded in understanding before lifting the two handwritten statements and began to peruse them, inwardly grateful that Iain's handwriting was not only legible, but the summary of facts was concise too.

Moments later, he laid down the two statement forms onto his desk and stared thoughtfully at them before lifting his head to peer at Iain, who dressed in a black coloured sweatshirt, jeans and a navy blue anorak, sat in one of the two opposite chairs.

"Look, Iain," he began, "I realise like everyone else you're keen to find Lesley or at least, find out what happened to her, but these…" he shook his head at the statements. Taking a breath, he slowly asked, "Just how credible are these two witnesses?"

Iain shrugged before replying, "I know May Johnson from occasional attendances to the casualty department. The doctor I'd never met before. However, neither of them had any idea why I asked them to recount what they heard so in my humble opinion, sir, they're telling the truth."

Morton tightened his lips as lost in thought, he reflected on what he had read.

Glancing at Irene, his gaze returned to Iain when he asked, "Don't take this the wrong way, but are you *absolutely* certain that what you've written here is what they told you? I mean, the nurse hearing the old man mumbling what she thought was Fullerton saying something about a white hat on the ground, hearing a splash and a woman screaming."

"That's what she said Sam told her, yes sir," he patiently nodded.

"Then this doctor, Pradesh is it?"

"Yes sir, Doctor Ajish Pradesh. He's Indian, but his English is excellent and quite pronounced. Speaks a lot more politely than I do," Iain grinned.

"Right," Morton drawled. "He alleges that the old man said…" he stopped and eyebrows knitting, smiled with curiosity. "He called Fullerton his uncle?"

"I asked about that," Iain said. "Seems in Doctor Pradesh's culture it's customary and respectful to address the older generation as uncle for the men and auntie for the women."

"Oh, maybe we could use some of that respect in our culture," Morton sighed, before continuing. "Anyway, the doctor told you that Fullerton said something about seeing 'him and her' and you believe the 'her' that Fullerton referred to was Lesley Rudd?"

"Yes, sir, I do."

Morton glanced again at the statement and said, "You've written that the doctor asked who 'him and her' were, but Fullerton didn't say? In fact, he made no mention of the 'her' being a police officer?"

"That's correct, yes, sir."

"The doctor then says that Fullerton said something about a hat on the ground and thinks Fullerton said something that sounded like the word splash."

"Yes, sir," Iain continued to nod, "that's correct."

"Was the nurse present when you interviewed the doctor? What I mean is I'm worried that they discussed what they *thought* they heard and agreed before you spoke with them?"

He took a breath before replying, "It did occur to me that they might have spoken about it, but I'm certain that neither of them gave any thought to what old Sam had said. In fact, it was only when I asked May Johnson if Sam had regained consciousness that she told me about him mumbling to her. Then when I pressed her, she thought but wasn't certain Sam had also said something to Doctor Pradesh so yes, I'm satisfied that they did not discuss what they each had heard."

Morton slowly nodded as though in understanding before asking, "Irene told me that you also heard the old man say something you believed significant and that's why you had the CID contacted. What was it again?"

He reached into his anorak pocket and fetching out his notebook, said, "I wrote it down verbatim, sir." Turning to the relevant page, he read aloud, "I didn't do anything to her. I mean, I didn't hurt her."

Morton chewed at the inside of his mouth, a habit he'd continued from childhood before responding with, "And this set you on the course that Fullerton might have either been involved or seen something of Rudd's disappearance?"

"Yes, sir," Iain answered, though his stomach was now knotted and he wondered if maybe he had made too much of Sam Fullerton's delirium.

"Irene?" Morton turned to stare at her.

"I agree with Iain. It's far too coincidental for both these witnesses to have heard the old man utter what he said and yes," she nodded, "I accept that their statements are third party. However, when put together what they both individually heard it seems to indicate that Sam *did* see something. Based on what Iain has learned," she turned to grimly smile at Iain, "I've taken the liberty of arranging for a Support Unit team to meet me at the dockside in an hour. I told them to bring tools because warrant or not, I'm going into all the locked and derelict warehouses because I've a sneaking suspicion that Sam might have been using one of them to doss down in and that's likely where he might have been when he saw what happened to Lesley."

"So, you're in no doubt these two statements are of evidential value?"

"No doubt at all, Colin."

They sat for almost a minute as Morton digested what he had heard then blowing through puckered lips, he reached for the phone and said, "Give me a minute."

Both Irene and Iain made to rise from their chairs, but Morton waved them down and said, "No, stay. I didn't mean for you to leave. I want you both to hear this."

When the call was answered, they heard him say, "Can you put me through to Detective Chief Superintendent Cruickshank, please." A few seconds later, Morton said, "Morning sir, it's DCI Morton at Govan. Yes, an early start," he smiled before continuing, "The missing person inquiry, sir, the young lassie, Constable Rudd. I've one of my constables sitting here with me whose dug up a couple of witnesses and from what he has learned," he stared pointedly at Iain, "I believe we're no longer looking for a missing person, but instead we're now dealing with a murder."

****

Entering the general office, Janie Wallace smiled when she was handed a mug of tea by DS Tam Whelan who then leaned in close to quietly whisper, "Just say the word, hen. I've an old balaclava and a pick axe handle that will sort out that two-timing bastard for you."

"Aye, and if that old fart can't handle it," his neighbour, Ian McDonald, called out from across the room, "then I'll do him proper, so I will. Arse that he is," McDonald muttered.

Raising her hand, Janie sighed loudly before replying, "Thanks, guys, but leave it to me. I'll be sorting this out when I get home tonight. But again, thanks for your support."

She took a breath and glanced around the room, taken aback and surprised at the level of support she was getting from her colleagues, both male and female, who nodded or gave her the thumbs up,

It was then that the detectives all turned and fell silent as Colin Morton, followed by Irene Crichton and Iain Meikle, entered the room.

They all knew that something was afoot, that one of Lesley Rudd's shift neighbours, Iain Meikle, had been cloistered with both the DCI and DI and that it meant something though nobody yet had an inkling as to what.

Calling the room to attention, Morton started by glancing around the room, then announcing, "First let me say from the outset that what I am about to relate to you is not at this time or under any circumstances to be disclosed to anyone outwith this room." He paused to let the warning sink in, before resuming, "Some able work last night by our colleague Iain Meikle has indicated that we're no longer looking for Constable Lesley Rudd as a missing person. From statements that Iain has obtained, we now have reason to believe that Lesley was murdered."

The shocked silence quickly became a hubbub of questions, halted when Morton raised his hand and continued, "I have informed Mister Cruickshank of the circumstances and he agrees that we will set up an incident room here at Govan. I will be the SIO while DI Crichton already has a number of inquiries regarding the disappearance of Lesley and will continue with those inquiries." He paused again and his glance sought out Tam Whelan who he addressed with, "Sorry, Tam, but I'm lumbering you with the role of office manager. Soon as I'm finished, get young Ian there," he nodded to McDonald, "to begin setting up from the murder box while you and I discuss who we'll need from the Pollok and Giffnock sub-Divisions to supplement the team. Right," he pointed to a stocky built Detective Sergeant with greying, tightly curled hair. "Janet, I'm leaving you to handle all the day to day inquiries and when Tam and I have sorted out the team, I'll let you know who you'll have on the book."

DS Janet Singleton nodded. The crime register that recorded all incoming reported crime and known by detectives throughout the city CID as 'being on the book,' was the system whereby crime reports to be investigated were issued in consecutive order to the detectives whose names were listed in order of seniority. In this manner crime reports received during the twenty-four-hour period would be fairly distributed unless the crime was of significance when crimes such as murder, rape or armed robbery and commonly tried at the High Court would be routinely allocated for investigation to a senior officer.

"In the meantime," Morton continued, "have a coffee and if you have any outstanding inquiries, pack them up together in case you're called upon to be part of the murder team Any questions so far?"

"What about the Serious Crime Squad, boss? Will you be bringing in the clipboard squad?' joked a portly detective.

Morton suppressed a grin at the slight against the Pitt Street based detectives and replied, "We'll work with what we've got the now, but if the inquiry takes off we might just have to call on the Serious to come and give us a hand. Any other questions? No? Right then," he beckoned that Irene and Iain follow him to his room, while calling out to Whelan, "Give me a couple of minutes, Tam."

Closing the door behind the two officers, he indicated they sit then taking his own seat said, "Irene. I know you've Lesley Rudd's former fiancée to interview and you also intend visiting Criminal Intelligence about the information she sent regarding Charlie Gallagher."

Morton didn't fail to notice the sharp glance that Iain gave the DI and explained, "Lesley had an interest in Gallagher, but we're not sure why."

"Is it anything to do with the arrest of Paula Menzies? Irene…I mean, Ma'am, mentioned it last night at the casualty department."

"Well, to be honest, Iain, we just don't know unless you have something to tell us?"

"Like I said last night, sir, I had no knowledge of Les trying to sign Menzies on as a tout nor did I know anything about someone taking an interest in her either."

"Okay," Morton nodded then to his surprise, said, "and if it's okay with you, Iain, I'd like you to remain on the inquiry." He raised his hand and added, "If you're agreeable, I'll square it with your shift Inspector."

"Sir?"

Morton spread his hands and continued, "You knew Lesley as well as anyone on her shift and you have a good working knowledge of the area where we suspect she was killed. If you're up for it, I'd like you to neighbour Irene here for the duration of the inquiry." He smiled and added, "I can't guarantee you an appointment to the CID, but in the meantime I want you to assume the role of acting Detective Constable. Is that okay with you?"

"Yes, of course sir," replied Iain who was quite clearly stunned.

"Right then," he laid his hands flat on the desk, "anything else before you guys go on your merry way?"

"Just one thing, Colin," Irene replied. "Likely Iain and I will be tied up with both the inquiry at Criminal Intelligence and interviewing her former fiancée, this guy DC Anderson. Can you arrange for someone to attend Sam Fullerton's PM? I'm sure you'll agree we really need to confirm if his death was accidental or not."

She left the rest unsaid, for if the PM discovered anything amiss with old Sam's demise it left open the strong likelihood they could be dealing with a second murder inquiry.

"I'll probably do that myself, Irene," he nodded. "Anything else?"

"What about informing Lesley's sister that we're now treating her disappearance as a murder?"

"It was young Janie Wallace who interviewed her, wasn't it? Her and that young lad, eh…"

"Peter Rossi," she reminded him.

"Aye, young Rossi," he nodded. "I'll send them both out there again. Leave that with me, too."

Rising from their chairs, Irene and Iain left the room.

****

Just over four and a half miles to the west of Orkney Street and north of the River Clyde is located the old, Victorian tenements in Lasswade Street not too far from the busy Dumbarton Road. The waste ground between Lasswade Street and the river was a jungle of overgrown trees and foliage, an exciting play park for the locals weans who frequently ignored the repeated warnings from their parents and elders regarding the dangerous river waters that flowed nearby.

However, kids being kids and dismissive of the adult's cautionary advice, the area was a popular haunt and in particular when they were playing truant from school.

And so it was that two thirteen-year-old, second year pupils from the local Knightswood High School had chosen to walk the two miles to Lasswade Street where they were certain they would not be discovered.

Smoking their illicit fags pinched from the older boy's mother, they were stood by the river's edge idly tossing stones into the murky waters when one of the lad saw what he believed to be a mannequin floating face downwards among the flotsam in the water. With a shriek of delight, the schoolboys began to pelt the mannequin with half bricks. When one of the lads scored a direct hit on the mannequin's shoulder, the blow caused the mannequin to slowly turn in the water. As they watched, the boys saw to their horror it was not a mannequin as they had thought, but the body of a woman; a woman who wore a dark coloured tunic with shiny buttons and whose blonde hair floated in the murky water like tendrils around her head.

CHAPTER NINE

In the passenger seat of the CID car with Iain driving and en route to Mavisbank Quay to meet with the Support Unit team, Irene turned to him and with a smile, said, "Didn't expect that, did you Iain?"

"No, I didn't," he admitted. "Still kind of taken aback to be honest." Glancing at her, his eyes narrowed when he asked, "Did you have anything to do with it?"

"No, not at all, though I have to say Colin Morton's a pretty good judge of character and if I'm reading him correctly, he believes you have something to offer this inquiry. Have you?" she stared curiously at him.

"Like what?"

"Well," she drawled and teasingly asked, "you can give us a better insight to Lesley for a start. I mean, she wasn't a girlfriend or anything, was she?"

"Irene!" he turned to stare at her. "What the hell do you think a smart, young lassie like Les would see in an old, divorced guy like me?"

"Oh, I don't know," she teased him with a half smile. "You don't give yourself enough credit, Iain. I'm sure there's a lot of life left in you yet."

"Yeah, maybe so," he nodded as though the very idea he was attractive to any woman was ludicrous. Softly laughing, he did inwardly wonder where this was going.

"Do you have your tickets?" she asked, referring to the police elementary and advanced examinations, known respectively and unofficially throughout the Scottish Police service as the Sergeant and Inspector tickets.

"I passed my sergeants exam a long time ago," he replied, "but never bothered sitting the Inspector's exam. Why?"

"Well, the sergeants ticket is enough to get you into the CID if you're interested."

He hadn't given any previous thought to joining the CID then wondered why she mentioned it. Glancing sharply at her, he saw she had turned away and was staring through the side window.

"Right, before we get to the Quay let me explain about this visit to Crime Intel," she turned back and adopted a professional voice. Quickly she related the search of Lesley Rudd's locker and reading the notebook that made reference to the submission of an Intel report.

"And that's why when we're finished with the Support Unit, we're visiting Crime Intel," he nodded in understanding before asking, "What about the visit to her former fiancée, this guy Anderson?"

"Did you ever meet him?"

He pulled a face and nodding, replied, "Once, briefly. About a year ago I think it was. At old Charlie Higgins retirement pay-off in the RNVR club in Whitefield Road. Les brought him along and introduced him."

"And?"

"And what?"

"Well, what was your impression of him?"

He exhaled through pursed lips before replying, "Well, you know how some of your CID colleagues are a bit up their own arse? Call us uniform guys woodentops, that sort of thing?"

She smiled and nodded.

"Let's just say DC Anderson belongs to that particular genre of detective. When Les introduced me his head was swivelling on his shoulders. Couldn't look me in the eye." He paused. "I got the impression he believed himself to be a cut above a woodentop like me, like he was looking for somebody more interesting to talk to. In fact," his eyes narrowed as he recalled, "I remember him asking Les if there were any CID at the doo, so let's just say once we were introduced I left them to it."

"And I ask again, your impression of him?"

"Based on that brief moment?" He shrugged. "The guy seemed to me to be a bit of a dick."

"Did Lesley ever speak about him?"

"Not much, Irene. I like…" he stopped as though suddenly accepting she was really gone and took a breath before continuing. "I *liked* Les and we got on well, together, but she wasn't one for talking about herself. I mean, it's only today when I was speaking with Janie Wallace I learned that Les has a twin sister. Who knew, eh?" he shook his head.

She sensed he was a little angry that Lesley Rudd had kept secrets from him and guessed he had been far more open about his personal life than had she.

"How was Lesley after she and Anderson split up? I mean, was she upset?"

"I didn't know they *had* split up," he shook his head. "At least, not till some time later, so I can't really answer that."

"Well, according to his boss, he's on duty today. Dayshift." She turned in her seat to face forwards, "So we'll meet with him at the Stewart Street office after we've been to Pitt Street."

He turned the car through the dilapidated entrance that led down to the Mavisbank Quay and drove slowly along the docks edge to avoid both the debris and pitted concrete surface.

"Looks like they're here," she said.

When Iain drew alongside then stopped the car by the double wheeled Support Unit Transit van, a uniformed sergeant got out of the front passenger seat. Approaching the CID both of them recognised the sergeant as a former Govan constable.

Greeting them with a wide grin, he said, "Right, Irene, I've got nine cops with me, so what do you need from us?"

****

The two young truants were panting for breath when they arrived in Lasswade Street and saw the old man at the car, his body doubled over as he bent beneath the raised bonnet and fiddled with the spark plugs.

"Mister! Mister!" cried one of the boys. "Can you phone the polis! We've found a dead body in the river!"

The man stared suspiciously at the two young lads before asking, "Should you pair not be at the school?"

They stopped and stared at one another for it had not occurred to them that they might get into trouble for dogging it from their secondary, but then as one decided that what they had found was more important than six of the belt.

"Mister, honest. There's a dead woman floating in the river and I think she's a cop!" the second boy gasped.

The old man's eyes narrowed for he had read in the "Glasgow News' just that morning the police were missing one of their young women. However, he was uncertain if he was being played for a fool and still wary of the two lads, said, "Show me."

As they made to return to the undergrowth, the man said, "Hang on, wait a minute," and turning towards the building, loudly called out, "Jessie! Are you there, hen?"

A sash window on the first floor was raised and a grey headed woman poked her head out to ask, "What is it?"

"I'm away down to the river with these lads. They said they've found a body…"

"We have," one the the boys protested.

"…and I'm away down to check. I'll be back in a couple of minutes, so keep your eye on the motor. I'm leaving the bonnet up and I don't want some bugger messing about with my tools. Okay, hen?"

Equally mistrustful of the two long haired teenagers, his wife replied, "Aye, okay, but don't be long. I've just put the kettle on."

Following the two eager schoolboys towards the river, the old man muttered under his breath that he could be doing without all this bloody nonsense just when he was trying to get his motor up and running, when they cleared the undergrowth.

"There," the two boys excitedly pointed.

Shading his eyes against the sunlight, the man stared at the shimmering water then taking a deep breath, muttered, "Oh, my God."

****

On the M8 motorway with Peter Rossi driving, Janie Wallace asked, "Do you think what the DCI said is right? That Lesley is dead after all?"

"There's really no way of knowing for certain without a body, is there? Anyway, I suppose the boss knows what he's doing and I can't see him setting up a murder inquiry without believing it himself. Now, digressing. You said there was no reply to the phone when you called Missus McNeil at home, but you remembered that she said she worked part-time in a personnel office, so can you check the map and find out where this Tunnock factory is?"

"Can do," she nodded and began to rummage through the glove compartment looking for an A to Z.

"What do you think?" he asked.

"About what?"

"Tunnocks. Think they might let us into their staff shop? I *love* their caramel wafers."

Horrified, she turned to him and said, "For heaven's sake, Peter, can't you…" then seeing his face, realised she was being teased and laughed loudly, inwardly grateful that he was trying to take her mind off her own problem.

While Janie concentrated on searching the map, Rossi gave her a brief glance and wondered how she was really holding up. Under no circumstances would he consider mentioning the "Glasgow News' report about Janie's boyfriend, though privately thought Fisher must be an arse to not only cheat on his partner, but to so publicly get himself caught with another woman; well, that just smacked of stupidity.

But then a thought struck him. What if that was Fisher's plan? What if he intended finishing with Janie and took the cowards way out because he was unable to face her and break off their relationship? It was no secret that some of the top English clubs had an interest in Fisher, so could it be that he didn't want to travel south with a girlfriend in tow? As his old nonna used to say, it is a youthful belief that the grass is always greener on the other side.

"Penny for them," Janie smiled at him.

"What? Oh, sorry, I was miles away."

"Aye, but we're not too many miles away from where Lesley's twin works, so get ready to take the Uddingston turn off," she replied.

"Righto, boss," he grinned at her.

****

The sergeant and constable who arrived in Lasswade Street in response to the panicked call from the old man and could see that he was still reeling in shock from what he had seen.

"And it was yourself that found the body?" asked the sergeant.

"No, it was them two lads that was dogging the school…" he turned around and was astonished to see the schoolboys had disappeared. "The wee shites, they're away," he muttered.

The sergeant glanced at her constable before she asked, "Can you take us down to where the body is, Mister, eh…"

"White. Archie White and it's down there in the river" he pointed then with a wave of his hand, added, "Aye, of course. Follow me."

As if suddenly realising his importance, the old man set a steady pace as he led the two officers through the undergrowth until at last they reached the river.

To his surprise, the body was no longer where he had seen it.

"It was there," he shook his head as though trying to clear it, waving his hand about his head to ward of the midges. "I'm telling you it was there," he pointed into the water.

"And you're definite the body was a police woman?"

"Aye," he was confused now, "a lassie with blonde hair. Wearing what you've got on," he pointed to the sergeant's tunic."

"Sarge," the constable nudged her and nodded towards the bank a little further up from where they stood. "The body's probably drifted in the water and…wait," he shielded his eyes from the bright sunlight, "I think I see her," he quietly added.

Telling the old man to remain where he was then carefully making their way along the slippery and muddy water's edge, the two officers stopped some twenty yards from where Mister White had first seen Lesley Rudd's body floating.

The constable began to search around for something to use to bring the body a littler closer to the bank, but the sergeant stopped him and in a quiet voice, said, "No sense in you getting wet, Tommy. You never know what you might catch from that murky water. We'll stay here to keep an eye on her and let the control room summon the launch."

"Do you think it's her?" he asked.

The sergeant's throat tightened and she swallowed with difficulty before nodding. She didn't need to positively identify the floating body to know it was the missing police woman and with that, she reached for her radio.

****

It was two of the Support Unit officers who after breaking into the padlocked warehouse, discovered Sam Fullerton's doss. Calling for Irene Crichton and Iain Meikle, the constables pointed to the food debris and with a grimace, the pile of faeces that littered one corner of the abandoned warehouse.

"Seems to be where your man used this as a toilet and waste bin, Ma'am," one of the officer's explained, then pointing to a gap further along the metal wall, continued, "There's a loose bit of wriggly tin in that wall back there, Ma'am, and we found some material snagged in the ragged edge of it." He showed them some threads that he had in his hand. "I'm guessing that's where your man squeezed through to get in here and caught his clothing on it."

"The thread's the same colour as the long coat Sam was wearing," agreed Iain as he examined it.

"Look here," she beckoned him to her.

Turning, he saw she was bent over and staring at the wall of the warehouse, but as he neared he saw she was actually peering through a hole.

"See what I see?" she asked, her voice betraying her excitement and as she moved to one side to permit him to peer through the hole, a small beam of light shone through.

He bent down and their heads almost touching, placed his eye against the hole and nodded. "This part of the warehouse is almost directly opposite where Lesley's hat was found."

"And seems to confirm what we thought. Old Sam was in here the night she disappeared and I'm guessing this is the place where he saw her and this man he mentioned."

She turned to one of the constables and said, "Daft though this may sound, can you guys nip back outside and find something heavy, say about the weight of a body then drop in into the river? I want to know if we can hear it from here."

"Ma'am," the younger of the two officers acknowledged with a nod then hurried outside.

Irene returned her eye to the hole in the wall then just under two minutes later, they clearly heard the sound of a loud splash.

"This place is deserted at night," Iain said, "and there's no backdrop of noise like the traffic on the Govan Road that we can hear during the day, so it's more than likely old Sam did hear…" he stopped and licked at his suddenly dry lips before continuing, "…that he did hear Lesley's body falling into the water."

There was an awkward silence in the warehouse, but broken when he asked, "So, does this take us any further?"

"Well," her eyes narrowed when she slowly replied, "it doesn't identify who Sam saw with Lesley, but what it does is add credibility to his mumblings and what he told the two witnesses you found, so yes; I think this has been a worthwhile exercise."

After a short discussion with the Support Unit sergeant, the three of them agreed there seemed little point in any further search and so thanking the sergeant and his team, Irene and Iain returned to the CID car.

"Pitt Street?" he asked as he started the engine.

"Yeah, I think we'll make that our first stop and while we're there," she grinned at him, "I'll treat you to a cuppa and bacon roll in the cafeteria."

"You really know how to impress a man," he returned her grin.

****

Unaware of the discovery in the Clyde waters near to Lasswade Street, Janie Wallace and Peter Rossi pushed through the doors of the Tunnock biscuit factory in Uddingston where the helpful receptionist's eyes confirmed that she had read the papers that morning, that she knew about Ellen McNeill's sister being missing. Almost with enthusiasm, she led Janie Wallace and Peter Rossi to a ground floor reception room and informed them that Missus McNeill would be with them shortly.

They thanked her and declining her offer of refreshments, sat quietly waiting for Lesley Rudd's twin sister to appear.

"I think it might be better if you broke the news," Rossi said. "I also think I might speak to her manager and ask if we can take her home. I can't see her wanting to work on, after this," he sighed.

She was about to respond when the door opened to admit Ellen McNeill who asked, "Is there news? Have you found her?"

They both rose to their feet before Janie replied, "Missus McNeill… Ellen. Please, sit down. I'm afraid we have some very bad news."

It took almost five minutes before Janie was satisfied that Ellen McNeill was composed enough to leave the room during which time Rossi had requested the young woman at the reception desk to inform Ellen's boss that she was not fit to continue working that day and that the CID officers would convey her home.

Fifteen minutes later in the McNeill's kitchen, Rossi was setting the kettle to boil while Janie sat in the lounge. Upstairs, Ellen was in the bathroom washing her face.

At last the three of them sat together in the lounge.

"Do you want us to contact your husband or a family member?" Janie asked the pale faced woman.

"No, I'll phone Jake later. The kids are at his sister's for the day. There's no need for anyone to be here," she replied then staring at them in turn, asked, "Do you know what happened to Lesley? Is there someone arrested for her…for what happened to her?" she said, unwilling to use the word 'murder.'

"The inquiry is still at an early stage," Rossi softly replied. "Like Janie said, we haven't yet discovered where Lesley's…where her body is and that's the boss's priority at the minute. Finding her."

She slowly nodded and with a sigh, said, "But you'll let me know when you hear something?"

"Of course," Janie nodded then with a telling glance at Rossi that indicated they should leave, she rose to her feet.

In the car outside, they sat for a moment in silence before Rossi said, "That's the part of the job I hate, breaking the news of a death."

"Aye, I've had my fair share of those," she agreed.

"It's a shame that we haven't found her sisters body yet because you know what she'll be thinking, of course," he turned to stare at her.

"What?"

"Well, the fact that we haven't found any body will sow the seed of doubt in her mind that her sister might not actually be dead, that Lesley might be alive somewhere."

"It would be nice of that were true," sighed Janie, "but I don't see the boss taking the decision to set up a murder inquiry if there is any doubt."

"No, you're right," he nodded and switched on the engine.

****

The sergeants radio burst into life with the message that *Semper Vigilo* and George Parsonage of the Glasgow Humane Society were both en route to assist with the recovery of the body.

"The CID and Scene of Crime have been informed too," added the controller, "and should be with you soon, over."

"Might be an idea to contact the Govan CID and inform them as well," responded the sergeant, but didn't add that as the poor lassie was one of theirs they'd likely want to know.

"Roger," acknowledged the controller.

****

After the pathologist concluded that though Samuel William Fullerton had suffered a blow to the head, there was nothing to positively indicate the blow was the result of being struck by another individual and concurred with DCI Colin Morton that it was possible the old man who clearly was seriously unwell, might have fallen where he was found and thus sustained the wound to the head.

Corroborating this conclusion was the lack of any defence wounds or any other injury consistent with being assaulted.

"So, in your opinion, it seems that his death is a tragic accident?"

"Well, yes, that and his apparent state of health," agreed the pathologist. "This poor man was a walking time bomb, Colin. His liver is shot to pieces, his kidney's are in a terrible state and look here," the pathologist pointed with a gloved hand to the open torso, "his lungs are almost black with tar and he seems to be in an advanced state of a number of terminal conditions. He was a walking example of the extreme harm alcohol and nicotine can do to the human body. I'm just surprised he lasted this long," the pathologist muttered almost to herself."

"Well, if you're happy the death is to be recorded as an accident," Morton sighed, "there's no need for me to be here any longer."

Turning to the scene of crime officer, he asked, "You have the fingerprints?"

"Aye, sir. I'll get them up to the Fingerprint Department right away."

"Thanks. His death will now be handled by the Inquiry Department at Govan, so ask whoever you speak with that any information about Mister Fullerton's family be forwarded to them. It would be a shame that the old man has to go to his grave without anyone mourning him," he shook his head, beckoning the young detective who had accompanied Morton to the mortuary to come with him as he made his way out of the examination room.

In the corridor outside, the mortuary assistant stopped him and said, "There was a phone call for you, sir. The controller at B Division. Said to tell you that some of his officers are standing by a body in the water at…" the older man glanced at his notebook, "…a place called Lasswade Street."

"Did they confirm its Lesley Rudd?" Morton calmly asked.

"No, sir," he shook his head. "All the controller told me is that what looks like the body of a blonde haired police woman is in the water and asked if you would attend. He also said to tell you that the police launch and George Parsonage are en route to recover the body from the water."

Morton turned and stared keenly at the detective before asking, "You knew the young lassie, did you?"

"Aye, sir, I did."

"Then before we call out the cavalry, son, let's head over to this Lasswade Street and confirm it is her, eh?"

****

It was Billy Madison's wife Sheila who wearing her knee length pink coloured housecoat, answered the heavy knock at the door in Langton Road to find a large, obese man dressed in a bright red coloured tracksuit stood there and glancing at the hulking figure through the glazed glass door, it didn't take a genius to work out why he was nicknamed Doughnut.

Pulling open the door, she inwardly shuddered because she never could tell if Doughnut's stare was one of pure idiocy or some lecherous desire for her and never, not in a million, fucking years would she….

"The man called for me?" he interrupted her thoughts in a shrill, almost falsetto voice that completely belied his hulk. Six foot four in his stocking soles with greasy black shoulder length hair and a face pitted with acne scars, the rubbery lipped forty-year-old Doughnut or to give him his Sunday name, Derek Stokoe, was well known in the City of Liverpool, but mostly for crimes of violence. Curiously though, Stokoe had never served a custodial sentence, but the reason for that was simple; his victims were terrified of him and to a man and woman, refused to give a statement to the police.

As for his victims, whether it be a man, a woman or a child, it didn't matter who was to be hurt for Stokoe had no sense of restraint and was a willing employee to any thug or gangster willing to pay him and that included his current boss, the drug dealer Billy Madison.

"Aye," she said at last, "he's in the front room. Beer?"

"No, tea will do nicely thank you and preferably in a china cup if you have one," he politely replied with a demonic smile that sent a shiver down her spine.

He knocked on the door and pushing it open, saw Madison sprawled on the couch watching a Betamax recording of a football game.

Born and though he also grew up in Liverpool, Stokoe was one of that rare breed of Scouser who had no interest in football nor the two teams that represented the city.

"You sent for me, Billy?"

Madison swung his legs till he was sitting upright on the couch then muting the sound on the television, indicated Stokoe sit in the armchair and replied, "I've a wee job for you, Doughnut. I've struck a deal with a Glasgow guy and I need the fifty kilo of the H delivered up there. Thing is," his face twisted, "I don't fully trust the bastard and I need someone I can depend upon to run the operation. You up for it?"

Stokoe stared at Madison before slowly asking, "What's the time frame, Billy?"

"That's to be arranged," Madison smoothly replied before adding, "but I suppose it's as quick as he can get the readies together. I mean, *we're* ready to go, aren't we?"

Nodding, Stokoe softly said, "The gear is under the floorboards of me mam's house, Billy. Nobody will touch it there. Stand on me about that."

It occurred to Madison that only an idiot would hide fifty kilo of smack under their mother's floorboards, but he knew that with Doughnut living there, nobody in their right mind would even consider screwing the house and the only threat was from the bizzies. But even they wouldn't believe that Doughnut would be so stupid to hide so much gear under the floorboards. Still…

"So, it's easily accessed then?"

"Yes, Billy."

"Right, I'll get on the blower with the Glasgow guy and set up the date for the delivery. What I need from you, Doughnut, is to stand ready to travel and ensure the collection of the cash from our punter. Do this right and there will be a good earner in it for you. You up for it, my son?"

"Yes, Billy."

The door opened to admit Sheila Madison who carried a china cup and saucer that she handed to Stokoe.

"That's very kind of you, Missus Madison," he formally thanked her, "but I think Billy is finished with me."

She stared with surprise as belying a man of his size, he quickly rose from his chair and towered over her, but she didn't miss the lengthy glance at her breasts.

It was then she remembered stories she had heard about Doughnut Stokoe, about his abusive treatment of women and tightening her housecoat about her, ever so slightly felt her knees wobble.

"I'll wait for your phone call, Billy," he turned to nod at Madison before making his way to the front door.

She followed him through the hallway when at the front door, he placed a large paw like hand on the door to prevent it being closed and with a soft smile, again openly stared at her breasts before telling her, "I'll be seeing, you, Sheila."

Locking the door behind him, she shivered then hurrying through to the front room, said, "That big bastard gives me the willies. When I opened the door and saw him standing there, I nearly peed myself."

"Yeah," he reached for the television control and turned up the sound as Kevin Keegan stuck the ball into the top corner of the net, "but put it this way. If that guy Charlie Gallagher in Glasgow tries to screw me over," he turned to grin at his wife, "can you imagine what Doughnut will do to him?"

CHAPTER TEN

Charlie Gallagher's visit to the private gym at Finnieston had nothing to do with his desire to increase his fitness, but everything to do with meeting his cronies and two trusted lieutenants of his criminal gang, Marty Boyle and Seamus O'Brien.

Gallagher would have been surprised to learn that his current squeeze, Paula Menzies, had been spot on, for here he now was stood with Boyle and O'Brien at the gymnasium rest area, each munching on a chocolate bar and sipping from a can of coke.

"So," O'Brien asked, "when is this deal due to take off, boss?"

Gallagher exhaled and replied, "Just as soon as we can collect the cash and that's why I need you two to put the hammer on our dealers. I want all of them who owe us to be squared up before the end of the week and I mean Thursday, not when they think they should pay up, understand?"

O'Brien glanced nervously at Boyle before replying, "That's a lot of running about. I mean, it isn't easy trying to pin some of they bastards down, boss."

Gallagher stared at his feet for a few seconds before slowly raising his head and staring O'Brien in the eye, said, "Are you not up for it, Seamus? Do I need to stand you down and get somebody else to do the job?"

O'Brien blanched before shaking his head and replying, "No, boss. It'll get done, stand on me."

"What about you, Marty," he turned to the smaller man and growled, "you got any fucking complaints?"

The small, shaven headed and plump Boyle grinned for he secretly coveted O'Brien's number two position and liked it when the redheaded bastard was taken down a peg. Extending his tattooed arms wide, said, "You know me, boss. I'm only too happy to do a bit of collecting."

Gallagher returned the smaller man's grin, aware that in the past the small man frequently used an open razor on the dealers who either were late with their payments or tried to stiff Boyle, claiming that they just didn't have the money, but with the six foot, redheaded hard man O'Brien at his back, none of the slashed dealers ever complained to the polis.

He stared in turn at the two men and smiled. Boyle, five foot two inches of mayhem. A typically small Glaswegian with the wee man chip on his shoulder who figured anyone staring at him because of his lack of height deserved a doing.

And then, he inwardly smiled, there is Seamus.

O'Brien's strict faith upbringing and fervent devotion to Celtic football club and the IRA, both of whom like many Glasgow Catholics he associated with Catholicism and his occasional sadism when dealing with awkward debtors made him the ideal choice to keep in line the numerous drug dealers that Gallagher had located throughout the city as well as the many he also run in Lanarkshire and Renfrewshire.

Aye, some team, he inwardly thought then graciously slapping a hand on both their shoulders, said, "When this deal goes through, guys, why don't the three of us catch a flight to Shagaloof over in Spain, spend some dough and have a time to ourselves, eh? My treat."

"I'm up for that," O'Brien nodded, relieved that Gallagher's mood had so quickly changed from aggression to calm.

"I'll need to square it with the missus," Boyle said, but then with a loud snigger added, "Oh, I forgot. The bitch fucked off and left me last year!"

That set the other two off laughing and backslapping their diminutive pal.

"Anything else happening in your world, boss?" O'Brien asked. "I mean, you still got that lassie with the big tits living with you? Paula, isn't it?"

"Aye, for the minute anyway," he nodded, then wickedly grinning, added, "but that might change anytime soon. As for my world," he paused and inhaled. "There was a wee hiccup when I found out she was speaking with the filth, but I've cleared that up."

"Cleared what up?" Boyle stared curiously at him.

Tapping the side of his nose with a stubby forefinger, Gallagher continued to grin when he furtively replied, "What you don't know can't hurt you, wee man."

They knew better than to press their boss and so both nodded as though in understanding, though neither man had a clue to what Gallagher referred and could not know that his 'clear up' had been to violently rape Menzies.

"Right," Gallagher finished his coke then crushing the can, threw it into a nearby waste bin, "time for me to be heading back home for my fry-up. You guys stand by your phones and remember," he stared keenly at them in turn, "all the dough in by Thursday, okay?"

"Bang on, boss," Boyle acknowledged for them both.

Watching Gallagher heading for the changing room, Boyle quietly said, "What the fuck is that supposed to mean, a wee hiccup and his bird speaking to the polis?"

"Fuck knows, but whatever he's done, whatever he's cleared up, he's right," O'Brien shook his head before adding, "I'd rather not know."

****

Sally, the young civilian telephonist who had commenced working just three weeks previously in the Govan control room hesitated in asking the advice of the police constable controller anything for she had on several occasions been subjected to his sarcastic wit. Instead she stared a little uncertainly at her handwritten note then finally made her decision. Excusing herself by pretending she needed a toilet break she made her way upstairs to the CID suite where timidly knocking on the door of the general office, she was relieved to see the friendly face of DS Tam Whelan sat behind a desk.

"Sally," he greeted her with a smile and waved her in, "what can I do for you, hen?"

"It's this, Mister Whelan," she shyly replied and swallowing nervously, handed him the note.

Reading it, his brow furrowed then glancing up at her, said, "What's it all about?"

"I'm not really sure. When she called in the woman asked to speak with Lesley Rudd. I wasn't too sure who to put her through to, so I said that Lesley was off duty the now and asked her if I could I put her through to somebody else? Then she said no, that it was only Lesley that she would speak with and that it had been Lesley who had given her the office number. I asked if the woman…"

"The woman didn't give you her name?"

"No," Sally shook her head then blushing, added, "I did ask, honest, but she said that it was only Lesley who could help her."

"Help her? That's the words she used? And she called her Lesley Rudd, not Constable Rudd?"

"Yes," Sally pointed to the note. "I wrote it down, see?"

"Did the woman know about Lesley being missing or did you mention it at all?"

"No, she never said and I didn't mention it either."

"So, likely she's unaware," he said almost to himself. He glanced at the note and slowly nodding, said, "I see you've also noted the time of the call. That's almost two hours ago. Why didn't you come up here sooner?"

She blushed and her heart thumping in her chest, replied, "I wasn't too sure if it might be important. Is it?"

Whelan knew who the controller on duty was and rightly guessed the lazy arse's attitude had intimated the young lassie and further guessed she had been too shy to ask the buggers advice.

"Everything about Lesley is important right now, hen," he sighed, "but don't worry about it. You did the correct thing bringing it to my attention."

He couldn't know those few words of approval calmed Sally down, but saw her visibly relax and so asked, "Now, can you tell me anything about this woman?"

He reached for a pencil and pad. "Her voice? Was she local?"

"Well," her brow knitted, "she sounded Glaswegian and she was a woman, not a girl. Not a young girl, I mean. Not polite, kind of a slang speaker, you know? Not posh or anything, like someone who lives in a council scheme."

"Like me," he smiled as once again, Sally blushed. "Did she say if she'd phone back or give you any kind of hint why she wanted to speak with Lesley?"

"No," she shook her head.

"Background noise? I mean, did it sound like a public phone box? Weans playing or a television on, anything like that?"

Sally's eyes narrowed and she bit at her lower lip as she tried to recall, then brightly said, "I think I could hear a radio in the background. Yes, I'm sure I could."

"So, it sounds like it might have been a private phone then," he made a note on the pad. "Did she say when she might phone back?"

"Yes," Sally eagerly nodded. "I told her that Lesley resumes on late shift today at 2pm so she said thanks and hung up."

"But she didn't *confirm* she would phone back at that time?"

"No," Sally was a little downcast, wondering if she should have done better with the call.

"Right," he smiled cheerfully at her. "I'll arrange for someone to be in the control room at 2pm just in case the woman does phone back. Thanks for that Sally, you did well and needless to say if the woman phones back before that time," he politely dismissed her with a wink.

When the young woman had left he stared at both her and his own notes and wondered; is this significant?

****

Irene Crichton and Iain Meikle just arrived at the Force Criminal Intelligence Department when Tam Whelan caught up with them by phone.

Watching her standing at the DI's desk using the phone, Iain saw her face pale as she nodded before replacing the handset. Turning to him, she calmly said, "Leslie's body's been found in the water near to some place called Lasswade Street down in Yoker. Tam says the boss is on his way there now to positively identify her when…" she paused and took a breath before continuing, "when they get her out of the water."

"There's no doubt?" he softly asked.

She shook her head as she replied, "Tam says the call that came in from the Clydebank control room described the body as that of a blonde haired woman wearing a police uniform so barring the official identification, it's more than probable it's Lesley. I'm sorry, Iain."

After all that had happened, all that had been said or assumed, he had already anticipated receiving the bad news, but when it came it still shocked him.

Les *was* dead, but how the *fuck* could that be?

He slowly inhaled then exhaled before asking, "What's the story then, Irene? Do we attend the locus or carry on with your inquiry?"

"There's nothing we can do in Yoker, Iain. The B Division CID will be handling the discovery of Lesley's body until such times Colin Morton formally identifies her and because it's a G Division inquiry, he'll take over. I'm sure if he needs us he'll give us a shout on the AS radio. Meantime," she sighed and nodding to the DI, said, "let's have a look at the report Lesley sent you guys."

It took just a few minutes for the report to be dug out from the extensive files and handed to Irene who reading it, blew out through pursed lips before passing it to Iain.

Quickly scanning the single page, his brow furrowed and he glanced sharply at Irene before telling her, "I had no idea about this, I swear it. I can only assume Les did this when she had Paula Menzies on her own."

Irene shrugged before replying, "Well, if it's true and I've no reason to doubt that Lesley believed it, either Paula was winding her up about offering to tout against Gallagher or she's providing us with a real opportunity to give him the jail."

****

Wading through the slimy mud made more difficult with the recent heavy fall of rain and his young DC by his side, DCI Colin Morton regretted not stopping by Orkney Street to collect his wellington's from the boot of his car.

Arriving at the river bank that churned up by the feet of the attending officers was now more like a quagmire, all thoughts of his heavily mud stained shoes and trousers were dismissed when he saw the body of Lesley Rudd laid out on a large and square, white plastic sheet.

On the river, the police launch *Semper Vigilo* with George Parsonage's wooden hulled lifeboat tied alongside, floated gently on the tide. A curious calm hung over the area as nearby a huddle of uniformed and CID officers stood smoking and in quiet discussion while a scene of crime officer photographed both the body and the surrounding locus. A middle-aged man kneeling beside the body wearing a worn, brown tweed suit and a weary expression nodded as Morton approached.

"Hello, Colin. Bad business this," Doctor Julius Mathias greeted him. "One of yours, I understand."

"Aye, doc, she is. I take it you're confirming life extinct?"

"Yes, though of course it's clearly obvious the poor lassie has been dead for a number of days," he indicated the white wrinkled skin of her neck.

"Anything amiss that you can see prior to a PM?"

"Well," Mathias bit at her lower lip, then removing his glasses, polished them with a handkerchief while he replied, "if you come a little closer, Colin, you can see she'd suffered a head injury to the left temple. Of course having been submerged in the water for…what is it now?"

"We believe she went missing on Saturday night."

"Well, the PM will probably confirm what I think, but I'm of the opinion that the wound to her temple is a deep gash and probably bled a lot, however, the time she has been in the water has rinsed the wound clean. That all said, at this time I am unable to confirm that the wound might or might not have occurred post mortem, perhaps when her body struck something in the water after she died."

"We found her cap on the edge of the dock at Mavisbank Quay and it had blood on it. I'm pretty sure now it's Lesley's blood, doc, so that seems to me to confirm she was struck before she went into the water," Morton sighed. "Here's a question, though. It seems to me as a layman and as you said that it's quite a deep gash. Does that mean it might have been a really heavy blow causing her to have bled significantly from such an injury?"

"Oh, well, the PM will confirm it, but yes, I believe the lassie will have suffered a serious blow to the head resulting in an extensive loss of blood. Why, is that significant?"

Morton frowned before answering, "We didn't find any blood on the ground at the point we believe she went into the water to suggest it occurred there. What I mean is, if she did bleed significantly, it must have been when she was in the water and if she went into the water as a result of the blow to the head then it's likely there wasn't time for her to bleed out onto the ground. A question for you. Would she have been rendered unconscious by the blow?"

"Possibly," Mathias nodded, "and if she was unconscious when she went into the water, it's unlikely she would have been able to save herself. The PM will indicate if there is river water in her lungs and that should determine if she was alive and breathing when she went in."

Morton's brow creased when he asked, "With the wound being on the left side of her temple, does that suggest it might have been a right-handed attacker?" He stopped then almost to himself, said, "Or she might have been struck from behind."

Mathias pursed his lips and said, "Possibly, but from where her temple has been struck I think it more probable that her attacker was stood facing her and did not strike her from behind. Then again…"

"The PM will confirm it," Morton finished for him. "Anything else of significance?"

He didn't miss Mathias glancing around him before the doctor quietly replied, "Without prejudice to her personal life, at the time of her demise the young woman's clothing seems to be undisturbed, if you get my meaning."

Morton stifled a grin at the prim doctor's polite reference and understood the subtle statement to mean that her intact clothing seemed to suggest the attack was not sexually motivated.

"Will it be your good self who is the reporting officer, Colin?"

"Aye, it is, doc, and thanks for attending today."

The police casualty surgeon nodded then stiffly rising to his feet, informed Morton his report would be on the DCI's desk that afternoon.

He watched the doctor walk off before turning to stare down at the body of Lesley Rudd.

In his twenty-three years as a detective Colin Morton had attended numerous murder locations and seen more dead bodies than he cared to remember; the young gang members stabbed or bludgeoned to death in senseless parochial disputes, the domestic killings that had started out as a drink-fuelled spouse beating, the young women raped then strangled and on two awful occasions, the child whose nightly crying had so annoyed the parent the weans had each been suffocated. Too many wasted lives, too many bad memories.

But never had he attended the murder of a colleague, a fellow police officer.

He glanced about him at the detectives who stood nearby, seeing them continue to quietly talk among themselves as they smoked and none who seemed aware of the young lassie lying dead on the plastic sheet. Yet he knew they were not indifferent to her death. It was just their way of dealing with the loss of a life and these same detectives would later that day return home to their families, their wives or husbands and their children as though today had just been another day at the office.

Dismissing his thoughts, he asked for the senior detective present to identify himself.

"That'll be me, boss," a suited, tubby man wearing a light blue shirt and loud jazzy tie, but with a worried frown and a cigarette dangling from his lips stepped forward. Extending his hand he introduced himself as Detective Sergeant George McPhail and continued, "Do you have any suspects at the minute?"

"Early days yet, George," Morton replied then formally requesting that the discovery of Lesley Rudd's body now be passed to himself for inquiry, Morton stood for several seconds contemplating what had to be done. At last he spoke, securing the assistance of the B Division detectives in the removal of Rudd's body to the city mortuary, the statement taking of all the witnesses involved in both the discovery of her body and recovery from the waters of the River Clyde.

As satisfied as he could be that everything at the locus had been done, he turned to his young detective and while walking with the younger man back to the CID car, said, "Better take me to Pitt Street, son, to deliver the bad news to ACC Kerr. While I'm doing that, you find a phone and tell Tam Whelan to keep everyone at the office till I get back. Oh, and tell him to phone my wife and ask if she'll drop by the office with a clean pair of trousers and shoes for me." Patting at his midriff, he smiled and added, "A pair of trousers that fit."

****

Peter Rossi smoothly drew the CID car to an halt in the rear yard then followed Janie Wallace through the back door that led to the uniform charge bar.

She pushed open the heavy door, to a barrage of cursing and swearing.

"What do you think it meant, all GA Division CID officers to return to Orkney Street?" she asked over her shoulder.

"Dunno, but I'm guessing it's got something to do with Lesley," he replied, ignoring the writhing, belligerent drunk who was being wrestled at the charge bar by two plain clothes officers, each with a foot stamped down onto the prisoner's feet to stop him kicking out at the bar officer who was down on one knee to search him and trying to get into the pockets of the prisoners tight jeans.

"What you looking at, ya fucking cow!" the man in his twenties screamed at Janie who ignored him, but turned sharply when the man gave a sudden yelp and saw him standing wide-eyed and stock-still while the bar officer grinned up at her.

"Seems he's not bothered about wearing underwear and I've just nipped his foreskin when I pulled open his zip," he explained.

Janie clamped her teeth together to supress a grin and closely followed by Rossi, pushed through the double doors where both burst into loud laughter.

"I felt my knees involuntarily draw together when I heard that," Rossi grinned at her.

But their hilarity ended when they arrived at the general office and immediately sensing an air of depression, learned of the discovery of Lesley Rudd's body.

Pale faced, Janie slumped down into a chair and said, "Even after this time, even though we'd found her cap I still thought that maybe, just maybe, it was all a mistake, that she'd turn up. Alive I mean," she added, her voice almost a whisper and her eyes brimming with tears.

"Here, drink this," she turned to see DS Tam Whelan thrusting a steaming mug of coffee at her. "If you need to take a moment, hen?"

"Thanks and no, I'll be fine," she replied, then sipping at the coffee, spluttered when she realised that Whelan had liberally added whisky to it.

"That will do you no harm," he tightly smiled before adding, "Away to the ladies' room and before you argue, I insist." Nodding, she rose to her feet and left the room.

"What's happening now, Tam?" Rossi asked.

"Nothing till the boss returns," Whelan replied, "then when we know what he's got in store for us and as this is now officially a murder inquiry, we'll likely break into teams and I'll issue you guys with your inquiries." He stared curiously at Rossi before asking, "Have you worked on a murder before?"

"Not as a CID officer, no," Rossi shook his head. "Stood by bodies and locations a couple of times and did some door knocking for the CID, but this will be my first murder."

"Hell'uve a one to begin with," Whelan sighed and turned away to prepare the murder box.

****

They skipped their visit to the headquarters cafeteria and decided instead to track down Lesley Rudd's former fiancé at Stewart Street.

Less than ten minutes later they were stood in the CID clerks small room and learning that yes, DC Fraser Anderson was on duty, but was currently out on an inquiry.

"Can you get him on the divisional radio and have him return to the office, please?" Irene requested of the elderly constable who agreeing, suggested they might wish to wait in the general office where they'd find a table with tea and coffee.

Nodding courteously to the lone detective sat at her desk, Irene took a seat while Iain tossed a fifty pence piece into the glass jar and made them both a coffee.

"You're a DI at Govan, Ma'am," the blonde haired DC stared across at her.

"Aye, DI Crichton," she then nodded to Iain who suppressed a smile when she introduced him as, "DC Meikle."

"I'm DC Liz Spencer," she called back to Irene before asking, "Any word on your missing policewoman yet?"

Irene glanced at Iain before she replied, "Yes, there is, I'm afraid. Her body was recovered from the Clyde just an hour or two ago. We're here to have a word with Fraser Anderson, her former fiancé."

"Oh," the younger woman paled. "I'm sorry to hear that…I mean, about the lassie being found dead. Eh, Fraser is out on an inquiry at the minute, but I expect he should be back soon. Is there anything I can do for you in the meantime?"

"No, we're fine, thanks."

Spencer bent her head to resume her paperwork, when a

thought occurred to Irene who asked, "Did you know her, Fraser's fiancé Lesley?"

"Ah, no, not really," Spencer blushed. "Well, I'd met her once when she picked him up here at the office."

Irene's eyes narrowed when she saw the younger woman's throat constrict and had the oddest feeling that there was more to what Spencer was admitting to. Thanking Iain who handed her a mug of coffee, she smiled and politely asked, "When was it? When you briefly met her, I mean?"

This time Spencer paled and Iain, sensing there was something amiss, sat quietly down at a desk, his eyes darting between Irene and the younger woman.

"Oh," Spencer's eyes flickered and she licked at her lips as though trying to recall the time before she answered, "It must have been what? Say, about four, maybe five months ago?"

"Four or five months," she quietly repeated before adding, "when they were still engaged."

"Yes, I suppose they were."

She continued to stare at Spencer then brightly smiled before saying, "Well, I suppose when we speak with Fraser he might recall, eh?"

An awkward silence fell in the room and when Spencer again bent her head to peruse her paperwork, he risked a curious glance at Irene who subtly shook her head to indicate for now, the matter was closed.

Just less than fifteen minutes later, the door opened to admit two men, the younger of who asked, "DI Crichton? I'm DC Anderson. I'm told you'd like a word with me?"

A tall and handsome man in his early thirties who projected an air of self-assurance and wearing a suit that Iain reckoned would have cost far more than he would have been prepared to pay, his impression of Anderson was…smug.

"Aye," the older man interrupted with a grin, "and keep your hands in your pockets, Fraser, or she'll be selling you raffle tickets for her favourite charity."

Irene smiled and standing, replied, "Well, as I live and breathe. Ricky Morrison. I thought you'd retired, you old heart throb." Grinning with pleasure the stoutly built detective sergeant took her hand and vigorously shaking it, said with a sly smile, "Still here, sweetheart and one step ahead of the posse of rubber heels that are dogging my footsteps."

Introducing Iain, she said, "If you don't mind, Ricky, I'd like to speak with your neighbour here. Is there somewhere private we can go?"

"Aye, of course, hen. Use the DS's room. Are you all right for coffee and tea?"

"Aye, we're fine, thanks."

Promising not to leave without having a word with Morrison, they followed Anderson to the Detective Sergeant's room where they seated themselves with Irene occupying the chair behind the desk, Anderson in front and Iain seated to one side. Before she could begin, Anderson turned to Iain and said, "We've met, haven't we? Your face is familiar?"

"Aye, we've met," he replied, but didn't elaborate.

"Right, DC Anderson," Irene interjected, "the reason we wish to speak with you is…"

"Before we start, Ma'am, is this a formal interview about Lesley being missing? What I mean is, do I need to be cautioned or anything?" he cockily smiled at her.

She didn't immediately respond, but then her brow crinkled when she said, "Why would you ask that, DC Anderson? Is there a reason you feel you need legal representation? Something that worries you? Something you do not wish to tell us?"

"What? No, of course not," his face betrayed his surprise as he waved his hands in front of him. "It's just that, well, I'm a bit surprised that you want to speak to me. I mean, I haven't seen Lesley since we broke up."

"And that was when?"

"Oh," his brow furrowed and he shrugged as though trying to recall, "I think it was about four and a half months ago."

"Why did you break up?"

He nervously licked at his lips before he replied, "Well, she got a bit suspicious; she thought I was seeing someone else."

"And were you seeing someone else?"

His eyes narrowed when he abruptly asked, "Of course not," he scoffed before asking, "Is that really relevant to your missing person inquiry, Ma'am? I mean, like I said, I haven't seen her for…"

He didn't get to finish for Irene held up her hand for silence when she interrupted with, "Let me explain, DC Anderson, this is no longer a missing person inquiry. It's a murder inquiry."

Watching in silence at Anderson's reaction, Iain was not entirely convinced the man's expression of shock was genuine as Irene continued, "So you understand, DC Anderson, *all* my questions are relevant. So, were – you – seeing – someone - else?"

Slowly, so very slowly, Anderson nodded and was completely taken aback when Irene asked, "Wouldn't happen to be one of your colleagues, would it? Say, DC Spencer?"

Iain glanced sharply at her and thought, how the hell did she cotton on to that?

Staring at her, Anderson again nodded, then, his voice quaking, said, "It was just a fling with Liz…I mean, DC Spencer. Honest. But Lesley? She went off her fucking nut at me. Told me we were finished and…and I tried to tell her it was a mistake, that Liz didn't mean anything to me but she wouldn't listen and I swear to God, Ma'am, I haven't seen her since she found out, since we broke up."

She didn't reply and simply stared pokerfaced at him, but then after almost a full minute had passed, said, "You're right, perhaps I should have cautioned you, DC Anderson, but in the meantime and in the absence of any other evidence that might implicate you in the murder of Constable Lesley Rudd, I will treat you as a witness and take a formal statement regarding your previous relationship with the victim. However, let me warn you that should you fail to disclose anything that might be of interest to the inquiry, should you prevaricate in *any* way I will make it my business to come down on you like the proverbial ton of shitty bricks. Do I make myself clear?"

"Yes, Ma'am," he sullenly replied.

"Okay, now that we're on the same page, DC Anderson," she coolly continued, "tell me where you were about eight o'clock last Saturday evening."

"Is that when she was…when she went missing?" he quietly asked.

"Just answer the question, please."

He fumbled with his fingers then with a sigh, replied, "At home and before you ask, I was alone. Catching up with some washing. I was supposed to go out with some mates, but," he shrugged, "overtime's been tight the last couple of months and my mortgage is killing me."

"So you have no alibi for that evening?"

"Are you telling me I need one, Ma'am," his voice now bristled.

"I'm telling you that if you wish to be eliminated as a possible suspect from the murder inquiry, DC Anderson, then you'll be truthful and answer my questions," she snapped in return.

"So, I am a suspect then?"

"How long have you served with the CID, DC Anderson?"

"The CID? Eh, almost three years now. Why?"

"Then in that time you should have learned that in a major inquiry such as a murder, *everyone* who is in some manner connected or related to the victim is a suspect until they are eliminated by alibi."

It wasn't what she said, but the way she said it that caused Iain to catch his breath. Something niggled at him, something he couldn't quite put his finger on, yet the feeling was enough to trouble him. He watched as Anderson's throat tightened, but the younger man refrained from answering.

"One final question, DC Anderson. When was the last time you visited Constable Rudd at her flat?"

He startled then shrugging, replied, "I don't know. I'm guessing here, but I suppose it was a week or so before we split, so say just under four months ago?"

She was about to turn to Iain, but then Anderson nervously licked at his lower lip before asking, "Will this affect my career, Ma'am? I mean, will me being interviewed about her murder, will that be on my personnel file or anything?"

She didn't respond, just simply stared at him with her lip curling in disgust, then turning to Iain, her voice calm, she said, "DC Meikle, would you be so kind as to fetch me a witness statement form, please."

CHAPTER ELEVEN

Colin Morton pointed to the security gate at the rear of Pitt Street's open air parking lot and instructed his driver, "Ask if there's a free parking space. Tell him we're going to visit ACC Kerr in the Command Suite."

Nosing the CID car up to the barrier, the driver wound down the window and explained as he was directed only for the uniformed commissionaire to bend down and staring at Morton, said, "Message for you from Detective Chief Superintendent Cruickshank for when you arrived, sir. Asks if you can call upon him before you visit the ACC."

Thanking the commissionaire, the DC drove the car into a bay and was told by Morton, "Once you've made your phone call to Tam Whelan, grab yourself a cuppa at the cafeteria, son. I'll come and find you when I'm finished."

A couple of minutes later Morton presented himself at Cruickshank's office where the DCS sighed, "The news is out here in Cowards Castle," he grimly frowned, using the popular nickname for headquarters. "Sorry business about the young woman, Colin. What's the mood of your team?"

"I haven't been back to Govan yet, sir. I came straight here," he took the chair that Cruickshank indicated and slumped down. "Thought I'd personally better present my case for more resources to our beloved ACC right away."

"Aye, well, I'll come with you. Maybe throw a bit of weight behind your application, though I have to warn you, the Special Branch have a major operation ongoing against some of our local Loyalists, so they might be getting a fair chunk of this month's CID budget."

"Anything interesting?"

"Who knows what the Branch get's up to?" Cruickshank shrugged. "You know that lot, tighter than two coats of paint when you try to get information out of them. It's a surprise to me they even admitted they are targeting the Proddies. "

Slapping his hands down onto the desk, Cruickshank abruptly got to his feet and said, "Right, no sense in hanging about. Now, before we visit him, is there anything that I need to know? Anything that might blow back on us?"

"Nothing I can think of, no," Morton shook his head.

As they expected, ACC Kerr kept them waiting for almost five minutes before he deigned to see them and making a show that their presence was a great nuisance to him, greeted them with, "I hope this won't take all day. I've a lot on."

Morton felt a cold shiver of anger sweep through him at Kerr's crass comment when he undoubtedly knew that he and Cruickshank were there to discuss the budget for the inquiry of their murdered colleague.

However, conscious that losing his temper would not help his request he sat down when invited and set out his case for more resources.

"I assume that Mister Cruickshank might have informed you that our SB have an ongoing major inquiry?" Kerr leaned forward onto his forearms and stared at Morton.

"He has, yes sir, but can I point out that while the Branch *might* be successful in putting away a handful of Loyalists for collecting funds for the Orange Cross or sending a couple of firearms to the Province to join the hundreds that are *already* in circulation there, I'm looking for the killer of a police officer. One of our own."

Kerr stared moodily at him, trying to decide if it was Morton's intention to rile him or maybe the bastard was just being cheeky. Still, the last thing he needed was some sort of dissension in the ranks over this bloody police woman's murder. That kind of thing might get back to the Chief and the last thing he needed right now was that bugger on his case. Taking a breath, he smiled humourlessly and turning to Cruickshank, said, "Perhaps if you can juggle the budget for the south side CID, Mister Cruickshank, we can help DCI Morton with his inquiry, eh?"

That'll be the Royal 'we,' thought Cruickshank, who recognised that by delegating the decision to him, Kerr was simply passing the buck in the knowledge that if anything went wrong, Kerr was in the clear, but would take full credit if Morton found the lassie's killer. However, if Morton gets his extra resources and something else kicks off, some other major inquiry that requires even further resources, the city CID could be left floundering. That and the rest of the divisional DCI's would be going ballistic if they were left bereft of detectives. With the the CID and the cash strapped Force of seven thousand police officers already ten per cent understrength, he could only pray that they hung on long enough for Morton to solve the murder as quickly as possible.

"Yes, sir," he quietly replied, "I'll see what I can do."

****

Returned to his office with a mug of coffee growing cold at his hand, Alistair Cruickshank stared thoughtfully at the window. It was not in Cruickshank's nature to be a disloyal or deceitful man, but working under ACC Martin King for the last two years had tried Cruickshank's patience beyond even his tolerance. While he had come to accept that the promotion that should have rightly been his was now out of his reach, he could not accept the manner in which Kerr did and continued to disrupt Cruickshank's beloved CID.

A detective for almost twenty-eight years and now three years past his date of retirement, in his time moving through the ranks Cruickshank had weathered bosses who were sleekit, incompetent, lazy and even one who was locked up for criminality, but never had he worked for such a self-serving egotistical prat like Martin Kerr.

The problem was as he saw it, Kerr had neither the brains nor the ability to cohesively lead his underpaid and overworked detectives in the fight against crime. When the media ranted and sought a statement from the Chief Constable about rising crime statistics, Kerr would find some excuse to blame one of his senior staff; a ploy that was becoming weary and overused for Cruickshank suspected that at last, the Chief was beginning to have misgivings that the head of his Force's CID was not just inept, but treacherous too, for Cruickshank also suspected Kerr's true ambition.

The bloody man wanted the top job.

His eyes narrowed as he folded his hands together. The problem is now, he thought, how do I scupper Kerr's chances without ruining what remains of my own career?

****

They had travelled in almost complete silence, but arriving back at Orkney Street, Iain Meikle parked the CD car in the rear yard then said, "Excuse me for ten minutes, Irene. I want to check my dookit to see if there's anything lying for me."

"Before you go, Iain, there's something I want to ask you."

"Yes?"

"What was your gut reaction to the interview with Anderson?"

"Well," he drawled, "you're the professional interviewer, Irene, and I have to say I thought you were spot on in what you said."

"That's not what I mean, I meant…"

He held up his hand and said, "I know what you mean. You're asking if I think Anderson is guilty or that he knows something? All I can say is," he exhaled, "if he's guilty of anything it's being a right shit for screwing around when he was engaged to Les, but does he know anything about her murder?" He pursed his lips and shook his head. "I just don't know. But tell me this, if they split up four and a half months ago like he said, why wait till now to try to get back with her, if indeed that's what you're thinking and why kill her? Just because it's likely she gave him a knockback?"

He paused a little before he continued, "Let me explain. I'm coming to terms that I didn't really know her as well as I thought I did, but the Les I knew wouldn't have take him back if she believed he was cheating on her," he took a deep breath. "One night Les and I were on late shift together and we got talking about me and my ex-wife, Carol. I told Les that just before we split and eventually divorced, I overheard Carol on the phone telling some guy…anyway," he wryly grinned, "I suspected it was a man, that she loved him too. Now, if Fraser Anderson for some reason tried to resolve his split with Les and she refused; well you saw him. He's a good looking guy and the DC he was messing about with, the one in the office, she's a right looker too. What I'm saying is that he's a guy who obviously plays around so, do you really think he would resort to murder just because he was spurned? I mean, that just doesn't seem to make any sense to me."

"Spurned?" she grinned at him before continuing, "You really *are* an old fashioned kind of man, aren't you Iain? But yes, you're right. I was thinking he might have tried to renew their relationship and it went sour," she sighed, "and when she refused, they quarrelled then he killed her and though maybe he didn't intend to, it just happened."

"Do you really believe that?"

"Not after listening to you I don't because to be honest, your explanation makes more sense."

She shook her head and pulling a face, a little hesitantly asked, "Do you think I was a bit hard on him? I mean, a wee bit bullying?"

"I don't think bullying is your style, but if I'm honest? Look, I don't know the circumstances, but I heard that your man, your husband I mean…"

"*Ex*-husband," she frowned.

"Yeah," he smiled, "your ex-husband. I heard he was shagging around when you were married so I suppose it must get under your skin when you're dealing with someone who does the dirty on their missus or in this case, fiancé. Would that be fair to say?"

"Yeah, I suppose so," she admitted with a tight grin.

"Well, for what it's worth, I don't like Anderson because of how he treated Les so truth be told I enjoyed watching the bugger squirm. Now, anything else?"

"Yes, there is something else," she said knowing that he was aware Rudd's flat had been broken into, told him about the fingerprint discovered on the underside of Lesley Rudd's toilet seat.

"The lift isn't public knowledge so we're keeping that to ourselves for the minute. However, as you're aware, when we join the Force all police officers are fingerprinted for elimination purposes at crime scenes so while you're checking your dookit, I'll ask the Fingerprints Department to check both Charlie Gallagher and Fraser Anderson's prints against the one that was lifted, then I'll see you upstairs, okay?"

"Righto," he grinned at her.

****

Walking through the rear door past the charge bar, Iain saw that the early shift was just handing over to his own shifts bar staff who were late shift. Seeing him pass by wearing a suit, they good-naturedly jeered with comments like, "Heard you joined the dark side," and "Next you'll be wearing a deerstalker, ya ponce."

Grinning as he gave them a two fingered salute, he made his way to the changing room where he saw his dookit contained a completed report. Scanning the report, he unconsciously nodded that it seemed correct and stepped over to the sergeant's room where he saw his shift supervisor, Jimmy Cole sitting at his desk.

Surprised, Cole asked, "What's going on? Why aren't you in uniform?"

"You didn't get the memo, Sarge?" he feigned innocence, but inwardly pleased the sod had been cut out of the loop. "DCI Morton has appointed me as an acting DC for the duration of the murder inquiry."

"Murder inquiry?" Cole paled. "You mean, they found Lesley's body?"

"You didn't know?" Iain stepped forward to lay the report on Cole's desk.

"Eh, no, nobody said anything when I arrived at the office," he muttered.

"Oh, well, I suppose the word is just getting out. Les's body was discovered in the River Clyde over in the B Division area somewhere. I don't know any of the details, but I'm sure that Inspector Kane will have more details when he briefs the shift."

"Right," Cole mumbled and Iain watched as his head drooped. And so it should, he savagely thought for in his mind Cole was partly responsible for Les's death by sending her out alone on a Saturday night in the busiest beats in the Division. Bastard!

Turning on his heel, he made his way through the muster room and opened the door to the wrought iron stairway that led upstairs to the CID suite.

It was while he was climbing the stairs that he had a thought, but almost as quickly dismissed it as irrelevant.

****

Driving home in response to his wife's distraught telephone, Jake McNeill was an agitated man.

Unaware that the police had that morning discovered Lesley's body, nevertheless, he believed it was just a matter of time and guilt wracked him.

His grip tightened on the wheel as he thought about his wife Ellen and considered the subtle change in their relationship. The last year and the increasingly frequent arguments seemed to him to be a definite indicator that they were slowly but surely drifting apart.

It was just a question of time.

He had always known he married the wrong twin, yet every time he looked at Ellen he could not help but compare her to Lesley. Yet though she never once mentioned it he suspected Ellen knew of his underlying feelings for her twin.

Lesley filled his thoughts and every occasion he was near to her his heart pounded. It had taken all the strength he could muster not to declare his feelings for her; to admit he was trapped in a loveless marriage to Ellen.

But then several weeks previously, that strength failed and one afternoon waiting outside her office for her shift to finish he had confronted her and admitted his love for her.

He had been shocked at the ferocity of her anger and reeled when she ridiculed and dismissed his feelings as nothing but infatuation, then threatened that if he even hinted to her sister what he had disclosed, she promised she would make it her business to protect Ellen and the children, no matter what.

Stunned, he had driven home in a daze, aware that he had completely fucked up and that his confession had inadvertently exposed himself not just to a divorce, but the loss of everything he had worked for.

The visit from the two detectives had scared him shitless for since that day when he had met with Lesley, he had lived in dread that she might expose his secret.

Now worried sick that the police might also discover his secret, he turned the car into Knowehead Gardens and drove slowly down the steep road to the house then turning into the driveway, switched off the engine.

****

Forty-seven years old Maggie McKenna had been using and dealing drugs on and off for over twenty years, mostly from her shabby first floor council flat in Dubton Path in the Easterhouse housing estate. Her downward spiral into drugs had cost Maggie her marriage, a number of partners thereafter and her four kids to foster parents, three who were so young when they were removed by social services they no longer remembered their birth mother.

Of course the local polis liked to believe they knew all about Maggie's activities and the uniformed constable tasked as the sub-Divisional Intelligence Collator in the local office had an increasingly thick file on the stick thin, bleached blonde woman. Not that the Force Drugs Squad had any real interest in Maggie for most of the entries by the beat officers described the addicted Maggie as constantly wasted on the drugs she sold, drugs that the officers incorrectly assumed to be cannabis. So, misinformed by the collator of her true pecking position in the local drug scene the Force's Drug Squad simply registered Maggie as a low priority target. Had they been better informed the story might have been completely different for the Drug Squad, with more pressing issues trying to contain the flood of smack that was plaguing the city and the west of Scotland in general, had no time or available resources to commit to any kind of surveillance on a woman who they believed was making a few quid selling pot.

And so Maggie was considered a sort of back-burner issue for when arrests slowed down; an easy capture to bolster the figures when statistical targets had to be met.

However, what neither the local officers nor the Drug Squad knew was that the drug ridden and Hepatitis B infected Maggie had earlier that year been recruited by Charlie Gallagher's man, Seamus O'Brien, and was now the main source in the area for users looking seeking heroin.

Lying befuddled on her brushed velvet but heavily stained couch, it was several minutes before Maggie realised the pounding was not in her head, but at her front door. Scratching at the stained football top, she first checked the street outside to search for the Drug Squad's plain clothes cars or marked police vehicles, then struggled to get into her tightfitting jeans. Falling heavily to the floor, she cursed but managed to zip the jeans closed then rising to her feet, lazily brushed the lank hair from her eyes and staggered through the hallway to open the door.

Through drug addled eyes, she saw it was Seamus O'Brien and her heart almost stopped. With a weak smile, she muttered, "Come away in, Seamus."

It was then her blood run cold for behind him was his pal, the wee bastard Marty Boyle.

She watched suspiciously as both men strolled through to the front room then closing the door, used both hands to sweep her shoulder length hair into a ponytail that she tightly bound with a rubber band from her wrist. That was when she heard Boyle say, "How the *fuck* can anybody live in shit like this?"

Taking a deep breath, Maggie adopted a smile though it didn't reach her eyes and following them into the room, invited them to sit down.

It was Boyle who snapped back with, "Are you fucking joking, hen? Your couch looks like it's infested. I'm thinking I'll need to wipe my feet before I step back onto the landing after treading these bloody carpets."

O'Brien, sick of Boyle's tantrums, took a breath and slowly shaking his head, said, "Ignore him, Maggie. We're here for what's due. Have you got it?"

She swallowed so quickly with fear she almost choked herself, then replied, "I've just over eight grand, Seamus. I wasn't expecting you till next week. If you come back then, I'll have…"

But stopped when he raised his hand and staring at her said in a quiet, but menacing voice, "I told you last week, Maggie. Today's the collection day. What the *fuck* is the holdup?"

She couldn't help herself, couldn't stop her wasted body from shaking and tried to plead, telling him that the money was coming in, that she'd get it all within two days if only…

The slap came so quickly she hardly saw his hand move, but the blow knocked her off her feet and onto her back, her head bouncing off the chipped and scarred coffee table before she hit the floor. Lying there stunned, she could taste the blood in her mouth as O'Brien stooped over her and in a calm voice said, "Now look what you've made me do. You know I don't like hurting you, Maggie, but we need the dosh right away, hen. So, I'll ask again. Are you pissing me about? Have you got it all and maybe thinking you can screw us over? Is that it, Maggie?" Tears of fear and hurt formed in her eyes and unable to speak, she could only shake her head.

O'Brien sighed as though in regret then standing upright was about to turn away, but to his surprise Boyle pushed past him and brought his booted foot down onto her vulva.

The pain was extraordinary, causing her to screech in agony as she instinctively folded her body in half, her hands reaching between her legs to protect and massage the soreness.

She could hear Boyle laughing as he reached down and seizing her by the hair with one hand, drew her head up and viciously twisted it round to face him.

His eyes like bright diamonds, he snarled, "You'll take this as a warning, Maggie. When we tell you we want all the dosh by a certain day, you better fucking deliver ya manky bitch! Now, go and get us what you have!"

Weeping, she turned onto her knees and still on all fours began to crawl to the door.

To add to her pain and humiliation she heard the laughing Boyle say, "If she wasn't so reeking, Seamus, would you do her doggy-style?"

O'Brien didn't respond, but inwardly thought that Boyle was just a wee stupid bastard. Yes, admittedly O'Brien wasn't beyond hurting people like Maggie, but thought it pointless to torture them when clearly they had taken the warning.

In the hallway, her genitalia wracked with pain, she managed to get to her feet and stumbled into the bedroom where she fetched an old biscuit tin from the bottom of her cupboard. Still crying, she carried it through to the front room and her hands shaking, handed it to O'Brien.

"Thanks, Maggie," he politely said as though the previous few minutes had been of no consequence.

Opening the box, he withdrew the bundle of notes and dropped the tin onto the couch.

Still in pain she stood fearfully watching him as he quickly counted out seven thousand, nine hundred and sixty pounds in a variety of used notes, then turning to her said, "I make it that you're two thousand and forty quid short, Maggie."

"Please, Seamus," she raised her hand defensively, her legs shaking so badly she thought she was about to collapse, but he slowly shook his head and staring at her, gently lid a hand upon her shoulder and drew her near so their faces were almost touching.

"You've two days. By this time Wednesday you'll have the money, Maggie. If you don't then I'll be really angry and," he paused, his breath reeking of onions, whispered, "You really don't want to make me angry, do you?"

Sniffling, the tears coursing down her cheeks, she couldn't trust herself to speak and vigorously shook her head.

Releasing her, he turned to Boyle and sharply said, "Let's go." He sensed the little man was annoyed they were leaving, that Boyle wanted to stay and humiliate her further, but even he wasn't having any of that and staring at Boyle, said again more forcefully, "Let's *go!*"

Head bowed, she remained standing in the middle of the room until she heard the front door slam then wrapping her arms about her, fell weeping to the floor.

****

DS Tam Whelan had been a busy man. An experienced and competent detective as well as a practiced major inquiry office manager, Whelan was knocking on the door for promotion to Inspector and if Detective Chief Superintendent Alistair Cruickshank was a man of his word, the next available DI's position in the city was Whelan's.

Stood in the general office behind his desk, he checked then rechecked that everything that might be required by an SIO or the team was available; every Action form readied to be allocated, the list that indicated which officer was paired with a suitable colleague, the dedicated phone line was in operation and even down to extra supplies of coffee, teabags and biscuits.

All that was needed now was the return of Colin Morton to provide the briefing before Whelan began sending the troops out.

"Penny for them, Tam," said a voice behind him.

"Oh. It's yourself, Irene," he nodded. "how did you get on at Pitt Street and with Lesley's former fiancé?"

Seating herself on the edge of a desk, she quickly brought him up to speed and when she was done, he asked, "What's your gut feeling about this guy Anderson?"

She shrugged and pursed her lips before replying, "He's quite obviously a cheating bastard, but that doesn't make him a killer. I've fired him and Charlie Gallagher into the Fingerprints Department with a request they check their prints against the one discovered in the lassie's toilet, so fingers crossed we should get a result sometime later today."

"But he's no alibi for Saturday evening?"

"No," she shook her head and turned when the door opened to admit Iain Meikle.

"Ah, Iain, just the man," said Whelan. "I've a wee job for you," then turned to Irene to ask, "That is if you don't need him right away, Irene?"

"No, not right away," she grinned, "but I might need my neighbour for later on."

Whelan's eyes narrowed at her odd response, but ignoring it told Iain, "The young lassie Sally on the early shift in the control room took a call from a woman asking for Lesley. The woman said she'd phone back after two. Can you nip down to the control room and take the call? It might be nothing, but by the same token it could be something. You were Lesley's neighbour…" he abruptly stopped then rubbing at his forehead, said, "I'm sorry, Iain. I wasn't thinking. How are you?"

Iain slowly shook his head and replied, "If I'm honest I'm not quite sure, Tam. Like I told Irene, I really liked Les and still can't quite believe that's she's gone."

"I suggested the bugger take a couple of days off," Irene interrupted, "but he's a stubborn man, is our Iain."

He smiled tolerantly at her and said to Whelan, "Right, if this woman does phone back, what questions do you want me to put to her?"

****

It was clear to the detectives who stood in the general office staring at him that DCI Colin Morton was not a happy man. Now wearing clean trousers and shoes, he stood with his back to Tam Whelan's office manager's desk, a cigarette in one hand and a mug of coffee in the other as he begun, "Needless to say, what is disclosed in this room remains among us. Under no circumstances what you are about to hear is to be discussed with any person not engaged in the inquiry. Is that clearly understood?"

A general "Yes, sir," and nodding of heads acknowledged his instruction.

"So, lads and lassies, this then is the story as we know it so far. Constable Lesley Rudd is sent out on foot patrol last Saturday night then sometime between her last contact with the control room downstairs at just after eight that night until two wee lads find her body earlier this morning, she's murdered. Now, I say murdered and yes," he held up a hand as though to dismiss any argument, "I know we haven't had the PM yet, but thanks to Ian Meikle's shrewd work and Doctor Mathias's expert opinion, I'm entirely convinced that is what's happened." Morton went on to disclose that Rudd's flat had been broken into and while it was uncertain if anything had been stolen, there was clear signs that the intruder or intruders had been looking for something. "What has been established," he said, "is that a witness confirms Rudd's door was secure at fifteen minutes past eight on Saturday night until it was discovered by Tam Whelan and Ian McDonald at twenty minutes past three on Sunday morning to have been broken into."

However, Morton did not disclose the discovery of a fingerprint nor the suspicion that the raised toilet seat seemed to indicate the culprit or culprits were male. That detail he decided in the meantime to keep between a tight group. Morton believed if the individual responsible was identified as a suspect and became aware he had left a fingerprint; it might give the suspect the opportunity to form some sort of explanation for being in the flat. If, however, the suspect was unaware he had left a fingerprint and during interview *denied* being in the flat it would catch him out in a lie and possibly strengthen a case against him.

Morton paused for breath before continuing, "Now I know you'll be asking yourselves, why am I so certain Rudd was murdered? Well, first we find her cap with blood on the headband then we have the dying words of Sam Fullerton, whom some of you might know as the old dosser who hung about the Paisley Road Toll area. According to two hospital staff who heard Sam as well as our own Iain Meikle who found him lying injured…" he cast a glance around the room before asking, "Where is Iain anyway?"

"Downstairs at the control room, boss," Whelan replied before adding, "I'll tell you about that when you're finished the briefing."

"Okay, right," he nodded, "Where was I? Sam Fullerton. Now, old Sam told Iain that Sam didn't do anything to her. 'Her' we assess as being Lesley Rudd," he added a little unnecessarily. "Then Sam tells Iain, that he didn't hurt 'her'. Now, in themselves that didn't mean much, but Iain got the old guy down to the casualty at the Southern General where before he died, two medical personnel, a doctor and a nurse, independently state that Sam also muttered something to them. To the nurse…" he turned to Whelan who glancing at the witness list on his desk, said, "Mrs May Johnson."

"To nurse Johnson he said something about a white hat on the ground, a splash and a woman screaming. Moments later, while the doctor…"

"Doctor Pradesh," Whelan prompted him.

"Doctor Pradesh is leaning across Sam, the old man mumbles something about a hat that fell on the ground and a motor that we assume Sam meant to be a car or certainly a vehicle of some sort."

A detective raised a hand to interrupt and ask, "Couldn't the motor have been some sort of generator, boss? I mean, it is the dock area."

"I thought about that, but if you know that area you'll be aware that there is nothing working around there and besides it was Saturday night so it's unlikely that any kind of business would be carrying on at that time. No, maybe it's a leap of faith but in company with his other comments I'm convinced old Sam didn't hear a motor but saw one, some kind of vehicle."

He paused and added, "Then Doctor Pradesh also believes though he's not absolutely certain, that Sam made mention of a splash and that seems to corroborate what the nurse also heard."

"Any likelihood these two witnesses discussed what they told Iain Meikle, boss?" asked another detective.

"Iain's convinced that they didn't, but on that point," he turned to Whelan, "have both the witnesses re-interviewed, Tam, just in case they might have recalled something else."

"Boss," he acknowledged and made a note on his pad.

Continuing for another five minutes, Morton related to a hushed room the discovery by two young boys of Lesley Rudd's body, both of whom had scarpered by the time the police arrived.

"Need them traced and interviewed, Tam. Likely from a local school and truant from classes this morning."

"Boss."

In the next few minutes, he disclosed Lesley Rudd's interest in the notorious Charlie Gallagher, but stressed that it might just be a work related issue and at this time Gallagher was not a strong suspect for Rudd's murder. Aware that some of her colleagues might have been aware Rudd had been engaged, Morton suggested Irene Crichton address the issue of her former fiancé, himself a serving officer.

In a calm and monotone voice, Irene related the interview that was conducted at Stewart Street police office, but simply said the relationship had broken up without disclosing Fraser Anderson's cheating affair with his fellow detective.

A young female detective called Sharon McGuire slowly raised her hand.

"Yes, Sharon," Morton smiled to her.

"I don't know if you recall, boss, but it's almost a year since I was appointed to the CID at Govan from Cranstonhill office where I served in uniform and did my CID aide."

"Aye, I remember."

The young woman seemed a little embarrassed as faces turned curiously to stare at her.

"Well, when I was doing my aide I sometimes was sent to the Stewart Street office when they were short staffed or to cover the Division during the late shift or the nightshift."

Sensing there was some purpose to her story, Morton nodded she continue.

"Well, it's just that on the odd occasion I was neighboured with Fraser Anderson and well…" Her face reddened and she seemed a little stuck for words.

Morton could see her throat working as she tried to swallow.

"Is there something about him, Sharon? Something you want to disclose?"

"Aye, he's a fucking sexist pig!" she unexpectedly burst out and much to the amusement of her colleagues.

Raising his hand to quieten the team, Morton calmly said, "Can you give me an example of him being a sexist pig, hen?"

McGuire, licking at her dry lips turned to stare at Irene, Janie Wallace and both her fellow female detectives in the room before bitterly replying, "It was wee things, boss. You know, the innuendos, the accidental touching my leg when he was changing gear in the car. Brushing up against me by accident. That sort of thing. Thought he was God's gift, but the guy's a complete arse."

It was Irene who then asked, "Did you know he was engaged to Lesley Rudd?"

"Oh, I heard he had gotten engaged to a policewoman, Ma'am,

but I didn't know Lesley at the time. I only met her when I started here at Govan."

"And these attempts at trying it on with you. Did you make a complaint to anyone, Sharon?"

The younger woman shook her head before tightly answering, "No, Ma'am. You know what it's like. There's still a lot of management who think the CID is a boy's only club and well…" she stopped and stared horrified and wide-eyed at Morton who quietly smiled as he said, "But that's not what I think, Sharon. I'm not interested in your gender, only if you can do your job. Now, did Fraser Anderson at any time try to inappropriately proposition you? Threaten you or anything like that? Or do you know if he tried it on with any other female officers?"

She shook her head and said, "No, he didn't actually try to proposition or threaten me, boss, but I do know he was the talk of the steamie in the women's locker room. If it's any use I can provide the name of a couple of female officers he did try to proposition."

Morton stared at her for a few seconds, before replying, "Thanks, Sharon. I know it can't have been easy admitting to that, but you've given us some background information on Anderson that just might come in useful. When the briefing's finished perhaps you can have a wee word with DI Crichton, eh? Now," he turned and pretended to stare threateningly at the team, "if any of you buggers try it on with our Sharon, she has my permission to batter the shite out of you. Is that clear?"

Relieved that her outburst had not been dismissed and to the sound of laughter, McGuire blushed furiously at the good natured banter that followed.

"Right, guys," Morton loudly called out and clapped his hands together for attention, "see Tam for your Actions, but grab a coffee first while I have a word with him."

Beckoning that Whelan and Irene Crichton follow him, Morton led the way to his office where with the door closed he told them of his visit to ACC Martin Kerr to plead for more resources.

"You've no chance with that slimy bastard, boss," Whelan spat out. "He's too busy looking after his own career to worry about us in the trenches. I heard a whisper he's after the Chief's job."

"I don't think that's any great secret," Morton sighed, squinting through a thick fog of cigarette smoke as he continued, "That was interesting what young Sharon told us, but unfortunately being a two-timing bastard doesn't make Anderson a killer, does it?"

"No, but it certainly lends weight to Lesley Rudd giving him the heave-ho. That is, if she knew about it," Irene added.

Morton nodded then asked, "Right then, where are we at with the fingerprint check against the one found in Lesley Rudd's house?"

"I've quoted Charlie Gallagher and also her former fiancé, DC Anderson," replied Irene, "but no word back yet. Other than those two, we can only wait to see if the Department themselves finger someone for the print. If you excuse the pun," she smiled.

"Excused," Morton retuned her smile then asked, "I saw that young Peter Rossi and Janie Wallace are back. How did they get on with the sister?"

It was Tam Whelan who disclosed the result of Rossi and Wallace's visit to Ellen McNeill's workplace and who added, "They were asking, boss, when you think it's convenient for Missus McNeill to visit Lesley's flat? We've still not ascertained yet if anything obvious was stolen?"

"Bugger, I'd forgotten about that," Morton's brow knitted before he continued, "Tell them to make the arrangement and have them both meet the sister there. Try to get it done as soon as possible, eh?"

"I'm on it," Whelan nodded then asked, "Anything else?"

"I suppose that when the sister arrives at Rudd's flat, it might be the best time to tell her that we've recovered her sister's body. Tell Janie to break the news and if they need to spend time with the woman," he finished with a shrug.

"Got it, boss. That it?"

"Yes, I can't think of anything else right now," Morton sighed, "but you're only a door away so if something comes to mind…" he left the rest unfinished.

When Whelan had left, Morton said, "I'm surprised to see young Janie here today. I thought she might have pulled a sickie after that article in this morning's 'Glasgow News.' Did you have a word with her?"

"I told her to take sometime off, but she's a game wee lassie and refused. Said she'd rather work on, so I agreed. I think if she's busy the she won't have time to worry about it or wonder what to do."

"Rotten that she finds out in the newspaper that her boyfriend is cheating on her."

"Rotten that she finds out at all," Irene cynically replied before adding, "He sounds a right bawbag."

Morton grinned then asked, "Okay, Irene, you're my number two; so, what's our next move?"

"As far as it goes, I believe we're currently on a hiding to nothing. We've no witnesses other than Sam Fullerton who has since died, no Forensic evidence unless the PM turns something up and currently, no motive as to why Lesley was murdered. If you're asking my advice…"

"Which I am," he nodded.

"Then I think we should go all out to try and trace the individual who Lesley's sister said was paying her unwanted attention."

"And how do you propose we go about doing that if we can't even confirm it was a man or a woman?"

"I'd start with her shift, just in case she might have taken one of them into her confidence and in particular, the polis women. As I recall, there is three…" she stopped and slowly shook her head. "No, two of them now Lesley's gone. I know, I'll get Iain Meikle to speak with his shift. He's long enough in the tooth to be able to sort out fact from rumour, hearsay and fiction and he knows them all too and they know him. It's likely they'll trust him more than one of us from the CID and probably open up to him. They're on late shift today so I'll suggest that he stays on and maybe catch up with them when they're on their beats, that way it won't come across as a formal interview."

"I agree," Morton nodded, "they'll be more relaxed speaking with him than somebody from the CID. I take it you're including his Inspector and shift sergeant too?"

"Yes."

Morton's face betrayed his doubt when he asked, "Do you really think Meikle to be an unbiased observer? I mean, if it is his shift, won't he be a little protective of them? Not press them like you might?"

"Oh, I think if someone on his shift knows something, Iain's more than capable of finding out," she wryly smiled, then added, "Iain's a lot brighter than he gives himself credit for. Trust me."

It was only after she had left the room that Morton realised there was something a little different about Irene Crichton. In the three years she had worked at Govan, he had never before known her to wear lipstick.

CHAPTER TWELVE

Janie Wallace put down the phone and turning to Peter Rossi sitting on the opposite side of the desk, said, "That's it arranged then. Missus McNeill will meet us at seven-thirty this evening at Lesley's flat." Her brow furrowed when she added, "She didn't seem particularly keen, though."

"Given the circumstance, I can appreciate that," Rossi shrugged.

"Aye, suppose you're right. Tam," she called across the room to Whelan. "Peter and I are meeting Lesley's twin at half seven tonight. That's the earliest she could make it," she added. Whelan grinned and replied, "Don't try to kid a kidder, ya mongrel. Tomorrow would have done fine, but likely the thought of a few extra hours on the OT persuaded you, eh?" "No, honestly, it's not that…" she stopped, smiling when she realised she was being wound up and said, "Aye, very good. Is there anything in particular you want us to ask her? Other than checking the flat over, I mean."

"I'll speak to the boss and get back to you about that. In the meantime, both of you take an Action between you and get there early. Speak to all the neighbours again. Ian McDonald and me chapped a few doors, but with the passage of time there might be something that somebody remembers. Try the closes on either side too just in case somebody was at their window having a fag or something. Take a note of any doors that don't answer and I'll get somebody to try them again tomorrow, okay? Oh, and ask if Lesley had any regular visitors."

"You mean like men?"

"Men *and* women. Could be that our housebreaker is a local. Find out if she was a good neighbour or had bother with anyone in the close or adjoining closes. The fact that nothing seems to have been stolen could suggest that maybe someone knew she would be out on shift and if there has been any kind of argument with Lesley, decided on getting a bit of payback by turning over the flat."

"Roger that," Janie acknowledged.

"Look," Rossi leaned across the desk and quietly said, "there's nothing doing here at the minute, so why don't we collect the Action and head out to Lesley's flat the now. Maybe pop into a café and grab something to eat on the way. I'm starving."

"Good idea," she nodded and grabbing her handbag, added, "I'll head to the ladies while you grab the paperwork and I'll meet you downstairs in the car.

****

Seated beside 'Hammy' Hammond the shift controller, Iain Meikle was idly working his way through that morning's edition of the 'Glasgow News' while Hammond and his civilian assistant, Hannah, a stoutly built woman in her fifties, routinely went over the call log for that morning to ensure the early shift had not missed anything, that every call was properly logged and dealt with.

"All correct," Hammond finally said with a sigh. Seeing Iain at the sports page he smirked and said, "That Sharkie seems to be getting a good write-up from the pundits for his move down south, eh?"

"Aye, and good riddance. He'll get eaten alive down there. He might be a big fish in a small tank up here, but when some of those cluggers get a hold of him," Iain smiled, "he'll be upended and on his arse so many times he'll think he's on a roller-coaster and wishing he was back here and hadn't done the dirty on our Janie."

"Aye, that was rotten so it was," agreed Hannah, a devout Baptist. "Such a nice lassie too. Is she working today or taking time off?"

"Oh, she's working," Iain replied. "Takes more than a bit of bad news to keep Janie down."

"She's better of without that prick…sorry, Hannah," Hammond apologised. "But you know what I mean. Janie's a looker. She won't be on her own for long."

"That's if she gives him up," Hannah sniffed.

"What? You think she'll stick by him, even though he's fucking about?" Hammond asked and again apologised.

Iain refrained from laughing for it was well known that John Hammond, who cursed like a trooper, did so unconsciously and just as unconsciously when working with Hannah, routinely apologised.

Before she could explain the idiosyncrasies of the female gender, the switchboard lit up with an incoming call that was answered by Hannah, who wearing her headset politely greeted the caller with, "Strathclyde Police, Govan. Can I help you.

Before Iain could speak, she reached out and with her stubby forefinger vigorously tapped the scrap of paper he had laid down on the desk that indicated any calls for Lesley Rudd be answered by him.

Donning a spare headset, he heard Hannah say, "I'll just put you though now, Madam."

He had practised how he would respond to the call if it came in, but now that it had he discovered to his surprise his mouth was dry and stuttered, "Hello, my name's Iain. Iain Meikle. I'm speaking on behalf of Constable Lesley Rudd. Can I help you?"

Conscious that both Hammond and Hannah were watching him, he licked at his lips as a woman quietly hissed, "I don't want to speak to you. I want to speak to her. To Constable Rudd. Fucking get *her* on the phone."

He swallowed and worked at getting some saliva into his mouth before carefully replying, "Look, hen, I know you've asked to speak to Lesley, but there's been…" he stopped and wondered, I know that voice, don't I, then thought should I admit Les is dead?

Seconds later he made his decision and said, "Lesley met with an accident. That's why I'm answering on her behalf. If it's important, I need to know."

"An accident? What kind of accident?"

He took a breath and said, "The fatal kind."

"Oh God! Oh, sweet Jesus! He knows!"

The line disconnected almost immediately and Iain was left with the broken connection tone. His thoughts were disturbed when Hammond asked, "Anything?"

He shook his head and staring into space, thoughtfully said, "I'm not certain, but I think I know who was on the phone."

****

Banging down the phone, Paula Menzies hurried to the bay window and glancing out into the street below saw Charlie Gallagher's black coloured Ford Capri drawing up outside the close.

"Shit!" she hissed and glancing around the room to ensure that everything was in order, nervously patted at her hair and tightened her ponytail in preparation for his arrival through the door.

Adopting a huge smile, she stood ready to greet him, but her mind was racing.

The polis lassie was dead and that could only mean one thing. Charlie had done her in. When he'd forced the Lesley's name from her, he'd hunted her down and killed her. No, she unconsciously shook her head. He'd *murdered* her.

She heard the key in the front door and involuntarily flinched, then heard his bag being thrown to the floor as he called out, "Paula! That's me home. I'm just going for a shite. Is dinner ready yet?"

"Oh, I'll just get it on," she called out and hurrying through to the hallway, saw the bathroom door close.

She stopped in midstride and clutched at her throat for that's when it occurred to her; that's when she realised that if the police knew or suspected it was Charlie who killed the lassie, they'd want to know who gave him her name.

She knew that Charlie wouldn't do her any favours and even though she'd tell the polis it was beaten out of her, she knew that they bastards wouldn't care. All they'd want was their pound of flesh and a conviction and with her record she'd go to the jail for a very long time.

A cold shiver swept through her when that thought led to another.

Only Charlie knew who had given him the name and that meant if the polis came calling for him, she could be used as a witness against him.

"Jesus!" she reached for the wall to steady herself, her legs about to fail her as she almost fainted with fright. If Charlie thought she might be a witness against him, that put her in the worst of danger. She had already accepted that he was going to dump her, that it was just a matter of weeks if not days, so why should he care what happened to her? Even worse, if he suspected that the polis could use her against him…

Hardly realising what she was doing, she staggered to the cutlery drawer and reaching in, drew out an eight inch, yellow handled butchers fillet knife.

Staring at the shiny blade, her mouth set grimly as she tested its edge against her forefinger and with an intake of breath, snarled and made her decision.

If one for second she thought Charlie intending hurting her or worse, he was getting it!

****

Derek Stokoe's mother Annie had taken to calling him 'Doughnut' since he was a lad and continued to deny his gross overweight was anything to do with her. What she conveniently ignored was the fact that being the lazy and slovenly woman she was, since he was a toddler she had bought and fed her son all sorts of inappropriate food and sweets rather than have to go to the bother of actually cooking nutritious meals for him.

At four feet and seven and a half inches tall, the small, dwarf like woman continued to limp on her left leg as she had done after giving birth to her eleven-pound baby and never let him forget that it was his delivery that ruined not just her life, but her sexual urges too. That said, not even on her best day could her own mother describe Annie as pretty for even on her very best day, a bit less than average looking would likely be the best the diminutive and overweight girl could have hoped for. And so in the fullness of time and finally accepting her lot with ill grace, the fifty-eight-year-old alcoholic Annie remained an unmarried woman with just the distant memory of a one-night stand; a knee-trembler with a tall and drunken stranger who in the darkness had stood her on a low wall in the yard behind the local hostelry and impregnated her.

Now resident in her council semi-detached home in Frampton Road in the Walton area of the city and less than three hundred yards from the pub where her one and only sexual encounter had occurred, she rarely left the house other than to attend her usual Tuesday and Friday night bingo sessions with her only friend, Gina, the sixty-year-old local illegal moneylender who used Annie's son Doughnut on a *ad hoc* basis to recover outstanding debts.

"I'm telling you, Gina," she sat at her kitchen table sipping at her gin beneath a haze of cigarette smoke, one bottle empty and a second almost empty between them, "that fly bugger is definitely up to something."

"Like what," her scrawny friend asked between hacking coughs that shook her body.

"Well, those bags he's dumped beneath the floorboards in the spare room upstairs. Thinks I don't know what in them, he does," she tapped a stubby forefinger against her misshapen nose and winked mischievously at her well dressed pal.

Gina, tipsy though not drunk and whose tolerance to strong drink was legendary, stared through myopic eyes and said, "What bags? What the fuck are you on about, you old git?" then frowning, suggested, "Maybe we should take a wee look, eh? Maybe just a peek?"

"Aye, let's see what my lad's hiding," Annie drunkenly sniggered and pushing herself to her feet, toppled over and fell onto the floor.

"Annie!" Gina reached down for her friend who began to giggle. Between them, Gina pulling and Annie pushing up from her chair, they got the stout wee woman to her feet then moments later, were upstairs in Doughnut's former bedroom where Annie almost fell to her feet. Lifting a corner of the old matted rug, she prised up the chipped and stained floorboards and reaching down into the space below, fetched out a clear plastic bag.

"What the fuck you got there, Annie?"

"I dunno. Sand I think. Anyway, it looks like sand, doesn't it?" she held up the bag for Gina to inspect and then bent down as she peered into the dark space beneath.

"There's loads of them bags in here," she said, her cheek pressed against the floorboard.

Gina was no fool and acting as an illegal moneylender in the Walton area for nigh a full decade had learned a thing or two in that time. Now, drunk as she was and eyes widening, she realised that bag didn't contain sand, but a drug of some sort and though the drug of her own choice was alcohol, was sharp enough to guess the sandy material was likely heroin. However, though in the past she had without conscience used Annie's son's brutality for her own debt collections, Gina was also aware how violent he was and could be and a shiver run down her spine. Swallowing with fear of the consequences if Doughnut discovered she knew of his stash of drugs, a cold calm overtook her.

"I think you should put that back, Annie. Yes," she vigorously nodded. "Just put it back, there's a love. We don't want Doughnut knowing we've been into his private business now, do we?"

Annie stared curiously at her and was about to argue when they both heard the front door open and Doughnut call out, "Mam? It's me. Where the *fuck* are you?"

"Quick!" Gina panicked. "Put it back!"

In her haste to shove the bag under the floorboard, Annie tore a corner of the plastic and both watched in horror as some of the powder spilled onto the floorboards.

Hastily, Gina dropped to her knees and with her bare hands helped Annie dust the granules of the powder into the open crack in the floorboards.

"Fuck!" they said almost in unison as Gina pushed the pissed Annie to one side and first shoving the floorboard into the space, dragged the mat across the spillage. Getting clumsily to her feet she heaved her stout friend upright then both tumbled out of the door into the upper hallway.

"Mam? You up there?" Doughnut called out as he began to climb the stairs.

Their hearts thumping, it was Gina, her voice squeaking who loudly replied, "Aye, we're here, Doughnut lad. Your mam was helping me in the toilet. I'm a bit under the weather with the gin," she forced herself to laugh then fetching her handkerchief from her trouser pocket, wiped off the powder adhering to her sweaty hands.

The bulky man reached the top of the landing and staring at them in turn, grinned widely.

"*You're* under the weather, Gina? Look at the two of you. You're *both* pissed."

"Yeah," she smiled disarmingly, though her heart was rapidly beating, "maybe you can give me a hand down these bloody stairs in case I fall," then looping her arm through his and followed by Annie, ushered him downstairs.

Minutes later and beating a speedy retreat from the house, Gina exaggerated her stagger along the road until she was certain she could no longer be seen from the house then face grimly set, straightened up and hurried home.

****

Stood in Colin Morton's room with the DCI seated behind his desk and Irene Crichton occupying the chair in front, Morton peered curiously at Iain Meikle before asking him, "You're sure about this? I mean, there's no doubt it was Paula Menzies?"

Pursing his lips and nodding, Iain replied, "I'm as certain as I can be without her actually telling me her name, sir. I've lifted Paula on two separate occasions in the last couple of months and yes, I'm certain it was her. And before you ask, she has a sort of lisping sound when she speaks. That's what alerted me to her voice."

"Did you let her know you were aware it was her that was calling? I mean, did you call her by name or anything?"

"No," Iain shook his head. "What I told you is exactly how the conversation went." He paused before continuing, "I *was* tempted to tell Paula I knew it was her, but I figured that you might wan to maybe bring her in and put it to her that you are aware she called the office looking for Les." He grinned when he added, "I didn't want to ruin your surprise for you."

Morton, nodded and returned his grin and said, "You did the right thing, Iain. We'll do that. We'll bring her in and ask why she was trying to contact Lesley, though I suspect you already guessed that, haven't you?"

He slowly exhaled then shrugging, said, "I'm thinking that when Les spoke with her, they've probably struck some kind of deal and the only deal that Les would have made is something to do with Charlie Gallagher, maybe persuaded Paula that any information she was willing to share might do her some good with the court. What I found interesting was when she said 'He knows' and I'm guessing she was referring to Gallagher. Sounded scared when she said it, too."

"Yes, you're right, that was interesting," Morton thoughtfully said.

He turned to her and asked, "What do you think, Irene?"

"It's like Iain says, Colin. Though we really don't have a clue why, it sounds like Paula is going to grass up her man. The thing is," she turned apologetically to Iain and shrugged, "I don't believe that Lesley had the practical experience or knowledge to just sign on someone like Paula Menzies. I think there might be more to it," she mused. "I mean, Paula has been through the system countless times and wouldn't give up Gallagher to a beat cop like Lesley just to get off a shoplifting and assault charge, would she? Christ, that would be like committing suicide if Gallagher ever found out."

Her eyes narrowed and chewing at her lower lip, then said, "It might be worth us taking a more in depth look at Paula. Given her extensive record, she must be well documented with the SCRO. Maybe there's something there in her criminal record that can explain this urge to assist the polis, something we're overlooking."

"You think there's a personal reason she's been trying to contact Lesley?" Morton asked.

She slowly shook her head and replied, "I think that Lesley just happened to be the cop that met Paula just at the right time and for some unknown reason, Paula needed a contact in the polis to fire in her information about Gallagher; someone she could trust."

The seconds of silence were broken when Iain slowly said, "You realise what you're suggesting? That if Charlie Gallagher discovers Paula is trying to speak to the polis, *was* trying to speak with Les, then he must be a strong suspect for her murder!"

They both stared at him, seeing his face pale, his cold fury and his fists clenched.

"What we think and what we know, Iain," Morton raised both hands defensively and softly said, "are two different things. What we can't do is go and drag Gallagher in here and charge him. Not without evidence. What we *need* to do is speak to Paula Menzies, get her away from Gallagher and on her own and find out exactly what she knows, what she was trying to tell Lesley. You realise that, don't you Iain?"

He stared wordlessly at Morton before nodding.

Inwardly relieved that Meikle wasn't going to hare off on some sort of vendetta, Morton continued, "I think it would be wise, Irene, for you to liaise with the shift Inspector and use his plain clothes guys to set up a surveillance at Gallagher's address and catch Paula Menzies when she leaves the flat alone. Bring her in and interview her. You *and* your neighbour," he caught the Iain's eye.

He was a Detective Chief Inspector and didn't need an officer of Iain's junior rank to concur, but with uncommon courtesy asked, "You agree?"

"That seems to be the best option, yes sir."

"Right then," he lifted some files from his desk and began to shuffle them before gruffly saying, "bugger off, the two of you. I've paperwork to attend to."

****

Parked near to Lesley Rudd's close in Baker Street, Janie Wallace in the passenger seat glanced at the folder in her lap and told Peter Rossi, "According to my list, we've covered most of the neighbours, so there's only three doors where there was no reply."

A car passing slowly by attracted her attention. "I think that's her now," she nodded towards it then pointed to the dark coloured, three door rusting Mark One Ford Escort. As they watched, the Escort stopped a few car lengths away and they saw Ellen McNeill alight from the driver's door.

Getting out of the CID vehicle they saw her startle, causing Janie to raise a hand and say, "It's okay, Ellen, it's just us."

"Oh, I'm sorry," she blustered. "I was miles away," and half smiled.

Aye, Rossi stared at her, and likely distracted too when she was driving here, but kept his thoughts to himself.

Entering the close, Janie led the way up the stairs to the first floor to the flat where they discovered that Hurry Brothers, the call-out firm of joiners who alongside their commercial and domestic business also served the city's police Divisions to effect temporary repairs to damaged shops and houses, had secured the broken door with a hasp and stout padlock.

Producing the key from her handbag, Janie unlocked the padlock and entering the flat, saw items and clothing strewn all over the floor of the hallway

"Oh, my God," she heard Ellen say and turned to find her stood in the doorway with her hand to her mouth, her eyes wide open and her free hand reaching out to hold onto the wall.

Placing a comforting hand on her elbow, Rossi said, "Let's find you a chair first," then turning to Janie, added, "Can you fetch some water?"

Minutes later they had the distraught woman seated in the lounge and slowly drinking from a mug of water, some of which had dribbled onto her coat.

"I'm sorry," she gasped, her head swivelling as she stared around her at the devastation. "I know you told me the flat had been broken into, but I never expected this."

"Believe me," Janie forced a smile, "it looks a lot worse than it really is. Other than needing a new front door and probably the insurance will cover that, there's no real damage. It looks worse than it is because everything is scattered about. Once Lesley's things have been tidied up and replaced in the drawers and the wardrobe, it will look just the same as before."

"What's that messy, silver coloured stuff there, on top of the glass," she indicated with a shaking finger towards an overturned coffee table.

Rossi turned to see what she pointed at and replied, "It's fingerprint powder. The scene of crime officer, we call them SOCO's, has been through the flat searching for fingerprints. Don't worry, it will wipe off the glass," he smiled at her.

Aye, thought Janie, but it's a bugger trying getting the bloody stuff off material or clothing.

"Did they find any fingerprints?"

Aware of Colin Morton's strict instruction re the dissemination of the discovery of the print, he lied, "No, not that I'm aware of. Sorry."

"So, are you feeling okay now?" Janie asked. "Ready to have a look around and tell us if there is anything that is obviously missing?"

Ellen nodded and getting to her feet, was closely followed by Janie as she commenced her search of the flat.

It took a little over ten minutes with her in and out of Lesley's bedroom, second bedroom, kitchen and bathroom before she sighed and shaking her head, said, "I'm sorry. I have no idea if there is anything stolen."

"You probably saw that her jewellery was tossed from the little jewel box onto the bed. Did Lesley own anything of particular value?"

Ellen pursed her lips and said, "The only thing she prized was our grandmother's brooch. It's emeralds and there is a matching set of earrings. I have the earrings and the brooch is lying on the bed, so other than that I can't think of anything else."

"When was the last time you visited Lesley at the flat?" Rossi asked.

"Oh, let me think. It would be, say, two, maybe three months ago? Lesley and I used to meet in the town. It was more convenient for us both. We'd have lunch…" she stopped and tears filled her eyes. "Sorry," she gasped, her face turning pale and hand to her mouth quickly made her way through to the bathroom.

They waited for several minutes before Janie decided to knock on the bathroom door. When it opened she saw Ellen's face had been scrubbed clean and her nose twitching, realised that a lemon scented aerosol had been sprayed.

"Sorry, I was a little…" Ellen didn't finish, but pointing to her mouth indicated she had vomited.

"It's the shock of what's happening and seeing this," Janie nodded in sympathy.

Closing the door behind her, she led the pale faced and embarrassed Ellen through to the lounge where Janie said to Rossi, "Can you give us a couple of minutes?"

He realised what was coming next and acknowledging with a nod, replied, "I'll see if any of the neighbours we missed are at home and meet you back here in the flat."

"Sit down, Ellen. Please," she indicated with her hand.

When they were both seated, Janie softly inhaled and said, "As we told you, Ellen, we already know that Lesley is dead. Well, it's my sad duty to inform you that earlier today her body was recovered from the waters of the River Clyde."

"Oh no, oh my God," Ellen burst into tears, her arms wrapped tightly around her as head down, she slowly rocked back and forth on her chair.

Though her inclination was to kneel beside Ellen and comfort her, Janie didn't move from her own chair, but sat silently watching.

Her shoulders heaving with her sobs, Ellen cried for a solid three minutes before raising her head, then dabbing at her eyes and nose with a handkerchief, said, "Where is she now? I need to see her."

"Yes, of course. Lesley has been taken to the City Mortuary at the Saltmarket. My instructions are to make an arrangement to take you there for a formal identification. I mean, we the police could do that, but we thought…"

"Yes, I understand," Ellen interrupted. "I'm guessing you'd prefer a family member for that."

"Only if you feel up to it."

"So, when I can see her then?"

Glancing at her watch, Janie replied, "I'm sorry, but it's a little late to attend the mortuary this evening." She stared at Ellen, knowing this was the hard part and continued, "Because of the… the nature of the inquiry, there will need to be a post mortem. It's preferable that the formal identification occurs before the PM…"

"When is the post mortem?"

"Ah, that's set for eleven o'clock tomorrow morning. If you like…"

Suddenly animated, Ellen sniffed back her tears and said, "Then I'll be there before that time. Will ten-thirty be okay?"

"Yes, of course."

"Have you arrested anyone yet?"

"No," she shook her head, "I'm sorry, not yet. Mister Morton, the DCI is in charge of the inquiry and…"

"When can I see him?"

"Tomorrow morning. He will be at the mortuary to attend the…the procedure and you can speak with him then."

As though abruptly deflated, Ellen's shoulders sagged. She stared at the carpeted floor then in a quiet, but firm voice, said, "He loved her more than he loves me, you know."

Janie's eyes narrowed. Rossi had already intimated his suspicion of Jake McNeill, but she had dismissed it as just that; a groundless suspicion.

But now this.

Not daring to move, she softly asked, "Who are you talking about, Ellen?"

"Jake, my husband. He thinks I don't know," she turned her

pale face towards Janie, her bottom lip trembling as she struggled against the tears. "But you can tell, can't you? When someone doesn't love you anymore."

Janie couldn't help it, but a sudden vision of the newspaper photograph of her boyfriend Paul getting into the taxi with the scantily clad blonde flashed through her mind and her heart racing, she swallowed deeply before asking, "Why would you think that, Ellen?"

"It's just the way he is about her, you know? Little things. The way he looks at her, the way he talks about her. Let's face it," she stared wild-eyed at Janie, her teeth bared. "Look at me and look at Lesley. The perfect *fucking* figure, the perfect *fucking* face, the perfect *fucking* career while I'm…I'm…" she thrust her face into her hands and again began to sob.

Janie was shocked at Ellen's revelation and fought an overwhelming desire to take this poor woman in her arms and cuddle her.

But she didn't.

She wasn't a cold-hearted woman, far from it, but realised that as a police officer she had her duty to perform and with a cold chill sweeping through her, recognised that whether knowingly or unwittingly, Ellen McNeill had just offered up her husband as a possible suspect for the murder of her sister.

But what shocked Janie even more was the sudden insight into Ellen McNeill's soul, the involuntary admission of jealousy and…she swallowed deeply, possibly hatred or at the very least an extreme dislike for her sister, Lesley.

CHAPTER THIRTEEN

Seated at the small kitchen table and his meal finished, Charlie Gallagher watched Paula Menzies as she stood at the sink with her back to him, washing the plates and the frying pan.

He sensed she was tense and at first put it down to his suspicion of her, that she was afraid he might again assault her.

Not that it bothered Gallagher for as far as he was concerned anyone who touted or was even suspected of touting to the cops was the lowest of the low and deserved no mercy. However, he was uncertain if Paula had been telling the truth, that the polis woman called Rudd really did try to sign her on, but what he couldn't decide if it was as she had claimed, that Paula wanted no part of it.

Eyes narrowing, he loudly burped, but the lingering doubt persisted and gave him some cause for thought.

As he watched her scrub at the pan he went over in his mind again what she told him and wondered; did she really take his warning seriously?

"Nice dinner, doll," he lifted his mug to toast her and arose from the table, then added, "I'm just going through to watch some tele."

Closing the front room door behind him, he stopped and holding his breath, listened for a few seconds.

Satisfied that Paula hadn't followed to listen to him through the door, he lifted the Trim phone and pressed the button for the last number called.

Seconds passed then he heard the connection and the number dialled.

His grip tightened and he almost crushed the handset when he heard a woman's voice say, "Strathclyde Police, Govan. Can I help you?"

****

Doughnut Stokoe had no reason to check the cache of heroin under the floorboards in the spare bedroom, but finding his mother and Gina upstairs had caused him to be a bit suspicious and so after dinner pretended he was going upstairs to use the loo, then sneaked into the room.

His heart sank when he saw the tattered rug had been moved a little and was no longer lying at the precise angle he had left it.

Dropping to his knees, he lifted the rug back and immediately saw traces of spilled powder on the floorboards.

His mouth tightening, he lifted the loose floorboard and feeling about under it, withdrew his hand and saw his fingers were covered in brown powder.

"Shit!" he exclaimed and with brutal strength, tore up the adjoining floorboard. Dropping his head, he could see that the top bag had been torn at a corner and it was from that bag the powder has spilled.

Gritting his teeth, he screamed, "Mam!"

He listened as she made her way upstairs, puffing and panting and the stairs creaking under her weight.

"Aye, son?" she poked her head into the room.

Now he was on his feet and looming over the small woman who was terrified of him, heard her stammer, "What is it, son?".

"What the fuck were you doing lifting the floorboards and going into my gear?" he snarled.

It didn't escape Annie's notice that Doughnut's fists were clenched and swallowing with fear, she stuttered, "It wasn't my idea, son. It was Gina. She made me."

"Did she take anything? Did she take some of the H?"

"The H?" she asked in such an innocent voice that even Doughnut realised she was clearly confused.

"The powder, mam! Did she take any of the powder?"

Backed against the wall and staring up at him, she vigorously shook her head and said, "No, son, no. I swear to God. We were just looking at it and then we heard you coming in the door, so we just shoved the bag back under the floor and it tore. That's when the powder spilled out of it, son. Honest."

He stared nastily at her for a few seconds, then leaning towards her said in a chilling, but calm voice, "You never again go near anything I leave in the house, mam. Do you *fucking* understand?"

Her tongue rattling in her dry mouth, she could not find the spit to speak and staring fearfully at him could only nod.

Backing off a couple of feet, he beckoned that she leave the room and watched as she scurried away.

Now he had a decision to make. Should he confront Gina about what she had seen or was his reputation enough to frighten her into keeping her mouth shut?

Sullenly, he sat down on an old armchair by the window and at length pondered the question for making decisions was not Doughnut's first skill.

If he did visit Gina it might make her all the more suspicious about what he was up to and if word got back to that plonker Billy Madison, word might also get around that Doughnut Stokoe couldn't be trusted and he knew that in Liverpool, reputation was everything.

With a sigh he finally decided that it would be foolish to come down heavily on Gina who was always good for an easy earner when she needed some of her debtors dealt with. Best to let sleeping dogs lie he thought and fetching a used handkerchief from his trouser pocket, got down onto his knees and began to carefully sweep the spilled powder into a small pile.

When the powder was returned to the burst bag he replaced the broken floorboards and decided to go downstairs and have a word with his mam.

****

While Peter Rossi spoke with Tam Whelan and pass the result of the calls to the neighbours doors in Lesley Rudd's close and the adjoining closes, Janie Wallace sat in front of Colin Morton to relate the information confided by Rudd's twin sister, Ellen McNeill.

Stood with her back to a wall, Irene Crichton listened intently as Morton asked, "And you're quite certain, Janie, that Missus McNeill is convinced her husband…"

"Jake McNeill, sir."

"Her husband Jake had a thing for Lesley?"

"Oh," she nodded, "I don't think there's any doubt about it, sir. To be fair, when we visited them at home the first time, Peter Rossi had a suspicion about the husband, but I kind of dismissed it," she blushed. "Anyway, what I mean is, it seemed to me that Ellen believes he has this thing for her sister, but whether that's true and he really did prefer Lesley…" she shrugged as though the answer was not one she could confirm. Continuing, she said, "If I might say this, sir, I knew Lesley slightly and there was no doubt she was a very self-assured and confident individual. Obviously slim and attractive too. Now, I'm no expert, but I don't think that Ellen has the same confidence, particularly in her appearance."

"What do you mean?" Irene asked from behind her.

"Well," she turned slightly to address the DI, "I only saw Lesley a couple of times off duty; you know, at payoff's, that sort of thing. No wait," he brow furrowed. "I did see her once at the Divisional dance up in the Rolls Royce club." She blushed again then continued, "What I'm trying to say is that she always made the best of herself. Dressed really nicely and turned quite a few heads. Her sister Ellen, however; she struck me as dressing a bit more…frumpy is the word I'd use."

"What, like me?" Irene teased her with a smile.

"No, Ma'am, I didn't mean…" Janie hastily replied.

"I'm joking," she grinned at the younger woman before adding, "Please, go on."

Her face flushed, Janie said, "Anyway, I got the distinct impression that Ellen was jealous of her sister. Maybe that's why she said what she said and that's why she is feeling insecure about her husband."

"Nonetheless," Morton made an arch with his fingers as he stared keenly at Janie, "it suggests that if Jake McNeill did have a thing for Lesley, it gives him motive. What about opportunity? Did you ask the wife if she suspected that Lesley might have returned his affection for her?"

"No, sir, I'm sorry, I didn't."

"No matter," he slowly shook his head. "What about opportunity? Did you ask where he might have been last Saturday night? If he was at home when Lesley went missing?"

Again Janie blushed as she shook her head, but any further

questions was prevented when Irene interjected with, "Given that the sister and her husband are close relatives and it's a sensitive time, perhaps we might consider taking a formal statement from the husband, Colin. Put it in such a way that we're eliminating all persons who had recent contact with her."

"Aye, maybe you're right," he sighed with a nod then said to Janie, "Don't feel bad about not asking questions, hen. We'll get round to asking them. What you've brought us is information that might prove to be more valuable than you think."

"Yes," Irene's eyes narrowed as she stared at Morton, "but there's one more thing that occurs to me." Turning to address Janie, she stepped forward to ask, "When the sister disclosed her thoughts to you, what was her demeanour? I mean, was she sad, confused, angry…"

"Oh, angry, Ma'am. Definitely angry."

"Mmmm, angry," Irene slowly repeated, then said, "Angry with her husband or angry with her sister?"

"Eh," Janie pursed her lips before thoughtfully replying, "both I'd say."

"Angry enough to hurt Lesley, do you think?"

She stared wide-eyed and open-mouthed at the DI, her thoughts from her time in the flat with Ellen McNeill coming back to her then shaking her head, replied, "I really…I really don't know, Ma'am."

The silence that fell between them was broken when glancing at his wristwatch, Morton said, "I trust you told Missus McNeill about the PM tomorrow morning?"

"Yes, sir. She said she'll be there at ten-thirty and hopes to have a word with you before the PM."

"Thanks, Janie. That'll be all for the night. You did a good job bringing this to our attention, so get yourself home and we'll see you tomorrow morning."

Rising from her chair, she nodded in acknowledgement and left the room.

Sitting herself down, Irene exhaled and said, "Well, that was a turn-up for the book, the twin sister not just offering up her hubby as a suspect, but we might have to consider her as the jealous killer too."

"Saturday night, though, Irene. As Janie said earlier, they have two young kids. If the husband was out during the material time Lesley went missing, it means the wife would have to have been at home caring for them. Likewise, if he was child-minding the weans, we'll need to alibi her. Bloody hell. Family relationships. Why do they always have to be a right can of worms?" he growled.

She let him brood on that thought before asking, "When do you want them interviewed?"

"Better wait till after the PM tomorrow."

"Anything else?"

He glanced down at his notes before asking, "Any word back on that fingerprint from the lavvy seat?"

She sighed before replying, "Both negative for DC Anderson and Charlie Gallagher. However, it simply suggests it might not have been them who broke into Rudd's flat, doesn't mean to say they're not the killer."

His brow furrowed when he said, "I thought if Anderson was engaged to Rudd his prints might have been discovered in the flat from the time he visited there?"

"I thought that too and gave Alex Murray a phone call and asked him that same question. Said that the flat was very clean and it was his opinion that Rudd was," she smiled, "more than house-proud; a right tight-arse about cleanliness. His description, not mine."

"Then no suggestion the intruder might have cleaned the place for prints?"

"No," she shook her head, "Not at all."

"Might be worth doing a speculative check with SCRO on this guy McNeill's name and address to find out if he's ever been charged with a crime and if he has…"

"Run his prints against the one found on the toilet seat," she finished for him before adding, "I'll get it done."

"Right then, a bit of bad news. I've had a call from the ACC's office to inform me that we will not be getting the extra resources that I asked for. I phoned Mister Cruickshank and passed on the news."

She frowned and asked, "What did Patches say about that?"

"Told me that he'd continue to work at getting me some more officers, but not to hold my breath. And while I remember, how did you get on with the surveillance for Gallagher's bird, Paula Menzies?"

"Inspector Kane agreed to lend me his two plain clothes guys, so I let them have the CID car that's running on three cylinders to sit in while they're watching the close. If they see Paula leave the close on her own, they'll follow her and give me a heads up so I can arrange to have her lifted."

"Good. What about Iain Meikle?"

"He's out and about on foot at the minute, away doing the rounds of the beats and speaking with his shift. I said I'd pick him up when I'm finished here and find out how he got on."

"Okay, right then, I'll have a word with Tam Whelan about the Actions and see you here tomorrow morning. We can travel together for the PM." He smiled when he added, "It'll be interesting meeting Rudd's twin sister."

With that, she bid him cheerio and left the room.

****

The bearded, scruffily dressed man sat in the saloon bar and nursing his Guinness, stared with watery eyes at Annie Stokoe's friend, Gina Poulson.

"So," he leaned across the table and softly said, "what you're telling me is that you and Annie Stokoe found a large number of these plastic bags filled with a sandy stuff hidden under the floorboards of her spare bedroom and she told you they belonged to her son Doughnut?"

"Yeah," she excitedly replied and opening her handbag that rested on her lap, rummaged inside and produced a clear plastic food bag that contained a soiled handkerchief.

"There's this," she handed the bag to the man who surprised, narrowed his eyes as he examined it before asking, "What the fuck is this you're showing me? Your snotty nose rag?"

Exasperated, Gina replied, "I wiped some of the powder from me hands onto me hankie," and pointed to the bag.

"Oh, right, and what do you expect me to do with this?"

Startled at his apparent lack of interest, she swallowed with difficulty and shrugging, mumbled, "I dunno. I thought you might want to test it or something."

"How many plastic bags, was there?"

"I dunno," she shrugged. "It was Annie who peeked under the floorboards and she said there was a lot, an awful lot." Gina decided a little exaggeration might be useful and upped the figure by adding, "Maybe a couple of dozen or so?"

He stared at her as though she were mad and though unable to determine how truthful she was, felt a twinge of excitement at what she told him. And he reminded himself the old cow had previously provided some good stuff.

Sighing, he lazily reached across the table to grab at the plastic bag and shoved it into the pocket of his worn anorak. Abruptly rising from his chair, he said, "I'll be in touch, but anything else, you know how to get in touch with me."

She watched him leave and blinked when he opened the door as the shard of bright daylight cut through the dimly lit pub.

She hated him, but there was nothing else she could do, not if she wanted to continue to run her profitable and highly illegal loan business. Finishing her gin, she smacked her lips together then stood up and followed the man out of the door.

****

Straddling her body he held her by down with one powerful hand on her throat, ignoring her frantic efforts to break his grip as she lay spread-eagled across the bed and watched through slitted eyes as she fought for breath, her face turning red as he slowly crushed her windpipe.

"Ya fucking slut!" he sneered at her. "Ya grassing bitch! Think I wouldn't find out you were telling the cops what I'm up to?" He drew back his free hand and punched her to the side of the head, but the blow was weakened as all his strength was in the right hand that continued to choke her.

Paula's eyes widened until the pupils rolled back so that she showed only the white and from her throat came a deep rattle. He knew she was seconds away from expiring and very gently, released the pressure on her windpipe to permit her to gasp for air, then continued to slowly remove his hand from her throat. He stood up from the bed and leaned over her, his hands bunched into fists as he watched her retch and rub with both her hands at her bruised trachea, turning her head back and forth, her lungs on fire as she snorted and breathing through her mouth and nose, fought for air.

"What did you tell them, Paula?" he calmly asked.

Terrified, she stared up at him and tried to speak, but Gallagher had done more damage than he intended and all she could manage was a croak.

Tears flowed from her eyes and she realised she had wet herself.

"I asked you a fucking question," he leaned down towards her, steadying himself on the bed with one hand on either side of her body.

His nose twitched, then he sniffed at the sharp smell of her urine and in that instant, his rage knew no bounds.

Snarling in apoplectic fury, he held her down with his left hand and began to pummel Paula's head with his right fist.

Again and again and again, he punched furiously at her face, ignoring the stream of blood that soaked his Tee shirt, the quilt covers and the now unconscious Paula.

Minutes passed before breathless, he stood upright and took a step back from the blood soaked bed and stared down at her, his face displaying disbelief as though surprised at what he had done.

"Paula?" he reached a hand to shake her by her leg. "Paula, wake up, ya dizzy bitch. Paula!"

He glanced down at his hands, seeing them covered in her blood and as though with sudden realisation took her face between her hands, but then to his disgust felt rather than heard the crack of her broken facial bones.

He stepped back in shock, his chest tightening and his breathing coming in spurts.

A long forgotten schoolroom lesson on First Aid came suddenly to mind and he grabbed at her wrist, feeling for a pulse with his own two fingers.

There was nothing. He reached for the pulse in her neck, the carotid pulse, but again there was nothing.

"Jesus Christ," he quietly mouthed.

She was dead.

He'd killed the grassing bitch.

He glanced quickly and fearfully around him as though the police were there waiting to handcuff him. Self preservation kicked in and he knew he would have to get rid of her body. And quickly.

He lifted her legs that drooped over the edge of the bed and folded them against her, then drew the quilt covers over her before bundling the ends together and dragging her body onto the floor.

Good, he thought as he peered at the mattress, the blood had not dripped through.

Help, he needed help. He needed Seamus and Marty to get their arses here, but before he did anything else, he stared at himself in the wardrobe mirror, he'd better shower and change.

****

In the darkening street outside, the two plain clothes officers sat in the smelly, rust-bucket CID car. While the driver watched the close entrance his passenger finished her greasy pie supper, both completely unaware that any expectation they had of spotting Paula Menzies, the infamous and prevalent shoplifter, was now totally futile.

CHAPTER FOURTEEN

Plodding around the Govan beats, Iain Meikle had just finished speaking with his mate, Eric Little who was in the Pollokshields panda with Shona Murtagh, the younger of the shift's two female constables. Both of them, like the rest of the shift Iain had spoken to had no knowledge of anyone having any interest in Lesley Rudd.

"And how did you get on when you spoke with the Inspector and that git Cole?" Murtagh smiled curiously at him.

"Well, Mickey Kane was fine but it was like drawing blood from Cole," Iain shook his head.

"And how are you getting on with our esteemed colleagues in the CID?" Little turned to stare at Iain in the rear seat.

"Ach, they're not a bad bunch and besides, it's not as if we don't know them. They've just got a different job to do, that's all."

"I heard you're neighboured with Irene Crichton. How are you getting on with her?"

"Irene's not so bad either," he smiled. "I like her. Doesn't treat me any differently to the other guys even though I'm just an attachment to the CID."

"Aye, and she's a looker too and not a bad body either," grinning, he winked at Iain before adding "or would be if she got her act together."

"As if a woman like her would pay any attention to me," Iain scoffed in reply.

"Oh, I don't know," Murtagh teased him. "For an old guy, you're not *too* bad looking. Anyway, what is is with you bloody men," she snorted at Little and in a comic voice, repeated, "Would be if she got her act together. What kind of thing is that to say about her? I've always found Irene Crichton to be really nice and yes, maybe she could use a wee make-over, but you got one thing right. She is a looker right enough. And as for you lot, if men had tits would you talk about each other like that?"

"If we had tits," Little laughed, "the shower room at the polis club in Pollok Park would be a lot more fun."

"Anyway, Iain's right," she continued and shaking her head, cheekily added, "I can't see a woman like Irene Crichton having an interest in an old guy like him."

That remark earned her a gentle cuff on the back of her head from the 'old guy.'

"Besides, isn't the story that after she dumped her man she cried off all men?" she added.

"So I heard, but you never know, Iain, a good looking guy like you," teased Little.

"Aye, very good," he cast a sarcastic glance at Little before using his radio to ask for the position of his next and final interviewee, Ian Harris.

Learning from Hammy Hammond the controller that Harris was currently in Drumoyne Road, he was grateful when Little offered to run him down to meet with Harris.

A little over five minutes later, he was stood with the young probationer and waving cheerio to the panda crew.

"On your own tonight, Ian?"

"Aye. Sergeant Cole said I would get a neighbour after six o'clock, but it's well gone that and he's not got back to me yet. Arse that he is," the younger man spat.

Iain knew that it wasn't right a short service probationer like Harris should be out on the beat alone, yet reluctantly sympathised with Cole who short-staffed, had twenty Govan beats to cover with less than ten constables and even less when three or four of the constables were at any one time in the office having their piece break. He inwardly smiled when he realised that with his temporary secondment to the CID, it made Cole's deployment of his shift even more difficult.

"It would make things a lot easier if the bastard was willing to come out in the panda sometimes or when he uses his own car to do his errands," Harris complained. "Expects results but won't do anything to help, but you know what he's like. Seldom if ever gets off his backside unless he's taking an hour off for himself to sneak away for something or other," he continued to grumble. "Does it nearly every bloody night too when the Inspector's not on shift. Thinks nobody notices, but can I get time off to attend my cousins wedding? Can I fuck! And he wonders why nobody likes him?"

Iain let the young cop have his rant before he said, "Anyway, the reason I'm here is to ask if Les ever spoke to you about her personal life?"

"Her personal life? What? The Ice Queen? Speak to a common probationer like me?" he grunted.

Startled and a little angry, Iain snapped, "What do you mean, the Ice Queen?"

Blushing, Harris held up his hand in apology and replied, "Sorry, Iain, that was just my nickname for her and I'm sorry she's dead. That was stupid of me to say that. Sorry," he said again then taking a breath, continued, "It's just that, well…" he paused to draw another deep breath, "Lesley was okay with you guys, but ask Shona Murtagh what she was like with us that just joined the shift. She barely said hello to me, let alone discuss her private life. She could be a real cow sometimes."

Iain found himself blinking at this surprising disclosure and asked, "You trying to tell me she was standoffish with you?"

"Standoffish? Jesus, Iain," he stared at him as though he were mad, "Lesley wouldn't give me the time of the day. The only time she ever spoke to me when I was neighboured with her and when she wanted me to do something. I could go a whole shift with her and she'd hardly speak to me. Look, ask Shona; she was the same with her too if you don't believe me. We were the new guys, not worth her attention. It was different with you older guys who have been on the shift a while. Don't tell me you never noticed it," he stared unbelievingly at Iain, "the way she kind of shunned us probationers?"

Iain didn't immediately respond, unable to get his head around what Harris was telling him. Of course it was common among a number of the older cops to treat the new probationers like apprentices, that they kept their eyes and ears open and mouths shut. It was an attitude that he himself neither approved nor condoned, but he never for one minute suspected Les of being like some of the bloody dinosaurs.

"I'm sorry, Ian, I didn't know she was like that."

Harris shrugged and replied, "The thing is, Iain, you're one of the good guys; you, big Eric, Laura and some of the others too. Lesley was very popular with all the guys on the shift and the men in particular, so I don't suppose it occurred to you that she could be a right…" he stopped, suddenly ashamed of how he was about to describe a deceased colleague.

They stood in awkward silence, before Iain said, "So, the long and short of it is that you have no idea if she was seeing anyone or if anybody had any kind of interest in her?"

"No, none at all," he shook his head. "I'm sorry, Iain. I know you and her were good mates."

Iain's radio burst into life with Hammy Hammond asking for his position.

"Drumoyne Road with Ian Harris," he replied and was told to remain there, that DI Crichton was en route and would be with him shortly.

"What, you've the DI chauffeuring for you?" Harris grinned at him.

"Aye," he returned the grin, "but that's only because I'm such a popular man."

****

The bearded, scruffily dressed man who had earlier that evening wandered through the gates at the rear yard of Merseyside Police's one storey, red bricked Walton Lane station headed for the back door.

He flashed a dog-eared warrant card and nodded to the bored officer who stood behind the charge bar, reading the sports section of that day's edition of the Liverpool Daily Post. Opening the door that led to the stairs the man wearily climbed to the upper landing, turned and made his way towards the Detective Inspector's office.

Knocking on the door, he entered and nodded to the bald man sat behind the desk before slumping down into the chair opposite.

"Detective Sergeant Webster," DI Frankie Solomon greeted him with a tight smile. "Nice to see you again," he said without any warmth, then asked, "What brings the Regional Crime Squad down to my patch?"

"I was meeting a source an hour ago, Frankie and learned something that might be of interest to you. Does the name Doughnut Stokoe mean anything to you?"

"Doughnut? That bastard," Solomon leaned forward and frowned. "What's he up to now?"

"So you do know him then?" Webster grinned.

"Oh, yeah, Doughnut's well known in these parts, Kevin. He's a right intimidating bastard, he is. Usually acts as muscle for anyone prepared to give him a wage and right now I hear he's working for a Jock by the name of Billy Madison, a dealer who lives over in the Wavertree area. Langton Road if I'm not mistaken. What's the Squad's interest in Doughnut then, lad?" he stared keenly at Webster.

Before he replied, Webster fetched the clear plastic food bag with Gina's handkerchief inside and laid it down onto the desk in front of Solomon.

"My source tells me that Doughnut has a number of plastic bags hidden under the floorboards of his mother's spare bedroom and that the bags contain a brown powder. Some of the powder had dusted off onto this hankie and I'm guessing that when it's forensically tested, it'll prove to be smack."

"How many bags are we talking about here," Solomon's eyes narrowed as he lifted the plastic bag to inspect it.

To provoke real interest, Webster decided to up Gina Poulson's lie of a couple of dozen bags and casually replied, "About forty bags I'm told."

"Bag's like these?" Solomon asked as he dangled the bag on his finger.

Give me strength, Webster thought, but kept his face straight and replied, "No, Frankie. That's a freezer food bag just to keep the sample intact. When dealers bag their gear it's usually in kilos, so we could be talking about forty kilos, here."

Solomon slowly smiled before replying, "It'll be nice to arrest Doughnut. That sod has terrorised the community around here for years, but we've never been able to convict him because people are too frightened to come forward as witnesses. He's not overly bright though, so I'm guessing the heroin belongs to his boss, Billy Madison. Thanks, Kevin," he reached for the desk phone, "I'll get a team organised right away."

"Ah, hold off for now, if you don't mind, Frankie. There's a little problem."

"Problem?"

"My boss at the RCS is having funding issues at the minute that's impacting on our operations and our access to resources, so he's looking for a headlining score to justify a bigger budget. Now, if we follow the drugs to wherever they're bound we could capture not just Doughnut and the courier, but whoever the drugs are intended for. Maybe even take down a complete syndicate, if we're lucky. However, if we raid the mother's house, all we get is the recovery of the drugs, possibly Doughnut and probably his mother. Not exactly the score that my boss might be looking for, if you get my drift, old son."

"What do you mean, *possibly* Doughnut?"

"Well," Webster drawled, "What if he puts his hands up and sells him mother down the Mersey, claims it's her house and he knows nothing about them? You've got a recovery, yes, and an old woman as the dealer? How is that headline going to read in the tomorrows Daily Post?"

Sensing a disappointment, Solomon slowly returned the phone to its cradle before asking, "Okay, I'm listening. How does your boss's budget affect me arresting Doughnut? What exactly do I get out of it?"

"Well, how does this sound to you?" Webster slowly smiled, for while making his way to Solomon, he had given it much thought. "I take this information to my boss and tell him that I have the full cooperation of DI Solomon who is willing to stand back to permit the RCS to conduct surveillance on both Doughnut and his mam's house. I also tell my boss that it was you personally who provided the intelligence and that means you get the credit that led to the arrest of Doughnut and if we get lucky, this guy Billy Madison you're talking about and the purchasers too. In short, with the RCS doing the donkey work, you don't need to provide any resources from your team here at Walton Lane, but will still get credit for being involved. And let's face it, Frankie, my boss would be bound to bring a good result to the attention of your Chief and it wouldn't do your promotion chances any harm, would it?"

Solomon's eyes narrowed as he considered Webster's proposal, before he asked, "If I'm to be credited with providing the information, then who exactly *is* your source, Kevin?"

Webster pursed his lips and extending his hands wide, said, "Maybe if you're asked and I doubt that you will be, you would consider explaining that for source protection you are unable to divulge that information?"

Solomon didn't respond as his mind rapidly worked overtime. It would be quite a coup for him personally to be recognised and credited by his management for providing the information that led to the arrest of Stokoe and in particular, that Scotch git Billy Madison. He took a deep breath and also realised with some reluctance that Webster was correct. In a complete reversal of the old saying, on this occasion and risky though it might be, two birds in the bush rather than just one in the hand would be more productive if an RCS surveillance rolled up a drug syndicate and wouldn't impact on his sub-Divisional budget either, particularly with the current restraint on overtime. As far as he could see, he slowly smiled, it was a win win situation.

He stared suspiciously at Webster before asking, "What I don't understand is why you come to me, Kevin, instead of taking this information directly to your boss at the RCS. I mean, you could quite easily have cut out us local guys, made this an RCS issue with no involvement by Merseyside; so, why didn't you?"

"Easily answered, Frankie. Politics. We both know the grief my boss gets if we fail to inform the local Force that we're running an Op on their patch. Coming to you and getting you on board negates that problem, that's all it is," he opened his hands wide and smiled.

"Is that all?" asked Solomon in the sure knowledge that it wasn't, that Webster was holding back on something.

Webster stared at him then taking a breath, continued, "Right, for your ears only, Frankie, and I mean it, okay? The source is Gina Poulson, Doughnut's mothers pal. I've been running her for a while now…"

"Poulson!" Solomon sat forward. "The fucking moneylender! She's your source? Have you any idea, Kevin, how much damage that woman has caused? Jesus! Half the patients at the city's casualty department are there because they can't keep up their payments and she uses Stokoe to deal out punishment! That and not one of them will come forward and give us a statement because they're too fucking terrified of what Stokoe will do to them and their families!"

Webster didn't immediately respond until Solomon asked, "What the *fuck* did you promise her for this info?"

Almost with reluctance, he replied, "I told her that if she continues to tout to me, you guys will back off from any complaints, at least for the next few months anyway. After that," he shrugged, "I'll be gone and as far as I'm concerned, she's open game."

Solomon shook his head then staring suspiciously at Webster, asked him, "What do you mean you'll be gone and what exactly do *you* get out of this, Kevin? You haven't answered my question."

"Me?" he smiled and cocking his head as though having an afterthought, replied, "My five-year secondment to the RCS is almost up, in nine weeks to be exact, but there's a Detective Inspector position becoming available soon in the the Crime Squad's Number Seven District, so by setting up this operation and if it goes the way I hope it does I could be in line for another five years as the DI."

Solomon didn't like the thought he was being used to further Webster's personal ambition, but the lure of getting Doughnut Stokoe and possibly Billy Madison off his patch was too tempting. That and the likelihood it might do his own career no harm and so quickly made his decision.

"Okay, we'll do it your way, but only if we keep this to ourselves, Kevin. If my bosses get wind of this deal…"

Webster hurriedly interrupted with, "Stand on me, Frankie. Just the two of us," he nodded.

Solomon paused, then said, "Okay, leave the bag," he nodded to it, "and I'll get it rushed to the headquarters Forensic laboratory at Canning Place. If it *is* heroin as you suspect, leave me your number and I'll phone you right away and we'll get the ball rolling."

Pushing himself to his feet, Webster passed Solomon a business card with his details and said, "I'll head off to speak with my boss and let him know it's time critical, see if I can persuade him to get a team together to latch onto Doughnut and his dear old Ma."

"What about Madison? Will you be watching him too?"

Webster pursed his lips and shaking his head, said, "No," he pursed his lips, "if Doughnut is storing the heroin then it's likely that your man Madison will conduct his business by phone. That being the case it's unlikely we'll know who the buyer is unless, as I said, we do a follow on Doughnut or whoever he decides to send with the gear to wherever it's bound for. Besides, because of the cuts we really don't have that many resources for a joint surveillance."

With a wave of his hand, Webster said, "I'll be in touch," and was gone just as a thoughtful Solomon called one of his detectives to his office to courier the small plastic bag to the lab.

****

The first thing Janie Wallace noticed when she drew up outside her house was that Paul's car wasn't parked there. Curiously, though disappointed that she wasn't immediately going to have the opportunity to confront him, she experienced a sense of relief that she could at least get into the house and get herself settled and readied for the forthcoming confrontation, have her argument prepared and her outrage waiting for him coming home.

Yes, she decided with a nod, I'll give it to the bastard when he gets here.

Closing the front door behind her, she flicked a strand of loose hair behind her left ear and just in case he was already at home, cautiously called out, "Paul?" but as she expected there was no response.

Dumping her car keys and handbag on the hall table, she went into the kitchen to boil the kettle and eyes narrowing, snatched at the note on the table.

Janie, it began, *I'm so sorry that you had to find out from the papers that things aren't working out between us. I know you'll be thinking I'm a right shit, but maybe it's better this way. I don't feel there is any need to explain anything because I know that you'll probably feel the same way, that when I move to England you had no intention of coming with me. I can't think of a reason why you would want to speak to me again, but if you do I'm staying at the Grosvenor on Great Western Road. Paul*

She closed her eyes, her teeth grinding and shuddered with rage.

Then a thought occurred to her.

Rushing upstairs she entered their bedroom to find the door of the wardrobe lying ajar and where his clothes hung there was now a row of empty hangers. Pulling open the bottom two drawers of the dresser, she saw that they too were empty.

He had gone and it seemed, as he had written, for good.

She sank down onto the bed, the note still clutched in her hand and staring at it, angrily tore it into a dozen pieces that she scattered on the floor.

You cowardly bastard! she thought and dropped her face into her hands.

****

The plainclothes officer in the passenger seat startled at the loud rapping noise on her window. Turning, she saw a small, fat and bald-headed man with piglet eyes grinning at her who indicated she should wind down the window.

"Can I help you?" she snapped at him.

"Evening, officer," he sneered at her. "Just wondering if you could tell me what time it is?"

"Time you fucked off, ya baldy wee shite," she snarled at him.

"Temper, temper," he calmly replied before turning to the tall, red-headed man beside him and saying, "No fucking manners, these filthy bastards, have they? Think I should complain?"

The redhead man took the smaller man by the arm and pulling him away from the door of the car, replied, "Leave it, Marty. Come on tae fuck out of it."

Marty Boyle stared at the policewoman and then quite deliberately, hawked and spat on the pavement beside the car. Turning away to follow Seamus O'Brien towards Charlie Gallagher's close, he glanced back at the car and mockingly grinned at the two officers.

Minutes later Gallagher answered the knock on his door and beckoned both men inside.

"Do you know you've got the CID sitting in a motor outside the close?" O'Brien asked him.

Gallagher paled and shaking his head, replied, "No, I didn't, but I can guess why."

Signalling they follow him, he led O'Brien and Boyle through to the front room where telling them to sit down, he walked to the bay window and furtively glanced out from behind the curtain.

"An old dark coloured Ford Escort?" he asked.

"That's the one," O'Brien confirmed. "It's got the extra aerial on the roof at the back. A dead giveaway."

"Aye, I see it. Who's in the car?"

"A guy and a bird in the passenger seat, but I don't think they're the CID," O'Brien screwed his face in thought.

"They're dressed more like plainers. And this stupid bastard," he added as he nodded at the grinning Boyle, "banged on the window and noised them up."

"So what," Boyle retaliated, "It wasn't as if we're doing anything wrong, were we?"

"Anyway, what's the problem, boss? Why are we here?" O'Brien asked.

"Maybe it's better if I show you," Gallagher replied and indicated they follow him through to the bedroom.

They stared at the huddle on the floor then O'Brien instinctively shrunk away when Gallagher pulled back the quilt cover.

"Fucking hell," Boyle muttered. "Look at the state of her face. Is that…?"

"Aye," Gallagher sighed as he pulled the quilt cover back over the body, "it's Paula. Bitch was grassing on us to the polis."

It had been with sudden intuition Gallagher decided that 'he' become 'us' with the thought that if both O'Brien and Boyle believed they were also being informed on by Paula, they would undoubtedly agree that she needed to be silenced.

"She's a right mess and no mistake," shuddered O'Brien in a hushed voice then nodding in agreement, Boyle, asked, "So, what's the plan then?"

"Well, the plan was to take her down and shove her in the boot of my car and dump her someone well away from here, but with those two sitting in the motor downstairs…" his voice tailed off as he reconsidered his options.

Boyle's brow furrowed as he said, "Why not stick a chamois cloth in her hand and shove her out of the kitchen window down to the back court? Then you can call an ambulance and say she was washing the window and fell out."

Gallagher stared expressionlessly at him then turning to O'Brien, said, "So, any ideas? I mean, any idea that *isn't* fucking straight out of a comic book?"

O'Brien inhaled then slowly exhaling as he thought, replied, "I think your first idea is the best, Charlie. I don't see they muppets downstairs in the motor being there all night. We wait them out then take her down to the back court and carry her through to…" he frowned. "What's that street behind you?"

"Skipness Drive," Gallagher replied as the plan dawned on him and smiled. "Yeah, I like it. Whose car did you use to get here?"

"Marty's motor, that old rusty Fiat he's got," O'Brien smiled at the small man's darkening face, "and the boot's big enough to take her. We can pretend we're leaving then drive Marty's car round to Skipness Drive and park there. After that we come back up here to the flat and then we carry Paula down and go through the back courts so even if the polis are watching the close entrance, they'll not see us in the dark going out the back."

"I like it," Gallagher repeated then indicating they return to the front room, added, "Let me get you boys a drink and we'll discuss where we're going to get rid of her and while we're at it, I've a call to make to an old pal who owes me a favour."
****

Irene Crichton tossed the car keys to Iain Meikle and said, "You drive. How many of your shift have you still to speak with?"

He shook his head and said, "Young Ian was the last and unfortunately, it was all negative. None of them knew anything about anyone having an interest in Les, though…" he hesitated, but his hesitation wasn't lost on her so she asked, "What?"

"I feel I'm kind of betraying Les when I tell you about this, but it has to be said. I learned something tonight about her, something that I didn't know and wouldn't have believed, but the more I think about it the more I now think it *is* true."

He told her of Ian Harris's admittance that he had thought of Lesley Rudd as the Ice Queen, of her arrogant attitude and snobbishness towards the junior members of the shift.

"And you never suspected that she was anything like that?"

"No, I didn't," he shrugged, then said, "I suppose because she was always friendly to me it kind of blinded me to how she was with the younger guys like Ian and Shona. Right," he sighed, "where are we going from here?"

"Turn eastwards onto Paisley Road West. I'll give you a shout when to stop," she replied before continuing, "Let me tell you something about men *and* women, Mister Meikle. Ninety-nine per cent of us look at a woman and see a pretty face, a plain face, a shapely figure, a fat lady. So few of us ever really get to know someone unless we're close to them or in a relationship with them. I'll bet you feel as if somehow you've been let down, that you think you should have known Lesley a lot better than you did. I mean, you didn't know she had a twin, you said; isn't that right?"

He nodded.

"Now, as for *really* knowing someone, take for example what happened this morning to young Janie Wallace. I bet she thought she was in love with that footballer, what's-his-name, then he sees a blonde bimbo wearing skimpy clothes and his relationship with Janie goes out the window. Rudely put, but as they say, a standing cock has no conscience. So, the guy she's living with and *thinks* she knows inside out does that to her. Oh, and I'm not criticising Janie, here. Look what happened to me with that bastard I was married to for eight years. Okay," she sharply called out, "stop here, between they two cars," and pointed at a space.

Reverse parking into the space, Iain switched off the engine then turned to stare at her. "So, what you're suggesting is that us guys on the shift couldn't see past Les's good looks, that we ignored her personality?"

"Something like that and not just you men, of course. Women tend to do that with other women, too. We see a pretty face and tell ourselves that the individual must have a nice personality to go with the face, but Iain," she slowly shook her head as though with an unspoken sorrow, "how wrong we all are and more often than we think."

"Well," he admitted, "I certainly got it wrong with Les on that issue. Not of course that she was bad. No, I liked her and she was good at her job, but it never occurred to me that she could treat some of her colleagues like that. In fact," he again shook his head, "when I think of what young Ian told me I realise now it's a form of bullying and whether or not it's Les or someone else who is acting like that, I would *never* condone it," he said with some feeling.

He glanced about him at the tenement building and the shops and curiosity in his voice, asked, "What are we doing here?"

"Oh, I should have told you," she smiled at him and pointing to a Indian restaurant, said, "I'm taking you to dinner."

He stared openly with surprise and dully repeated, "You're taking me to dinner?"

"Yes," she firmly nodded. "I know it's usually the man who invites the woman to dinner, Iain, but I like you. Have done for quite a while in fact," she shrugged, "so I decided tonight there was no reason why I shouldn't tell you."

Her chest felt tight at her open admission and he could not have known how hard it was for her to admit it as gazing keenly at him, she asked, "Are you okay with that?"

"Eh, a little taken aback to be honest," he found himself blushing, something he couldn't recall having done for a very long time, but then he smiled and added, "But yes, Irene. I'm okay with that."

****

With the body now wrapped in half a dozen black plastic bin bags, tied with string and being awkwardly carried by Charlie Gallagher and Seamus O'Brien, the two men followed Marty Boyle down the tenement stairs to the rear exit that led onto the darkness of the back court. The only heart stopping moment had come when Boyle, a flight of stairs ahead of them to check no one was coming up the stairs, encountered an elderly neighbour on the first landing who opened her door to permit entry to her mewing cat.

"What the fuck you looking at!" he had snarled at the old woman who in fright, closed her door so quickly she almost caught the cat's tail.

Sniggering with relief, Boyle loudly whispered, "Right, we're clear."

Though believing their regular attendance at their gym made both Gallagher and O'Brien fit and strong, the two men were soon breathing heavily as they struggled with the plastic wrapped body. It was when they were about to exit the close into the rear back court that O'Brien realised the plastic bag that had been wrapped around Paula Menzies head had worked itself loose and his hands were now soiled with her blood. Squealing in fright, he shrank back and dropped his end of the load causing Gallagher to stumble and fall. Glancing in rage back at O'Brien, he saw the red haired man frantically wiping his hands on his jeans to rub off the blood.

"Ya fucking nancy boy!" he sneered at O'Brien. "Pick her up!"

Minutes later, the coast cleared by Boyle, they exited onto Skipness Drive and at last dumped Paula's body into the empty boot.

"Right," wheezed Gallagher, "let's get to fuck out of here!"

CHAPTER FIFTEEN

Engrossed in the antics of the two naked women in the porno video, Doughnut Stokoe killed the sound on the television and reaching for the phone on the side table, discovered it was Billy Madison.

"How's it hanging, big fella?" Madison asked.

"Same old, same old," was the bored reply.

"Doughnut, I want you to be certain that you're happy to make the delivery."

"No problem, Billy," he replied, his eyes glued to the television and wishing Madison fucked off for the two women were now getting to the interesting part, but Madison continued with,

"Listen, big man. I want this kept tight. Too many prying eyes and loose tongues wagging and I can't afford for this to go bad. I'm in deep shit if anything happens to the…you know? I got it on tick so we can't afford to let anything go wrong or it's my balls in the noose."

"What do you mean, deep shit? With who?" Madison now had his full attention.

"The London team that I got it from. You know, that big darkie guy?"

"Fuck, Billy!" he sniggered, "Don't tell me you did business with the Jamaican!"

"Aye," Madison warily retorted, "It seemed like a good idea at the time. Anyway like I asked; is it still safe?"

Stokoe decided not to mention the incident with his mother and her pal Gina and replied, "It's safe. When do you want it moved?"

"I've been calling the buyer all night, but there's no reply so I can only think he's out bevying somewhere. Anyway," he sighed. "I'll give him a phone in the morning and by that time we should have a better idea when it can go north."

"North? You mean Manchester? Leeds?"

"No, the *real* north. Glasgow."

"Fuck me, Billy," for never the sharpest tool in the box, Stokoe was confused. He'd never visited Scotland and had no idea where Glasgow was. "How long will it take me to get there on the train?"

He listened to Madison chuckling, who then replied, "Shouldn't take any more than three and a bit hours, big man if you get a train through to the Central Station in Glasgow."

"I won't have to stay there overnight or anything, will I?"

"Not if you get an early train, you won't. Don't worry about it, Doughnut. It's an easy trip

Stokoe's brow furrowed. He didn't like this, didn't like it at all. In fact, Stokoe didn't like leaving his comfort zone that was his neighbourhood, let alone his city and as far as he knew, Scotland was a foreign country. He was about to ask if he'd need a passport, but then Madison continued, "Listen, Doughnut, the money we'll make on this deal will sort us out for quite a while and with your share of the profit you'll be able to get yourself a bird to spend your money on, eh? Maybe a good looker, eh?"

That perked Stokoe up and grinning, he decided maybe after all the risk *was* worth taking.

"Okay," he slowly replied. "You'll let me know when and where?"

"Soon as I hear from the buyer, aye," Madison confirmed before ending the call.

Replacing the phone onto the table, Stokoe turned as his mother entered the room and in a low voice, said, "Do you want a cuppa before I go to my bed, son?"

Turning, he stared at her, focusing on her black eye and felt almost regretful about hurting her, but inwardly sighed; lessons had to be learned. Shaking his head, he replied, "No, mam. You just go to your bed, love. I'll see to myself if I need anything."

When the door closed behind her, he smiled at the thought of the money he would earn and the women he could buy, then turned the sound on the TV back up to loud.

****

Their meal over, Irene Crichton leaned onto her forearms and staring across the table at him, said, "Tell me about yourself, Iain."

"What's there to tell?" he shrugged. "You know I'm divorced. I've nobody in my life…" he paused and smiled, "Well, I didn't have anybody in my life, but if you're seriously thinking about us two getting together that might not be quite true."

Then she surprised him by asking, "So, when was the last time you *had* a relationship with a woman?"

His eyes squinted and he sucked at his lower lip as he thought before replying, "Let me see. I did a week in Malaga two, no three years ago and there was a woman in the hotel. Joyce, that was her name. Let's just say that during the holiday we spent a pleasant few days together. What I suppose you could call a holiday romance."

"You didn't keep in touch?"

"I might have considered it," he wryly smiled as he stirred his coffee, "but to be honest, Irene, I got the impression that though like me she was on holiday alone, there might have been someone at home. She was English and she didn't really speak much about herself other than to tell me she worked in a bank and came from somewhere in the London area, or that's what she said. So no, I think I got the impression right away that staying in touch wasn't on the cards. And what about you? I know you're divorced too. Nobody since?"

"What, me?" she almost scoffed, then shaking her head, continued, "Let's just say after that last disaster married to Teflon Bill, I have trust issues."

"Teflon Bill?"

"Aye," she smiled. "That was my pet name for him. Treated every woman like a challenge and thought whatever shenanigans he got up to would never stick to him and get back to me," she sighed before adding, "How wrong he was."

His brow furrowed when he asked, "So, what made you decide to, ah, invite me to dinner?"

She pursed her lips before replying, "I like you, Iain. Have done for some time. If what I'm seeing is true, you're a very decent man and seem to be honest too. I don't mean honest in that you're not…"

"I think I know what you mean," he interrupted with a smile, then shrugged. "Anyway, I've no reason not to be honest. I find that lies and deceit always seem to come around and bite you in the arse, so it's easier being truthful with people. Besides, a liar needs a good memory and I can hardly recall what I had for dinner last night."

"Do you mind that I invited you here tonight?" she waved a hand around her.

"Actually, had I known you had an interest in me, I'd like to have been the one who invited you, but…well…" he paused and grimaced. "You have this kind of reputation that you're weren't really interested in seeing a man." He quickly raised his hands and waving them, explained, "Not that I'm unhappy we're here having dinner, not at all. It's just, I suppose, you're an attractive woman, Irene, and doing well in your career. I didn't think you'd be interested in someone like me."

"Someone like you?"

"Aye, well," he pulled a face, "I'm not exactly a highflyer in the polis. I'm just a cop seeing out the remainder of his career walking the beat and happy with what I'm doing. I'm not ambitious or keen to progress through the ranks or anything…"

"And what makes you think that matters to me?" she suddenly reached forward and took his hand in hers. "Tell me you don't think I'm the sort of woman who worries about things like that, Iain. I'm not your ex-wife and nothing like her, believe me," she vigorously shook her head.

Their fingers entwined, he tightened his grip on hers and quietly said, "You do realise that it won't do your reputation any good if you do want to continue to see me? People will gossip and, well, it's just that I don't want anyone thinking anything bad about you."

She smiled happily and replied, "See? One date, Iain, and already you're worrying about me. I knew I did the right thing, asking you out."

****

Marty Boyle had a tendency to drive fast, but not tonight, for the last thing he wanted was to be stopped by the Traffic beasties carrying a body in the boot of his car.

"Where are we going?" Seamus O'Brien leaned forward to ask from the rear seat.

Pointing through the front windscreen, Charlie Gallagher replied, "Drive down towards Port Glasgow, wee man. When you get to the roundabout before you go into Port Glasgow, there's a wee park and a pier off to the right hand side. It's usually quiet at this time of the night. Maybe we'll find a winching couple in their car, but there's plenty of wooded area there. We'll get her out there and while I think about it," he turned to stare at Boyle, "do you still carry that hatchet in the boot of the car?"

In the back, O'Brien felt his blood run cold for he guessed where this was going. Boyle, slower on the uptake, nodded and replied, "Aye, I do. Why?"

"You'll find out," Gallagher smirked, but said no more.

Boyle turned quickly to glance at him before asking, "This place we're going to, boss. If it's near the water and if we dump her, won't she float back up again? I mean, the polis will eventually find her, won't they? And if they find her and identify her, won't they come looking for you? I mean, don't they know she lived with you?"

Gallagher evilly grinned at him and asked, "Who said anything about dumping her body?"

"What, you're not going to just leave her there? What if someone finds her?"

As though explaining to a child, Gallagher said, "No, wee man, we're not just leaving her there. It's nice and quiet there and nobody around to see us when we cut her up, you fucking dolt. Once we do that, we're going to visit that friend of mine who owes me a favour, the one I phoned and who owns a pig farm over in Lochwinnoch."

Boyle was confused and didn't understand why at that time of the night they were going to visit a pig farm, but rather than endure further sarcasm, decided to keep his mouth shut.

In the rear seat, O'Brien felt sick at what he guessed was to come.

****

Lying in bed, Janie Wallace had given up forcing herself to try and sleep and rising, slipped on a dressing gown and headed downstairs.

In the kitchen, she fetched a small pot from the cupboard and filled it with a mugful of milk then set it to boil.

She had given up cigarettes years before, but suddenly found she craved the comfort of a fag and regretted that she had none. Standing waiting for the milk to heat up, she thought again of Paul's note, that he intended staying at the Grosvenor Hotel and her eyes narrowed. She guessed that he knew her pride wouldn't permit her to go running after him and she wondered; was he really booked in to the Grosvenor or was that another of his lies? Was he really staying elsewhere, perhaps with the blonde photographed with him in the newspaper?

With a start she realised what she was doing. She was torturing herself with his betrayal.

Bastard! she viciously thought, her eyes closed tightly together and her fists clenched.

She took a deep breath then opening her eyes, saw to her dismay the milk had boiled over the rim of the pot and was cascading down onto the cooker. Reaching with her right hand for the pot to lift it from the gas ring, she jerked back when she touched the metal handle and instinctively shrieked, her hand knocking the pot's handle and causing it to fall to the floor, the milk cascading everywhere.

Rushing to the sink, she shoved her reddening hand under the cold water tap and left it there for almost five minutes to cool. With a sigh of relief, she saw that other than a small blister on the pam of her hand, her quick reaction had prevented any real damage.

Turning, she glanced down at the mess on the floor and muttered, "Bugger."

A sudden tiredness overtook her and reckoning that she'd had enough excitement for one night, decided to clean up the mess in the morning and went back to bed.
****

Pacing the floor of his lounge, Billy Madison cursed loudly at the phone in his hand, but wondered where the hell Charlie Gallagher had got to.

"Leave it for now, our Billy, and come to bed," his wife Sheila yawned.

"I can't leave it," he hissed through clenched teeth. "I've the H ready to go north and that big black bastard in London is waiting on his payment. If I don't come up with the cash by the weekend, there's a penalty and that fucking penalty is him sending somebody to do my legs," he wailed.

Leaning against the door jamb, Sheila yawned again and arms folded, soothingly replied, "Well, it's gone two in the morning so if you want to worry yourself half to death, do it without me and do it quietly because I'm going to me bed."

With that she turned and closed the door behind her.

Madison slumped down onto the couch and leaning forward, dropped his head into his hands.

Sheila had warned him about doing business with the Jamaican, with the reputation the big man had. Madison knew of at least one Liverpool dealer who had crossed the Londoner and if the rumours were true, he was last seen taking a trip down the Mersey, though not on a boat but with a large concrete block chained to his feet. No matter whether or not the rumours were true, the dealer had never been seen or heard from again.

His stomach rumbled and swallowing rapidly, he realised that his nerves were getting the better of him and if his nerves were acting up it usually resulted in his bowels exploding.

Clenching his teeth and knees together, he rose from the couch and hurriedly made his way to the downstairs toilet.
****

In the rear seat, Seamus O'Brien wound down the window and fighting the nausea, gasped as the cold night air filled the car that was preferable and more tolerable than the sticky, sweet smell of dried blood that clung to their clothes.

In the front, he listened to Gallagher directing Boyle while they both giggled like weans.

"Did you see the way her head bounced away?" laughed Gallagher.

"I thought I was going to puke," Boyle sniggered.

Turning in his seat, Gallagher stared at O'Brien for a few seconds before asking, "You all right there, Seamus? Not going to throw up again, are you?"

The question sent Boyle into another fit of the giggles.

O'Brien was grateful for the darkness in the car for he could feel his face flushed and promised himself, when he and the wee man were on their own, the bastard was getting a right good slapping.

"No, I'm fine boss," he forced a smile and fighting the sarcasm that he wanted to really scream at them both, instead replied, "It's the first time I've ever seen anybody dismembered, know what I mean?"

"Dismembered. Oooh, get him and his fancy words," Gallagher teased in a shrill voice.

Taking a breath, he continued in his own growl, "Well, that aside, the bitch won't be telling anybody and not least the polis about us, eh boys?"

"Fucking right," Boyle agreed while O'Brien in the back seat, nodded before asking, "What about…" he paused, his mouth dry, then licking his lips, said, "What about her body parts. Should we not just have slung them into the water? Wouldn't that have been the best thing to do, boss?"

"How do you mean?" Gallagher stared beady eyed at him.

"Well," he shifted nervously in his seat, "I just thought carrying her bits in the plastic bags in the boot…"

"And that's why we're visiting a pig farm, you idiot," Gallagher lightly cuffed Boyle on the back of the head. "Did you not know that pigs will eat almost any-fucking-thing?"

In the darkness at the back of the car, O'Brien swallowed with difficulty and mentally vowed that never again would he eat bacon or pork sausages.

CHAPTER SIXTEEN

Showered, shaved and dressed, DCI Colin Morton made his way downstairs to find his wife Alice had prepared breakfast and was waiting for him to join her at the kitchen table.

"What kind of day do you expect to have, dear?" she asked as she poured the tea.

"A bad one," he gloomily replied. "I've the young policewoman Lesley Rudd's PM this morning, so likely there were will be snot and tears from everyone concerned. Not that I'm unsympathetic," he hastily added, "but these things are best dealt with without emotion."

She stared sombrely at him across the table and reaching for his hand, said, "Don't kid yourself, Colin Morton. You pretend that the post mortem of a young lassie, a colleague if you will, won't affect you, that you're only doing your job, but I know you too well. You'll have that stiff upper lip of yours and get through it and no doubt be very professional about the whole thing, but rest assured; there will be a dram waiting for you when you get home this evening."

He smiled without humour and nodding, replied, "Well, it's a dram of my favourite, I'll be looking forward to it, sweetheart."
****

Across the city, Janie Wallace awoke surprised that after all, she had managed to get a couple of hours sleep. Instinctively, she reached across the bed to Paul's side, but then quickly withdrew her hand when she remembered that he wasn't there nor ever would be again.

Of that she was damned certain.

Yawning widely, she stretched then wearily rose from her bed and headed for the bathroom.

Fifteen minutes later and refreshed, she returned to the bedroom and tying back her red hair into a tight ponytail slipped on a black coloured sleeveless and fitted knee length dress and a lemon coloured jacket.

Turning back and forth to check herself in the mirror, she nodded with satisfaction and headed downstairs to grab some breakfast before heading to work.

It was while she was driving down Broomloan Road towards Orkney Street that she guiltily smiled for though she could not admit it to anyone but herself, she looked forward to working that day with Peter Rossi.

****

Dressed in the newer of his two suits, Iain Meikle decided that as the weather had taken a turn for the better he would leave his eight years old red coloured Vauxhall Viva in the driveway and walk the two and a half miles from his house in Tealing Avenue to the office in Orkney Street. Setting off with his overcoat across his arm, his first thoughts were of the previous evening and the surprise revelation that Irene Crichton had a romantic interest in him.

Unconsciously smiling, he nodded to a passing neighbour then turning onto Paisley Road West, wondered just how long she'd had this interest for never in a million years had it occurred to him that Irene would even give him a second look. As for him, he involuntarily nodded, he had to admit that she was quite a catch for any man; smart and not bad looking either, he continued to nod.

He had enjoyed their dinner together and even after their meal had finished they had sat for almost an hour talking about everything and nothing until the pokerfaced waiter caught Iain's eye and subtly pointed to his wristwatch.

He inwardly smiled when he recalled that he had tried to insist he paid for the meal only to be reminded that not only was it she who had invited him to dinner but she outranked him, too, then jokingly suggested that on their next date he pay for their foreign holiday together.

But *was* she joking?

He couldn't quite decide and let the comment slip by.

In the cold outside the restaurant he courteously helped her put on her coat and drew the comment, "See? I always knew you were very much the gentleman," then driven them both back to the office. Letting her out at the front door, he frowned when he asked, "You're not going up to the office at this hour?"

"No," she had smiled through the open passenger door, before replying, "I'll let you hang up the keys to the car and see you in the morning."

It was as she turned and before he could react, she had blown him a kiss.

Before he realised it he was turning from Helen Street into Edmiston Drive and was just over five minutes' brisk walk from the office when a newish bright red coloured 340 Series Volvo drew alongside him.

Bending down, he was surprised to see the driver was Irene, who beckoned him into the passenger seat. When the door closed, she said as she pulled away from the kerb, "Morning, Iain. Sleep well?"

"Fairly well, yes," he replied, then brow furrowing, added, "Might not be a good idea to let people see me coming out of your car so early in the morning, Irene. Like I told you, you've got to think about your reputation."

"Oh, bugger what people think. As long as you don't mind us being seen together," then thoughtfully asked him, "Do you?"

"No, of course not," he smiled.

"Well, then," her heart racing, she took a breath and continued, "maybe we should make a habit of it, you and me arriving together at work. What do you think?"

He turned in his seat to stare at her then slowly nodding, replied, "I'd like that, yes."

He could not know how relieved she was that he had so swiftly responded and continuing to smile, she said, "Good. Then when we're done tonight, Mister Meikle, what say you that I bring a bottle of hooch to your place and you can make me dinner?"

Once again he stared at her before replying, "Tatties, mince and turnip do you?"

"God, Iain," she grinned, "you really know how to impress a woman."

****

When at four-thirty that morning Marty Boyle dropped him off at his Georgian flat in Buccleuch Street in the city's Garnethill area, Seamus O'Brien had showered twice and used almost a full can of BRUT aerosol spray before he was satisfied that the stink of dried blood and pig manure had disappeared from his skin. All his clothes and his training shoes had gone straight into the washing machine at the hottest cycle, yet he'd already decided once they were washed they were for the bin.

In bed beside his current girlfriend, he had tossed and turned so often the young woman bitterly complained, causing him to angrily wrestle her from the bed by her wrist and her hair and yelling that if she didn't like it, she could use the fucking couch in the front room!

He knew though that his anger was not really directed at her, but to Charlie Gallagher and his poisonous sidekick, Marty Boyle.

When the girl had gone weeping from the room he had thrown the sheets back onto the bed, yet still sleep eluded him for he could not erase the memory of the previous night, of what the two of them had done to the body of Paula Menzies.

It was just after eight o'clock he heard the front door loudly slam and realised his girlfriend had gone to work, though whether or not she would return to the flat was anybody's guess and surprised himself by thinking he couldn't give a damn if she did or not.

Lying there with an arm carelessly thrown across his face, his thoughts kept wandering back to their actions the night before at the waters edge; Gallagher wielding the hatchet and Boyle chortling and dancing about like some demonic, psychotic dwarf as he stuffed the body parts into the plastic bags.

By his own admittance, O'Brien was no angel and had done some bad things in his life. He'd hurt people, men and women, young and old, some on the orders of Charlie and because of business and some simply for pleasure, but he had never before been involved in anything like this.

What worried him now was that at some point in the future, Charlie Gallagher would consider what he had done and realise that there were two witnesses to the murder of Paula and the desecration of her body, for that's what it was.

A desecration.

O'Brien had been brought up by strict Catholic parents, though as a young teenager he had given up on the religion. However, those early years of indoctrination had left their mark on his consciousness and whether he realised it or not, what Charlie did to Paula had left its imprint in his mind.

But that wasn't the problem or what really worried him.

The real problem was when Charlie did recognise that both he and Boyle were the only two witnesses to the murder and disposal of Paula's body; witnesses who, if the polis ever found out, could put the big man away for a very long time.

O'Brien was increasingly concerned about Charlie's behaviour and he now believed that the big man was losing it, that he was becoming increasingly erratic. If Charlie, ever considered that he and Boyle might be a threat to him, that they could give him up to the polis…he shivered for he now knew realised that he had one person to look out for; himself.

He glanced at his wristwatch and saw that it was almost eight-thirty.

Cursing loudly, he wearily gave in and rose from the bed.

In the kitchen he fetched out the wet clothing and hung it to dry on the ceiling pulley.

Making himself a coffee, his mind kept revisiting the scene at the pig farm; Charlie Gallagher and Marty Boyle, their laughter and clowning as the pigs noisily swarmed round the body parts.

With a shudder, he threw the coffee into the sink and opening the larder, reached for the bottle of whisky.
****

Unlike their fellow gangster, both Gallagher and Boyle had no problem getting to sleep in the early hours of the morning. Twenty minutes after being dropped off in Skipness Drive, Gallagher peeked from behind his front room curtain and saw that the CID car with the two officers seemed to have departed from the front of his close. Minutes later, he was showered, dried and changing the sheets on the bed he had both shared with then murdered Paula Menzies.

His head had barely touched the pillow when he was fast asleep.

It was almost forty minutes later that Marty Boyle, after dropping off O'Brien, returned home to his fourteenth floor flat in the multi-storey building in the Sighthill area of the city.

Unlike his two pals, Boyle, who lived alone, simply stripped off his clothes and dumped them on the bedroom floor before climbing into his bed.

Lying on his back, he sniggered at the memory of what he and the others had done.

The more he thought of it, the more excited he became then closing his eyes tightly to visualise the scene again, reached a hand under the soiled sheets and began to rapidly stroke at his groin.
****

"Come in," Colin Morton called out, but the door was already opening to admit Irene Crichton who was dressed in a light coloured blouse and maroon coloured knee length pencil skirt with matching maroon coloured high heels and with her jet black hair curling down to her shoulders.

"Morning," he greeted her, then his eyes narrowed and his brow furrowed, for it was evident that she had made an effort that morning and not just with her dress, but with make-up too. He smiled and said, "My, but you're a picture this morning, DI Crichton. Got a man in your life?"

It was meant as a joke, but to his surprise she grinned and teasingly replied, "Maybe, well, yes, actually. I think so."

He stared at her with open curiosity before she added. "We had a first date last night, dinner together," she explained, "and it seemed to go well."

"Okay, I'll not ask, but no doubt I'll hear in time," he returned her grin, then business-like, handed her a file as he added, "This arrived for you from SCRO. Paula Menzies record."

Taking the file she sat down and opening the file, asked, "How did the surveillance get on last night?"

"No trace of her leaving the close," he sighed. "in fact, I had a note on my desk from the shift planers who said that he was visited by two males earlier in the evening. They didn't recognise them, but left descriptions and the registration number of the car the males arrived in. They did a PNC check and the car is registered to a Martin Boyle and from the description of the other male, tall with red hair, it sounds like Seamus O'Brien, Gallagher's two henchmen."

He paused and smiled when he continued, "The plainers said the smaller of the two, who fits the description of Boyle, noised them up so left no doubt in Gallagher's mind we were watching his close. Anyway, O'Brien and Boyle, if it was them and I have no reason to doubt it, left after about twenty minutes. There was no sign of Menzies or Gallagher leaving the close and the plainers stood down at…" he glanced at the note on his desk, "two-thirty this morning."

"Were the lights still on in the flat at that time?"

He pursed his lips and replied, "The note didn't say. Why do you ask?"

She shrugged before replying, "Maybe I'm being a bit paranoid, Colin, but if I know the polis are watching the entrance to my close and I wanted to go anywhere, I'd skip round the back court and get out that way."

"Well, if they did," he sighed and sat back in his chair, "we'll not know now."

"Are you ready for the morning briefing?"

"Give me a couple of minutes," he replied.

"If you don't mind, I'll remain here with you and have a look through this file, see if there's anything in it that might indicate why Paula wanted to speak with Lesley Rudd. On that point, have you decided who will accompany you to the PM?"

"I'd like you to come, if you don't mind. I believe the presence of a ranking female officer will provide some dignity to the procedure and we'll take young Sharon McGuire to handle the productions from the PM."

"Okay," she nodded, "I'll make sure I'm available too."

While he glanced through his briefing notes Irene perused the file then gave a start.

"What?" he asked.

She grimly smiled at him before replying, "I have an idea why Paula Menzies was keen to speak with Rudd.

****

Seated at a desk in the general office, Janie Wallace stared wide-eyed at Iain Meikle and said, "I didn't know you actually owned a suit, you old bugger."

"Well, Miss Smart-arse," he retorted, "I *actually* own two suits and before you start, they both fit."

She grinned and replied, "For what it's worth, Iain, you look very smart. For an old guy, I mean."

"I'm not old," he protested with his own grin, "I'm experienced and that, young lady , is something that only comes with age as undoubtedly you will find out with the passing of the years."

"Haven't you learned anything in all *your* years, Iain? Women don't age, we only grow more graceful."

"Aye, as the women who have run through my life kept reminding me," he pretended cynicism.

"What women are we talking about here, Constable Meikle," came the voice behind him and turning, saw Irene Crichton stood in the doorway with Colin Morton beside her.

Blushing, he replied to laughter, "The ones that got away, Ma'am."

"Very good, Iain," Morton interjected with a grin before loudly clapping his hands and calling out, "Right, settle down. Briefing time."

When the room quietened he begun, "As of this morning, there is no news to indicate that we have positively identified any suspect for the murder of our colleague, Lesley. However, I can share with you and let me stress," he stared around the room, "this information is for you alone and not to be divulged outside the inquiry team, that we are looking at Charlie Gallagher whom I know most of you will be aware of, as a possible suspect."

The room broke into a mutter of angry comments and expletives, silenced when Morton raised his hand and said, "Let me be absolutely clear, guys, this is a possibility only and will be explained by DI Crichton."

Turning to her, he said, "Irene?"

Acknowledging him with a nod, she said in a loud and clear voice, "This morning, Paula Menzies SCRO file was delivered to us from headquarters. Many of you will know Menzies is Gallagher's partner. Now, the reason we requested the file is that a couple of days ago Menzies attempted to make contact with Lesley Rudd. The call was answered by our own Iain Meikle," she smiled at him, "but Menzies refused to speak with him. However, Iain reports that when Menzies was told of Lesley's death, she sounded very upset. That does not sound like the Menzies we usually deal with for those of you who know or have had dealings Menzies will be aware that she is definitely *not* pro-polis and truth be told, probably hates us. But why did she try to contact Lesley, we wondered?"

Shrugging, she pursed her lips and, continued. "At first, we couldn't quite work that one out, but inquiry had already led us to discover that Lesley had an interest in Charlie Gallagher and submitted an intelligence report to Criminal Intelligence at headquarters about him. There isn't anything of real evidential value in the intelligence report; however, it's just another thread that connects Gallagher to Lesley."

She paused before further continuing, "Now, let's talk about Paula Menzies. Her SCRO record indicates she had a younger sister called Catherine who according to the file, lived until several months ago at the parental home in Possilpark. I've spoken with the local collator who informed me that the house was often the subject of domestic abuse calls, the father getting steaming and beating the hell out of his wife and daughter, Catherine. The collator was also able to inform me that when Menzies, who as you can guess is well known to the cops in Possil, moved over here to Govan and moved in with Gallagher, Catherine took over Menzies council flat in the multi-storey's in Sandbank Street. That's in Summerston, I think?" she glanced for confirmation to Tam Whelan who nodded in agreement.

"Anyway, to continue. About six weeks ago and acting upon an anonymous phone call, the local cops broke into the flat occupied by Catherine to discover her unconscious with a needle stuck in her arm. She was rushed to the Gartnavel casualty, but died shortly after her arrival there. The post mortem concluded she died of a heroin injection. Not an overdose, as you might think, but it seemed that the heroin had been adulterated with some kind of commercial starch," she paused before adding, "I can't recall the name of it, but the Forensic report later indicated this starch is the kind used when you're ironing shirt collars and the like. Anyway, Catherine's death was one of three deaths within that month in the Glasgow area as well as six emergency admissions to hospital with the same symptoms and in all the fatal cases the same adulterant was detected. Now, where is this going, you must be asking? Well, I've spoken with the DI in the Drug Squad and according to her it seems that though there is no proof, their intelligence indicates the adulterated heroin was supplied by a local dealer who in turn gets his smack from a lowlife called Martin Boyle who *again* in turn, is one of the two enforcers used by Charlie Gallagher."

She paused again and stared around the room.

"It is our belief that Menzies is aware that her sister's death was likely the result of Gallagher's adulterated heroin and our assumption that she wants revenge, hence the reason for the contact with Lesley Rudd. Is she intent on providing information to Lesley? We're really not sure. Now," she shrugged as though not certain, "did Gallagher know of Menzies intention to inform on him? And if he did," she glanced at Morton, "it might have been enough for him to wonder what Menzies could have told Lesley, perhaps enough for him to consider Lesley a threat that he had to deal with."

A hand was raised and nodding to the detective, she said "Yes?"

The stocky man asked, "No offence, Ma'am, but isn't this all conjecture? If I'm correct, we've no hard evidence against Gallagher, much as I'd like there to be," he finished with a growl.

However, before Irene could respond Colin Morton stepped forward to answer, "No, Sandy, you're absolutely right. This *is* all conjecture and it all hinges on Paula Menzies. If we can get her on her own and away from Gallagher's influence, we could maybe break this case." He saw some brows furrowing with curiosity and realising an explanation was called for continued, "Last night, I instructed that the late shift plainers conduct a surveillance at the Gallagher's close in the hope of catching Paula Menzies on her own because quite obviously, we need to know if she will be willing to give us a statement about what she knows if indeed she knows anything about Lesley's murder. During their surveillance, the plainers saw two men, later identified as Martin Boyle and Seamus O'Brien, enter Gallagher's close in Burghead Drive where they stayed for about twenty minutes. Regretfully, Boyle and O'Brien sussed the surveillance and even challenged the plainers. However, during their time watching the close the plainers did not see Paula Menzies. Now, as you'll probably guess, our priority is to interview Menzies so I'm instructing Tam Whelan to put a team of you together with the express purpose of tracing her and bringing her in for interview. We'll start with watching the close, but if we don't manage to detain her by this evening, I intend asking for a Sheriff's warrant to detain her for interview and with the warrant in our hand, we'll knock on Mister Gallagher's door first thing in the morning and take her from the house. Any questions?"

There was a general shaking of heads before Morton turned again to Whelan to ask, "Tam, how are we on that billing request for Lesley's house telephone?"

Whelan glanced down at the summarised log of Action and sighed heavily before replying, "The Post Office Telecommunications Branch assured us that we would have the billing details for the preceding two months by start of play yesterday, boss. Let me chase that up and I'll put a fire under their arse."

"Do that," Morton agreed then continued, "In an hour I'll be leaving with Irene to attend Lesley's post mortem. In the meantime, Tam has some Actions to be distributed that I want completed by close of play today. Any questions?"

Again there was no reply. His eyes searched out Janie Wallace and Paul Ross who he beckoned to him.

"Before you go anywhere, I want a word with you two in my office," he turned away and indicated that they follow him.

When Morton had left the room, Irene sidled over to Iain Meikle and running a finger under his lapel, quietly said, "Quite the handsome detective today, Constable Meikle."

"Aye, but remember, it's only for the inquiry, Ma'am," he smiled at her, before adding with a cheeky grin, "The suit I mean, not me being handsome."

At his desk, Tam Whelan watched the exchange and slowly smiled. It seemed, he thought, that things might be looking up for Irene.

****

He slowly opened his eyes with the feeling that they had been glued shut and his mouth felt like he had been eating sand. At first a little disorientated, Charlie Gallagher wondered what the ringing noise was then realised it was the phone on the bedside cabinet.

Snatching at the receiver, he grunted, "What!"

"Hello, me old mucker, it's me, your pal from way back. Can you speak?"

Stifling a yawn, he realised it was Billy Madison and replied, "Aye, okay. What's up?"

"I've been trying to get you all last night. Out on the bevy were you?"

"Aye, I was clubbing all night," he glibly lied, then eyes narrowing, asked, "Is this about the delivery? Is there a problem?"

"Yes, it's about the delivery, but no, there's no problem, pal. I'm ringing to ask if you've the readies arranged and if you're prepared to receive the delivery?"

His head thumping from lack of sleep, Gallagher thought quickly. Seamus and Marty should have all the money collected within the next two days and so made his decision. "This Wednesday evening suit you?"

"Tomorrow? I can do that," Madison eagerly agreed. "I'm thinking of sending my man by train up to the Central Station and having him return the same night. Think you can arrange for a meeting place for the exchange somewhere close by?"

Lying on his back with the phone clamped to his ear, Gallagher run his free hand through his mop of unruly hair and exhaled as he thought, before answering, "How about the Waterloo Bar in Argyle Street."

He listened as Madison snorted before replying, "Bloody hell, is that place still there? Many's the time I've got pissed in there," he cheerfully added with a hint of nostalgia in his voice.

"Aye, it's a busy shop and if memory serves correctly it's usually not too big a crowd on a Wednesday night. Your man can mingle and won't have any difficulty meeting with my guys and I'll make sure my man has the readies to hand over. All I need from you is a time and what your man will be wearing."

"Right, then," Madison said. "The trains are pretty regular, so I'll get my man to catch a train that arrives at the central round about seven o'clock. I'll make sure my man is wearing a local top, if you get my meaning."

"Local top?" Gallagher repeated then eyes narrowing, understood and asked, "As in the Reds?"

"That's it, as in the Reds," Madison agreed.

"Anything else?"

"Nothing, lad. Just make sure the readies are all there. I wouldn't like us to fall out over something like a short change. Not when we can do business again, if you get my meaning."

"Don't worry, wee man," Gallagher growled. "If the stuff is the same as what you sent up before, there won't be any problem from this side. Understand?"

"Understood," Madison agreed then ended the call with, "I'll be in touch when it's all arranged."

Gallagher lay on his back cradling the phone in his hand until the loud tone noise became irritating. With yawn he yanked the cord from the wall socket then pulling the duvet over him, tightly closed his eyes and returned to sleep.

****

The two Regional Crime Squad officers squatting in the rear of the rusting Bedford van that was parked in Frampton Road a hundred yards from the junction of Knighton Road had a clear view through the glazed rear window of Annie Stokoe's front door.

"Bloody hell, Dave," moaned the younger of the two who screwing his face wafted a newspaper in front of him, before asking in a thick Geordie accent, "Can't you plug that arse of yours or what?"

His Scouse colleague Dave mischievously grinned before replying, "It's me wife's home made curry, lad. I can't help it if it disagrees with me bowels, can I?"

The Geordie snorted in disgust then startled and sharply said, "That's him." Reaching for the radio, he snapped out, "Tango One exiting the house and seems to be heading south on foot, over."

The message was acknowledged and within minutes, ten officers on foot and in three unmarked cars who were dispersed throughout the Walton area converged in the streets and roads around Frampton Road where unknown to Doughnut Stokoe, he became the subject of an intensive follow.

Throughout that day, the surveillance continued, watching Stokoe as he lazily strolled through the city before visiting a semi-detached house in Freehold Street in the Fairfield area. Logging the address in their report, none of the surveillance team were familiar with Gina Poulson, the local illegal moneylender who occupied the property. Five minutes later, Stokoe emerged from the house having obtained from Gina the fee for his services tucked into an inner pocket and the names of two debtors who had fallen behind with their payments.

The surveillance watched him leave Poulson's house and followed him to a mid-terraced house in Devonfield Road in the Orrell Park area where he spent fifteen minutes there, again uncertain why he was visiting the property.

They were unaware that in the house he not only slapped and punched the occupant, a slightly built young single mother then laughed as he cruelly manhandled her, tearing off her blouse and bra, then groped her in front of her terrified children. He left smiling at the traumatised woman and in the knowledge she would be too terrified to report the sexual assault to the police, but not before warning her that if she did not pay her dues within twenty-four hours he would return and rape her.

They continued to follow him and saw him enter a second mid-terraced house in Drake Crescent in the Fazakerly area of the city, but again knew not why for they could not see him break the nose of the elderly drunk householder nor did they see him take the man's wife by the throat, then warn them that if they failed to pay their due within twenty-fours he would return and really hurt them.

The followed him as he lazily made his way to a hostelry local to his house where two officers acting as a couple entered the saloon bar and covertly watched him order a meal and consume several pints of his favourite ale. In their report they noted that when Stokoe arrived in the pub, the place quietened and several patrons quickly left. The officers noted it was their opinion that not only was he unwelcome, but that the staff were too frightened to refuse serving him or to throw him out of the pub. When later that evening he returned home, the team were stood down but not before handing over to a nightshift team who would continue the twenty-four-hour surveillance at Annie Stokoe's house.

In the front room of the house and his mother banned to her room, Stokoe sat before the television watching yet another pornographic video, but sighed and paused the screen to answer the phone.

"It's me," Billy Madison said. "It's on for tomorrow, lad. Here's what I need you to do."

He listened patiently, his eyes on the screen and wishing the Scotch git would hurry up because the video was getting to the really good part.

"You got all that, then?" Madison asked.

"Aye, buy a ticket to Glasgow Central Station to make sure I get there at seven o'clock," he repeated in a bored voice. "Find a pub called the Waterloo Bar that's not far from the station. Wear a Liverpool top so the guy will recognise me. Make sure the bag he gives me has got the dough before I hand my bag over to him. Get the overnight train back home. Bring you the dough first thing on Thursday morning for you to pay the Jamaican. Anything else?"

"No, lad, I think I've got it all covered. One thing, though. The guy I'm dealing with is called Charlie Gallagher. If anything should go wrong…"

"It won't. Stand on me about that," sighed Stokoe, wishing the bastard would just get off the fucking line.

"I know, lad, I know. I'm just saying. If anything *should* go wrong, remember that name, Charlie Gallagher. He's well known in Glasgow and easy to find for what you do best. Got that?"

"Yeah, got it."

****

It had been a long day in the SRC control room monitoring the team's broadcasts. After reading the dayshift's log of events, Detective Sergeant Kevin Webster contacted DI Frankie Solomon of the Merseyside Police and requested that his officers make a discreet inquiry as to who resided at the Devonfield Road and Drake Crescent houses and what connection they had with Doughnut Stokoe.

There was no requirement to check the Freehold Street address in the Fairfield district that had been visited by Stokoe, for Webster already knew who occupied that house.

What he didn't tell Solomon was his opinion that Stokoe's visits to the two unknown addresses had nothing to do with the heroin, but everything to do with the big man acting as a debt collector for Gina Poulson; no, no need at all he privately sniggered. After Solomon's complaint about Stokoe sending more than his fair share of the local citizenry to the local casualty department, Webster decided there was no need to wind the DI up any further.

Sat back on one of the unyielding plastic chairs, the only thing that bothered Webster was that at no time during the surveillance did Stokoe use a vehicle. Yes, the PNC indicated that Stokoe was a banned driver, yet local intelligence indicated he was not beyond ignoring the ban and on several occasions made use of vehicles. Did it mean, Webster wondered, that Stokoe was merely storing the heroin to be collected by a courier and that in turn begged the question.

Who was the recipient for the heroin and more importantly, when was it to be shipped out from Stokoe's house?

He licked nervously at his lips, his fingers beating a tattoo on the brown cardboard file held in his hand.

He knew he was gambling with his career, lying to his boss that Solomon had provided the information to him, then urging his boss to mount an expensive surveillance operation against Stokoe and persuading him that it would net not just the big thug and possibly Billy Madison too, but more than likely roll up a major dealer somewhere in the country. He had hinted that the heroin was probably bound for Leeds or Manchester where there had recently been several drug related deaths and where the media were hammering at the local police to sort the situation out.

"If we can seize this shipment and make some high profile arrests, boss," Webster had eagerly encouraged him, "it'll definitely help with our funding issues."

Besieged as he was, the boss of the area RCS was willing to go along with any operation that might somehow improve the Squads current financial predicament, so with some nervous reservation, agreed.

And now, Webster inhaled, it *had* to go well or any hope he had for appointment to the soon to be advertised DI position was scuppered.

CHAPTER SEVENTEEN

In his office, Colin Morton slumped down into his chair and pointing to the other side of his desk motioned that both Janie Wallace and Peter Rossi do likewise.

"The reason I called you in here for a private chat is that I don't want what I'm about to say to be divulged outside this room. Clear?"

"Yes, sir," they replied in unison.

"Janie," he turned to her. "I've been giving some thought about what you said. When Lesley's sister disclosed her suspicions about her husband," and reminded her, "you said Ellen told you she believed that Jake had a thing for Lesley? Why do you think she told you what she did?"

"Well," she grimaced, "I felt that Ellen needed to unload her concerns about her husband Jake and she only did because she was at a low ebb. I don't know if she would have said anything if she hadn't been so distraught about Lesley's murder, sir."

"After our discussion yesterday, do you have any further thought that she might have deliberately fired him in? That she herself might have killed Lesley?"

Janie swallowed hard, for her answer might determine whether or not the DCI took a closer look at Lesley's sister as a potential suspect and frankly, she wasn't that certain herself. Finally, she replied, "I have to admit it did occur to me, but I really don't know, sir. That is," she nervously tucked a loose hair behind her ear, "I'm not sure."

Morton was astute enough to realise that by asking her to make such a judgement he had put the young woman in an impossible situation and gently explained, "Don't worry about it, Janie. I know that you think what you tell me might influence my decision, but rest assured; if we do treat Ellen McNeill as a suspect it is my decision, nothing to do with you. All you are providing is what I lack and will never understand," then he smiled. "A woman's intuition."

"Sir," she blushed.

"What about you, young Rossi," he addressed him. "What's your thoughts on the matter?"

"Me, sir? Well, to be honest," he quickly glanced at her, "when Janie and I first visited the McNeill's to inform the sister that Lesley was missing, I first got the impression that the husband Jake just didn't like Lesley's fiancé, Fraser Anderson, but the more I thought about it," his brow furrowed, "I realised it was more than that. In fact," he held up a warning hand, "and it was only my impression you understand…"

"Understood," Morton nodded.

"I thought that maybe Jake McNeill was jealous of Anderson."

"Then, from what Janie has learned from the sister, maybe you weren't too far off the mark," replied Morton with a slow nod.

"Right," he abruptly said, "again, the reason I have you both in here is that I want you to formally interview Jake McNeill about his relationship with his sister-in-law. If he asks if he's a suspect for her murder, inform him that until the killer is apprehended, everyone is s suspect. I also have to tell you that I had Tam Whelan do a speculative check on Jacob McNeill and we had a hit. It seems that when he was a student at Glasgow University, McNeill earned his one and only conviction for attempting to pass a stolen cheque and for which he received an admonishment at the Glasgow Sheriff Court. However, the conviction was enough for the police to record his fingerprints that remain on file today."

It was Janie who asked, "How do his fingerprints help us, sir? I mean, wasn't Lesley assaulted then drowned?"

"Well, the PM will establish that fact, Constable Wallace," he pretended to reproach her, but then smiling, added, "What you both know and this time must remain confidential is that the fingerprint discovered on the toilet seat in Lesley's flat remains unidentified. According to Alex Murray who dusted the flat, apart from a number of prints that have since been identified as Lesley's it is his opinion that the flat had been wiped clean. Now, as you might guess, our problem is that we cannot categorically say that the flat was broken into by the killer; however, it is too coincidental that on the night she went missing, her flat was the subject of a break-in. Was it the killer and if so, what was he after? Might it have been the brother-in-law, Jacob McNeill or maybe even his wife, Lesley's sister?"

He shrugged then continued, "You were both there when Alex Murray told us he suspected the print belongs to a man, so as a matter of urgency, McNeill's print is being checked at the Fingerprint Department against the print discovered in the flat." Slightly irritated, he sighed before adding, "However, the Fingerprint Department's sense of urgency differs slightly from that of an SIO running a murder inquiry. What I want from you two is that during his interview, you need to determine where McNeill was between the hours that Lesley went missing and the time the flat was discovered broken into. I'm meeting with the sister this morning at the PM, so Irene Crichton and I will deal with her and obtain her formal statement."

"Are we at liberty to mention the discovery of the fingerprint, sir?" Rossi asked.

Morton inhaled before replying then nodding, slowly replied, "Judge for yourself how the interview goes. If you've got him on the ropes and if need be, mention the discovery of the fingerprint after the break-in and see how he reacts."

"Anything else, sir?" Janie inquired.

"That will do for now. Oh, one more thing. When Tam Whelan phoned this morning to offer Missus McNeill a lift to the mortuary for the formal identification of her sister, she told him that she'll be driving herself and that her husband will be at home minding the children."

"He'll have his children there, sir, at the house with him when we're interviewing him?" her face reflected her concern.

"Yes, Janie, and I know it's not the best situation for an interview, but like it or not, he is still a grieving relative so you'll have to remember to be sensitive when you're speaking with him. That's why I'm sending you two. He's already met you under circumstances when you broke the bad news about Lesley and likely will assume that you are sympathetic to their grief. Do what you can to obtain the information without causing too much alarm. Do you think you can handle this?" he glanced from one to the other.

"Yes, sir," Rossi nodded for them both, unaware that Janie had reservations about the interview, but thought it better at that time to keep them to herself.

****

He'd taken the day off work and now making the kids their breakfast, Jake McNeill thought it was a bad idea keeping them off school that day. Buttering the toast, he couldn't understand what he had done wrong.

Since Ellen had returned home from visiting Lesley's flat with the detectives, she had been cold and uncommunicative unless spoken to. Not with the children, though. For some unknown reason, she was even more motherly towards them, hugging and kissing them both.

It was almost as though she was intent on lavishing her affection on them rather than him, making him watch as she did.

He turned as his wife appeared in the doorway and saw that she had not applied any make-up, her blonde hair was tied up in a tight bun and was wearing a white blouse as she fiddled with the cuff on the jacket of her black, trouser suit.

"You look…" he hesitated searching for the right word and settled for, "nice."

"Nice," she repeated and he could not help but wonder how a woman could turn that one word into a derisory form of scorn. A cold shiver run down his spine.

Could it be…did she suspect?

"Any idea how long you'll be at the…you know."

"No," was the curt and very abrupt response, before she stared at him and asked, "Is that a problem? You looking after *your* children?"

"Of course not," he tried to smile, but couldn't refrain from turning the smile into a grimace.

She turned away into the hallway and loudly called out, "Fergus, Nicola. Be good for your daddy. I'll be home later."

He heard the front door close and the throaty roar of her old Ford Escort as it raced away.

He gritted his teeth. He had warned her time and time again about speeding up the hill, reminded her over and over that their own children and their neighbours kids played in the street of the quiet cul-de-sac.

Placing the toast and cups of juice onto a tray, he carried them through to his children watching television in the front room.
****

Ellen McNeill turned at the Cross onto Uddingston's Main Street, crunching the gears as she did so with tears of anger smarting her eyes.

"The two-timing bastard!" she snarled through gritted teeth.

So engrossed in her own rage she failed to see the pedestrian crossing lights turn to red and in panic stamped onto on the brake, completely forgetting to declutch.

The car stalled and shuddered to a halt a mere three feet from the elderly woman on the crossing who shrank back in terror as the tyres squealed, drawing the attention of all the pedestrians shopping nearby.

Wide-eyed, her mouth hanging open, she watched in disbelief as the old lady lifted her rolled up brolly and brought it crashing down onto the rusting bonnet, then haughtily marched off.

It was the driver behind sounding the vans horn that brought her out of the stupor and starting the engine, she slowly rolled forward into an empty parking bay below the Park Church, then slowly resting her forehead on the steering wheel, her shoulders shook as she began to weep.

****

As a matter of routine that morning in the fifth floor conference room at Police Headquarters, Detective Chief Superintendent Alistair 'Patches' Cruickshank and his fellow DCS, Bobby Baxter, the head of the city's north side CID, met with the Chief Constable and Assistant Chief Constable (CID) Martin Kerr for a roundup of the monthly crime statistics for the city's Divisions.

The four men sat at the highly polished table with the Chief as befitting his rank seated at the top of table, Kerr to his right and Cruickshank and Baxter to his left, the barrel-chested Ayshireman with a pipe firmly clamped in his teeth.

Taking a few minutes to read a synopsis of the statistics, the Chief stubbed out his cigarette and sighing, removed his reading glasses then said, "It makes for painful reading, gentlemen. Needless to say when the press gets a hold of these latest figures," he held the stapled sheets of paper up as though they offended him, "they'll have a field day."

Turning to Kerr, he asked, "Is there any light in this report, Mister Kerr?"

"How do you mean, sir?"

Cruickshank could almost sense that like him, Baxter was holding his breath at the stupidity of the bloody man for not recognising what the Chief was asking of him.

Slowly, the Chief replied, "What I'm asking is, is there anyway we can improve upon these figures in the constraints of our current budget?"

"We can always lie," Kerr joked, but his attempt at humour fell flat when he saw that not only the Chief but both his DCS's did not find it funny.

He swallowed with difficulty and continued, "What I mean is yes, of course I'll find some way to improve the stats, sir."

"I'm not so worried about improving the stats, Mister Kerr, I'm wondering how we can improve our crime detection," the Chief dryly replied.

Thinking fast and wondering why it was so bloody hot in the room, Kerr said, "Perhaps we could downgrade some of our unsolved minor crimes to offences and that way *pro rata*, the detected crimes will seem to have increased."

"So," the Chief stared thoughtfully at him, "you're back to your original suggestion. By playing with the statistics, we lie to the public."

"Oh, well, what I mean…"

The Chief held up his hand for silence and sighing heavily, interrupted with, "If you will forgive me, Mister Kerr."

Turning to Cruickshank he asked, "What's your take on this report, Alistair? And yours, Bobby?"

It wasn't lost on Kerr that the Chief used Cruickshank and Baxter's forenames while *he* was always addressed as 'ACC Kerr' or 'Mister Kerr.' Bristling, he remained resentfully silent, but with a sidelong glance at the Chief longed for the day when he would take the bastards job from under him.

With a glance at Baxter who nodded that Cruickshank respond to the Chief's question, he replied, "It's public knowledge that the Force is currently ten per cent understrength, sir, and obviously that includes the CID too. Crime levels haven't increased, it's just that our numbers have not and until this proposal by the Home Secretary Merlyn Rees, that Lord Edmund Davies review police salaries, we will continue to struggle with these figures. I'm sure you are already aware that the senior officers in the Divisional CID's strive to improve on these statistics, but…" he held his hands wide before adding, "a lot of the crime is being committed by the same criminals. If our people are fortunate enough to arrest an offender and libel charges against that individual, it does of course improve the detection statistics. However, when you have one individual committing two, five, ten crimes then getting bloody bailed to commit *more* crime before the arresting officers have the opportunity to convict him for the ones he was arrested for in the first place!"

He left the rest unsaid.

"Bobby?" The Chief turned questioningly towards Baxter.

"It's like Alistair says, sir," he shook his head, his Ayrshire accent strong and pronounced. "We're being overwhelmed by numbers. In fact, I'm getting to feel I'm more of a fucking accountant than a detective," he bluntly exclaimed.

It didn't escape Cruickshank's notice that while Kerr frowned at Fullerton's ripe language, the Chief forced a cough to hide his grin.

Hunching his shoulders, Baxter half-smiled when he continued, "And again like Alistair says, a lot of the crime is being committed by recidivists who when we put them to court are out that day on bail and back to screwing houses, breaking into cars, shoplifting, etcetera. Perhaps if you might induce the Procurator Fiscal to consider requesting the courts to refuse bail for the persistent offenders…"

"Which in turn places a greater strain on the prison system and to be frank, I've already had that complaint from the Chief Executive who like me is working to a tight budget," the Chief shook his head.

"Aye, maybe so," Baxter agreed, "but consider this too, sir. When these buggers are released on bail and committing further crime, our lads and lassies are stuck in their offices preparing time-consuming statements and reports for the Fiscal's Department for the crime the buggers were locked up for in the first place, not out hunting more of the buggers like they should be. It's a vicious circle," he slowly shook his head. Feeling he was being excluded from the conversation, Kerr wracked his brain to come up with something to say, some idea that would impress them, then brightly said, "Why don't we use our own Divisional cells for holding these persistent offenders and that might relieve the pressure on the prison service?"

The Chief didn't immediately answer as an embarrassed silence fell upon the room. Then conscious that he could not make Kerr look like a fool in front of two subordinate officers, he tactfully replied in an even voice, "An interesting concept, Mister Kerr. However, I believe there exists the problem that if the courts did remit accused individuals to our police cells, we would then be responsible for guarding these prisoners, a job that we as a service are not as experienced as our colleagues in the prison service. I also believe there is a number of regulations in force that requires prisoners to receive adequate food and drink during their period of confinement for which we do not have a budget. Then of course prisoners are entitled to exercise during the day and we would require to take a large number of our constables off the street to guard and supervise this exercise that in turn, I'm sure you will agree, would cause a public outcry about a further lack of officers on the beat. However," he graciously smiled, "we won't completely dismiss your innovative suggestion."

Both Cruickshank and Baxter kept their faces straight, but knew that not just the Chief, but the general public would never condone such a preposterous idea.

For his part, Kerr was tight-lipped and staring down at the table, his face reddened and he simply nodded at the Chief's decision.

Deciding there was little need to go over ground already covered, the Chief dismissed the meeting, but as Cruickshank rose to his feet, he said, "Perhaps a moment, Alistair, if you don't mind. I'd like to hear how DCI Morton is progressing with the inquiry into the murder of Constable Rudd."

When Kerr and Fullerton left the room, the Chief gestured that Cruickshank sit back down and then lighting his sixth cigarette of that morning, with a long sigh asked, "Now that we're alone, Alistair, what's happening in Govan?"

"From what Colin Morton tells me, sir, here's no real leads at the minute. They're looking at a local drug dealer called Charlie Gallagher who might have had some resentment against Constable Rudd in the belief she was receiving information about his business from Gallagher's live-in girlfriend, a convicted shoplifter called Paula Menzies. However," he shook his head, "regretfully there is no direct evidence to link him to Rudd. My understanding is that Morton and his team are hoping to persuade this woman Menzies to give up Gallagher, but as of this morning they haven't yet traced her."

"What about the break-in to Rudd's flat? Is that connected to the murder?"

"More than likely, but Morton hasn't yet discovered why the flat was broken into."

"So in short, we're no further forward in arresting anyone?"

"No, sir, regretfully not."

"I've perused Rudd's personnel file. I gather her only close family is a sister, her twin?"

"That's correct, Missus Ellen McNeill. Morton informs me that after the PM today he intends interviewing the sister."

"I feel I should be meeting this woman, giving her the Force's condolence for her loss and to assure her we are doing everything to trace the person responsible for her sister's murder. We *are* doing everything possible are we not?" he stared keenly at Cruickshank.

"Of course, sir. If there is to be an arrest in this inquiry I'm confident Colin Morton will make one."

Tempted though he was, his ingrained sense of pride prevented him from mentioning that ACC Kerr had blocked Morton's request for extra resources.

"However," he continued as he inwardly struggled with the decision, but finally decided the Chief should know, "I'd be grateful if you would consider deferring your meeting with Missus McNeill for now."

"Why?"

"DCI Morton wishes to positively eliminate the sister and her husband as suspects before you call upon them."

The Chief did not immediately respond but then nodding, rose to his feet then said, "In that case, keep me apprised of how the inquiry is going. A daily update by phone will suffice."

"Of course, sir," Cruickshank nodded as they left the room.

In the corridor outside the Chief suddenly stopped as though recalling something then turning, gently poked a forefinger into Cruickshank's chest and taking the DCS aback, said, "I had the most curious chat the other day with Mister Kerr, in which he reminded me that apparently I gave a speech about the solidarity of the police brotherhood?"

He pursed his lips and stared accusingly at Cruickshank with a twinkle in his eyes before continuing, "Now, Alistair, remind me again. When was this and what was it that I said?"

****

The Regional Crime Squad officers in the Bedford van had just split a flask of coffee between them when they saw Doughnut Stokoe emerge from the front door of his mothers house.

While one cursed furiously as he spilled the steaming hot liquid down the front of his sweatshirt, his neighbour quickly grabbed the handset and alerted the surveillance team that their target was on foot and making his way along Frampton Road towards the junction.

Like a smooth, well oiled machine, the team's vehicles surrounded their target in the adjoining streets and roads while three footmen were deployed to trail him in the standard ABC pattern of foot follow.

Completely unaware of their interest in him, with a lumbering stride the heavy built Stokoe made his way northwards until half an hour later he at last arrived at Walton railway station. A female officer was quickly dispatched to enter the booking office where fourth in the queue behind Stokoe, she heard him loudly ask about the price of a return ticket to Glasgow.

"Are you travelling today, sir?"

"Tomorrow."

"First thing, sir," the ticket assistant helpfully replied, "you need to travel to Lime Street station and the second thing is if you book today you can get the ticket cheaper. What time do you intend travelling at?"

"What times are the trains that will get me to Glasgow for around seven in the evening?" grunted Stokoe

Behind him, the detective refrained from smiling but thought, this is pure gold.

"Well," the assistant reached behind for a timetable and replied, "there's around thirty trains a day. Of course that is during a twenty-four-hour period and…"

"Just give me the time of the train I want that will get me there for seven," Stokoe snapped at him.

The woman in front of the detective, sensing trouble was brewing from the monster of a man, stepped away from the queue and hurriedly left the ticket office. The detective moved a little closer and saw the assistant turn pale before he crossly replied, "There's a train departing Lime Street at fourteen-ten…" he paused then staring at Stokoe, cheekily said, "Ten minutes after two in the afternoon. There's a couple of stops but it will get you into Glasgow Central at ten minutes to seven. Will that do you…sir?"

"What about a train back that night?"

"The same night?"

"Yeah, you fucking deaf or something? The same night."

So, it's a delivery he's making, the detective thought and knew she *had* indeed struck gold.

"The sleeper train to Penzance departs Glasgow at eleven-thirty, but stops at Preston where you can change and catch the Liverpool train at twenty minutes after two in the morning."

"What, nothing overnight to Liverpool?"

"No, now I've other customers to see to, lad, so do you want a ticket now *or what*!"

To the assistants astonishment, Stokoe didn't respond but merely turned away and made his way out of the ticket office. The detective remained standing where she was but the fingers of her hand inside her anorak pocket worked furiously, rapidly clicking the transmitter button of her covert radio to alert her colleagues that Stokoe was exiting the building.

Minutes later the voice in her earpiece informed her that the target had moved away from the railway station and it was now safe for her to leave the ticket office and re-join her vehicle.

****

Iain Meikle was reading the handwritten note from the sergeant in charge of the Inquiry Department downstairs when he sensed he was being watched.

"Care to accompany the DCI and me to the mortuary," Irene Crichton leaned across the desk to quietly ask him.

Conscious there were others about, Iain hid his smile and nodding, replied, "Of course, Ma'am. I'll grab car keys and meet at the front entrance when you're ready to leave."

"Colin Morton's in his office with young Janie and Peter Rossi, so it might be another couple of minutes or so," she sighed, "which gives you time to work out where you're taking me this evening."

"Oh, going out are we?" his face expressed his surprise.

She pursed her lips and replied, "Thought maybe you'd like to take me to a movie or does the offer of you cooking me tatties, mince and turnip still stand?"

He broke into a slow smile and said, "I make a great gravy to go with the mince. One of my better achievements."

"Red or white?"

"Oh, if you're not fussed, I fancy a bottle of red."

"And shall I bring an overnight bag?"

Staring at her, he felt his throat tighten and wondered, was this going too fast?

His hesitation was misread by her and he saw her eyes narrowing, so quickly whispered, "I think that would be a great idea."

Her chest tightened with relief and forcing a smile, she said, "I don't know what time we'll be done here today so we'll just need to play it by ear, if that's okay with you?"

"Fine by me," he continued to stare at her.

They both turned when Colin Morton called out from the doorway, "You ready for the PM, Irene?"

"All set," she replied before adding, "Iain volunteered to drive us there."

"Good man, Iain," Morton responded then said, "We'll get you down at the front door."

"Sir," he acknowledged.

On the way down the stairs to the car park in the rear yard, Iain paused and let out a breath. Irene was coming on strong he thought then smiled for curiously, he didn't really mind and if anything, was more than pleased.

Starting the engine, his thought was that he'd better remind himself to buy some mince from the butchers on Paisley Road West.

Oh, and change the sheets on the bed.

CHAPTER EIGHTEEN

DS Tam Whelan answered his desk phone to find it was DS Jack Fleming calling who with three DC's, was charged with conducting the surveillance outside Charlie Gallagher's close in Burghead Drive to watch for Paula Menzies.

"Anything yet?" asked Whelan.

"No, nothing so far," sighed the DS.

"Where are you calling from?"

"I'm out getting coffee and rolls in a wee shop in Langlands Road. The woman in the takeaway shop let me use her phone in the back, but don't worry, Tricia's in the car with an eyeball on the close and she'll radio me if Menzies appears. Me and Tricia have been here since six-thirty this morning," he continued. "I've put the other two onto a late shift to relieve us at four this afternoon and they'll remain in situ till after midnight. Frankly, I don't see the point in staying there overnight because if Menzies shows up at that time of night she'll likely be wasted on the bevy and my understanding is that the boss wants her sober for interview."

"Well, you're in charge of the surveillance so that's your decision Jack, but for what it's worth, I agree. Any movement at all that you can see in the flat?"

"From where we're sitting in the car we can see the windows, but not into the flat. It looks like the curtains are still drawn. Gallagher left just after nine o'clock in his motor, dressed in a tracksuit and carrying a wee bag so I suppose he's on his way to that gym he uses over in Finnieston. If the boss wants, we can go up to the flat and knock on the door and if she's there, we can bring her out and down to the office?"

"No," Whelan shook his head. "The boss says to give it today to see if we can get her away from him on her own without snatching her. Besides, you don't know who else might be in the flat and if we chap the door and there is somebody there when we ask her to come out and play she might bottle it and refuse to speak with us."

"Point taken," Fleming agreed before asking, "Anything happening back at the office?"

"Nothing in overnight," Whelan sighed with evident disappointment. "The boss and Irene are away to Lesley Rudd's PM and I know they intend interviewing her sister while they are there, so I don't expect them to be back for a couple of hours at least."

"Right then, I'll away back to the car with our breakfast. I'll use the radio if there's any update."

Whelan acknowledged the report then settling down to his paperwork, idly wondered what if anything Paula Menzies had to tell the inquiry.

****

Driving again out to Uddingston, Peter Rossi said, "You're quiet this morning, Janie. Are you okay?"

"Yes, just a few things on my mind," she tiredly replied.

"At the risk of being nosey, how did you get on with your boyfriend when you got home yesterday?"

"I didn't," she sharply snapped, then taking a deep breath added, "Sorry. That wasn't fair. Paul has moved out. Left a note saying me and him wasn't going to work anyway and that he's moved into the Grosvenor Hotel in Great Western Road."

"The Grosvenor?"

"Aye, you must know it, it's…"

"Yes, I know it, but I would have thought he'd maybe have family or friends he could go to. The Grosvenor seems…" he hesitated.

"Seems what?"

"Well, kind of temporary, as if he knew he wasn't going to be there for long and certainly," he chuckled, "not at the prices they charge."

Her eyes narrowed in thought then she said, "Wouldn't his club foot the bill?"

"I don't think so," Rossi replied. "It's not their responsibility to house their players during a domestic…" then stopped and a little more conciliatory, added, "Sorry, but you know what I mean. Perhaps he's only there for a night while he makes alternative arrangements for one of his family or friends to accommodate him."

She didn't immediately respond, but then in an instinctive flash of intuition, slowly said, "Or perhaps the deal has already been struck with one of the English clubs and he knew he was moving out anyway, that it wasn't worth his time moving in with someone else."

He didn't reply and could not know that like him, she now believed that might be the real reason for him being caught with the blonde; that Paul couldn't face her and break off their relationship like a man.

Fucking coward, she angrily thought.

Staring through the windscreen, her hands in her lap tightened into angry fists and she almost winced as her nails dug into the soft skin on the heel of her hand.

Rossi didn't know how to respond to this awkward silence for he really didn't want to get involved in Janie's breakup other than perhaps to offer his support as a friend. However, against his better judgement he said, "Look, I've a mate who works part-time in the Grosvenor. He's a barman going through his Masters degree at Glasgow Uni. If you want, I can give him a phone call later today, ask if he's heard anything?"

Again she hesitated, then her curiosity got the better of her and she nodded, "Yes, please."

"Now," he exhaled and anxious to change the subject, "how do you want to handle this interview with Jake McNeill?"

****

The surveillance team followed Doughnut Stokoe to a row of shops in a tenement building on Walton Road adjacent to The Clock public house. The eyeball footman saw Stokoe suddenly stop and then enter an Army and Navy surplus store that was displaying ex-military items in the window with second-hand military clothing hung from wire hangers at the door entrance. "I'm hanging back, the shop's too small for me to go in after him," the footman radioed the convoy before taking up a position at a bus stop on the other side of the road from where he had a clear view of the shop door.

They waited for a little under ten minutes before Stokoe emerged with a parcel wrapped in brown paper that he carried under his left arm.

While the convoy continued their surveillance, the footman and one vehicle to pick him up were instructed to remain in Walton Road and make inquiry at the shop to find out what Stokoe had purchased.

A small bell jingled when the footman pushed the door open before entering the dimly lit and claustrophobic shop. Dust mites floated in the air as his nostrils were assailed by the smell of old leather and unwashed clothes.

"Help you, mate?" a large swarthy man wearing washed out jeans and a leather waistcoat with a shaven head and heavily tattooed arms stepped out from behind a laden counter to stare suspiciously at the slightly built footman.

"The big guy who was just in here," the footman smiled genially at him. "Can you tell me what he bought?"

The storekeeper stared warily at the footman before asking, "Why the fuck would I do that?"

Fetching a crumpled, laminated warrant card from his trouser pocket the footman held it in the palm of his hand as he presented it to the shopkeeper and said, "Because I'm the police and I'd like to know, please."

The storekeeper sneeringly grinned and repeated, "Like I said, mate, why the *fuck* would I do that?"

The footman shrugged and glancing around him at the packed shelves and clothing hung all over the shop, calmly replied, "Because with all the gear you have stacked here, it looks to me like it's a firetrap and if you don't tell me, *mate*, in half an hour I'll have the Fire Brigade round here checking your fire safety certificate and doing a fire safety assessment check on this place. And let's not forget there are people living in the flats above the shop and we both know how rigorous the Brigade can be when they're doing their checks, don't we, *mate*? Might even have to close you down till you get this place sorted out, *mate*. Might even be closed for weeks or months, *mate*."

A few minutes later the footman was out of the shop and when he returned to the pick-up car, used the radio to inform the convoy commander that the target had purchased a heavy duty ex-army canvas kitbag, having told that shopkeeper that he needed something strong for travelling and tough enough to carry a heavy load.

****

They had stood silently and watched as Ellen McNeill, red eyed and her body shaking, a handkerchief clutched in her hand that she used to dab at her nose and eyes, stared through the window into the small anteroom and formally identified the body of her sister, Lesley Rudd.

Her lips quivering as she tried to compose herself, she had turned to ask Colin Morton "What happens now?"

It had been Irene Crichton's idea and so nodding to the young female detective who would take possession of any sample seized from the body at the time of the PM, he had replied, "With my colleague I'll attend your sisters post mortem. In the meantime, DI Crichton and DC Meikle will take you to a quiet room to get you a cup of tea and take a statement from you."

"A statement?"

"It's a formality, Missus McNeill. We need a statement from the closest member of Lesley's family and since you have also made the formal identification..."

He didn't finish, but watched as Irene gently took the distressed woman by the arm then followed by Iain, lead her along the corridor.

In the room reserved for bereaved family members, she bade Ellen McNeill to sit down then gave a subtle nod to Iain that he organised a pot of tea.

"Do you understand the procedure of eliminating witnesses from an inquiry, Missus McNeill?" she asked as she fetched her notebook from her handbag.

"Ellen, please. Yes," she nodded, then a little self-consciously, added, "I read crime books and I like crime drama on the television."

"Well, you understand that I have to ask you some questions about your whereabouts last Saturday night, when Lesley was first reported missing."

She took a deep breath and nodding, replied, "Of course."

"So, can you tell me where you were?"

"At home, with the children."

"And with your husband?"

It was the hesitation in her eyes that Irene saw, before she replied, "No, well, yes. What I mean is that Jake was at home in the early part of the evening, but he sometimes goes to the pub on a Saturday night for a pint and to play dominoes."

"What time did he leave the house and what time did he return?"

Nervously, she dabbed at her eyes with the handkerchief before replying, "He left about seven or maybe it was half past. The kids were still up because I remember Nicola and Fergus asking him to bring sweeties home."

And if she's home with the kids, Irene inwardly sighed, that kind of alibis her, though as a matter of course they would check.

"And the time he returned home?"

Ellen inhaled, her hands twisting the hankie back and forth.

"Ellen?"

"I'm not sure," she quietly said, "You see if he's been drinking he snores a lot and I can't sleep if he's tossing and turning and snoring so I usually just go to bed with Nicola. Curl up with her."

"So you don't know what time he arrived home?"

"Not usually, no, because I normally go to bed early on a Saturday night and I'm usually sleeping when he gets in. But on Saturday night, I remember he got in a few minutes after ten that night. I remember," she took a breath, "because I had to get up to go to the loo and I heard him creeping in the front door."

"You're certain that was the time?"

"Yes," she slowly drawled, "because I looked at the digital clock in the kids room and I thought he was back from the pub earlier than usual."

"And what pub does he drink in and play dominoes?"

The door opened to admit Iain who carried a plastic tray with a stainless steel pot of tea, mugs, sugar and milk.

"Nothing fancy, I'm afraid," he apologised.

Though she tightly smiled, Irene inwardly cursed the inopportune time of his arrival and when they each had a mug in their hands, she continued, "You were about to tell me what pub Jake drinks in?"

"Oh, it's usually the Anvil on the Bellshill Road."

"The Anvil," Irene softly repeated as she bent her head to write in her notebook. "And is that within walking distance of your house?"

"It's about a five minute walk away."

"So your husband won't have taken the car with him?"

She watched as Ellen's eyes narrowed before she slowly replied, "Yes, he did have the car on Saturday night. Perhaps he wasn't drinking that much. He doesn't always drink heavily, I mean. Sometimes he just takes a pint or two. He really just goes to play the dominoes," her voice faded almost to a whisper.

Irene caught Iain's eye and they both had the same thought. The husband had his car with him on Saturday night. Turning to Ellen, she asked, "Do you know any of the patrons that your husband plays dominoes with or drinks with?"

"No, not personally," then hurriedly continued, "Look, I know what you're getting at, but Jake wouldn't have hurt Lesley. He…"

"He what, Ellen? Liked her? Perhaps liked her a little too much?"

Iain watched Ellen McNeill closely, then saw tears forming in her eyes when she quietly replied, "She told you, didn't she? That other police woman. She told you that I think Jake…" she stopped and clutched at her throat as tears began to trickle down her cheeks.

"Yes, Ellen," Irene gently replied. "She told me what you thought because she is a police officer and like the rest of us, we're trying to find out who killed your sister. You want to know too, don't you?"

She couldn't speak, but nodded.

"Do you think your husband hurt your sister, Ellen?"

She raised her head to stare Irene in the eyes and while tears continued to run down her cheeks, softly replied, "I don't know."

****

They had both decided that the interview would be conducted under formal conditions, that they would address him as Mister McNeill and regardless of their previous visit, decline to use his forename.

Jake McNeill was waiting by the door when they got out of the car and with a smile, said, "I saw you turning the car. Can I offer you a tea or a coffee?"

From the outset it was obvious that he was extremely nervous. Before Rossi could respond, Janie Wallace held up her hand and replied, "No thanks, Mister McNeill. We're on a tight schedule."

He led them into the front room and explained, "I've told the kids that we need a bit of privacy, so they're up in their room watching television." He shrugged and added, "I really think that they should be at school, but Ellen insisted on keeping them off."

Inviting them to sit, it was Rossi who fetched his notebook from his jacket pocket and explained, "We're taking statements from everyone who knew Lesley, Mister McNeill, and trying to verify their whereabouts on the evening that Lesley went missing. Can you tell me where you where last Saturday night, say from eight o'clock onwards?"

He had worried all night about their visit. Again and again he had gone over in his head what he would tell them, but now confronted by them both his nerve failed him.

"I...I was out," he stammered."

"What time did you leave the house, Mister McNeill, and where exactly where you and with whom?"

He unconsciously licked at his lips, but it was noticed by both the officers before he replied, "I usually go to the pub for a couple of pints and a game of doms…dominoes," he corrected himself and cleared his throat.

"And is that what you did last Saturday night?" Rossi calmly asked.

"Ah, no," his throat constricted as he tried to swallow. "I, ah, decided just to go for a drive. Alone. To clear my head."

"To clear your head," Rossi slowly repeated, then added, "Alone."

He stared inquiringly at McNeill before he asked, "Why did you need to clear your head?"

He took a deep breath, but they saw him anxiously fiddle with his fingers and continued to lick at his lips and he wondered why his mouth was so suddenly dry.

"I had things on my mind, things I couldn't discuss with Ellen."

Rossi pursed his lips and shrugged as he asked, "What, job related things? Personal things? What were these things that caused you to go driving alone? And on that point, where did you drive to?"

"Eh, down to Strathclyde Park. I sometimes go there if I'm worried about something. Sit by the loch, that sort of thing," he shrugged.

"And what was worrying you on Saturday night?"

He cleared his throat as he fought against the rising bile and taking a deep breath, said, "Look, I know what you're getting at, but you have to understand. I didn't do anything to Lesley. I couldn't because…"

"Because?"

"Daddy?"

They all turned to see Fergus standing in the doorway staring at them in turn.

Almost with relief, McNeill stood and reaching out his arms to the small boy who run into them and said, "The tele's not working."

"I'll just be a minute," he told them and led his son out of the room.

They listened as he tramped upstairs, both annoyed at the interruption.

"What do you think?" Rossi quietly asked.

"Well, he's shit scared and that's a fact, but does he know anything about Lesley's murder?" she shook her head. "I'm not getting that vibe. What about you?"

"Me neither. I think he's more worried about what his wife told you, about her finding out he fancied Lesley."

Three or four minutes later, McNeill returned to the front room and it was clearly obvious he was a lot calmer.

They could not know that in that brief interlude he had made up his mind to tell the truth.

"So," Rossi was clearly surprised, "what you're telling us is that you had this thing for Lesley and when you disclosed your feelings, she knocked you back? Threatened to tell your wife?"

"Yes," he nodded. "To be honest it was a kind of wake-up call. I realised I didn't love Lesley as I thought. It was just a stupid crush I suppose you could call it."

"When did you tell Lesley about your feelings?" Janie interrupted.

"Oh, it was weeks ago. I went to her office…"

"You went to Orkney Street police office?"

"Yes. I knew from Ellen talking about meeting Lesley for a lunch that she was on an early shift and finished about two in the afternoon, so I took a couple of hours off work and, well," he took a breath as though the memory disturbed him, "I waited on her and when I got out of the car she thought something had happened to Ellen or one of the kids. I asked her to get into the car so that I could speak with her, but she seemed…I don't know. Distracted. I acted like a complete fool and told her how I felt and she just…she just told me I was a fucking idiot and that's when she threatened to tell Ellen and told me that if I didn't grow up," his face reddened, "that she'd make sure Ellen would leave me and take the kids."

"Did that make you angry?" Rossi asked.

"Angry?" his face contorted. "No, it made me feel stupid, like the idiot she called me."

He leaned forward and rubbing at his brow, continued, "Since then I've been worried sick that she told Ellen. Look," he reached his hands out as though in plea, "I know I've been an idiot, but I wouldn't hurt Lesley. All I worry about now is that if Ellen finds out, I'll lose her and the children too."

Rossi glanced at Janie and said, "The problem we have now, Mister McNeill, is that by disclosing that Lesley threatened you, you have provided us with a possible motive for you harming her and particularly as you do not have an alibi for your movements on the night she went missing."

"Look, if I could I…" he stopped and his eyes widened. "Last Saturday night," he almost stopped breathing, then said at a rush, "When I was coming home from the park, I saw a police car with its blue lights on. It had stopped a car on the Bothwell Road. Yes," he cried out, "opposite Douglas Gardens. It was a Traffic car." He made a circle with his finger over his head and added, "The policeman was wearing one of those white covers on his cap, you know?"

"What time was this," Rossi's eyes narrowed.

"Oh," McNeill squeezed his eyes tight as he tried to recall, then said, "I'm only guessing but I think it was about ten o'clock or maybe earlier? I'm not really sure."

Again Rossi glanced at Janie and said, "The time between eight-thirty and ten o'clock still gives you time to travel to Glasgow and back, Mister McNeill, so that doesn't really alibi you for the time your sister-in-law went missing. However, we'll check out what you've told us. Janie?" he turned to her. They had agreed that it was she who would deliver the gut punch and so she asked, "When was the last time you visited Lesley at her flat?"

"Her flat?" his face betrayed his surprise. "Oh, let me think," his brow furrowed. "I'm not certain, but I'm guessing it must have been some months ago and if I did visit the flat, I'd certainly do it with Ellen and the kids," he shook his head when he added, "never on my own."

He seemed so sure of his reply that it occurred to Janie that maybe he was telling the truth, but that didn't stop her from commenting, "So, if it was some months ago like you say, there's no likelihood we might find your fingerprints in the flat?"

"No, none at all," he shrugged and seemed confident it couldn't have been his fingerprint.

She paused to permit him to say something else, perhaps recall that yes, he did recently visit the flat; however, he said nothing further.

"Our boss will probably want us to speak with you again, Mister McNeill," she said at last, then decided that he likely deserved what she was about to disclose.

"One thing I should mention. You might want to consider telling your wife what you told us about your affection for Lesley because I don't think she'll be too surprised."

****

The RCS surveillance team followed Stokoe to his mother's home and continued their static watch. However, in the control room there was a tense excitement among most of the officers at the news Stokoe intended travelling the next afternoon to Glasgow and likely take with him the drugs hidden in the house.

Well, most of the officers celebrated, but not DS Kevin Webster, for he realised that instead of being the main man in the operation that he had wrongly assumed would be a Regional Crime Squad coup, once Stokoe reached the border protocol dictated that he would then be handed over to their Scottish counterparts, the Scottish Crime Squad. In fact, it now transpired that Webster's only contribution to the whole affair that would be recognised by his boss was that DI Frankie Solomon had allegedly informed Webster of the information; information that Webster was dutifully obliged to pass on. Shit!

He had been too smart.

Now, instead of covering himself in glory the prospect of promotion had slipped away and there was nothing he could do for he could no more admit his part in the collusion with Frankie Solomon than admit that the source was his, for that would reveal that he had inveigled Solomon to assist him in duping his RCS boss.

Miserably, he rubbed at his brow as the officers around him grinned at the prospect of the Jocks taking down not just a persistent offender like Doughnut Stokoe, but also recover a substantial quantity of heroin.

Worse still for Webster was that though the Jocks would make the arrest and seize the heroin, the credit for the source information and eventual arrest and seizure would go to Frankie *fucking* Solomon!

****

Returning to Govan police office with Iain driving, Colin Morton in the front passenger seat and Irene Crichton in the rear, Morton turned to her and asked, "What is your opinion of Ellen McNeill?"

"Well," she slowly began, "if you want my guess, she's not responsible for her sister's death. When Janie Wallace spoke with her last night in her sister's flat, Janie said that she thought Ellen was jealously bitter that Lesley was doing well and had the makings of a successful career ahead of her while she was married, two kids and in a lowly paid clerical job. You saw for yourself how she was dressed this morning, as though she had taken no time about her personal grooming, so add that to her suspecting her husband was no longer interested in her, that instead he preferred her sister, the slimmer and more fashionable Lesley. If you ask me," she testily added, "that's enough reason for any woman to be bitter and vengeful, yet I didn't get the impression she wanted her sister dead. However, what did arise is that she isn't certain about her husband, but we'll need to wait and find out how young Janie and Peter Rossi got on with him."

"And what about the time Lesley went missing. Has Ellen an alibi?"

"Not the best alibi, I'm sorry to say. Says she was at home with the children, so we'll need to either accept that she wouldn't leave the children on their own or have them spoken to, but I think it's unlikely that they'll remember and," she sighed, "any interview with kids that young must take place with a parent or a responsible person present and that obviously brings its own problems because how do we prevent the parents from being present unless we tell them they're suspects? I'm certain they would want to be in the room to hear what we're asking their kids."

Her eyes narrowed when leaning forward, she continued, "That said, I also didn't get the impression that she and Lesley were as close as she might have liked us to believe. What do you think, Iain?"

Concentrating on his driving but nevertheless listening, he replied, "It still bothers me that in the years I knew Les, she never once mentioned she had a twin sister. I don't have any siblings so I'm no expert, but it strikes me that if I *had* I'd have at least mentioned them from time to time and particularly to the people I work with. The fact that Les didn't say anything strikes me as odd so yes, I'm inclined to think maybe they weren't that close. What I'm trying to say is that if they were close, surely Les would have mentioned Ellen, you know, things like, 'I'd lunch the other day with my sister'; things like that."

Morton nodded as though agreeing with their assessment before he said, "I'm of the opinion that her grief was genuine. What do you think, Irene?"

"Seemed to be, though it might have been tinged with a little regret too that she and her sister weren't as close as perhaps she'd have liked them to be."

"Iain?" he turned to him.

He guessed that the DCI didn't really need his opinion on Ellen McNeill's demeanour, but was pleased that Morton had the courtesy to include him in the discussion and replied, "In my limited experience, sir, real grief is difficult to pretend so yes, I think she was truly sorry that Les is dead. However, that doesn't mean to say she might not be responsible."

A slow smile crept across Morton's face as he replied, "Good answer, Iain. In *my* experience, people tend to get taken in by signs of grief and it's a good way to hide their true feelings. So I'm guessing that her grief aside, you remain suspicious of Missus McNeill?"

He didn't immediately respond, but then said, "A couple of years ago I attended at a flat in the tenements in Copland Road, an old woman who called us turned out to be a moaning faced old git going on about her neighbour across the landing coming home drunk at night. There was nothing going on when I got there, but I thought I'd knock on the neighbour's door anyway and advise her that a complaint had been made and if she was coming in late at night with a drink in her, to do herself a favour and keep the noise down. That's all I intended, just a wee quiet warning."

He turned from Paisley Road West into Broomloan Road, then continued, "The door was opened by a wee boy aged nine. When I asked where his mammy was, he said she was out with her boyfriend. Turned out he was alone in the house with his six-year-old brother, several packets of crisps each, a bottle of Irn-Bru between them, the television on and a four bar electric fire burning away in the front room. I had no option but to call the duty social work team who arrived at the same time as the mother and her boyfriend, though he scarpered at the sight of us. Needless to say the mother was very sorry and assured us it wouldn't happen again, blah, blah, blah. My point is," he glanced in the rear-view mirror at Irene Crichton and guessed she was probably recalling him telling her about his ex-wife Carol, "no matter how loving a mother might be or tell you she is, you know as well as I do that people can be very selfish and their needs come first. In that occasion, it was the mother's boyfriend who came before her weans. So my question is and difficult though it might be to prove, how can we be sure that Ellen McNeill didn't leave *her* weans tucked up in their beds and go to meet with Les?"

Morton turned to stare at Irene and sighing, said, "He's got a point. We can't dismiss the sister because she said she was at home with the children."

They were getting out of the car in the rear yard when Iain caught her eye and subtly nodded that she hang back.

"I'll just be a minute, Colin," she called out and asked, "What?"

He passed her the note from the Inquiry Department sergeant and as she read it, he said, "Think the boss will give me a couple of hours off for the service tomorrow morning?"

"Has there been no word of any family being traced?"

"No," he shook his head. "I don't think it's right that old Sam shuffles off this mortal coil without someone being there."

Surprised, she stared at him before replying, "I didn't know you were a Shakespeare fan and you're just a soft-hearted bugger too, aren't you, Iain Meikle?"

He smiled as returning the note, she added, "I don't think this will be a problem, though I regret I won't be able to attend with you. If we haven't traced Paula Menzies by this evening, we're knocking on her door first thing in the morning and I'm down for the interview. But we're still on for dinner this evening?"

"Oh aye," he grinned with forced enthusiasm, "and looking forward to it."

However, when she turned away he could not help but feel that this new and sudden relationship with Irene was moving fast and inwardly though he hated admitting it to himself, thought it might be moving too quickly for him.

CHAPTER NINETEEN

They had moved from the gym to a shabby pub on Dumbarton Road.

It was a dimly lit, smoke ridden premises where the ceiling was stained by the nicotine of thousands of cigarettes, where large faded travel posters of far flung cities were thumbtacked to the walls to hide the dampness that seeped through the wallpaper, where tables were occasionally given a cursory wipe with a ragged cloth but failed to remove the greasy smears, where upholstered chairs were patched with black masking tape, where the sullen owner was sympathetic to those regulars who had shady dealings to discuss and where new faces were always viewed with suspicion.

Ordering three pints at the bar, Charlie Gallagher and his trusted lieutenants Seamus O'Brien and Marty Boyle moved to a corner booth where two old men, one in his seventies and the other in his sixties, sat playing dominoes.

"You'll be more comfortable over there, I think," Gallagher nodded to the other side of the pub.

It seemed as if the elder of the two men was about to object, but his friend hastily gathered up the domino chips and replied, "Aye, okay, we're moving, big man."

Boyle sneered and stood his ground, forcing the pensioner to squeeze past him as he shuffled out of the corner seat.

Sitting themselves down with Gallagher's back to the wall and a clear view of the door, he quietly asked, "How's the money situation?"

It was O'Brien who replied, "We did some of the rounds early this morning and most of its collected and counted, boss. We'll get the rest tomorrow and it'll be ready to be delivered when you give the say so."

"Well, I'm giving you the say so now, tomorrow night just after seven o'clock in the Waterloo Bar," he said, then stopped speaking as the busty, gum chewing tattooed barmaid delivered the beer to the table.

Boyle grinned and was about to speak to the young woman, but was foiled when Gallagher growled, "Let's not get distracted, wee man, eh?"

Nodding, Boyle turned his head and like O'Brien, bent forward to listen to Gallagher.

In short, terse sentences, Gallagher related the plan for the collection and handover of payment for the heroin.

"So, this guy coming up will be wearing a Liverpool shirt and arriving at about seven in the evening at the Central Station. Is it not a lot easier to just meet him there?" Boyle asked.

"Aye, why don't you do that?" Gallagher's voice oozed sarcasm. "Then, when the choo-choo polis that haunt the fucking place ask you what you are doing with a bag load of my money and handing it to a guy right off a train who's handing you *his* bag that's loaded with heroin, you can say, 'It was a lot easier than meeting him in the Waterloo pub, officer,' ya fucking halfwit!"

Chastened, Boyle's face turned red as across the table, O'Brien grinned at him before turning towards Gallagher to confirm, "It's the Waterloo Bar then, big man."

Taking a deep breath, he bit nervously at his lower lip before asking, "Have you given any thought to just taking the H and keeping the money?"

Gallagher's eyes narrowed as he stared at him before he replied, "You're suggesting we screw over Billy Madison?"

"Why not?" O'Brien shrugged. "If I remember correctly, someone once told me that the wee shite slashed some big noise gangster up here then buggered off down south to escape being murdered. You know Glasgow as well as I do, Charlie. People have got long memories and particularly if they've been wronged, so I reckon it's unlikely he'll risk his life to come back here to start a war with us; am I right?"

Gallagher inhaled, his brow knitted and he stared vacantly into space for a moment as he gave thought to O'Brien's proposal. He sipped at his beer as his mind worked overtime and thought, it would be a real coup if he agreed to O'Brien's suggestion and the money would be useful to purchase more of the H, though of course he'd need to find a new supplier. The problem was though that being a middle man Madison was a reliable source for the drug with access to English based suppliers that Gallagher did not have and suppliers, as he knew, could be far more dangerous to deal with than the Liverpool based Weegie. In the short term he could be cutting off a useful route for the H and other commodities for the sake of nearly fifty-eight grand when over a period of time he could likely earn himself a lot more if he continued to use Madison.

However, the suggestion to retain the money was very tempting indeed and so he replied, "Let me think about that for the time being. In the meantime, we'll go ahead with the plan as it is." O'Brien nodded as if in consent, but what Gallagher could not and would never know was that his red-haired enforcer was making plans of his own.

For some months, O'Brien had considered ripping Gallagher off, stealing the money they'd collected and fulfilling a long time dream; disappearing to one of the Spanish islands and opening a bar. What had held him back was that prior to this large deal with Madison, he and Boyle never collected any amount in excess of eighteen grand. But now with this big deal looming and fifty-seven and a half thousand pounds to be collected in total, he'd have enough to make a start abroad. His mind racing, he also considered that if he stole the heroin he could take it to London and finding a buyer, maybe make a quick profit on the H too.

He involuntarily swallowed, for what had finally decided him was the killing of Paula Menzies and the dismemberment of her body for he knew in his gut that somehow or other, the polis would eventually cotton on to her disappearance and they'd be all over Charlie, Marty and him like a bad rash and there was no way he was going down for murder; not for Charlie fucking Gallagher anyway.

"I said are you listening, Seamus?"

He startled and turned to see Gallagher staring at him.

"Sorry, big man, I was away there, thinking about the handover. What was that you were saying?"

"I said, do you think you and Marty will be enough to do the handover or do you want to bring in some extra muscle in case that bastard Madison has his own idea about ripping us off?"

Exhaling through pursed lips, O'Brien's brow furrowed for the last thing he needed was more bodies to worry about. Boyle he could handle and maybe the courier too, but extra muscle?

He replied with a forced a grin, "I think the less punters that know about your business, the better. I mean there's nothing that me and the wee man can't handle, eh Marty? Particularly if we go tooled up."

Grinning widely and flashing his yellowing teeth, Boyle eagerly nodded and butted in, "Aye, I'd be happy for some bastard to have a go at us, eh, Seamus?"

Gallagher turned to stare from one to the other before hissing, "Listen! This is a handover you're dealing with, ya pair of clowns. You're not looking to start a fucking war!" Then bending his head closer to Boyle, he muttered, "You start anything in a public place like the Waterloo Bar, you're going to have the cops down on top of you faster than shit off a hot shovel and how do you think you'd explain two bags, one filled with cash and another filled with smack?"

Embarrassed, the two men stared down at their pints. Realising that he needed to keep them onside, Gallagher sighed and nodding to the barmaid who was a couple of tables away, grinned and said, "How about bending her over the table here and us taking turns to give her one, eh?"

Keen to avoid any further chastisement from Gallagher, Boyle eagerly seized upon the suggestion and in lurid detail, described what he would do to the young woman while O'Brien grinned and nodded as though in agreement.

However, try as he might he could not shake the thought that even if Gallagher disagreed with stealing the heroin and if the courier wasn't too much of a handful, he would give serious thought to battering Boyle senseless and if need be, the courier too before making off with both the money and the H.

That and if it got to the rough stuff, hidden in his flat he had a wee persuader that he'd never told the other two about.

He watched as the two men sipped at their pints and continued to discuss the barmaid's physical attributes, then quietly smiled as though listening; but his thoughts were elsewhere for he was already making plans for hiring a car, travelling to London to sell the heroin and then onto Spain and what clothing he would pack when he returned home that afternoon to the flat.

****

Thomas Preston, the Detective Superintendent in charge of the Regional Crime Squad team responsible for the operation against Derek 'Doughnut' Stokoe sat at his desk and stared down at the handwritten notes he had made prior to the phone call. At last he took a deep breath and dialled the number.

As he waited for the few seconds for his call to be answered, he gave some thought about the man he was about to speak with. There was no love lost between the two police officers, not since a year previously when both attended the Bramshill course where the Jock bastard had beaten him to the prize awarded to the top student on the prestigious, senior management 'Surveillance and Counter Terrorism' course. What made it more difficult for the embittered Preston was he had privately, but vociferously complained to the head of the Police College that it was he who was the more suitable candidate for the prize; a complaint that was completely dismissed and then to his acute embarrassment thereafter leaked by persons' unknown to the rest of the students.

"Scottish Crime Squad, DCI Richards," the droll voice echoed in his ear.

"Good day, Maurice, it's Thomas Preston from the RCS," he snappily replied.

"Hello, Tom," Richards cheerfully replied, "How're you doing?"

Preston smarted, for he hated his forename name being abbreviated and suspected that Richards knew this. Exhaling, he said, "I'm on with some information that was gleaned from a source and might be of mutual benefit to our respective Squads."

At his side of the call, Richards choked back a laugh and thought, trust the snobby Preston to use a dozen words when a couple would do, then tongue in cheek asked, "So, you're looking for some help, then?"

In short, sharp detail, Preston informed the DCI of the pending visit by Doughnut Stokoe to Glasgow who was assessed to be bringing a kit bag full of heroin.

"But no idea how much heroin he's bringing with him or who he's meeting here?" Richards asked as he scribbled on a notepad.

"No," Preston drily replied, "but as per previous agreements between your Crown Office and our own Crown Prosecution Service, my officers will follow him to the Glasgow Central Station where they will hand the target over to you. I presume you will have a team standing by?"

"Oh, absolutely. You say he's planning to return home to Liverpool the same evening?" Richards squinted as he spoke.

"That's his travel plans, yes," Preston sighed.

"So, that would suggest he doesn't intend travelling far from the station or possibly even making a handover at the station or nearby, then?"

Keen to end the call, Preston huffily replied, "I'm sure that you have assessed that correctly, Maurice."

"Well, I look forward to acting on this, Tom," he cheerily said, "and I'll get my guys to contact your team. Of course I'll ensure that when we nab this guy the report to the Fiscal will make mention of the provenance of the information being your own Squad and I'll formally request that the Fiscal forward a copy of the indictment to your CPS as well as your boss in London. Well," smiling as he imagined Preston's outrage at having to hand over such a significant target and particularly to Richards, he added, "I'll personally give you a phone to update you when we have made an arrest. Nice speaking with you again, Tom."

"Yes, thank you. Goodbye," Preston abruptly ended the call. Replacing the phone, Richards slowly shook his head and grimaced as he muttered, "Arse."

****

Driving home, Ellen McNeill's thoughts were filled with the picture of her sisters body lying beneath the white sheet in the small anteroom, her face deathly white.

Stood in the visitors' room staring through the glass window, she had worried that the police officer Mister Morton might have suggested or tried to encourage her to enter the anteroom, perhaps wrongly assuming she might wish to touch or embrace Lesley but that, she inwardly cringed, would have been more than she could bear.

When the curtains had closed for one awful moment she thought she might collapse in a dead faint and probably would have but for the presence of the woman detective who stepped forward to tightly hold and support her.

Later, seated in the small room with the woman and the man, try as she might she could neither remember what questions they had asked her nor even their names, recalling only that they had probed her relationship with Lesley and her husband and supposed that whatever answers she had given them seem to have satisfied them.

Driving through Kyle Park towards her home, her thoughts turned to Jake and she wondered what he had told the officers who visited him.

She wasn't stupid and stomach tightening, realised the police suspected that she might have harmed Lesley just as they obviously also suspected her husband too.

Several hundred yards short of the junction with Knowehead Gardens, she stopped the car in Old Glasgow Road and switched off the engine.

Staring listlessly through the windscreen, she thought about the next ten minutes, how she would greet Jake, what she would tell him, what she would ask him, then asked herself; could she ever again trust him?

More to the point, *would* she ever again trust him?

Her teeth gritted and lips tightly set, she made her decision.

Switching the engine on, she drove home.

****

Iain Meikle read the note in his dookit and frowning, made his way to the sergeants room where he saw Sergeant Jimmy Cole seated at his desk, but to his surprise saw Cole to be dressed in a light blue sweater and jeans.

"Looking for me, Sarge?" Iain held up the note as he greeted him.

"Ah, the very man," Cole smiled then indicated he sit.

As he did so, his nose twitched when he got a whiff of Cole's scent and thought the bugger must have spent an hour walking back and forth through a Boots perfume department.

"How are you getting on with the CID?"

"Fine," Iain pursed his lips, surprised that Cole would have any interest in anything his shift constables did, then reluctant to spend any time in the sergeant's company, asked, "Was there anything specific you wanted to see me about?"

"Oh, yeah," Cole turned away and began to sift through his basket before lifting a stapled sheet of papers. "This report came down from the typists for you to sign. I thought you might be busy with the murder inquiry and was going to 'PP' it for you, but thought you might want to read through it first."

Iain stared at him. It wasn't like the shift supervisor to be so attentive to any of his constables. Shrugging, he took the report from Cole's outstretched hand and glanced through it.

"Seems fine to me," he said and fetching his pen from his jacket pocket, added his signature before handing it back to Cole.

"Great," Cole smiled widely. "So, like I said, how's things? Think you'll be making application to join the CID?"

Iain stared at him as though he were mad before replying, "I've only been with them for a couple of days, Sarge. I'm not even officially attached as an aide, but just there to assist for the period of the inquiry. I mean, it could wind up tomorrow or…"

"What!" Cole's eyes narrowed, "Have they got a suspect already?"

"No," he shook his head, then in that instant realised why Cole was being sociable. He wanted to know what was going on in the inquiry, Iain thought. He's still worried that some blame for Les's death would attach to him.

"I'm not saying it will end tomorrow. What I'm saying is that I'm only there for as long as the inquiry runs, then it's back to the shift. If the inquiry takes a week, a month or whatever, then at the end of it I'll give some consideration to whether or not I want to make application to join them, but right now…" he left the rest unsaid.

"It's a bad business," Cole scowled. "Lesley is the first…I mean the only officer I've known to die in service like that. I hope they get the bastard," he vehemently burst out.

Meikle stared at him then nodding in agreement pointedly glanced at his watch before saying, "I better get back."

"Aye, right, of course," Cole turned back towards his desk. He'd pulled open the door before it occurred to him, then turning, asked, "This is your variable rest day, Sarge? What you doing in the office?"

Cole shrugged and replied, "When Lesley went missing it was all hands on deck, so I kind of got behind with the paperwork. Her indoors was nagging the arse off me to take the kids out for the day," he smiled humourlessly and flicking a hand at his basket, continued, "so I kind of worked a flanker and instead headed in here to catch up."

"Oh, right then, I'll see you," Iain said and closed the door behind him.

It wasn't the first time Iain had heard about Cole taking time away from his wife and had heard the sergeant was a bit of a ladies' man, but dismissed the rumours and accepted that being disliked as Cole was he was an easy target for office gossip.

Besides, he gave a quiet grimace, he didn't like the lazy bastard and had no interest in what the slimy bugger got up to.

****

An increasingly dejected DCI Colin Morton sat in the chair beside Tam Whelan's desk to be told, "No, boss, there's been nothing new since you left this morning. I've also been in regular touch with Jack Fleming who's at the close watching for Paula Menzies, but there's no show there either. The only thing he did report was that Charlie Gallagher left earlier this morning and Jack hasn't contacted me to say if Gallagher is back yet, so I can only assume he's not returned to the flat."

Slowly shaking his head, Morton reached into his jacket pocket for his cigarettes then offering one to Whelan, lit them before before asking, "What about the media appeal? Anything back from Jimmy Donnelly in the Media Department?"

"Nothing, boss. Do you want me to give him a call?"

"No, no need. If Jimmy has any information he'll be on the blower right away. What about the fingerprint?"

Whelan shook his head before replying, "No word yet, but I'll give it to the end of the day and see if they have any results, particularly for the lassie's brother-in-law, that guy Jacob McNeill."

Morton rose from his chair and said, "Do that and when Irene gets back, ask her to join me in my office."

"Right, boss. Where has she gone, did she say?"

"She's away to try her luck with the Fiscal's at the Clyde Street office, see if she can persuade one of them to apply for an arrest warrant for Paula Menzies as a person of interest in the murder."

Whelan's face expressed his doubt, to which Morton added, "I know, I know. We're clutching at straws here, Tam. I don't see a Sheriff signing a warrant for Paula without any hard evidence that she might be have information about Lesley's murder, but we have to try," he sighed.

Returning to his office, he took a deep breath and read through the typed and worryingly thin synopsis that was the investigation into the murder of Constable Lesley Rudd.

Nothing in the report indicated a witness of any value and the only tentative suspect was Charlie Gallagher and that simply because of a phone call from Gallagher's live-in partner.

He laid the report back down onto his desk and rolled his head to ease the ache in his neck.

The door knocked and was almost immediately opened by 'Patches' Cruickshank, who said, "Don't want to be a nuisance, Colin, but thought I'd pop in to see how the inquiry is going?"

Courteously, Morton respectfully stood for the Detective Chief Superintendent and indicating a chair, asked, "Coffee?"

Cruickshank smiled and replied, "I poked my head into the general office. Tam Whelan says he'll send someone in with two cups. So," he settled himself into a chair, "anything doing?"

Morton inhaled before replying, "Sorry to say, sir, no. We seem to have come to a standstill. No witnesses, no Forensic evidence and more importantly," he sighed, "no suspects. Well, that said," he related the phone call from Paula Menzies and the intention to bring her into the office to interview her as to why she wanted to speak to Lesley Rudd.

"And you're certain it was this woman Menzies who made the call?"

"It was one of the team, a uniformed cop who knew Rudd and worked with her that I've drafted in to assist the inquiry. He recognised Menzies voice, so yes. Iain Meikle is a sound guy and I've no hesitation in believing him to be correct."

"And you're trying to get a hold of this woman?"

"Aye, but so far without luck. I'm a bit reluctant to take her from the flat she shares with Charlie Gallagher just in case and as I hope, it's Gallagher that she wanted to speak to Rudd about. Irene's hoping to get a warrant to detain Menzies for interview, but I'm doubtful she'll succeed."

"Okay, I'm aware you think Gallagher might in some way be

implicated in Rudd's murder, but what do you base that suspicion on?"

His brow furrowed when he replied, "Rudd had an interest in Gallagher and had submitted a report to Criminal Intelligence about him. I'm of the opinion that if Gallagher suspected Rudd was nosing into his business, he might have presumed her to be more than a nuisance, though at this time I don't know why. It's a leap of faith, but to be honest, sir, it's the only lead we have."

"I recall you saying when we met at headquarters that you were looking at the family. Her sister and brother-in-law, was it?"

"That's correct, but again," Morton shook his head, "there's no direct evidence against either of them. I met with the sister, who by the way is her twin, at this morning's PM and she was formally interviewed by Irene Crichton. Irene is of the opinion that the sister was jealous of Rudd and most of that is assessed because it seems the brother-in-law, Jacob McNeill, had a thing for Rudd."

"Happy families then," Cruickshank shook his head. "I'm guessing if you're looking at them both then they are not alibied?"

"The sister says she was at home with the young children, two of them, when Rudd went missing so unless she took them with her or left them alone in the house in Uddingston…" he shrugged and left the rest unsaid. "The two officers I sent to interview the brother-in-law report that he doesn't have a strong alibi for the time, so he's not out of the frame yet."

"I understand you were at the PM this morning. Was the pathologist able to confirm the cause of death?"

Morton squeezed his lips tightly together before replying, "According the the pathologist the lassie was struck on the head by a blunt instrument," he wryly smiled, then added, "Her description, not mine. She reckons the force of the blow would have at the very least stunned if not caused Rudd to lose consciousness and from there it's likely she either fell or was pushed into the water. That's obviously open to conjecture.

What is definite is that she was certainly alive when she went into the Clyde for her lungs were full of water and she has drowned. The pathologist is of the opinion she was unconsciousness when she drowned."

"But nothing to suggest she might have tripped and fell in?"

"No," Morton vigorously shook his head. "What little we know is that the witness Samuel Fullerton," he paused and sighed, "regretfully, now deceased, apparently told two hospital staff that he saw Rudd with a male figure and thereafter heard the splash as she presumably went into the water."

"And what about this blunt instrument?" Cruickshank allowed himself a small smile.

"No trace of anything at the locus that would fit the bill," Morton shook his head. "According to the measurement of the wound taken by the pathologist it was something similar to a round baton, though fractionally larger."

The door was pushed open to admit Irene Crichton who carefully carried two china mugs of steaming hot coffee.

"Met Tam in the corridor on his way here with this," she laid the mugs down onto the desk then turning to Cruickshank, said, "Hello, sir. How are you doing?"

"Fine, thanks Irene," he smiled at her as she drew up a chair. "Colin had just been telling me about the lack of progress in your inquiry. You anything to add to that?"

She took a deep breath before replying, "No, I'm afraid not. Likely he's mentioned the thing about Paula Menzies?"

"Yes. How did you get on at the Fiscal's office?"

"Well," she began, "after I explained the circumstances and after they burst into hysterical laughter at my request…" she finished with a shrug.

"So, Colin, what do you intend now then?"

"I still need to have Menzies interviewed so what I intend is for Irene along with a couple of the heavies I've got in the Department to knock on Gallagher's door first thing in the morning," he grinned at her.

Cruickshank pretended to scowl as he asked, "No other option? I mean, won't you consider taking her off the street?"

"That was the original plan, but again that relies on getting her alone and it seems that when she leaves the flat she's usually in the company of Gallagher. At least if we take her from the flat even though Gallagher is there, it lessens the chance of a public kick-out in the street."

"And if she refuses to come with you?" he turned to her.

"Then, sir, I might need to invoke the Ways and Means Act."

He stared moodily at her as though deep in thought, before reminding her, "You realise that if you take her, forcibly or otherwise, you might leave yourself open to an allegation and possible complaint against you for false arrest?"

"Then I'll just need to be my usual charming self, won't I?" she smiled.

****

Arriving back at Orkney Street, Peter Rossi suggested he commence typing Jake McNeill's statement while Janie Wallace excused herself and headed for the female toilets on the ground floor.

Five minutes later and irritably shaking her head at the usual lack of a clean towel, she opened the door into the corridor and almost collided with Sergeant Jimmy Cole who she was surprised to see was out of uniform.

"Hello, Janie," he stopped and turning, greeted her with a wide smile. "How's things going?"

She didn't like Cole and had always thought him to be a little too attentive, too tactile for her liking, but politely replied, "Fine thanks, Sergeant, and you?"

"Oh, so so," he shrugged. "Just popped in today to clear up some outstanding paperwork. Gives me the chance to be away from her indoors and the kids for a couple of hours," he grimaced as though sharing a secret. His eyes narrowed and he raised his hand to gently stroke at her arm before continuing, "Sorry to hear about your break-up."

She couldn't explain why, but inwardly shivered at his touch and forcing a smile, replied, "Yeah, well, it's old news now."

"And you're with Iain Meikle on the murder inquiry? I suppose we'll soon be seeing you transferred to the CID?"

"Oh, I don't know if I'm ready for it," she continued with a fixed smile.

He grimaced and slowly shook his head when he said, "Iain's a good man and I'd be sorry to lose him off the shift. One of the stalwarts, he is. He tells me that you're struggling for a suspect at the minute. Hopefully, something will turn up, eh?"

"Yes, hopefully," she agreed with a nod then added, "and on that point, I'm supposed to be submitting a statement right now, so if you'll excuse me?"

"Oh, right, of course," he took a step back and raised his hands before continuing, "And Janie," he shrugged, "if you need someone to talk to, about the break-up I mean, you can always knock on my door."

"Thanks, Sergeant," she forced another smile, but turning away from him her face fell for she thought Cole would be the last person on earth she would want to be in a closed room with.

CHAPTER TWENTY

Established in 1969 and stationed at Strathclyde Police's Stewart Street police station, Lothian & Borders Police Headquarters at Fettes in Edinburgh and at Tayside Police's Stonehaven police office, the Scottish Crime Squad was run and financed by Scotland's eight Police Forces Chief Constables.

In 1977 the Squad comprised of over ninety volunteer detective officers drawn from the eight Forces who were seconded to the Squad for anything between three and five years. Primarily set up as a ready means of tackling travelling criminals and major crime that affected more than one police area and thus not limited to Force boundaries, the majority of the officers were surveillance trained. However, as the years passed the Squad were increasingly focusing on drug dealers who travelled not just between the major cities and towns and from England, but also to the outer reaches of the country.

Sat at his desk in the top floor in the Glasgow office, DCI Maurice Richards, a Strathclyde Police officer now in his third year of his secondment to the Squad and aware that at some point in the future he would return to his parent Force, was politically astute to know that if he was to seek further career advancement it was wise to maintain a regular and fruitful contact with the Force's senior management. Lifting the telephone Richards called DCS Alistair Cruickshank's office at Pitt Street Police Headquarters. However, learning that Cruickshank was unavailable he left a message requesting a call back.

****

As it happened at that time Cruickshank was chewing the fat with DCI Colin Morton while Irene Crichton sat smiling tightly, but acutely conscious that if she was as she planned to turn up for dinner at Iain Meikle's house looking irresistibly dazzling, she first needed to nip home to her detached bungalow in Newland's Quadrant Road to shower and change into something short and slinky.

"What do you think, Irene?" Cruickshank caught her unawares.

"About what?" she blushed before smoothly fibbing, "Sorry, I was thinking about the plan to knock on Paula Menzies door tomorrow morning."

"I was saying to Colin, what do you think about the sister or brother-in-law as suspects for Rudd's murder?"

She didn't immediately respond, but then said, "I'm probably hanging myself out to dry here, but no, I don't think the sister killed Lesley. As for her husband though," she shrugged, "he's not fully alibied for the material time and we're still waiting for a result of his fingerprint check on the toilet seat, so maybe we'll get lucky." Making a point of glancing at her wristwatch, she continued as she arose from her chair, "I hope you gentlemen don't mind, but I have an appointment later this evening so I'll head off and be here sharp in the morning, Colin," she nodded to him.

"What time do you intend knocking on Gallagher's door?"

"I've arranged for DS Jack Fleming and his team who are watching the close to accompany me, so with your permission…?"

"Yes," Morton waved at her, "of course and have a good night."

"Nice seeing you again, Irene," Cruickshank gave her a wave as she closed the door.

"Very competent young woman," he remarked after she'd left.

"Aye, she is that," Morton smiled before adding, "and I don't suppose you noticed that she's wearing lipstick and looking a bit, I don't know, like she's paid a wee bit more attention to the way she dresses?"

He stared at the DCI before grinning, then admitted, "No, I didn't, but you're inferring she might have a man in her life?"

"I think so, yes and not before long. That git she was married to," he shook his head. "Everybody and their mammy knew he was a two-timing bastard, but of course it's usually the wife or the husband that's last to find out. I only hope whoever she's tied up with now treats her well."

"She's a big girl," Cruickshank stiffly rose to his feet and rubbed at his increasingly aching lower back, "so let her worry about herself. You, my lad, have a lot more on your plate right now."

"Aye," Morton grinned humorously, "and I have to admit it's bloody keeping me awake at night."

He was about to bid the DCS farewell when his phone rung and answering it, said, "It's for you, sir, your office," and handed Cruickshank the phone.

He listened as Cruickshank took the call and heard him say, "Yes, I'll phone him from here. Thank you."

Holding onto the handset, he told Morton, "It seems Maurice Richards from the Squad is looking for me. If you don't mind

I'll call him from here."
****

Billy Madison put down the phone and slowly exhaled before glancing at his wife Sheila and try as he might he couldn't prevent the rivulet of sweat that slowly coursed down his spine. However, no matter that he loved her more than life itself he could not tell her the whole truth and croaked, "That was the Jamaican to remind me that the bill for the H is due this Saturday.'

Her brow creased as worriedly she asked, "You'll have the money, our Billy? Won't you?"

"Yeah, of course," he scoffed with a lot more feeling than confidence. "Doughnut's going up to Glasgow with it tomorrow and he'll be back on the overnight train, so I'll have it in my hands for Thursday morning. Relax, doll, it'll be fine."

But she had been with him for nearly twenty-eight years and knew her man inside out and could see it in his pale face that he was frightened, so asked, "What else did he say? Did the bastard threaten you, Billy?"

Deciding she'd only worry if she knew the truth, he replied, "Yeah, doll, just the usual shite that if I don't have the cash, what he'll do to me, you know? But don't worry," he faked a laugh, "It's sorted. Trust me."

"Well," she angrily cleared her throat, "if the sod turns up at our door, he'll be very fucking sorry he did! Threaten my man, will he? Bastard!"

With that, she pushed herself up from the armchair and went into the kitchen to fetch her husband a beer.

He slowly lowered his head and inwardly shivered for he couldn't tell her what had been said, knowing that the truth would terrify her.

The Jamaican threatened if he defaulted on the payment he would regret it then followed that with some quietly spoken, but blood chilling vicious threats, mostly describing what he and his team would do with a machete and explaining in detail what bits they would cut off.

But the threats had not been against Billy.

No, the threats had been made against Sheila.

****

Derek 'Doughnut' Stokoe grunted as down on his knees he fumbled beneath the floorboards for the bags of heroin. His sausage like fingers were already caked in the drug from the burst bag causing him to growl and regret that he had punished just his mother when he should have smacked that old hag Gina Poulson, too.

Grabbing what he believed to be the last of the bags he thrust it into the canvas kit bag and fumbled again beneath the floorboards to ensure that he hadn't missed any. He'd counted fifty bags, though of course one bag was a little short due to the spillage, but didn't think that would make much difference and definitely didn't imagine that the guy he was delivering it would want to check it in the middle of a pub.

Satisfied that he'd got the lot, he turned to sit on his wide haunches and slowly let out his breath.

With a slow smile, he thought about Billy Madison and the money he was making for the weedy Scotch guy and that's when the idea came to him. His eyes narrowed as he wondered exactly what would Billy do if instead of handing over the money, Doughnut kept it all to himself?

He didn't for one second consider keeping the heroin for though he was acquainted with most of the heavies on the Liverpool scene and while a large number of them were into the drug trade, Doughnut wasn't good with numbers and wouldn't know how much the H was worth, let alone negotiate a sales deal. If he sold it too cheaply the word would get out that he was an easy mark and Doughnut had a reputation to consider; however, if he priced the H too high, he'd be left holding the bloody stuff and he'd made enough enemies to realise that word would eventually get around and some bastard would tip the wink to the rozzers who'd be on his case faster than a rat up a drainpipe.

No, he slowly smiled, he'd be better off with the cash than the hassle of trying to get rid of the heroin.

But what would our Billy do if he screwed the weasel faced Jock git over, he again wondered?

Apart from Doughnut himself, what heavies did Billy know who he could call upon to set against Doughnut?

Continuing to squat on the floor, his mind worked overtime as he considered the number of real hard men that Madison might contract to get revenge against him.

There was the Anfield Pair, but almost immediately dismissed them when he recalled that the older brother Steff was doing an eight stretch for GBH and his kid brother what's his name, his eyes narrowed, wouldn't dare tackle Doughnut on his own. Not if he wanted to keep his balls in their sac.

Or maybe Billy would bring in some of those right wing nutters that hung around Blonde Bab's house in Tintagel Road. Those fuckers would shag then murder their granny if they thought it would earn them a tenner. Yes, he slowly nodded, they were a definite possibility.

He unconsciously scratched at an itch on his chin and smiled. Maybe even Elvis would get the job of taking him down. Elvis, he continued to smile, the karaoke king of the Red Lion in Bootle who last year was said to be responsible for the shooting of Ernie Jarvis after Jarvis grassed up the team who were responsible for almost a dozen post offices armed robberies; and Jarvis was only *suspected* of touting to the rozzers, for it was never proven.

His brow creased and he sighed for he had to admit the list of possible heavies available to Billy was endless. Too many people would be more than happy to have a crack at Doughnut for with a smile he knew that anyone who could take down Doughnut Stokoe would become legendary and even more feared than he was.

Yet the lure of all that money was overwhelming and sitting there he thought about what he could buy with almost fifty-eight grand instead of the poxy three grand that Madison had promised him. The birds, the bevy, maybe even buy a place in the sun, though he'd never actually been abroad. His eyes shone at the thought as his imagination took over.

Clumsily getting to his feet, he lifted the bag with one hand, surprised at the weight but knew that it wouldn't cause any problem once slung across his shoulder. Still, it might be an idea to pack something across the top of the bags and leaving the bag in the room, collected some old towels from the closet on the landing that on returning he stuffed into the top of the bag.

Drawing the cord closed, he tied it tightly in a bow and once more hefted the bag, but this time onto his shoulder.

With a grunt of satisfaction, he dropped the bag to the floor and headed for his bedroom for he now had a lot to think about.

****

She had hurried home and changed into a black coloured, sleeveless, knee length tightfitting dress with a low cut lace collar, matching high heels and after her shower, had spent more time doing her hair and makeup than she had done in the preceding years.

Now, parked outside Iain Meikle's lower cottage flat in Tealing Avenue and her stomach in knots, she nervously wondered what the hell she was doing.

Though she had never disclosed it to anyone, it had hurt her deeply when she discovered her former husband was cheating on her and to add shame to the shocking revelation, discovered that he and his latest fling were the talk of the steamie with her being the last to know.

Her eyes narrowed and her brow creased at the memory for it still rankled, even after all these years.

But then bashfully, she slowly smiled. My God, she thought and glancing in the rear-view mirror, saw that she was blushing. Here I am, almost forty-one years of age and chasing a man. She tightly closed her eyes and arched her back into the driver's seat. What must he think of me, she wondered?

Slowly she opened her eyes and reaching up, tilted the rear-view mirror to again stare at her grimly set face. She frowned at the white, creased line on the underside of her chin where all those years ago she had been struck with the broken bottle. "Nothing you can do about that, my girl," she muttered to herself with a wry smile, "and besides, you've earned that war wound."

Her thoughts returned to the man she was about to spend the evening with and, she slowly exhaled through pursed lips, if things went well possibly the night too.

She had fancied Iain from the moment she met him, though had never hinted at her affection for the tall, rather sombre man. She liked to believe she had quickly seen through his quiet reserve and realised that there was a depth to him that others did not appreciate.

Like all businesses and professions, the police were inundated with rumour and gossip mongers and it wasn't long before she learned that he was divorced from his wife Carol, who it was whispered lived her life well beyond the means that Iain could afford.

In the years she had known him, their paths frequently crossed professionally though with her senior CID rank and his rank of constable, never socially.

At least not until now.

She could hardly believe that it had been just a few days previously when she made the decision that enough was enough, that for once she would take control of her personal life and taken the plunge.

Now she could only hope that she didn't regret it, that wearing her heart on her sleeve wouldn't be a huge mistake.

Taking a deep breath, she muttered, "Well, you've made your decision, my girl, so let's see what the night brings." Grabbing her jacket and the bottle of red wine from the passenger seat she opened the car door.

Making her way to the gate, she pushed it open and almost laughed out loud for unused these days to wearing high heels she found she had to walk very carefully along the slabbed path through the neat and tended garden. Passing Iain's red coloured and aged, but highly polished Vauxhall Viva parked in the driveway, she squeezed between the high hedgerow and the car before stepping forward to the door at the side of the building. For a heartbeat she hesitated, then steeling herself, rapped with her hand loudly on the door.

A dozen thoughts passed through her head in the seconds it took for Iain Meikle to open the door.

She could not know that standing back from the window in his lounge he had seen her getting out of the car and watching her entering the path was equally nervous about their forthcoming evening together.

Now staring at her, his eyes fluttered in surprise for he didn't recognize Irene Crichton as the Detective Inspector he knew who worked upstairs in the CID office, for the sometimes plainly dressed and perhaps even dowdy DI had transformed into a sleek and extremely attractive woman.

"Hi," he greeted her, conscious that his mouth was dry and the practised welcoming speech suddenly gone from his head.

"Hi, yourself," she smiled at him.

A few seconds passed before she beamed and asked, "Well, can I come in?"

"Oh," his face reddened. "Sorry, yes," and stepped to one side to permit her to enter.

His mind registered that she hadn't brought her overnight bag and inwardly wondered if that was significant.

Taking the bottle of wine from her with a "Thanks," he was about to lead the way through to the lounge, but stopped and staring at her, said, "You look *amazing*."

He couldn't have chosen a better thing to say then turned and led the way to the lounge where her nose twitched at the appetising aroma of cooked food coming through the open door from the small, compact kitchen.

"Please," he took her jacket from her and indicating an armchair, watched as she gracefully sat down. He could not help but admire as her knees demurely together, the tightfitting dress slid halfway up her thighs.

Her first impression was of surprise that the room was neat and tidy with solid and comfortable if slightly worn furniture. In the corner by the window she saw that a drop leaf gate leg table with two folding chairs was covered with a crisp white linen tablecloth and had been set for two.

"To be honest," he saw her glance at the table then admitted with a shrug and a half smile, "I'm still a little surprised that you're actually here."

It was then she realised that he was as nervous as was she and felt a little relieved.

"Well," she slowly replied as she stared at him, "how about you open that bottle of wine and serve me up that mince and tatties you promised?"

****

Driving home that evening, Janie Wallace tried to remember the interview with Jacob McNeill. In fact, she had to force herself to think about the interview for otherwise her thoughts kept drifting back to her cheating boyfriend, Paul.

Yet try as she might she could not concentrate on anything other than his betrayal and even trying to convince herself that she was better off without him, that the hurt and embarrassment he had caused her was worth it to be rid of him.

Tears of self-pity almost blinded her and gritting her teeth to stop herself from bawling out loud, she used the sleeve of her blouse to wipe at her eyes.

"This is crazy," she muttered and indicating, pulled the car over to the side of the road and braked sharply. When the car came to a sudden halt, she took a deep breath and let it out slowly to calm herself.

Sitting there with her hands tightly gripping the steering wheel and ignoring the curious glances of passers by, she finally accepted that she was more upset than she was initially prepared to admit.

"Get a grip, you idiot," she quietly chastised herself and forced herself to think of Paul.

Yes, she admitted, he was good looking and charming. Yes, on occasion he would be thoughtful and bring her flowers. Yes, he could also be big-headed and her eyes narrowing, recalled that he could also be opinionated on issues he knew little about, a fact that often caused her to privately question how bright he really was.

But he was lazy around the house and refused to cook even the simplest of meals, preferring the easy option of buying in a takeaway that was a constant source of complaint by Janie. And he could be moody too, even petulant when he didn't get his own way; another cause of many arguments.

Her mouth grimly set, Janie thought about the frequency of their arguments and realised that more often than not she usually gave in to Paul for the sake of peace, even when she knew she was right.

Now, she wondered, why would I do that when I would never do it with anyone else? Was it because I loved him or *thought* I loved him?

She almost startled for even in her thoughts, this was the first time that she could recall ever doubting her feelings for Paul and in turn this questioned whether she had really loved him as she had convinced herself.

No, she shook her head. What she had thought was love was really a strong affection bordering on adoration.

But it was over, she sighed and felt almost relieved.

True to his word, Peter Rossi had contacted his friend who worked at the Grosvenor and learned that Paul Fisher had booked a room for one night only, but all the rooms were doubles so was unable to confirm if Paul had been alone.

But do I really care now, she asked herself and without realising it, she had taken a huge step forward and felt as though a weight had lifted from her.

Curiously too, she also realised she no longer had any strong feelings for Paul, though knew it would take her some time to get over his betrayal.

Starting the engine, she edged out into the traffic and calmer now continued her drive towards her home.

****

In the bedroom of his flat where he had murdered Paula Menzies, Charlie Gallagher stood in front of the wardrobes mirrored door and hummed along to the radio as he dressed in an open necked black shirt and black suit.

Critically examining himself in the mirror, he turned when the phone by the bed rung.

"Hello, it's me," Seamus O'Brien greeted him. Conscious of Gallagher's instruction about discussing details on the phone, he said, "We're all set for tomorrow night. Most of the dough's collected with just a call tomorrow at a pitch in Easterhouse to get in the last of it in. The wee man will keep it in a bag at his pitch, so like I said boss, it's a go. Any last instructions?"

"Nothing I can think of, pal, just make sure that wee shite stays on track. I don't want him starting a ruckus and bringing the scummies down onto you guys. I've too much riding on this deal."

"Can I ask, have you given any consideration to what we discussed in the pub? I mean…"

"I know what you mean," Gallagher interrupted and continued, "Aye, I did, but I've decided against it for the time being." He sighed into the phone, "The way I see it, it would be a quick profit against a long term business arrangement. That's not to say when the time's right we wouldn't go ahead with your idea if the money was right. Get me?"

"Okay," O'Brien slowly replied before asking, "What you up to the night?"

"I fancy popping up into the town, maybe calling in at a few pubs and," he grinned, "getting myself a bird for night. Just someone to tide me over till I get a replacement for you know who," he sniggered at his own black humour.

O'Brien didn't immediately respond, but shivered for he had a fleeting memory of that night when they had taken Paula's body to the river's edge, what Gallagher and Boyle had done to her body with the short handled axe and then, he choked back some bile, thrown her remains in the plastic sacks into the boot of Boyle's car before transporting them to the pig farm.

"You still there?" Gallagher's voice thundered in his ear.

"Eh? Oh, aye, still here," he gasped.

"Why, you want to join me?"

"Join you?"

"For a couple of pints, ya numpty. Have you not been listening or what?"

"Oh, aye, maybe," O'Brien shrugged. "Where were you thinking of starting off?"

"Probably the Horseshoe Bar, but it gets crowded pretty quickly in there so after a quick pint I'm thinking of meandering up towards Vicky's on Sauchiehall Street. How about I see you in say an hour at the Horseshoe then?"

"Aye, see you then," O'Brien ended the call.

Stood in his kitchen nursing a whisky, he took a deep breath. The last thing he wanted to do was go bevying with Charlie, but neither did he want the big man to become suspicious for after giving the idea a whole lot of thought and his mind made up, O'Brien was committed to the idea.

Rising from the chair he threw back the remains of the whisky then made his way through the flat to the spare bedroom. Moving an old and very heavy armchair to one side, he lifted the corner of the carpet to expose the floorboard then pried up a loose plank. Reaching underneath he fetched out an object covered with an old towel. Unwrapping it, he stared at the .38 Smith and Wesson short barrel revolver. The lightly oiled six shot handgun felt good in his hands and still on his knees, held it at arms length and squinted along the barrel. The handgun and twelve cartridges had cost him almost two hundred quid and he'd bought it simply as an insurance if he ever required extra protection when carrying out any of Charlie's deals. To date though, he never had the need; at least not till now.

Now, he grimly smiled, it was going to help him rip off Charlie for tomorrow night, he was going to rattle that wee bastard Boyle and if the courier interfered, he was getting it too.

Then, smiling at a plan that could not go wrong, it was down to London to sell the H and off to Spain with a bag full of dough.

****

"That was excellent," she smiled at Iain before asking, "can I help with the washing up?"

"Not at all," he returned her smile, pleased that the meal had been a success.

The conversation throughout the meal had become personal, each disclosing details of their private lives and with tacit agreement steering clear of work related issues.

He learned of her hurt and pain caused by her husband's infidelity and her mistrust of men in general, "But only in a social sense," she had smiled, "for I've a lot of good male friends in the job."

"And is that why…" he knew he was entering dangerous territory, but decided to be honest, "you never make the best of yourself? I mean." He blushed, but continued, "You are one hell of a good looking woman, Irene, and yet you seem to dress as though you don't care about your appearance. Am I being too rude?" he grimaced.

She wasn't offended as he'd feared, but stared curiously at him before answering with a teasing, yet pleased smile, "So, I'm one hell of a good looking woman am I, Iain Meikle?" She paused, then said, "No, you're right. I probably didn't bother about my appearance. Maybe I just didn't think it was worth putting myself out there and risk getting hurt again in another relationship. Well," she stared meaningfully at him, "not until now, anyway."

"And here you are," he quickly held up his hands, "and I'm so very, very pleased you've chosen to be with me. More than pleased," he added with a grin, but then biting at his lower lip he asked, "You're not worried about what people might think if this gets out? I mean, you and me going out and me being just a constable…"

"And me being a Detective Inspector?" she interrupted, waving her forefingers in the air like italics. She shook her head and added, "No, it doesn't bother me, Iain. What about you? Does it bother you?"

His smile said it all as he replied, "Not in the slightest."

They sat for a moment in silence, reflecting on what she had disclosed and finishing their wine, then as he relaxed she learned of his attempt to patch his marriage with a spendthrift wife who used their son as a bargaining tool for more maintenance from Iain, yet denied him regular visits.

"I saw the photos on the shelf there," she nodded towards them. "He's a fine looking lad and obviously takes after you."

That pleased him and he smiled widely.

They had lingered a little longer at the table because both were acutely aware that moving from the table to the comfortable chairs would mean the inevitable; there would be nothing between them, no barrier as the table was, nothing to stop them drawing close.

It had been a long time since Iain had entertained or been in a one to one situation with a woman and frankly, he was feeling a little out of his depth.

Irene sensed he was uncomfortable and her heart beating a tattoo in her chest, decided to take the initiative.

Rising from her seat, she saw him also attempt to rise, but waved him back down and then moving round the table, bent and took his face in her hands and kissed him full on the lips.

To her surprised pleasure, he returned her kiss and pushing the chair back, awkwardly stood upright then took her in his arms and crushed her to him.

"I have an idea," she whispered breathlessly to him. "If you take my car keys, you can collect my overnight bag from the boot. That will give me a couple of minutes to powder my nose."

He was uncertain how to respond, so simply nodded before releasing her.

Minutes later in the bathroom, she heard the front door close and critically examining herself in the mirror, patted at her hair before stepping out into the hallway where she saw him coming out from the bedroom.

"I put your bag in there," he nodded through the door. "I thought that maybe…" but he got no further for she reached out and taking him by the hand, led him back into the room.

CHAPTER TWENTY-ONE

She woke in the semi-darkness of the room, for a few seconds unsure of where she was, but then involuntarily smiled.

Turning her head as slowly as she dared she saw that Iain was already awake and lying on his side, was watching her.

"Morning," he softly said.

"Hi there," she smiled back, then asked, "What time is it?"

"Just gone five-thirty. Why," he grinned at her, "have you somewhere to be? No, let me guess. Now that you've used my body, you're going to shove a tenner under the pillow and be gone from my life for ever."

She turned towards him then playfully punched him on the chest, but remembering that she was naked under the sheet was suddenly embarrassed and said, "Thank you."

"For what?"

"Well," she drawled, "for dinner and for…you know."

He sighed and wrapping his arm about her shoulder, drew her into him and replied, "No, Irene, it's me that should be saying thank you. Last night was…" his brow creased as he sought the right word then with a cheeky grin said, "interesting."

"Interesting!" she pretended to be annoyed and they tussled for a few seconds before she wrapped her legs about his waist and straddled him.

He didn't protest when her hands pinned him by the shoulders and her hair hanging loose, she stared down at him. Feeling him become aroused she lowered her head till their noses almost touched and quietly whispered, "Five-thirty, eh? Well, I don't need to be at the office till about seven, so…"

****

Just after seven-thirty that morning in the flat on Burghead Drive, Charlie Gallagher woke with a blinding, alcohol induced headache and groaned. Fighting a wave of bile that rose in his throat, he turned to the dark haired teenage girl lying beside him and nudging her on her shoulder, roughly told her in a hoarse voice, "Get your arse into the kitchen and fetch me a glass of water."

"Let me sleep," the girl grumbled, but was suddenly awake when he grabbed a handful of her hair and snatching her head towards him, snarled, "Do as I fucking tell you, ya wee slapper or it'll be my fist, not my hand!"

With that he used his feet to propel the girl from the bed and watched as naked, she slid from the silk sheets and fell onto the floor.

Shaking both with fright and in the cold of the room, the girl gathered up her mini dress and underwear from the floor and getting to her feet, stumbled towards the door.

Lying back with his hands behind his head, Gallagher exhaled then loudly burping, tasted the spicy kebab he had eaten in the early hours that he'd purchased from the dodgy food caravan parked at the taxi rank, but that only brought on another rise of bile.

The door was pushed open by the young girl carefully carrying a pint tumbler of cold water, her dark hair dishevelled and now wearing her mini dress.

"I can't find my shoes," she whined.

"Try the front room," he took the water from her and with some dribbling down his chin drank almost the full pint in several gulps then gasping, laid the tumbler down onto the bedside cabinet.

He knew as soon as he'd finished the water that it had been a mistake, gulping it down like that and loudly belched as he expelled foetid wind.

The girl turned away in disgust, but then he added, "And phone yourself a taxi, hen. I want you gone by the time I get up."

She stared at him, her face pale and in a low voice, stuttered, "I don't know what the address is here, Charlie. Where am I?"

He shook his head, but that brought on another spasm of pain then snapped at her, "There's a phone in the hallway and a taxi number in the book beside the phone. Tell them to pick you up in Burghead Drive, okay?"

"But I've no money. You said you'd take me home in the morning, remember?"

"Did I?" he pretended to express surprise. "Well, then," he sneered at her, "looks like I was fucking joking, doesn't it?"

"You bastard!" the girl angrily retorted, but shied away in fear when he threw back the quilt cover and made to get out of the bed, his face betraying his intention to go for her.

"Fuck you!" he screamed at her and pretended to grab at the young girl, but she was too quick for him and with a frightened squeal run from the room.

"Bitch," he muttered then his head thumping and his legs shaking, reached for the wall to steady himself while with his free hand he massaged his temple that seemed ready to explode.

A half minute later, he heard the sound of the front door being slammed and tried to grin, but even that brought on a stabbing pain. The wee cow was gone and good riddance for he couldn't even remember her name.

Making her way downstairs with her shoes carried in her hand, the young girl sobbed more with embarrassment than fright. It had seemed a good idea last night, ditching her mate for a chance to go home with *the* Charlie Gallagher, but if ever in her young life she had made a fucking mistake…she shivered.

Her embarrassment slowly turned to anger as reaching the ground floor she stopped and listened, but he hadn't followed her as she'd feared.

Sitting on the cold stone stairs, she slipped on her high heels and muttering to herself that included a wide knowledge of choice expletives, walked to the entrance with her hand rising to shade her eyes against the bright sunlight.

She stopped and glancing around her, mumbled, "Where the *fuck* am I?"

At last she made her decision. With a sigh, she wrapped her arms around her in a vain attempt to keep warm before turning left and began to stroll in the direction of Govan Road, completely unaware she was being watched.

Across the road in the parked CID car, DS Jack Fleming and his female neighbour observed the young girl walking off from the close entrance.

"Somebody's had a good night," his neighbour chortled.

"If my daughter wore a dress that short, she'd be grounded for at least a year," Fleming grunted.

"That's not short, ya old fogey," his neighbour Tricia replied. "You should see what some of my pals wear when they're out at the dancing."

Turning, he grinned at her and replied, "Give me an invite and I'll come for a look."

"Pervert," she sighed, then asked, "When did Irene Crichton say she'd get here?"

"She told me she was leaving a note for the boss, so she should be here with the other two…" he glanced in the rear-view mirror before adding, "Speak of the devil."

The second CID car driven by a male detective stopped smoothly behind Fleming's car.

Getting out of the vehicles, the five detectives grouped together and listened as Irene said, "You know the drill. "You three wait on the half landing while Jack and I try to talk our way in, but if there's any nonsense from Gallagher or Menzies, come running. The last thing I want is a scrap at the door and the chance of me getting a sore face at this time of the morning. Not when I've got you lesser beings with me," she grinned at the good-natured scowls. "Right then, everybody clear what we're doing?"

The detectives nodded and all five headed towards the close. A minute later she was knocking on the door that was answered by Gallagher who she and Fleming could see was clearly hung-over, his face flushed and wore nothing but a black silk, knee length dressing gown emblazoned with a colourful dragon on the right breast.

"What the *fuck* do you lot want at this time of the morning?" he greeted them with ill-grace.

"If you let us in for a chat we'll tell you," Irene replied with a smile.

It worked in their favour that Gallagher was still intoxicated and not at his best for it never occurred to him that the police would dare call at his door without a warrant and so, mistakenly believing them to be in possession of such a document, shook his head as he stood to one side to admit them.

However, as he did so a myriad of thoughts invaded his mind, most prominently that the cops had somehow learned he'd murdered Paula.

A sudden panic overcome him and the bile rising in his throat, he knew he could not hold down the vomit.

Clutching a hand to his face as his mouth filled with half digested kebab and alcohol, he pushed past Fleming and hurried to the bathroom where squatting in front of the toilet bowl, his stomach erupted and he puked the contents. Such was the force of his heaving that his bladder loosened and caused him to pee on the floor, but with the vomit splashing up from the enamel toilet bowl and onto his face that for the minute was the least of his concerns.

Staring at him from the toilet door, Fleming screwed his face against the awful smell and winced at the sight, then seeing the puddle of piss leak from between Gallagher's legs supressed a grin. Giving a nod to the DI, he watched as she ducked into the main bedroom.

The curtains were tightly drawn and the room was lit by the overhead light. She almost gagged at the strong smell of body sweat, stale alcohol and cheap scent, so overpowering she guessed the scent must have been applied by a paint sprayer. To her disappointment the unmade bed was empty and taking advantage of Gallagher's distress, she quickly glanced into the other rooms, but again those too were empty.

A thought occurred to her and returning to the main bedroom she opened the fitted wardrobe doors and saw an array of female clothing hanging there. Checking the clothes and aware of Paula Menzies reputation as a prolific shoplifter, she saw that many of the garments carried designer labels that she assumed might not actually have been purchased and were of the size she reckoned Menzies to be; it seemed reasonable to Irene to surmise that the frocks were stolen and likely for wearing by Menzies.

Pulling open a couple of drawers in the dressing table she also saw items of makeup and underwear, all neatly arranged. It was when she rummaged through the drawers she saw a pair of crumpled tights lying discarded on the floor beside the bed that seemed at odds with the tidy clothing, but at that time gave the tights no further thought.

In the bathroom, Gallagher sat back from the toilet bowl and gasping, turned to harangue the two detectives, but saw only the big guy stood there watching him. Before he could question where the woman was another bout of nausea overtook him and muttering, "Oh, God," once more began to heave into the bowl.

Closing the drawers, Irene returned to the hallway where Fleming continued to watch Gallagher heaving and shrugging, she shook her head to indicate there was no sign of Paula Menzies in the flat.

"He's still talking to God on the big white telephone," Fleming smirked as he nodded at the sickly Gallagher.

Curling her lip at the bad smell and waving a hand in front of her face, she politely called out, "Sorry to see you're a bit indisposed at the minute, Mister Gallagher, so we'll maybe just call back another time, eh?"

Gallagher, both hands on the rim of the bowl, tried to turn his head to protest but once more his stomach's reaction to the excess alcohol and the dodgy kebab took over his bodily functions and, his head dipping back into the bowl, continued vomiting and farting in turn.

"I think we'll leave him to enjoy himself," she smirked at Fleming.

On the way back down the stairs, Fleming asked, "Shouldn't we have asked him where Menzies was? I mean, just in case they might have broken up."

Shaking her head, Irene replied, "I don't want him to know we have an interest in her and no, I don't think they've split. I had a quick look in the bedroom and it looks like all her stuff is still there."

Fleming's eyes narrowed as a thought occurred and he said, "If Menzies wasn't at home and maybe I'm jumping to conclusions, but just as you were drawing up behind us a young lassie was leaving the close. She was dressed like she'd been on a night out and heading home. Looked a right state, she did, too. Think she was maybe visiting our Charlie?"

Recalling the discarded tights in the bedroom, Irene slowly nodded and replied, "Maybe."

"So, what now?" Fleming asked when they emerged back onto the pavement.

"Right now, we'll grab some rolls and sausage and head back to the ranch. The boss will want to know that we didn't find Menzies," she sighed.

****

Iain Meikle still couldn't believe in his good luck and finishing his shower, was still smiling when he returned to the room to get dressed and make the bed. Before she left for the office, Irene showered and changed into a skirt and blouse from her overnight bag, then grabbed the coffee and toast he'd made her and hurriedly kissed him goodbye.

Selecting his best suit, he slipped on a white shirt and black, clip-on police tie and checked the clock. The Inquiry Department sergeant had said that the council service was due to commence at nine o'clock and with the cemetery just under a mile away, decided there was little need to take the car, that he'd walk there.

As he strolled along towards Paisley Road West, Iain reflected on his evening with Irene.

It had gone much better than he anticipated and for that he was tremendously relieved. His inner thoughts about Irene had at first confused him; why would she, an attractive, smart woman with a successful police career, take such an interest in an ordinary beat cop like him? Yes, with self-effacing humility he knew that he wasn't an unattractive man, but he had never been ambitious, had never sought promotion and in general, his failed marriage aside and lack of regular contact with his son, was happy with his life.

And now this budding relationship with Irene.

If he were honest with himself, it troubled him that if they continued as a couple and he really hoped they did, word would soon get out and the rumour and gossip mongers would have a field day. He'd been truthful when he told her that he didn't care what people thought of him, but it did bother him that Irene might be subjected to some form of discrimination for Iain was realistic enough to know that no matter how much the police had recently begun to beat the drum about fairness and parity in the ranks, there still existed a glass ceiling for females. His brow creased when he tried to recall how many women he knew or heard of who had achieved the rank of Superintendent, let alone senior rank and apart from a female officer he'd heard of who had recently been appointed to the rank of Assistant Chief Constable in charge of the Personnel Department, he could not name more than four.

He stopped at the traffic lights and crossed to the other side of the road before continuing north onto Berryknowes Road.

She was ambitious, of that he was certain for during dinner she had mentioned that within the forthcoming year she hoped to be appointed to the Chief Inspector rank and thereafter perhaps return to the CID as a DCI somewhere. It worried him though that he might be the cause of some harm to her career prospects if it became publicly known she was having a relationship with a junior officer.

Lost in thought he passed by the large, ornate wrought iron gates then stopping and feeling a little foolish, turned back and into the cemetery.

Iain was no stranger to the large cemetery having on many occasions been tasked to attend there and get rid of the local alcoholics, teenage glue sniffers and junkies who used the grounds as a drinking den or to score their drugs. However, walking on the wide dirt path through the graveyard he was distressed to see the mid-nineteenth century lairs were in an awful state with many if not most of the headstones damaged by falling over or tipped over by vandals.

As he trudged along he recalled that on one of the occasions he was tasked to attend a drunken brawl in the graveyard, he met one old and infirm gentleman called Alex whose hobby was researching the history of the cemetery and during conversation, told him a little of the history of the graveyard and of those interred there; local politicians, a hero of the Titanic disaster, early twentieth century footballers, Captains of industry whose companies continue to flourish, decorated soldiers from both world wars and even an American who had married a Glasgow girl and been killed during the Vietnam conflict.

And all now left and forgotten in this wilderness, he sadly shook his head.

At last he reached at the crematorium and saw a hearse already arrived. Two men formally dressed in the attire of undertakers were placing a plain, light oak coffin onto a wheeled trolley.

"Can I ask, is that Samuel Fullerton you have there?" he respectfully asked.

"Are you a relative, sir," the older of the two asked.

"No," Iain shook his head, "I'm just someone who knew Sam from his days at the Paisley Road Toll."

He waited till the men pushed the trolley through the entrance then slowly followed them inside.

There were no other mourners.

****

Lying in his bed, Doughnut Stokoe woke to the squeaking of the door and saw his mother entering with a mug of tea in her hand.

"You said I'd to give you an early morning call, son. It's nearly nine o'clock. Is that early enough?"

"Aye, mam, that'll do me," he wheezed and pushed himself upright on the bed.

Watching her lay the mug onto the chair beside the bed, he said in dismissal, "Close the door on your way out, mam."

When she'd gone, he turned awkwardly and reaching under the pillow for the porn magazine, with a lewd grin turned to his favourite page.

****

Billy Madison had a sleepless night. Confident as he was that Doughnut would have little trouble taking the heroin to Glasgow there remained a nagging doubt that something unforeseen would happen, some unpredictable event that would delay or interfere with the payment that he so desperately needed if he was to to pay off that black bastard, the Jamaican who'd threatened Sheila.

"Do you want another cuppa, our Billy?" his wife called through from the kitchen.

"No, I mean, yeah, please," he shouted back.

God, he thought, I'm so rattled I can't even make a bloody decision about whether I want tea or not. What the hell kind of state am I in?

Reaching for the phone, he was halfway through dialling Doughnut's mother's house, then stopped. The big man got irritable when he called him there and had even accused Madison of checking up on him.

His foot beat a tattoo on the carpet as he slowly chewed at his nails.

What the fuck am I worrying about, he told himself. Nothing will go wrong. Charlie Gallagher is as keen to get the H as I am to get paid, so it *will* happen.

"Here you go, love," his wife appeared at his elbow and handed him a steaming mug of tea, then softly placed the back of her hand onto his brow.

"What you doing?" he stared up at her.

"Just making sure you don't have a temp, love. You're looking a little flushed there. Are you feeling okay?"

"Yeah, yeah, I'm fine," he snapped at her, but was immediately contrite and apologetically said, "Sorry, hen. Just a little tense about the handover this evening."

"Well, I can't think why," she snorted, then cheerily added, "You're sending that big bloody gorilla Stokoe up there. I mean, who's going to mess about with him, eh?"

"Aye, I suppose you're right," he smiled at her, but still there remained that lingering doubt.

****

DCI Colin Morton braced himself before he gave the morning briefing for he knew that he had nothing solid with which to motivate his team. No breakthrough, no real update and worse of all, no suspects. Not even Charlie bloody Gallagher.

Now stood at Tam Whelan's desk facing the detectives, he begun, "Morning, guys and gals. The word has likely got out that we didn't locate Paula Menzies this morning and we can't even be certain she still resides there. The reason I say this is Gallagher *might* have had another bird staying with him last night. What does this mean? Is Gallagher simply cheating on Paula or have they split up and she's moved out, though Irene Crichton saw what seems to be her clothes still in the flat. The truth is though, we don't know," he shrugged, "and it's disappointing that in the preceding thirty-six hours' the surveillance hasn't seen her at the flat."

He raised a hand as though to quell a protest and added, "Don't worry, Jake, nobody's inferring your guys missed her or anything."

"Boss," Fleming acknowledged, though with a defensive frown.

"However, we still need to locate Menzies so Tam Whelan will issue some of you with a list of addresses that she has been known to reside at or frequent and I want her traced as a matter of urgency. You know the drill. When she *is* traced, get her back here for interview by any legal means possible and guys, I do mean legal. If she does provide us with solid information about Gallagher I don't want it contaminated by any allegation of coercion on our part, understood?"

A general nod and grunting acknowledged his warning.

"Now," he continued and turned towards Janie Wallace and Peter Rossi who stood together, "I want you guys to dig deeper into Jacob McNeill. By his own admission he's not alibied for the time Lesley Rudd went missing, so be discreet and I mean, discreet. I don't want a complaint logged against us that we're harassing the family of the deceased, understand?"

"Sir," Peter acknowledged for them both.

"What I'd like you guys to do is confirm with Q Division the time of the accident that McNeill says occurred on the Bothwell Road. Sorry," he rubbed at his forehead, "not the actual time of the accident, but if I recall correctly from his statement, he said the Traffic cops were in attendance, is that right? That he saw an officer wearing a white cap and there were blue flashing lights."

"That's correct, sir," Rossi replied.

"Then find out when the cops arrived and how long they were at the locus. Once you have that information, drive the shortest route between the locus of the RTA to where Lesley Rudd went into the water at Mavisbank Quay. I want to know if it is possible for McNeill to have killed Lesley then seen the accident. Got that?"

"Yes, sir," they replied together.

"Iain Meikle?" Morton's head swivelled as he looked for him.

"Ah, he's attending the funeral this morning, boss," Irene piped up. "The old guy who fell and dunted his head, Samuel Fullerton."

"Ah, yes, of course. When he comes in," he turned to Tam Whelan, "ask him to come and see me."

Irene Crichton's eyes narrowed and she wondered why Morton wanted to speak with Iain.

"Tam," Morton turned to Whelan, "any word back from the Fingerprints Department re McNeill?"

"Nothing yet, sir," he shook his head.

It was clear that Morton was not a happy man and curtly said, "Keep trying. Now then," he continued again, "those of you with outstanding Actions continue with those but before we break, any questions?"

There were none and so Morton dismissed them to their tasks, but not before beckoning that Irene Crichton join him in his office.

****

Seated at his desk in Police Headquarters, Detective Chief Superintendent Alistair Cruickshank reflected on the previous evenings phone call when he had gratefully acknowledged DCI Maurice Richards heads up about the arrival of a large quantity of heroin on Wednesday evening at the Central Station and agreed that the arrest would be handled by officers of the Scottish Crime Squad; however, Cruickshank was in no doubt why Richards had informed him rather than the Criminal Intelligence at Pitt Street, who should have been the proper recipient for such information.

The bugger was keeping his name in the frame for his return to Strathclyde Police.

"No, sir, there is no suggestion that firearms are to be used," Richards had assured him. "Our intelligence is that it will be a straight forward handover from a known courier travelling by train from Liverpool to person or persons' unknown, but we will have sufficient resources on hand to deal with any number of individuals who might be involved in the transaction."

"What about vehicles? As you know, Mister Richards, the city centre on any given evening is a very busy place. Am I to assume that there is no likelihood of a vehicular pursuit? What I'm getting at is this," tongue in cheek, Cruickshank was thinking on his feet, "I understand why you wish the handover to take place, you want to arrest the customers of the heroin and possibly seize whatever cash is to be paid for the drugs. But my main concern is the public. Can you assure me you have carried out an adequate risk assessment and there will be no danger to the public, particularly at any location where the handover is to take place?"

Thinking that by contacting Cruickshank and as the DCS so rightly surmised, Richards believed he would be congratulated and earn himself some kudos for the intelligence; however, Cruickshank's question set him back on his heels and he had blustered that all precautions would be taken. At the conclusion of the call he took a quick breath and quickly gathered his team leaders together then set them the task of assessing the risks of the operation, but slyly neglected to inform them the idea had not been his own.

Muttering and complaining under their breaths, the officers dispersed and to a man wondered when and why Richards had come up with this crap notion.

"What the fuck is a risk assessment anyway?" grumbled one bearlike DS. "I mean, isn't the plan that when it's time to make the arrest we go in hard, baton any bugger that gets in the way and give the bad guys the jail. Is that not what we usually do?" he'd glanced about him for support from the nodding heads of his sour faced colleagues.

Now, the morning after their phone call, Alistair Cruickshank sat back in the comfortable swivel chair and thought about Richards, who he knew only slightly.

He had little doubt the DCI was feathering his nest for when his secondment to the SCS was completed. Not that he was much different from any other ambitious officer who sought senior rank, Cruickshank wryly knew and his thoughts turned to Martin Kerr, the man who had usurped him to the Assistant Chief Constable (Crime) position.

It still galled him that Kerr had acquired the rank by subterfuge rather than talent, but to complain or whine would only make him sound bitter and that just wasn't Cruickshank's style.

Well, what's done is done, he exhaled having long ago resigned himself to the decision.

With a sigh, he sat forward and looked up the phone number for the city centre's Chief Superintendent, the A Division commander, for regardless of Richards request that the information be treated as confidential the DCS's protocol required that at the very least the local police chief should be aware of what was about to occur in his Division.

****

Unlike Charlie Gallagher, Seamus O'Brien had consumed very little alcohol and so that morning woke clearheaded and sober. The night had gone very much as he'd predicted, with Gallagher throwing back the bevy and the usual sycophants hanging onto him like leeches, keen to be seen with the noted gangster. Minutes after their arrival at Victoria's nightclub, the already tipsy Gallagher was leering at a young dark haired teenager who flashed her tits at the middle aged gangster then dumped her pal to hang onto Gallagher's arm.

It was after he'd bought another round for the table that O'Brien heard Gallagher tell the girl, "Stick with me, hen and I'll see you home in the morning," a clear invitation for her to spend the night with him.

The girl, herself drunk and foolish, giggled and agreed. However, hard man that he was and though he'd caused a lot of hurt and harm in his time, O'Brien was embarrassed by Gallagher who openly pawed at the teenager who had barely attained the age of consent and realised that he intended taking the lassie back to the flat and shagging her on the very bed where he'd murdered Paula Menzies.

He couldn't explain why and on hindsight thought maybe after all these years it was his Catholic upbringing kicking in, but the thought of what Gallagher intended disgusted him and any respect he had for his former boss that had been rapidly dissipating, was now gone.

What worried him too was recalling sitting with the drunk Gallagher in the booth at the club and casting a glance around the patrons, saw more than a few guys watching them, seeing how drunk Gallagher was and here and there, some were openly sniggering. Particularly the young team, he had noticed, some of whom he knew by name or reputation. Mostly young men in their twenties; wannabe gangsters who were keen to make a name for themselves.

He was convinced now that Gallagher was losing it, that the once shrewd, respected and feared underworld figure was on a rapid downward slope to self-destruction.

If anything Gallagher's increasingly erratic behaviour made O'Brien's decision to rip off the heroin and the money that much easier.

As the night drew on he had feigned a headache and excused himself from Gallagher and the girls company, though now so intoxicated and with Gallagher's tongue down the girl's throat, they hardly heard him.

In the taxi he thought about Gallagher, how angry he would be that he'd been ripped off and what steps he would take to find O'Brien and idly wondered who he would send after his trusted lieutenant. When he arrived at the flat it was as he suspected; his live-in girlfriend had gone for good, though he'd hardly been surprised.

Curiously it was when he'd poured himself a whisky and been walking through the empty flat that the idea formed in his head and with a smile, went in search of a pen and paper.

****

"Sit down, please Irene," Colin Morton indicated the chair in front of her desk.

She sensed there was something troubling him but thought it better to let him tell her than ask. She didn't have long to wait. Swallowing as though he were worried, Morton said, "How well do we know Iain Meikle?"

Her chest tightened and forcing a smile, she replied, "As well as anyone else in the uniform side I suppose. What's this about, Colin?"

He raised his hands as though in apology and said, "It occurred to me last night when I was thinking about the inquiry. We've interviewed everyone…or rather, I had Meikle interview everyone on Rudd's shift. But we haven't interviewed him, have we?"

"What," her face paled, "you think he might be a suspect?" Morton shrugged before responding, "It's just a thought, Irene. He's already told us he liked the lassie so maybe *liking her* isn't the full story, if you see what I mean."

"But at the time she disappeared, he was with his neighbour, eh…" the name momentarily escaped her, but then she said, "Little. Eric Little. Surely that alibis Iain?"

"Yes, of course," Morton rubbed wearily at his brow. "I'm sorry, Irene, I'd forgotten that. Stupid of me."

Shaking his head, he continued, "It's this bloody inquiry, it's wearing me down. Yes," he held his hands up as though in surrender, "I know it's been less than a week, but from the first day there has been absolutely nothing to go on. No eye witnesses, no Forensic evidence. Zilch. I've never managed or been involved in an inquiry where there has been so little to work with. We're really grasping at straws, looking at the sister and brother-in-law or wondering if one phone call might lead us to Charlie Gallagher. It's all so much…" he was lost for words, so with a gentle smile she suggested, "Distressing?"

"Distressing?" he stared curiously at her then returning her smile, said, "Yes, I suppose that's as good a word as any. I'm

distressed that we haven't yet identified anyone to account for the lassie's murder. Oh," he waved his hand again, "I'm not concerned about my reputation or any of that shite…"
And she believed him.
"…it's just that I don't want to go down in police history as the man who failed to find our colleagues murderer."
"For heaven's sake, Colin, listen to yourself," she soothingly chastised him. "It's early days yet. Granted," she shrugged, "we've not had a break in the case, but you've been a detective long enough and run enough major inquiries to know that at some point we'll get that break. We work and push hard enough and something *will* turn up."
He slowly inhaled then let his breath out through pursed lips before replying, "Thanks, Irene. I know it's my job to motivate the team, but sometimes I need my own arse kicked." He stared at her and added, "You're a good prop and I'm lucky to have you."
She decided that maybe this was the right time and biting at her lower lip, then took a breath and said, "There's something you should know, Colin, something that for the minute I'd like to keep between us."
****
In his pocket Iain Meikle had brought a multi-striped tie to the ceremony and when it was over headed into the small toilet to change from the black, police tie, for he'd decided that he'd not bother going back home for his car, but catch a bus down to the Govan office.
Twenty minutes later he was entering the general office where Tam Whelan spotting him, said, "The boss is looking for you, Iain. Says you've to knock on his door when you come in."
"Cancel that," Irene Crichton's voice interrupted from the door. "It's dealt with," then addressing Iain added, "Can you come with me, please?"
He saw her about turn and followed her through the door where glancing along the corridor she saw they were alone and said,

"It's nothing, I'll explain later, but tell me. How did the funeral go?"

"Pretty sad," he shook his head. "I was the only mourner."

"Whether it's one person or a thousand," she smiled at him, "at least someone was there to say goodbye." Her eyes narrowed and she gently squeezed his arm as she asked, "How are you?"

"Me?" he was surprised by her question. "Eh, fine, I suppose. Why do you ask?"

"Well, you didn't really know the old guy, yet you felt the need to attend his funeral service and that," her eyes twinkled, "is half the reason I really fancy you, Iain Meikle. You're a good man," she hesitated before adding, "a *really* good man and I never listen to rumours."

"Rumours? What rumours," his face showed his confusion, but then he grinned, realising he was being teased.

Her voice lowered when she continued, "I'm going home after work and thought I'd collect another overnight bag but this time, why don't we get a home delivery?"

"Seems like a plan," he smiled.

"Sorry, am I disturbing you?"

They hadn't seen or heard Janie Wallace leave the general office and Irene dropped her hand from his arm like she'd been scalded.

"Janie," she found her voice, what can I do for you?"

"Peter Rossi and me are heading out to Q Divisional headquarters in Hamilton to check the files for the RTA that Jacob McNeill said he passed by, Ma'am, and we're wondering if there is anything else the boss might want us to do when we're there? I mean about the sister, Ellen McNeill."

"Ah, no, not that I can think of, but if there is anything we'll get you on the car radio, okay?"

"Ma'am," Janie nodded and walked off, but with her back to the DI, she gave Iain a knowing smile.

"Oh, and there's another thing I might want to tell you later," Irene whispered and left him wondering what the hell that might be.

****

Despite what Charlie Gallagher had told him, Marty Boyle was looking forward to the handover that evening and more so because there might be the likelihood of some kind of bother. As a six-year-old Boyle and his three elder siblings, one boy and two girls, had been removed from the parental home by the social services and placed in a number of foster homes with couples well used to dealing with the children of alcoholic parents and violent fathers. Not that the mother herself was any angel for unable to fight back against her bullying husband, she took her anger out on her kids and when they were taken from her all four were found to have fresh bruising as well as historic injuries. Brought up in a tenement environment in a dilapidated housing scheme where the enemy was anyone in authority or from the council, none of the four would ever dare admit that their parents were responsible for the beatings.

It was unfortunate that the diminutive Boyle's formative years had been so steeped in violence for the little lad knew nothing else and regardless of the care and attention lavished on him, was unable to conform to the rules of good behaviour in his many foster homes. It was with extreme reluctance the social services finally admitted defeat and placed Boyle, now ten years of age, in a council run orphanage that accommodated disruptive children.

It proved to be a very bad decision.

The home, a large sprawling former mansion situated in the affluent Pollokshields area where many of the well-heeled and genteel folk of Glasgow resided, was a housebreaker's paradise and within a short time Boyle and three likeminded associates began to plunder the houses about them. But it wasn't the theft or property that worried the police and the social workers, it was the wanton and malicious damage that occurred within the houses that culminated in an extremely serious assault upon an elderly woman who in the middle of the night had the misfortune to disturb the intruders.

Of course the polis didn't have far to search for the culprits and it wasn't long before they were arrested. During questioning, three of the snot nosed weans quickly admitted to their involvement in the break-ins, but not the tight-lipped Boyle. It soon became clear to the detectives that the assault had been carried out not by the three associates, but by the young and nasty wee dwarf like child and so began his lengthy criminal career.

Having exhausted all kind of verbal persuasion about right and wrong, the social services finally admitted defeat and following a judgement at the Children's Hearing placed Boyle in a second, but secure children's home on the outskirts of Barrhead where in the evening and through the night the occupants were locked in their rooms and constantly monitored.

However, that didn't stop the enterprising Boyle.

Three escapes from the home in two years ended with Boyle being returned by the police after committing numerous thefts and housebreakings and on two occasions when he was on the run, also resulted in some innocent individual being harmed. At the age of sixteen without any formal training and barely literate, Boyle was released from the social services care to make his own way in the world and tasted three days of freedom before being arrested for a serious assault.

And so continued his run-ins with the law that, aside from his time spent in children's homes, culminated in twelve of the thirty-five years old Boyle's life being spent in custody. However, upon his release three years earlier he had soon come to the attention of Charlie Gallagher who curiously kept him out of the clutches of the police, for Gallagher recognised Boyle's brutishness and his potential as an enforcer.

Partnered with Seamus O'Brien from the beginning, Boyle did as he was told, hurt whom he was ordered to, was ruthless in carrying out Gallagher's instruction and loved it all. His only complaint that he wisely kept to himself was that he believed O'Brien to be too soft on the punters they shook down and secretly craved the bigger man's job as Gallagher's number two.

In fairness to Gallagher, he was astute enough to know that he could demand loyalty if he paid well and so he did; however, unlike O'Brien, Boyle wasn't bothered about the money for Boyle was the stereotyped Glaswegian reputed to characterise the 'wee man syndrome.' At five feet two inches tall, he had throughout his life suffered numerous jokes and cracks about his height and wasn't averse to using an open razor to settle disputes about his lack of inches. So, getting paid for battering and slashing punters?

It was almost a dream come true for the psychotic Boyle.

In his 14th floor flat in the high-rise building in the Sighthill area of the city, Boyle stood in his front room and carefully used a leather strop that was attached to the wall to sharpen his razor while happily daydreaming for the opportunity to use it that evening.

****

Glancing at the clock in the kitchen, Doughnut Stokoe saw that time was marching on and using a fourth slice of bread to wipe the egg yolk from the plate, stuffed it into his mouth then loudly burped.

"That was the business, mam. Hit the spot, it did," he congratulated his mother on the large breakfast.

"Thanks, son," she replied with a wide smile, pleased that all acrimony now seemed to have been forgotten and lifting the pot from the cooker, poured him yet another mug of tea. Her nose was bothering her and so she hesitantly asked, "I see you've a travelling bag in the hallway, son. Are you thinking of going away somewhere?"

He glanced sharply at her, but then seeing the fright on her paled face, relaxed and said with a stubby forefinger at his lips, "Just a wee business trip, mam. Nothing for you to worry about or tell anyone, get it?"

"Okay, our Derek," she nodded. "My lips are sealed."

"Aye, well, they fucking better be," he jovially warned, but the inference was there and she weakly smiled in reply.

Wiping his bearlike hands together, he pushed back the chair and got to his feet while his mother busied herself at the sink.

"I'll be back tomorrow morning," he told her and with that, left the kitchen and went into the hallway where he grabbed his jacket from a coat hook and after putting it on, hoisted the kitbag onto his shoulder.

"See you, ma," he loudly called out and closed the door behind him.

The Regional Crime Squad detective squatting alone in the rear of the rusting Bedford van that was parked one hundred yards from the mid terraced house regretted finishing a full flask of coffee for just as the front door opened he was kneeling on the floor of the van as he urinated into a plastic container. Seeing Stokoe leaving the house he cursed as he peed across his hand and down the front of his jeans then grabbed at his microphone and excitedly whispered, "Standby, stand by, standby. Tango One exiting the house and now turning left, left, left," he hesitated before adding, "That's south, I think. Tango One wearing a black coloured rain jacket and carrying an army type kitbag on his shoulder. Now towards Knighton Road, over," he added before disgustedly staring at the puddle seeping into the knees of his jeans.

From five cars surrounding the Stokoe house, detectives were deployed on foot to take up the surveillance while back at the control room, a half dozen RCS officers grimly smiled.

The follow was on

****

Making his way to the local newsagent to grab that morning's edition of the 'Glasgow News' and four rolls for his breakfast, Seamus O'Brien also purchased a book of first class stamps. Attaching one stamp to the envelope he brought from his pocket, he smiled and thought, what's the harm then added a second stamp.

On his way back to his flat he slid the envelope into a nearby post-box and thought, there's no going back now.

CHAPTER TWENTY-TWO

Seated in his office just off the muster room Inspector Mickey Kane was tired of reading reports, tired of correcting the most basic spelling and grammar, tired of seeing the same names time and time again on the charge sheet, tired of the whole bloody thing and worst of all, suffering from toothache. Sitting back in his chair he threw down his pen in disgust and rubbed at the ache in his jaw as he reflected that the fourteen months he had left to serve just couldn't come quick enough.

Popping two aspirin, he swirled them about in his mouth before washing them down with a sip of tea then glancing at the wall clock, yearned for the end of the shift.

Since his first promotion to sergeant back in the old Renfrew and Bute Constabulary days, he had never lost an officer under his command and realised it wasn't really the bad tooth, but the death of young Lesley Rudd that what was really bothering him, why he couldn't concentrate and why he felt so damned depressed.

That and this bloody complaint.

He stared unhappily down at the sheet of paper.

With a sigh he picked up the paper from the desk and perused what he had written.

A practising Baptist and deeply devout man, Kane at first found it difficult being transferred from the relatively quiet Johnstone office to the Glasgow Division where the old religious divide between the Catholics and the Protestants still flourished. At first he had kept his beliefs to himself but soon made it known he would not tolerate any member of his shift using language or behaviour that reflected their dislike of an opposing faith. Not that the officers under his command paid much attention to him

for he later learned he had been awarded a moniker, The Padre.
With a smile he inwardly admitted it could have been a lot
more offensive and in time had come to accept the nickname.
But even more than religious intolerance, Kane hated bullying.
And now this.

Young Ian Harris, one of the three probationers on his shift,
had requested a private chat. The lad had been uncomfortable
and clearly ill at ease, but at last disclosed that he believed the
shift sergeant Jimmy Cole was picking on him because he was
a Catholic. Stuff and nonsense, of course, but Kane had
patiently listened to the young man's complaint and finally
persuaded Harris that no, Sergeant Cole was not bias against
Catholics or Harris, that Cole was simply being strict with the
young constable who still had a lot to learn and particularly
about report writing, then cited several reports that had frankly
been very poorly worded. Nevertheless, Kane promised he
would speak with Cole and hoped that the matter was now
resolved. Harris had seemed satisfied with Kane's response and
promising to buck up his ideas, agreed that if the Inspector
dealt with the issue, no further official action need be taken.

"But the sergeant will know it was me that made the complaint,
won't he sir?" Harris worriedly asked.

"Leave it to me to sort that out, Ian," he had reassuringly
replied.

What bothered Kane though was he had lied for he knew that
as soon as he instructed Cole to lay off the lad, the vindictive
bugger would do everything he could to pile it onto Harris, for
the lad had been correct.

It irked him that someone like Jimmy Cole was in charge of
officers on Kane's shift for the man *was* a bully of the worst
kind, using his rank to hide his incompetence and lack of
leadership ability. He wouldn't dream of trying it on with the
more experienced members of the shift like Eric Little or Iain
Meikle, but young cops like Harris or Shona Murtagh, another
probationer, were fair game to him; someone he could exert his
authority over and who wouldn't argue back.

However, there was no way Kane could get rid of him without a plausible excuse and one complaint from an acned teenager wouldn't cut it with the management.

Well, to Kane's inward shame he had tolerated it for long enough and rubbing again at his aching jaw decided it was now time to put a stop to Cole's nonsense, vowing that the first time the sergeant slipped up, he was gone.

****

In the muster room on the top floor of Stewart Street police office, twenty-two detectives of the Scottish Crime Squad were being briefed by DCI Maurice Richards about the pending arrival of the drug courier Derek 'Doughnut' Stokoe.

Richards was aware that there had been some muttering about the number of officers he had tasked for the job, but under no circumstances did he want anything to go tits up because of a lack of resources for he was determined that having been provided with the information by the RCS and in particular, that torn faced bastard Thomas Preston, the operation must result in an arrest and seizure of the heroin.

Surveillance photographs of the target that had been couriered overnight from the Regional Crime Squad were handed around to whistles of surprise and comments of, "He's a right big fucker, isn't he?" or "I think I'll be looking out my pick axe handle for this boy," and "He must have bounced off every branch on the way down when he fell out of the ugly tree."

What was generally agreed was that if Stokoe resisted arrest as it was presumed he would, it would take more than one officer to contain him and so three detectives were assigned the job of taking down the big man. Chosen for the task were three of the burliest detectives present; two hulking men and a female detective, who though she stood at six foot two inches tall without her high heels and weighed a little over seventeen stone, for some unaccountable reason was nicknamed Twinkle. Stories of Twinkle's sexual prowess abounded and were legendary, but it was generally agreed among her male colleagues that nobody in the Squad had the balls to quiz her about them. However, it was commonly agreed that at the many Squad nights out, if Twinkle wanted you to sit on her knee nobody dare argue.

Once tasks were allocated, Richards informed the team leaders to dismiss their guys for a couple of hours to grab some grub, have a kip or in the case of the Grampian detectives, phone home to speak with their favourite sheep.

****

Standing in the front room staring out of the window to the street below and nursing a glass of hair of the dog, Charlie Gallagher hated even thinking about it, but was intensely worried that something would go wrong that evening at the handover. He had orchestrated plenty of drug deals in the past, but there was more money riding on the success of this deal than he had previously arranged.

Now showered and changed into a clean light blue coloured track suit and feeling a damn sight better than he had when he awoke, his thoughts turned to the visit earlier that morning from the CID.

He hadn't recognised the bird, the female detective, though the face of the big guy who was with her was vaguely familiar.

But what had they wanted, he asked himself.

Sipping at the whisky he turned over in his mind what happened, but all he could recall was they arrived at the door, asked to come in then watched as he'd vomited into the toilet and pissed himself, before leaving.

No search of the pitch, no interview, no questions about Paula. Nothing.

That confused him and deeply suspicious of the intention of their visit wondered what the fuck *that* had been all about?

His eyes narrowed and he glanced anxiously about him.

Had they left something? A listening device, maybe?

He recalled watching the tele a couple of months previously when the investigative programme 'World in Action' had reported a case down in the Smoke where the Metropolitan Police had bugged a drug dealers flat and slowly rising from his chair, laid down his glass and began to suspiciously search the room.

The first thing he checked was the telephone, but he had never been technically gifted and turning it back and forth, didn't really have a clue what he was looking for. Better to be safe than sorry he thought and unplugged the line from the socket in the wall. Convinced now in his mind that was why they had come to his door he carefully lifted ornaments, peeked behind photos on the wall, stood on a chair to check the light fitting on the ceiling and tried to do what he recalled seeing James Bond do in the movies.

But as the minutes passed and he failed to find anything, he became increasing obsessed and began to ransack the room, ripping stitched cushions from the settee, checking underneath the couch and armchairs that he then tipped onto their side, then ripping up the corner of the carpets.

Breathless, he found nothing and apprehensively turned to stare at the door.

Rubbing at his brow, he seemed to recall the female detective had moved away from the toilet door while he was vomiting and decided to check the other rooms.

Over an hour later with perspiration running down his spine, he still hadn't found anything and slowly turned to look at the devastation he had wreaked on the flat.

But that doesn't mean there isn't a bug here, he thought.

His hands shaking, he returned to the front room and plugged in the phone. Dialling Seamus O'Brien's number, he heard the ringtone then when O'Brien answered, snapped, "Don't speak, just listen."

"Charlie?"

"I said don't speak," he hissed, "I want you to listen, okay?"

He lowered his voice as though that might defeat any cop who was monitoring the call and said, "They came to my pitch this morning, but didn't question me or anything. I think they might have left a you know what."

Of course O'Brien didn't have a clue what a 'you know what' was and shaking his head as if to clear it, was also conscious that tempted though he was to ask, this was clearly to be a one-sided conversation.

"The thing we're doing," Gallagher continued to whisper, "don't tell anybody about it, okay?"

O'Brien raised his eyes to the ceiling and confused, thought, who the fuck would I tell that me and the dwarf are meeting a guy tonight to buy heroin.

"Don't contact me when it's done. I'll contact you," Gallagher finished the call.

On the other end of the line, O'Brien returned the phone to the cradle and shaking his head, slowly released his breath. If nothing else, the phone call settled it and confirmed that he made the right decision to steal the H and the money, for there was little doubt now that Charlie Gallagher had most definitely lost it.

The bastard was now completely off his rocker and though he wouldn't realise it was now not just a liability to himself, but to O'Brien and Boyle too.

****

Getting off the bus in London Road, Doughnut Stokoe lumbered the half mile towards Liverpool's Lime Street railway station with the kitbag carried almost effortlessly across his shoulder.

He had given himself plenty of time before catching the Glasgow train for it was his intention to grab some grub and a couple of pints for the journey.

Behind him trailed the surveillance team, confident in the knowledge they knew the big man's destination for one car had already gone ahead and deployed three footmen, two males and one female detective, inside the station's concourse.

One footman stood by the newsagent stall reading a newspaper under the large clock while a second footman enjoyed a pint in the station bar. The female detective sat reading a glossy magazine as she sipped her coffee at the station café and like her colleagues, listened to the chatter in her earpiece as the officer with eyeball on Tango One updated his movements.

A few seconds of heart stopping panic ensued when Stokoe glanced about him and stopped to speak to a swarthy and furtive looking man, then lowered the kitbag from his shoulder to the pavement. However, it soon became clear the unknown man was merely someone Stokoe knew and after a few minutes of conversation, they watched as Stokoe first cheerfully slapped the man on the shoulder, lifted the kitbag and settling it onto his shoulder then continued on his way.

The convoy commander, aware that the meeting might have some significance, wisely deployed two footmen to follow the swarthy man in an attempt to identify him.

As it later transpired, he was of no real consequence and the meeting was logged as a chance encounter by Tango One with an acquaintance.

A few hundred yards from Lime Street station, Stokoe surprised the surveillance when he unexpectedly nipped into a café.

In the event this was a meeting of some sort, two female officers were deployed to enter the café where over the course of thirty minutes they watched Tango One consume a large meal and two sweets.

Exiting the café, Stokoe continued to the railway station where upon entering the concourse and to the relief of the footman who stood in the queue directly behind him, he first purchased a return ticket to Glasgow before slowly making his way to the station bar.

****

DS Tam Whelan was at his desk when Peter Rossi phoned in from Hamilton police office to report that he and Janie Wallace had traced the Traffic report regarding the accident on the Bothwell Road.

"We got a copy printout of the RTA from the control room here at Hamilton then I spoke with the Traffic sergeant who attended the call on the phone, though he wasn't happy about getting woken up off the nightshift," Rossi snorted. "He was a bit grumpy till I reminded him that this was a murder inquiry and that the DCI had a special interest in what he had to say. He told me that the accident occurred about nine-twenty-five on the night Lesley went missing and the times are logged on the printout. Him and his neighbour attended at the locus at nine-forty-one and again the time of the Traffic cops' arrival was logged by the control room," he explained. "The sergeant said it was just a rear-end bump with no injuries so suggested the driver's exchange details and there was no police involvement."

"You mean they were knocking off at eleven that night and didn't want to get bogged down in paperwork?" a cynical Whelan grinned into the phone.

"Seems that way, Sarge," Rossi cautiously replied and Whelan guessed he was in an open office and didn't want to sound too openly critical of their Traffic colleagues.

"I take it you and Janie will still do the drive between the locus and Mavisbank Quay to time if Jacob McNeill could have made it to Glasgow, murdered Lesley and got back in time to see the RTA?"

"We will do," he heard Rossi sigh, "but we're conscious that Iain Meikle spoke with the two council guys who said they saw Lesley half-seven and eight o'clock that night. If the timings are correct give or take five minutes either side, it's unlikely McNeill could have made it back and forth and had time to kill Lesley."

"But not impossible?"

"No, not impossible," Rossi agreed, then added, "The other thing that kind of corroborates his story is that in his statement, McNeill said he was travelling west on the Bothwell Road from the Strathclyde Park when he saw the RTA. If he had been returning to Uddingston from Glasgow it's more than likely that he would have come off the motorway at the Glasgow Zoo exit onto the Hamilton Road as that would have been a more direct route to his house."

"I'm not familiar with that area, so you're point is?"

"Well," Rossi slowly drawled, "if he had come that way fro Glasgow, he couldn't have passed by the RTA, so Janie and I are of the opinion it's likely he was at Strathclyde Park as he said."

"Oh, right. But you'll still do the run anyway?"

"Yes, of course."

"Right then, do that Peter and I'll see you when you get back. I won't tell the boss what you've found out until you've completed the run."

With that, they ended the call.

****

Sitting among the carnage that had been his front room, Charlie Gallagher decided that whether or not the polis were listening to him he would phone Billy Madison to ensure that everything was on course for the evening's delivery of the heroin. He slowly stared about him and decided once that was done he would arrange for a couple of nights away to a city centre hotel. Tomorrow he'd arrange for a guy he knew who was into technical stuff to properly search the flat and who undoubtedly would find whatever the black bastards had left hidden.

His call was answered almost immediately and he greeted Madison with, "Don't say too much on the blower. I'm just checking to ask if the deal is still on?"

Recognising Gallagher's voice, Madison was momentarily confused, but recalling the big mans irritation when they'd previously spoken on the phone, reassuringly replied, "Nothing to worry about, mucker. Everything's on track. My guy's en route as we speak. I take it everything is okay at your end?" he hesitatingly asked.

"Right as rain, right as rain," Gallagher forced some joviality into his voice before finishing, "I'll give you a call when it's completed. Okay pal?" and ended the call.

He sat for a moment staring at the phone in his hand.

It occurred to him that maybe he might take a wee trip to the Waterloo Bar to watch the handover take place, but on hindsight just as quickly rejected the idea for two reasons.

If Seamus and the wee man saw him there it might cause some confusion; that and if for any reason the exchange went sour and the polis arrived, there was no need for him to get snatched too.

No, he'd leave it in the hands of his guys and smiling, arched his fingers then leaning back in the armchair, dialled the number for the Thistle Hotel.

****

Radio reception between the four-man team who had accompanied Doughnut Stokoe on the train and the Regional Crime Squad was intermittent; however, during a five-minute layover at Carlisle station, one officer left the train and took the opportunity to make a hurried phone call to his control room to update his controller that there was no change, that Stokoe had steadily consumed the six cans of ale he had purchased prior to boarding the train.

"Is he drunk?" the controller had asked.

"Hard to say," replied the footman. "He's sitting sleeping and snoring like a buzz saw. Oh, oh, need to go," the footman quickly ended the call and raced for the train.

But it was enough and so the information that Tango One was en route was quickly passed to the Scottish Crime Squad control room.

Located in the Squad's control room on the top floor of Stewart Street police office, DCI Maurice Richards sat comfortably on an old and much repaired armchair beside the Detective Sergeant who sat huddled over the base set and who was designated the liaison between the SCS and the RCS.

"Tango One still on the train and en route to Glasgow," he repeated.

Richards breathed a sigh of relief. If this operation went well he thought, it wouldn't do his return to Strathclyde Police any harm and might even enhance his promotion opportunities as he idly contemplated how he'd look in a Superintendents uniform.

When the DS left the room to grab them both a coffee, in his mind Richards composed a brief for the media, how he'd managed the team who successfully prevented the scourge of a large shipment of heroin hitting the streets of Glasgow.

With a smug smile he relaxed his body and settled in for the next couple of hours.

****

The Central Railway Station in Glasgow, busy with thousands of commuters making their way home after a hard day in the city, was also awash with SCS footmen.

Seated at the cafe drinking coffee or in the food court having a burger, stood under the Train Information Board with backpacks padded out with cardboard sides to make them seem heavy or pretending to be couples meeting or saying farewell, the detectives were all connected via their earphones and regularly updated from the DS at the base set who assured them Tango One was still en route while urging them to stay alert, for they still did not know where the handover was to take place. The DS also took the opportunity to remind the footmen it was possible that the recipients for the heroin were already in the station and to keep their eyes peeled for any known faces.

In the streets outside the station, surveillance vehicles, most illegally parked, listened to the radio chatter while the drivers like their footmen scanned the surrounding pavements for any sign of dealers who were known to them.

One van painted a nondescript grey that advertised a bogus plumbing firm on the side contained the arrest team who sitting in the rear among an array of batons and pick axe handles, played cards.

The woman known as Twinkle glanced at her wristwatch before removing it and carefully placing it in her jacket pocket. "Don't want it getting broken when we grab this bugger," she explained to her colleagues, then with a grin threw down a winning hand.

****

Marty Boyle practised swishing the razor back and forth through the air at an imaginary face and grinning, hoped that tonight at the handover some bastard would try to intervene and he'd get the opportunity to use it. Shrugging on his jacket, he slipped the razor into the side pocket then running a hand across his bald head, critically examined himself in the wardrobe mirror.

Happy with what he saw, he made his way to the front door and decided though he was a little early, he'd wait downstairs for O'Brien in the forecourt.

****

In his flat, Seamus O'Brien carefully loaded the Smith and Wesson revolver and cocked the weapon. Though he did not know for certain he had been told by the seller it took about five pounds of pressure to pull the trigger and briefly regretted that he had never actually fired the bloody thing.

However, he grinned, if he did need to fire it he'd be close up and personal against whoever was getting the working end of it, but hoped that the very sight of it would be enough to make someone back off.

With a sigh, he glanced again at the handgun and carefully stuck it in the trousers waistband at the small of this back, then slipping on a loose fitting dark coloured anorak, turned to the mirror and twisted his body. He was pleased that he could not see the bulge of the handgun under the jacket. Four time he practised pulling the gun from the waistband and finally satisfied that he could achieve this without any problem, took a deep breath and lifted his holdall from the bedroom floor.

He stopped dead at the front door and laid the holdall down onto the floor. It worried him that the meeting was to be in the Waterloo Bar among what was usually a pub crowded with punters. That's why he'd made the decision that he'd park the hired car in the bay in Wellington Street then intercept the courier before he got there. That and he'd persuade the wee man to leave the money in the boot of the car, that they'd take the courier to the Lane and make the exchange there rather in the pub; or so he'd tell Boyle.

All he had to do was watch for the courier in the Liverpool top coming off the train and follow him from the station into Wellington Street, take the bag of heroin from him and with the bag of money already in the boot, he'd be off Scot-free.

Glancing at his wristwatch he saw that it was about time he left to pick up the wee man and the money then making his way to the front door, took a last look at the flat before closing the door behind him.

****

Seated in his office, DCI Colin Morton was a frustrated man. Yet another possible suspect, Jacob McNeill, seemed to be out of the frame for Janie Wallace and Peter Rossi, at his instruction, had timed the run between the murder locus and the RTA McNeill had witnessed and concluded it was unlikely the brother-in-law had the time to murder Rudd and returned home. Not impossible, they admitted, but unlikely. That and their observation that it was just possible McNeill had been telling the truth; that his route home passing the RTA inferred it was more than likely he had been in Strathclyde Park at the material time of Lesley Rudd's murder.

He was also frustrated the rest of the team had so far failed to find any trace of Paula Menzies at any of the addresses they had been given to check.

Sitting in front of him, Irene Crichton studied him with critical eyes and said, "Can I make a suggestion and don't go jumping down my throat?"

"Go ahead."

"Well, I don't think a good night's sleep will do you any harm, Colin, and if anything it might gee you up a bit, so for once why don't you have an early night? I mean, the guys on late shift and night shift can always phone you if anything comes in. It might even perk you up," she smiled at him.

It went against the grain as far as Morton was concerned to leave the office while some of his team were still out on inquiries, but with a grunt he knew that Irene was correct.

"Are you hanging on for a bit?" he asked her.

It wasn't her intention to stay too late, but she realised that if she were to persuade Morton to go home, he'd feel better about leaving early if she were still here in charge so nodded and replied, "Yes. Iain and I are having a late dinner so I'll hang on for another hour or so."

"Okay then," he sharply rose from behind his desk. "It won't do me any harm to get home before it gets really dark and kiss the wife while she still remembers who I am," he grimly smiled.

Grabbing his coat from the hook he quietly added, "Thanks Irene. I'll see you in the morning."

When he'd gone, she rose from her chair and went to find Iain Meikle, then calling him from the incident room into the corridor, explained that she'd be a little late getting to his place.

"No problem," he smiled. "Why don't we cancel the takeaway for another time. I'm guessing you want won't a heavy meal last thing at night before you…" he stopped and smiled, "before we go to bed, so I'll stick something on. I've plenty of vegetables in the house so I'll rustle up a broth if that's okay with you?"

"Sounds great," she nodded with a smile, then asked, "What are you working on at the minute?"

He closed his eyes for a second, then opening them replied, "I'm going through what statements there are in the file, not that there's many," he sighed. "I know it sounds really daft, but someone recently said something to me and its kind of stuck in my head. I can't for the life of me remember who said it or what it is, but the bloody thing has niggled me all day." He shook his head, a little embarrassed and added, "It might not even be of any importance, but you know that feeling you get? That kind of feeling that you know there's just something at the back of your mind," he grimaced and as though to make his point, clenched a fist, "and you just know it's there but you can't reach it?"

She smiled and suggested, "Try to stop thinking about it and maybe it'll come back to you."

He slowly shook his head and grinning replied, "You're right. At the minute I should be concentrating on us."

"Now there's a good idea," she continued to smile.

****

Standing in the forecourt of the high rise flats and smoking with two teenage girls, Marty Boyle, the bag containing the money at his feet, didn't recognise the light coloured Mark Four Cortina when it stopped outside the main doors, but then saw it was Seamus O'Brien in the driver's seat waving at him. "Got to go, ladies," he smirked at the fifteen-year-olds and flicking the cigarette away onto the nearby scrub of dirt that once boasted a lawn, lifted the bag made his way to the car.

"Ready?" O'Brien asked.

"All set," Boyle confirmed.

They had been driving for just a few minutes when O'Brien said, "I got a phone call from Charlie. There's been a wee change of plan."

"What change?" Boyle stared suspiciously at him.

He'd carefully thought it out, what he would say and playing on Boyle's fondness for violence, replied, "Charlie's worried the courier might have some muscle with him, so he's told me that he wants you in the pub to grab a table and have a look at the punters to see if there's any known faces. I'm to watch for the courier arriving on the train and tail him to the pub to ensure he's not got any back-up with him. When he gets there you've to wave him over to the table while I watch your back from the bar. Charlie wants you to make the handover, but not in the pub in case someone's watching. You've to bring the courier out into Wellington Street and we'll do the exchange there. I've to keep the money in the boot of the motor so we've no chance of getting ripped off in the pub," he lied with a cheerful smile, knowing exactly how Boyle would react.

As he'd predicted, the smaller man's face turned brightly crimson with outrage before he boastfully exploded, "Who the *fuck* would try to rip off me and you, big man! No fucking way!"

"That's what I told Charlie," O'Brien shrugged, "but you know how he is, so we've to do it his way."

Sensing that Boyle was swallowing the lie, he added, "Once you've checked the H is in the bag, bring him out to the motor and we'll give him the money."

"No problem," the unsuspecting Boyle did not question the new arrangement, being just so pleased he had been given the pivotal role in the exchange.

Inwardly relieved the smaller man had not argued the change in the plan, in his head O'Brien again went over the real plan. It was his intention to meet with the courier off the train then lead him to the car parked in Wellington Street where he'd use the handgun to relieve the courier of the heroin. If the guy resisted, then he'd use the Smith and Wesson to batter the guy or in the worst case scenario, shoot him in the leg and be away to London before the cops had an inkling something had gone down.

Resisting the urge to laugh out loud, he idly wondered how long Boyle would sit in the pub until he realised that no one was coming.

****

The two uniformed British Transport officers were slowly meandering across the wide concourse at the Central Station when the young woman officer quietly said, "Don't turn your head to look, but there's two guys with backpacks who have been standing under the information board for over an hour."

"And that's odd, why?" her older male colleague turned with a bemused smile to stare at her.

"Well," she frowned, "you'd think they'd be watching the board for train information, but their heads have been swivelling on their shoulders as though they're watching for something."

"Or someone," he softly replied. "Maybe, hen, they're just waiting for a pal who's going with them to wherever they're going. After all this *is* a railway station."

She stopped walking and turning to him, took him by the arm and determinedly said, "I'm going to have a word with them. I think they're up to something."

He was about to respond when to his annoyance and without any further ado his neighbour marched off towards the two men.

Hurrying after her he saw her approach the men and heard her politely ask, "Hi guys, where are you off to, then?"

As he joined her, the younger of the two men quietly hissed, "Nowhere, but do us a favour, will you? Fuck off sharpish. We're the Scottish Crime Squad and you're about to blow an operation by speaking to us."

Before she could respond her colleague stepped forward and blood up that he and his neighbour were being so rudely dismissed, angrily replied, "Then if you'd had the common sense and courtesy to inform our control room you are in our station we wouldn't be having this conversation now, would we?"

A tense standoff was averted when the older of the two detectives quietly raised a hand and smiling through gritted teeth, said, "I apologise, pal, but he's right," he nodded to his fellow detective. "Speaking to us does compromise the two of us, but maybe the operation can continue, so if you don't mind we'll quietly walk away and leave the station and you can continue on your patrol."

It would have been resolved without any further acrimony for the older detective realised that they had probably been burned and the correct thing to do was get the hell out of Dodge.

However, as the older detective turned away, his colleague, annoyed and a little embarrassed that they had been made by a wee polis lassie, stupidly used a stage whisper to make a derogatory comment that incensed the older cop when he said, "Fucking choo-choo polis."

Turning back to the detective, the red-faced cop loudly barked, "And fuck you and you secret squirrel operation! Anyway, how do I know you're who you say you are! Let me see your warrant cards! *Now*!"

The hostility between the older uniformed cop and the young detective immediately attracted the attention of the nearby commuters who turned to stare at the four officers.

With dismay at the loud exchange, none of the footmen nor the four officers saw or paid attention to the tall and powerfully built, red haired man who having just entered the station concourse through the Hope Street entrance, stopped dead twenty yards from the foursome and with a quick, panicked glance about him, retraced his steps and headed for the exit.

CHAPTER TWENTY-THREE

Watched by the Detective Sergeant manning the base set, an irate and extremely angry DCI Maurice Richards paced the floor for he had a decision to make.

The senior detective at the locus, having watched his two colleagues and the BT officers become engage in a bawling match, reported that the operation might be blown and requested instructions.

Rubbing a worried hand across his brow, Richards quickly realised that it was unlikely the courier on the train would have knowledge of the confrontation. However, if he was to be met at the station it was also likely the purchasers of the heroin had been alerted by the argument and would not now make the exchange. It would mean that the purchasers would not be identified and the handover cash was lost, but the courier and his bag of drugs could be seized and besides, who knew what information they could prise from the him?

However, if the exchange was to take place *outwith* the railway station, then nothing was lost and the surveillance could continue. His team would follow the courier and with a bit of luck, bag both the courier and the purchasers.

He decided that the team would stay in place and with a bit…no, a lot of luck, the operation was still a goer.

Nodding to the DS, he listened as the message was broadcast.

"Stay on site and continue the surveillance."

****

There seemed little point on hanging on, Irene Crichton decided.

The last of the team had returned to the office with the news that Paula Menzies was neither at the address they checked nor had been seen there for some months.

"Might as well wind it up for the night, Tam," she tapped Whelan on the shoulder, "and get home to the wife and the weans in time to see them to bed."

"Only if I must," he pretended to grumble, before asking, "What about you, Irene? Anything planned for this evening?"

"A hot date," she grinned at him, "with a plate of soup and a sexy man."

"So, the rumours are true?"

Startled, she stared wild-eyed at him.

His eyes narrowed when he continued, "I *was* joking, but I'm guessing you weren't?"

She blushed and lowering her voice, replied, "You'll keep it to yourself for now?"

"Scout's honour,' he raised two fingers, but in a rude V rather than the proper promise.

She took a deep breath when she said, "Iain Meikle and I have an interest in each other."

He pursed his lips before he said, "I admit to being surprised, but if there is to a be a man in your life you'd be hard pressed to find someone as decent and as good a guy as Iain. I've known Iain for a number of years now and it's about time he got a break of the ba'," he smiled at her, then added, "You two will be good for each other."

"Thanks, Tam," she said and then scowling, continued, "I'm off to the ladies to apply some lippy, so when I get back here, Detective Sergeant, I want to see you gone."

"Yes, Ma'am," he threw her a casual salute.

On her way to the female loo, she felt that some kind of hurdle had been achieved, that apart from Colin Morton she was able to admit to someone that she had a real interest in a man. Smiling, she pushed open the door and looking forward to again visiting Iain, realised too that she was hungry.

****

Worried that he might have been identified and was being followed, Seamus O'Brien hurried back to Wellington Street and approaching the hired car turned to glance behind him, but seeing just a number of pedestrians milling about the street was unable to tell who was or might be an undercover cop.

Jesus, that had been so close!

At the car he tried to insert the keys into the door lock, but his hands violently shaking, dropped the keys onto the street. Finally getting the door opened he sank into the driver's seat and almost immediately cringed, for the handgun stuck into the rear waistband of his trousers snagged on his jacket and the very act of sitting back caused the gun to dig painfully into his spine. With a yelp he twisted and managed to yank the gun from his waistband and threw it to the footwell on the passenger side.

His hands still shaking, he inserted the key into the ignition and with a quick check over his shoulder pulled out into the traffic. Driving off, he began to slap at the steering wheel in excitement and laugh uproariously.

He'd missed out on the heroin, but was only partially disappointed for he had a bag with almost fifty-eight grand in the boot and heading for the M8 motorway, prepared for the long road journey to Heathrow Airport.

****

The senior detective within Central Station, his eyes glued to the Train Information Board, told his team to standby that the Liverpool train was arriving three minutes before scheduled. Tensely, the detectives switched on to the imminent arrival of the courier who aside from already having seen his photograph had learned from their RCS colleagues that Tango One was wearing a distinctive Liverpool football top and carrying an army style kitbag.

As the train shuddered to a halt at Platform Four, the footmen began to disperse to their designated sectors to cover all the exits including the stairs to the lower platforms and out to the 'Hielanman's Umbrella' in Argyle Street, the two exits that led out to Hope Street, the stairs down to Union Street and stations main entrance onto Gordon Street where two surveillance vehicles sat ready near to the taxi stand.

In the the vehicles outside the station, the long wait was over. Detectives arched their backs or stretched their legs to ease the ache of sitting for a prolonged period in a cramped space.

In the rear of the grey coloured van, the two male detectives wondered where the hell Twinkle had got to for her comfort break, but sighed with relief when the van door was jerked open and the large woman cheerfully said, "Sorry lads, I thought I was peeing for Scotland, there."

"Too much information, hen," grimaced one of her colleagues. In the control room, DCI Richards used the back of his hand to wipe at his mouth. This was the moment when they would find out if Tango One was being met at the station or if the surveillance would continue.

This was the moment, thought Richards, when they'd know if they had half a capture or a full arrest.
****

Janie Wallace didn't quite fully understand why she'd accepted Peter Rossi's invitation for a Chinese meal, but was glad she did.

Seated opposite each other in Sauchiehall Street's Loon Fung Cantonese restaurant, Rossi said, "Did you know this is reputed to be the best Chinese restaurant in Glasgow?"

"And you know this how?" she teased.

"Well," he slowly drawled and nodded about him, "have you seen the number of *Chinese* people who eat here?"

"Oh, no I hadn't noticed," she glanced around her.

They sat in awkward silence for a moment before he asked, "How are you doing? After the…you know."

"You mean my complete humiliation?"

"No, I didn't mean…."

"I'm joking, Peter. I know you didn't mean that. Well, how am I feeling?" she pouted. "I suppose I could say I'm feeling a little vulnerable right now. The man I trusted and thought I loved turned out to be a cheating rat. I suppose you should ask, how do I feel about him?"

"How do you feel about him?"

"Nothing," she quickly replied. "I have no feelings for or about him. Whatever I thought we had together," she shrugged, "it's a bad memory. No," she hastily shook her head. "That's not true. There *were* some good times, but the way it ended is how I'll remember Paul and now that he's gone from my life I feel I'm ready to move on. Case closed," she used her hands as though pretending to close a book.

"Good," he softly smiled.

"Why here?" she suddenly asked.

"Eh, what?"

"Well, I'd have thought if you intended wooing a girl and with your family background you'd have taken me to a Pizza place or Italian restaurant for lasagne or something."

"Is that what I'm doing?" he smiled at her. "Wooing you?"

"Isn't that what you're doing?"

Her repeated question took him aback and licking nervously at his lips he replied, "I suppose I am. I just didn't want to step in just as you've come out of a difficult relationship. What I mean is…"

She reached across the table and taking his hand, interrupted when she quietly said, "I think you've stepped in just at the right time."
****

The rich aromatic smell of home made soup assailed her as soon as she stepped through Iain Meikle's door.

Taking her coat from her, he tossed it onto the couch and sliding his arms about her waist, pulled her close.

"Hungry?"

"Very," she nodded and smelling the soap and scent from him, guessed he had recently showered.

"So," he half smiled at her, "do you want to eat first or…"

"Or what?" she teased him.

He stared for a few seconds then narrowing his eyes, replied, "Soup first I think. You look starved."

"I am, actually," she agreed and inwardly blessed the intuition that made her decide to disclose her feelings to this thoughtful man.
****

His mouth felt as though he'd been chewing a dirty sock for a week and reckoned the half dozen cans of ale he'd drunk on the train must have been off.

Dragging the kitbag along the narrow passage he stepped from the train on to the platform then hoisted the kitbag onto his shoulder.

Following the crowd to the gate he flashed a ticket at a weedy ticket collector who hardly glanced at it, preferring to avert his eyes from those of the large and rough looking man pushing the kitbag on the trolley.

On the concourse, Doughnut glanced curiously about him and thought the Scottish railway station didn't look that much different from Lime Street and brow knitting, wondered where the fuck were all the poofs wearing the tartan skirts?
****

For one heart stopping moment, the female detective watched the arriving train disembark its passengers thought she had missed the target who was said to be wearing a bright red Liverpool football top, but then among the last of the passengers, spotted the large lumbering man along with the kitbag in a trolley he pushed and sighed with relief when she saw that he had his jacket fully buttoned.

Pressing the transmitting button in her coat pocket, she whispered, "Tango One static at the exit gate, over."

****

He handed over his ticket to be punched then decided he'd better find out pronto where this pub was located. Seeing a small Pakistani man wearing a porter's uniform, Stokoe headed for him.

****

"Tango One now off, off, off…wait one. Seems like he's looking for directions from a member of the station staff, over. Standby, now heading towards the Hope Street exit, over."

From all the other exits, footmen began to hurry to leave the station and work their way round to Hope Street to get there before or at the same time as Tango One.

In the SCS control room, Richards breathed a sigh of relief. It seemed then that Stokoe was not being met, that he had instructions to go somewhere and gleefully rubbing his hands together, considered that maybe the operation would not go tits up like he'd dreaded.

****

Colin Morton might have been angry, disappointed or perhaps even a little thankful if he had known that shortly after he left the Govan office to return home, Irene Crichton had phoned his wife to suggest that she offer him a couple of halves with his dinner.

"It might help him sleep," Irene had suggested. "It seems to me that he needs a right good night's rest," she added.

Alice Morton was grateful that Irene had persuaded her husband to knock off work early and agreeing, admitted, "I've been a wee bit concerned about him. He's never usually this worried about solving an inquiry, but I think the fact it's one of

your own is preying on his mind. Thanks, Irene, I'll see to him tonight."
****

In his Burghead Drive flat in the Linthouse area of Govan, Charlie Gallagher sipped at the whisky with one eye on the clock and walked to look out of the window to the street below. His eyes darted back and forth as he tried to spot the CID car that he guessed was watching his close.

He'd ordered a taxi to take him to the Thistle Hotel in Cambridge Street where he was booked in for the next three nights and grinning, thought, that would fool the bastards. Now his holdall was packed and a clean jacket and trousers suit in the suit holder for he planned a night out to celebrate the success of the handover and imagined the wealth that this, the first of many such deals with Billy Madison, would bring. Staring at the chunky glass in his large fist he swirled the whisky about the glass and thought about Seamus O'Brien.

In the recent few weeks there was something definitely off about Seamus, something that he couldn't quite put his finger on.

He had seen the way the red headed sod had shirked from getting involved in cutting up Paula's body, saw the disgust on his face when he and wee Marty had piled her body parts into the plastic bags then squirmed and looked away when they'd thrown the meat to the pigs.

Aye, he'd definitely need to keep an eye on Seamus he decided and sipping again at his whisky, saw the Hackney cab draw up in the street below.
****

Irene Crichton finished off the last of her soup then licking at her lips said, "That's definitely what I needed."

"What's that you needed? Just the soup?" he pretended surprise.

"You've definitely come out of your shell, haven't you Mister Meikle," she chortled. "I thought it was me that was supposed to be pursuing you?"

"Well," he quietly said, "you've caught me, Miss Crichton, so now that you have, you won't find me so easy to get rid of."

"And who says I want to get rid of you?" she leaned across the table to stare at him.

He didn't immediately respond, but then in the same quiet voice replied, "That sounds like a commitment to me."

"Would you like it to be a commitment?"

"Yes," he slowly nodded, "I think I would like that."

"Well," she pretended to be confused and asked, "is there anywhere in this place we can go and relax and talk a little bit more about this?"

He stood up from his seat and offering her his hand, smiled and replied, "I know the very place."

****

Marty Boyle had never drunk in the Waterloo Bar, indeed he seldom if ever drank in the city centre preferring instead to do his drinking in the Shettleston area of the city among the local Celtic fans and Irish Republican patriots. Besides, he glanced suspiciously around him, he'd once heard a rumour that this was a poofs pub.

Now sitting with his back to the wall in a booth in the Waterloo Bar and a clear view of the doorway, he had searched the faces of the couple of dozen or so customers and thought they were mainly staff from the nearby offices, but none jumped out at him as any kind of threat. Indeed, most of those who caught his eye quickly glanced away, some inner sense telling them that the small man exuded an air of unprovoked violence.

Nursing his second pint of lager Boyle as hid fingers idly played with the closed razor in his pocket, he continued to stare at the doorway and the customers in turn, unaware that the two barmaids and male manager had already marked him down as trouble and were not only keeping their own discreet eyes on him, but also stayed within reach the large wooden batons behind the bar.

It did strike Boyle as odd that quite a few of the customers seemed to be funnily dressed and some of the guys were wearing too tight jeans. Look like poofters, he inwardly smirked but was conscious of Charlie Gallagher's instruction not to draw attention and so kept to himself any derisory comments he might have thought to make.

Pity that neither Gallagher nor O'Brien had thought to mention to Boyle that popular with locals and tourists alike, the Waterloo Bar was also reputedly one of Glasgow's oldest and most popular gay bars.

****

The station porter's directions had been spot on and as Doughnut Stokoe lumbered across Hope Street into Waterloo Street, he continued walking to the junction of Wellington Street where he turned left, coincidentally passing the bay where just twenty minutes previously, Seamus O'Brien had been parked.

To the alarm of the footmen following him, Stokoe's head swivelled on his shoulders as he searched for the Waterloo Bar that according to the porter was on the corner of Argyle Street and where he'd arrive after a couple of minutes walk.

Unfortunately, the footmen mistook Stokoe's observations as counter surveillance and began to hang back and frantically advise their colleagues to be aware.

In the control room and listening intently, DCI Richards, acutely aware of the balls-up in the Central Station was conscious of a rivulet of perspiration running down his spine and indecision wracked him as he wondered; should he call a strike, just go for the courier and the heroin?

However, with the kitbag on his shoulder, the big man plodded along and had he the sense to turn and look behind him, he might would have been surprised to see a half dozen footmen trailing behind like a bride's train while the remainder and their vehicles closed in from the adjoining streets and roads.

****

"Standby, it's a stop, stop, stop," the excited footman who had eyeball almost screamed across the radio. "He's stopped and...he's dropped the kitbag and is unbuttoning his coat.

Bag's back upon onto his shoulder and…wait one…Tango One now entering the…it's the Waterloo Bar, corner of Argyle Street and Wellington Street, over!"

The channel was overwhelmed as the footmen all came in at once, each volunteering to enter the pub with one thought in mind.

A couple of pints on expenses.

However, the convoy commander who had overall control of the vehicles and footmen cut through the excited radio chatter and instead instructed that the three footmen who would enter the premises would be the arrest team who in situ would decide if any further resources were necessary.

Within ninety seconds of his instruction, Twinkle and her two neighbours were stood at the bar ordering three pints of heavy while they covertly watched a dwarf like man beckon Tango One to join him at the smaller man's table in the rear of the pub.

****

"You've got the payment?" Doughnut asked as the big man wearing the Liverpool top dumped the kitbag onto the floor then slumped down into his seat before wiping a meaty hand across his face.

"Aye, if you've got what I think you've got in that bag there," Boyle nodded down to the kitbag, then subtly turned his head to watch for Seamus O'Brien entering the pub.

"Oh. I've got it, Jock. Now," his eyes narrowed as he turned to stare at the floor and the seat next to Boyle, "I see my bag with the H, but where's yours with the dough?"

So wrapped up in his thoughts at seeing the bearlike Liverpudlian walk through the door of the pub, it then occurred to Boyle that O'Brien still hadn't followed the courier in. Where the fuck is he, he thought and wondered; O'Brien was supposed to be acting as a stopper for any muscle the courier might bring with him. Was there someone else outside that Seamus was dealing with and who, he turned to gaze through slitted eyes at the three large guys…no, fuck me, one's a bird…who stood at the bar with their backs to him and had followed the Scouser into the pub.

His mouth suddenly and unaccountably dry and his ingrained distrust of everyone, Boyle decided that something was wrong; aye, something was definitely wrong!

In that split second he stared again at the trio at the bar and yes, the guy on the end had turned to glance at him.

Already hyped up, he switched his gaze to the hulking figure sat beside him and felt his blood run cold.

That's it, he decided and licked nervously at his dry lips. The three at the bar are with this bastard sitting next to me!

It was a set up!

The bastards were after the money and likely they had already done for Seamus.

He took a sharp breath and as slowly as he dared, slipped his right hand down to his jacket pocket.

"Fucker!" he screamed and in one swift movement his right hand withdrew the razor from the jacket pocket, his thumb already practised at opening the razor as his hand drew back and then forward, drawing the razor down across the face of the courier.

Completely taken unaware, Doughnut screamed, his hand instinctively reaching up to clutch at his slashed face as blood spurted through his fingers and across the table, spraying the razor wielding Boyle who drew back his hand to strike again.

But Doughnut wasn't yet down and out. Ignoring the pain and for all his size he swiftly reached a large hand towards Boyle and grabbing the smaller man by the jacket, pulled him across the table toward Doughnut.

In that heartbeat of indecision, the large man decided to try and close the gap between him and the smaller man, but had he a split second longer he might have instead decided to reach for the hand wielding the razor.

In the meantime, Boyles first screaming assault upon Tango One had caused uproar among the customers who turning to see the commotion and the blood, began to flee the pub, but inadvertently prevented the three detectives from racing the few yards across the floor from where they stood at the bar ready to pounce and arrest the two men.

While the manager quickly dialled nine-nine-nine, the two barmaids, completely unaware that the two hulking men and one woman were officers of the Scottish Crime Squad and more than capable of dealing with the fight, mistakenly believed the three intended to involve themselves in the brawl. As one the barmaids worsened the situation by grabbing the batons from behind the bar and launching themselves across the bar began to hammer into the three detectives.

Mayhem ensued with Doughnut ignoring the pain and now with both hands about Boyle's throat and strangling the smaller man who fighting for breath, continued to repeatedly slash at the bigger man, striking him several times and cutting through the sleeves of the flimsy jacket and Liverpool top into Doughnut's powerful arms.

Meanwhile the three detectives were wrestling with the two furious barmaids and trying to fend off the women's baton strikes before they could turn their attention to the blood soaked pair who continued to grapple across the table in the booth.

While her two neighbours fought to subdue the struggling barmaids and all the while shouting, "We're the polis, ya pair of fucking nutters!" Twinkle, grabbing one of the batons from a barmaid and sporting a bleeding head wound and a bruise across her forehead, launched herself across the room to reach for Boyle's right hand to relieve him of the razor. However, the wee man who was by now fast losing consciousness had a final lunge at Doughnut who unfortunately was at that second lowering his head to avoid the blow.

But Doughnut was not quick enough for the ale he had drunk prior to boarding the train at Lime Street and the six cans of ale he had consumed on the train combined to dull his wits and thus he paid the consequence.

The clumsy strike by Boyle's razor slashed across Doughnut's throat and the tip caught him squarely on what is frequently referred to as the common carotid artery.

Not that Doughnut was particularly interested in the medical term for all that he cared about right at that time was the slicing razor resulted in a gaping injury, causing a massive surge of arterial blood that spurted from his neck in a scarlet projectile that shot across the room and landed on anyone or anything that got in the way.

Feeling faint from the loss of blood, he instinctively let go of Boyle who gasping for air, was suddenly pummelled into unconsciousness by the baton wielding Twinkle before she turned her attention to the mortally wounded Tango One.

"Get me some cloths or something!" she screamed.

Almost as one, the shocked detectives and barmaids turned to see the large woman using her hands to compress Tango One's throat and watched as the blood seeped through her fingers.

Quick as a flash the manager threw a pile of bar towels at the two detectives and the barmaids who crowding around Twinkle thrust them at her and watched as her lifesaving attempt to stem the flow of blood proved to be of no avail.

Try as she might, within minutes the life seeped from the large man and finally she could no nothing but lay him awkwardly down onto the bench seat of the booth.

She sobbed and took a deep breath and oblivious to the fact her hands were covered in Tango One's blood, inadvertently wiped her hand across her face.

As one of her neighbours later commented, "If Twinkle was a scary woman before that bloody incident, you should have seen her when she was covered in blood. Demonic she was," he had shuddered.

A curious and almost respectful silence had fallen among them, broken when a head was raised from the other side of the bench seat and Boyle, his scalp bleeding from Twinkles baton strike, slowly come to consciousness then politely asked, "What the fuck happened?"

He got his answer when Twinkle reached across the table to grab him by his ear and painfully hauling him across the table, shoved his head against the dead body of Doughnut Stokoe and hissed, "*That* happened and see you, ya wee bastard! You're getting done for his murder!"

TWENTY-FOUR

Listening to the morning news on the radio in the kitchen while he gulped down his coffee, DCI Colin Morton wondered at the circumstances that led to the death of a man in a Glasgow city centre pub where the reporter said the police were actually inside the premises at the time of the incident.

"Sounds like somebody is going to get their arse kicked," he muttered as he bit at his toast.

"What was that, dear?" his wife Alice asked.

"I said I love you to bits," he solemnly replied.

"Aye, I'm sure you did," she gave him one of her 'that'll be right' looks before asking, "Did you sleep well?"

"I did, thanks. Why didn't you come in beside me instead of using the spare room?"

"Let me think," she poked a forefinger at her chin and pretended to ponder. "Me in beside you after you've had a couple or three of drams then snoring like an express train or me in the spare room having a restful night. Oh, what a hard decision *that* was," she sighed.

"Sarcasm, my dear, does not become you," he politely said.

She stood up from her chair then leaned across to kiss him on the forehead and gently replied, "Well, sarcasm or not, you've had a good night's sleep and you're looking all the better for it. Now, I'm off to work so I'll see you when you get in tonight," and waved him cheerio.

He heard the front door closing and finishing his coffee, reached for his suit jacket from behind the chair and carried it with him through the hallway while he wondered what the day would bring.

****

When the previous evening Charlie Gallagher had arrived in his hotel room he'd changed his mind about going out and instead run up a bill in the hotel bar for which he was now paying with a severe hangover. But drunk though he had been, before going to bed he'd phoned both O'Brien and wee Marty's numbers, but neither man had answered.

Now stood shaving in the en suite of his fourth floor hotel room, he was more than a little concerned that his early morning calls to Seamus O'Brien's flat had gone unanswered. It was then the worry began to kick in, that the unthinkable had happened.

They had been arrested.

Either that, he stared at his reflection and gritted his teeth, or that *bastard* Billy Madison had screwed him over and done for the two of them.

Drying his face, he threw the damp towel to the floor and stepping into the bedroom pulled a clean set of clothes from his holdall and dressed in a clean shirt, jeans and training shoes. Reaching across the unmade bed he grimaced at the throb in his head and switching on the digital radio clock, turned the dial to Clyde One.

There was still a few minutes before the eight o'clock news began so brewed himself a coffee while he contemplated what might have occurred at the handover.

Should I phone Madison and find out if his courier arrived back, he wondered.

Idly stirring at the coffee, he sat down heavily on the edge of the bed; however, his mind was on what had happened to O'Brien and Boyle and he carelessly spilled some of the scalding coffee onto his jeans.

"Fuck!" he cried out, but getting to his feet only succeeded in spilling more coffee that this time scalded his hand.

Throwing the cup with rage across the room, he stomped into the en suite to run his hand under the cold tap.

It was then he heard the jingle that announced the start of the news bulletin that commenced with the shocking news of a murder within a city centre pub.

His painful hand for the minute forgotten, with eyes widening and mouth gaping he listened as the reporter related the story of a fight the previous evening in Argyle Street's Waterloo Bar that resulted in one man dead and another arrested.

"According to witnesses," the reporter continued, *"plain clothes police officers were in the premises at the time, but a spokesperson for Strathclyde Police refused to comment on an ongoing investigation other than to say police inquiries are continuing. Neither the dead man nor the individual arrested has been named."*

Numbly, he turned off the tap and slowly made his way through to the bedroom where confused, he walked to the window and stared unseeingly down at the street below.

His mind was in turmoil.

What could have happened and who was dead?

Worse, who had been arrested and what did it mean for me, he thought?

He took a sharp breath as a feeling of dread took hold of him.

Marty Boyle, he confidently knew, would never grass on him and months ago he might have said the same thing about Seamus O'Brien. But these days, his eyes narrowed, the way Seamus had recently been acting he didn't have the same confidence about the red haired bastard.

And my money, his stomach tightened.

What the fuck has happened to my dough?

****

While Iain Meikle showered, Irene Crichton prepared a breakfast of bacon and eggs in the tight little kitchen and set the table in the room.

She turned as Iain, wearing a shirt and suit trousers but barefooted, appeared at the kitchen doorway as he roughly towelled his damp hair.

"I could get used to this," he smiled at her.

She returned to flipping the bacon in the frying pan and slowly nodding, said, "Then why don't we talk about that, say, this evening?"

"You're serious?"

She swallowed, her throat suddenly tight and wondering if that was perhaps a step too far. Still with her back to him, she forced her full attention to frying the bacon then quietly replied, "Only if you think it would be a good idea."

She wasn't sure how he would react to such a proposal, particularly as they had just got together and tensed herself for a rejection, but was surprised and relieved when he stepped forward then dropping the towel onto a chair, wrapped his arms about her waist. Nuzzling at the back of her neck, he whispered, "Okay, but why don't we discuss it at your place." He jokingly continued, "I'm beginning to think you're homeless and that you only want me because you need somewhere to live."

She turned a little awkwardly in the tight space that was his kitchen and he was taken aback to see she was tight-lipped, holding back the tears in her eyes.

She took a breath then in a soft voice, she asked, "You mean it? You'd give some thought to us living together?"

Some inner instinct warned him that flippancy was the last thing she needed right now, so instead he nodded and quietly replied, "Absolutely."

She held on so tightly he thought she would crush him to death, but then lightly said, "Well, if that's settled then, sit yourself down, Mister Meikle. Breakfast is ready."

****

The early shift bar officer stared curiously at the envelope and decided to place it to one side.

He'd watch for the DCI arriving and hand it to him personally.

****

The first thing that the Chief Constable did when he arrived at Pitt Street that morning at his usual early time was peruse the typed report sitting forefront on his desk, the twenty-four-hour synopsis of major incidents within the Force area. Speedily reading through the document, he called for his ACC (Crime) who regretfully had not yet arrived at Pitt Street for Martin Kerr was not as fastidiously punctual as his boss.

However, the Chief's aide, a uniformed Superintendent who stood in front of the desk reminded him that the Detective Chief Superintendent (South CID) was in *his* office. It was then that Martin Kerr's belligerent attitude to his subordinates became his undoing for the Superintendent who disliked Kerr, cannily suggested, "If you wish sir, I can ask Mister Cruickshank to attend here?"

Less than three minutes later, Alistair Cruickshank, who carried a file in his hand was shown into the Chief's office and bluntly being asked, "What the hell happened last night at that city centre pub?"

Before he replied, Cruickshank nodded to a chair to which the Chief said, "Yes, of course. Sorry, Alistair, sit down, please. Now, give me the story, warts and all."

"I take it Mister Kerr is…" he paused, his eyes narrowing, "unavailable?"

The Chief scowled and said, "Don't try to score points, Alistair, it's beneath you," then sighed before adding, "As you have rightly guessed, not everyone is as dedicated as you or I. Now, the story," he impatiently asked.

In short, concise sentences, Cruickshank related the conversation he had with DCI Maurice Richards who had assured him that the drug courier arriving from England, an individual known as Derek Stokoe who was known to the Merseyside colleagues, would be the target for the Scottish Crime Squad, that it was to be a straight forward arrest and that the assistance of local officers of Strathclyde Police was not necessary.

"However," he wheezed, "it seems the individual who was to take receipt of the drugs, a Martin Boyle who is well documented with us met with the courier in the Waterloo Bar. Three Squad members followed Stokoe into the bar where along with some bar staff, they there witnessed some sort of disagreement resulting in a fight during which Boyle used an open razor to cut Stokoe's throat. Despite a valiant effort by one of the Squad detectives, Stokoe bled to death in the pub," Cruickshank added.

"And this man Boyle?"

"In custody charged with murder and other offences and due to appear at two o'clock this afternoon at the city's Sheriff Court where undoubtedly he will be remanded."

"What do we know of these two individuals?"

"Well, starting with Stokoe. I've learned from the Head of the CID at Liverpool that Stokoe is predominantly an enforcer for hire and occasional employee of a former Glasgow gangster called William Madison who now resides in Liverpool and has done for some years. I'm also told that Madison is well well-known in the drug scene down there. It is surmised the drugs that were recovered…"

"What kind of drug and quantity are we talking about here?"

"Fifty kilo of Class A heroin that I'm told by our own Drug Squad has a street value in excess of around two hundred thousand pounds. Perhaps more if it's adulterated further."

The Chief whistled then said, "That's quite a recovery."

"Yes, sir, it is. The man arrested, Martin Boyle, is a known associate of Charles Gallagher who…"

"Charles Gallagher? Isn't he a suspect in the murder of my constable, the young lassie Rudd?"

"That's still being investigated, sir," Cruickshank tightly replied.

The Chief was about to ask more, but recognising that Cruickshank didn't expand further, held his tongue and simply nodded that his DCS continue.

"The SCS have assessed that if Boyle was the meet and greet for the courier it is likely that Gallagher was the recipient for the heroin."

"What is Boyle saying to all of this?"

"Regretfully, he remains tight-lipped, sir, and refuses to cooperate with either the murder or the drug investigation."

"What, you're splitting the two into separate inquiries?"

"Ah, yes and no, sir. I've suggested with…"

He got no further for the door was loudly knocked then almost immediately pushed open by a red-faced Martin Kerr who blundered into the room and apologetically said, "Sorry I'm a little late, sir. Traffic, you know. What have I missed?" then without being asked, sat heavily down onto the chair beside Cruickshank.

"Good morning, Mister Kerr," the Chief greeted him in a voice dripping with sarcasm before continuing, "Mister Cruickshank was just bringing me up to speed about the murder in the pub last night."

"Murder? Ah yes, that murder," Kerr blustered, but he had given himself away and it was evident he had no knowledge of the murder, that he had not taken the time to read the daily synopsis but likely hearing that Cruickshank was with the Chief, rushed straight round to the Chief's office.

An awkward silence fell between the three men, broken when the Chief calmly said, "As you have just arrived at your office, Mister Kerr, and as Mister Cruickshank here has filled me in with the details of the murder, I don't believe there is anything that you can add to what I need to know, so please; do not let me keep you from whatever duties you must attend to."

The rebuke was embarrassingly obvious, yet Cruickshank felt no sympathy for the blustering ACC for as far as he was concerned, Kerr had brought it upon himself for it was generally understood that a man of Kerr's rank should be in his office if not before then certainly at the same time as his boss. But then to attend at the Chief's office without having knowledge of a major incident that occurred the night before; well, that was unforgiveable in Cruickshank's book.

Though he took no real pleasure in it, it seemed to him that as far as Kerr was concerned the writing was on the wall. However, he continued to stare straight ahead and did not see Kerr's face pale or his lip curl as the ACC realised that he was summarily, if at least with some courtesy, being dismissed. Rising to his feet he choked back a retort, but his face revealed his fury and nodding he left without a word, though it took all of his inner strength to avoid slamming the door behind him.

Seconds passed before the Chief passed a hand across his face then quietly said, "I'm sorry you had to witness that, Alistair."

"Sir," was all Cruickshank replied.

"Now, what were you going to tell me about splitting the murder and drug inquiries into two?"

****

No matter how many times Billy Madison phoned Doughnut Stokoe's number, all he got from his mother was that her son had not yet returned home.

"But have you heard from him?" he almost begged her.

"Not today, Billy lad, no. Why, is it important? Will I get him to phone you when he gets home?"

"Important!" Madison almost screamed down the phone, when what he really wanted to shout was that if the big bastard doesn't get my money to me my wife's going to have her fucking *tits* cut off you drunken, useless hag!

Instead, he took a breath and forced himself to be calm before telling the old woman, "Just get him to phone me, hen. As *soon* as he gets home. You can do that, can't you?"

"Aye, Billy, I'll get him to phone you when he gets home," Annie Stokoe replied, but wondered what kind of trouble the big bugger has got himself into this time?

But then she turned when the doorbell rung and through the glazed glass window, could see the outline of two uniformed rozzers.

****

It had started as a suggestion then almost turned into an argument, but now sitting in Irene's passenger seat, Iain Meikle accepted it made sense and smiled.

"Look," he turned to her, "I know I didn't think it was a good idea us travelling in the same car to the office, that people would talk, but now that we are together I kind of like the idea that everyone knows I'm having an affair with the DI."

She turned towards him, her face aghast and asked, "Is that what this is? An affair? I'm some kind of trophy on your bedpost! You cheeky bugger, Meikle! I'll…" but stopped when she saw him grinning and realising she was being teased, bunched her left hand into a fist that she thumped off his chest.

"Ouch. We've only being together for a few days and already you're subjecting me to domestic violence," he pretended to whine.

She laughed with him then said, "It makes sense taking the one car if we're going to my place tonight. Besides, I like the idea of having a boyfriend, even if it's an old scruffy guy like you."

"Scruffy?" he glanced down at his suit. "I'll have you know that ten years ago this suit was the height of fashion."

"Aye, and maybe it will come back into some kind of retro fashion in the future," she pretended to sigh.

She parked outside the office in Orkney Street and when they were getting out of the car saw a couple of CID officers also arriving at the same time. Whispering across the roof to him, she said, "Don't look now, but I think we're going to be the talk of the steamie."

"So, no quick winch before we go into work then?" he smiled.

"Wait till tonight," she grinned mischievously at him.

They walked together upstairs to the CID suite where in the general office serving as the incident room, DS Tam Whelan, who first stared curiously at Iain, told Irene, "The boss said when you got in that he wants me and you to go and see him right away."

"See you later," she smiled at Iain then followed Whelan into the corridor towards to Colin Morton's office.

"I take it that it's public knowledge now, you and Iain?"

"Didn't see any point in keeping it quiet any longer," she shrugged. "Thought it better that we were seen to be a couple before the tongues started wagging."

"Trust me, they'll still wag," he grinned at her before knocking on Morton's door then pushing it open.

"Ah, good, you're here," Morton greeted them then waving a hand added, "Draw up some chairs."

They were both curious to see that on his hands Morton wore a pair of light blue coloured, Forensic gloves.

When they were comfortably seated or as comfortable as they could be on the tubular leg and unforgiving plastic bum torturers, Morton waved an envelope at them before handing it to Irene.

"This was handed to me when I arrived at the office this morning by the bar officer downstairs. It's been well handled, so I'm not too bothered about prints," he added. "This however, is a different story. The envelope you have there contained this handwritten letter," he added as he held up a sheet of A4 paper. She could see the excitement in his eyes as she glanced at the envelope that had scrawled upon it, *'Head of the CID, Govan police office, Govan, Glasgow'*.

Handing it to Whelan, she wryly commented, "Whoever sent it was keen it got to you because I see it's been posted with two first class stamps."

"And when I read you the contents, you'll understand why," he grinned at her.

After Whelan handed the envelope back, Morton carefully laid it to one side then said, "You'll be wondering at the gloves. There's no signature on the letter so after we have it copied," he glanced at Whelan, "I'll be wanting it taken to Pitt Street, Tam, and tested by ninhydrin for fingerprints and before you ask," he smiled, "I've a suspect in mind."

He was about to continue, but the door knocked and was

opened by DCS Alistair Cruickshank who poking his head into the room, seemed surprised before he asked, "Sorry, am I disturbing a meeting?"

Both Irene and Whelan respectfully got to their feet, but were waved back down into their chairs by Cruickshank as Morton said, "No, you're all right, sir, come in," Irene thought Morton seemed pleased to see him, then suggesting that Cruickshank also draw up a chair, told him of the delivery of the anonymous letter.

"Okay," Cruickshank slowly replied before adding, "Tempted though I am to ask who your suspect is, I'll wait till you're ready to tell us. Go on, please."

"Right, spelling, punctuation and grammar aside, the handwritten letter is quite informative and as I said, unsigned. However, the information it contains does not in itself contribute to the murder of Lesley Rudd, but might prove to be very useful. It begins," he started to read out loud:

"I am not telling you who I am but I want you to know that Charlie Gallagher who you will know lives in a pitch in Burghead drive was living with a bird called Paula Menzis but he killed her. He killed her in there bedroom on the bed. He battered her to death with his fists. When he done that he got me and a guy he knows called Marty Boyle who is a wee guy and lives in the multis in Sitehill on the 14 floor I think it is. Me and Boyle went to Charlies pitch in Boyles motor, an old rusting black colored Fiat. When we got there we saw Paulas dead body lying on the bed. I wanted no part of it but Charlie said we had to help him get rid of her body. He told me that if I didn't help he'd kill me to. I am scared of Charlie and I did as he said because I was scared. There were two cops in a CID motor outside charlies close, a guy and a bird that wee Boyle had noised up. Anyway we wrapped Paulas body in plastic bags and carried her down the stairs and out in to the back court then in to the nearby street where Boyle had parked his motor then put her into the boot. Like I said I did not want to take part in this but charlie made me. Then Charlie made wee

Boyle drive down towards Port Glasgow and told him to drive into a wee park where there is a peer and were winching cuples go to snog and have sex. Then Charlie asked wee Boyle if the wee man still carried the hatchet in the boot of the car and wee Boyle said he did. Then…"

Morton stopped and staring at them in turn, quietly said, "I'm sorry, but from here on the letter gets a bit graphic."

He continued, *"Then Charlie and wee Boyle got Paulas body out of the boot and I thought at first that Charlie was just going to dump her into the river but then they took turns in using the hatchet to cut Paulas body up into small bits. That sickened me and I took no part in it, but Charlie and Boyle were dancing about like fucking maddies and laughing and joking when they were doing it to her. Wee Boyle in paticulir was laughing when Charlie cut Paulas head off. I was sick and they thought that was funny to. Then when they had finished cutting her up they put her bits into the same plastic bags again and then Charlie made wee Boyle drive to a pig farm up somewhere in a place called lockwinik or somewere that sounds like that."*

Morton, swallowing, paused again to comment, "Likely he means Lochwinnoch."

He continued, *"When we got there Charlie spoke to the guy who owns the farm and they know each other and the guy is an old guy with a white beard and looks like he likes a drink and I think he was drunk when we got there. Charlie called him smudger or something like that. Anyway, the farm guy told Boyle to drive the motor round to the back of the house and there was a big fenced off area with a lot of pigs there and the place stunk rotten enugh to make me want to throw up again and the pigs sqeeling was horrible to. Then Charlie and wee Boyle opened the boot and got out the plastic bags with Paulas bits in them and emptied the bags into the field where the pigs run over and started to eat them. I had to look away because it turned my stomach. Then Charlie gave the guy smudger if that's his name some money but I don't know how much. Then wee Boyle started moaning because some of Paulas blood had*

spilt from the bags into the carpet of his motors boot. If you are
looking for the hatchet that cut Paula up wee Boyle has kept it
and it shoud be in the boot of his motor and I think the gloves
they wore are in there as well. This is all true and I did not
want any part of it and that's why Im not giving you people my
name."

Morton glanced up and said, "That's it."

"Fuck me," Whelan muttered, "I'm never going to eat bacon again."

"And who do you suspect to be the author of this letter?" asked Cruickshank.

"Well, the only member of the unholy trio who is not named in the letter seems to be Seamus O'Brien who intelligence suggests with Boyle is Gallagher's main trusted lieutenant. The information the letter contains is too precise for the author not to have been present at the dismemberment of Menzies and particularly when he describes the pig farm. I can't imagine Gallaher being so foolhardy to call upon anyone other than Boyle and O'Brien to assist him with the disposal of Menzies body, so I think it's fair to assume that Mister O'Brien is our author. You might also note that in the letter the author refers to attending at Gallagher's flat when two police officers are in a CID vehicle outside Gallagher's close and that Boyle 'noised them up.' Well, we have it documented that two plain clothes officers were indeed on surveillance when both Boyle and O'Brien arrived at Gallagher's flat and were spoken to by Boyle. That's why I intend having O'Brien's fingerprints compared against any that our esteemed colleagues at the Fingerprint Department manage to find on this letter," he flourished it.

"Tam," he turned to Whelan, "please contact the office local to Lochwinnoch and make some inquiry as to a pig farm with a tenant or owner called Smudge or Smudger or something similar."

"On it, boss," Whelan watched as Morton carefully laid the

letter onto a sheet of paper then lifting it from the desk, rose from his chair and left the room.

"So Colin, what's your next move?" Cruickshank asked.

"Well if the letter is genuine and I have no reason to doubt its veracity, unfortunately this seems to explain why my guys are unable to trace Paula Menzies." He grimly smiled, then continued, "The first thing I'm going to do is arrange for this Marty Boyle to be arrested and his car seized for Forensic examination and hopefully, we'll also find the hatchet mentioned in the letter. Then I'll arrange for a warrant to have Gallagher's flat Forensically searched too and…"

Cruickshank raised a hand at which Morton stopped speaking, then told the DCI, "About your suspect, Martin Boyle. I have some news on that particular individual."

****

Twenty minutes later with the inquiry team assembled in the incident room, Colin Morton, with Alistair Cruickshank and Irene Crichton at his back, commenced his morning briefing. To a shocked silence, he related the circumstances of the anonymous letter and followed that with the revelation that Martin Boyle, one of the suspects in the disposal of Paula Menzies body was in custody for the murder of an English drug courier.

"In short, ladies and gentlemen, there is a lot of work to do. Actions will be allocated to interview Boyle, the search of his flat and the seizure of his vehicle. Actions will also be allocated for the Forensic search of Gallagher's flat in Burghead Drive and the outcome of that search will determine if he is to be arrested."

"Can't we just lift him anyway, sir?" a DC called out.

"Not without substantive evidence and regretfully, an anonymous letter does not fill the bill. However, before we look at Mister Gallagher, Actions will be allocated for a team of you to attend at a pig farm run by a…" he paused and turned towards Whelan who said, "Philip Smith also known as Smudger who runs a pig farm in Lochwinnoch. I have the address and," he added to some laughter, "I suggest that those of you going there find yourselves wellies and waterproofs." Smiling, Morton raised his hand for quiet before continuing, "I also want Actions raised to trace and interview Seamus O'Brien. At the minute he is not a strong suspect, but depending on the result of an Ninhydrin test he might very well be the third man who was at the disposal of Menzies body and disturbs me as it does, might prove to be more valuable as a witness than an accused. So, when he is traced, kid gloves please. Any questions?"

It was Iain Meikle who raised a hand to ask, "If bloodstaining is discovered at Gallagher's flat or in Boyle's boot, sir, how will we know if it belongs to Paula Menzies?"

A silence fell on the room and they watched as Morton grimly shook his head and replied, "Unfortunately, we won't so the blood will be circumstantial evidence alongside anything else we can pin on Gallagher. The upside is that we can bring him in and interview him about Lesley Rudd's murder."

As he watched, Iain broke into a slow smile and slowly nodding his head, replied, "Perhaps I can help you there, sir." Morton felt a tension in his stomach and staring at Iain, asked, "In what way?"

Aware that all eyes were on him, Iain took his time to explain, "Some months ago Lesley Rudd and I attended at the Cooperative Hypermarket to arrest Menzies on a shoplifting charge."

"Yes, I'm aware of the incident," Morton was curious where this was going, but decided to let Iain continue.

"Well, Menzies had stolen a woollen jacket and during a fight with the staff, she not only inflicted some damage to them, but had her own nose burst to."

Morton could feel a growing excitement in his stomach as Iain added, "She bled onto the woollen jacket that I seized as a production in the case against her. It was Lesley's case, but to assist her I bagged the jacket in a paper bag and to tie up the evidence against Menzies I had the casualty surgeon obtain a specimen of her blood that I later sent with the jacket to the Laboratory at Pitt Street where I'm assuming it's still logged there."

Excited, Morton had to refrain from punching the air and quickly turning to Whelan, said, "Tam, issue Iain with an Action to attend at the Lab and ensure they still have the specimen."

Turning back to Iain he took a breath before telling him, "Well done, Iain. That good police work might just earn us a conviction against Gallagher for murder."

CHAPTER TWENTY-FOUR

A new impetus was driving the team, an energy that had during the preceding days, been seriously lacking.

Granted, they were no closer to positively identifying Lesley Rudd's killer, but the possibility that Charlie Gallagher might still be in the frame was driving them on.

The four detectives assigned the Actions for the Lochwinnoch pig farm first met with a local constable who accompanied them to interview the owner, Philip Smith, who was also known locally as Smudger. Within minutes of their arrival, the alcoholic Smith was blubbering like a child and confessing that not only Charlie Gallagher had used his services, but to the astonishment of the detectives named three other notable Glasgow based gangsters who also had brought bodies to be fed to Smith's pigs and thus opened a veritable can of worms.

When news reached him of the pig farmers confession and conscious that the investigation would encompass many lines of inquiry, DCS Alistair Cruickshank awarded this new inquiry to the Force's Serious Crime Squad, recognising that neither the K Division CID who were responsible for investigating crime in the Lochwinnoch area nor Colin Morton's overworked G Division murder team had the resources to deal with this new and in all likelihood, major investigation. However, what was important to Morton was that though Smith positively identified Gallagher who was known to him, he also recalled that the two men who accompanied Gallagher that night were a short, balding man who assisted him in feeding the body parts to the pigs and a tall, red haired man who took no part but stood aside.

The tall red haired man, Morton was convinced, had to be Seamus O'Brien.

However, Actions to trace O'Brien at his home address proved negative and though a warrant to enter his flat was granted, no trace of his current whereabouts was found. Inquiry with neighbours and his landlord also proved negative.

****

DS Jack Fleming was one of the two detectives assigned to interrogate Marty Boyle and so with his neighbour arrived at HMP Barlinnie where Boyle was on the Remand Wing at the bleak Victorian jail.

In a cold and graffiti covered interview room, Boyle, who had refused the services of a lawyer, sneered at the detectives and arms folded persistently replied, "No comment," to their questions.

However, bored with the repetitive 'No comment' replies and conscious that there was no lawyer present and there would be no record of the interview, Fleming blatantly lied that Charlie Gallagher was in custody and had confessed that it was Boyle who murdered Paula Menzies.

"You're lying, ya bastard," Boyle sneered, but his eyes betrayed the fact the seed of doubt had been sown.

"Why would I lie, Marty? I mean, let's face it, Gallagher tolerated you because you were useful. Seamus O'Brien was the real number two in your organisation. I mean, he's the *real* hard man, isn't that right?"

"No, that's not right. Seamus was…" he hesitated. "Is on his way out. Charlie knows who the real muscle is, the guy that does all the real work. Seamus is there to support *me*," he boasted, tapping a forefinger at his chest.

But then Fleming unwittingly made an error, for he said, "If that's the case and let's suppose for a minute you're correct, Marty, that it's his job to support you, where was Seamus when you were getting the jail in the Waterloo Bar?"

Boyle frowned and for one erroneous moment, Fleming thought he had scored a point, but what he had done was set Boyle to wonder; where *was* O'Brien when the shit hit the fan?

Boyle unfolded his arms and leaning forward, his forearms resting on the scored wooden table, said, "If like you say Charlie did get the jail too, how come I haven't heard anything about it in here? How come the whisper hasn't reached my ears?"

Thinking on his feet, Fleming smiled and replied, "Because he got lifted at eight o'clock this morning and as you know, he won't go to the court till tomorrow, so at the minute he's lying in a cell at the Govan office."

Boyle's eyes narrowed as he stared at the detective, but Fleming didn't flinch.

Then the DS leaned forward and quietly said, "Tell me about the murdered polis woman."

He didn't need to be a detective to realise that by his expression, Boyle didn't have a clue what he was on about and particularly when the small man replied, "What the *fuck* are you talking about?"

****

Fleming and his neighbour used the phone in the prison gatehouse to phone DS Tam Whelan.

"He's a right wee shite, so he is, but he's saying nothing," Fleming sighed into the phone.

"What about Lesley Rudd. Did you mention her, if the name meant anything at all?"

"Oh, he knows *of* the murder, just like anybody else that reads the 'Glasgow News,' but we're of the opinion he doesn't know anything *about* her murder," he glanced for confirmation at his neighbour who silently shook his head, "and to be honest if he did we're the last people on the planet he'd burst to."

"Didn't happen to mention where Seamus O'Brien might be?"

"Like I said, Tam, told us hee-haw, but I got the impression that him and O'Brien are no longer bosom pals. I take it from your question the team that went for O'Brien didn't get him then?"

"No, either he's on his toes or he's got another address we don't have. Are you on your way back now?"

"Aye, be with you in twenty minutes so get the kettle on, sweetheart," then grinning at his own joke he ended the call.
****

Tam Whelan had just hung up the phone when it rang again, but this time it was Iain Meikle who confirmed the Laboratory still had Paula Menzies blood sample and the blood-stained woollen jacket.

"Said they've been overwhelmed recently and were about to get round to it," Iain related, "but I've a feeling it was on a back burner. Thing is, it's still here so that's some good news, eh?"

"Aye, good news at last," Whelan agreed and said, "While you're at Pitt Street, Iain, pop into the Fingerprint Department and do something for me. We've been hanging around for days waiting on a comparison result of the fingerprint discovered in Lesley's flat. Ask if they've managed yet to check it against Jacob McNeill. If they give you that old chestnut about being busy, tell them Detective Chief Superintendent Cruickshank has authorised it gets done as a priority."

"Did he?"

"Course he didn't," Whelan scoffed. "Just keep your face straight when you lie."

"Jacob McNeill," Iain repeated. "Right oh, I'll phone you back when I've got a result."

"No need. Just bring the information with you when you get back here."
****

Armed with the information provided by the now arrested pig farmer, Philip Smith, and the details contained in the anonymous letter, Irene Crichton led the team of detectives and Scene of Crime personnel on the raid at Charlie Gallagher's flat.

When their knocking provoked no response, she stood to one side and gave a nod to a burly uniformed officer who used the key in his size twelve boot to open the door.

To their surprise it went in a lot easier than she had expected. "Don't make doors like they used to," the big cop grumbled.

A quick search of the flat revealed that it was empty, but looked like a crime scene for the furniture in every room had been turned over or toppled, with both male and female clothing scattered around the bedroom.

"Check with the neighbours if they've seen him recently," Irene ordered two detectives then turning to the SOCO supervisor, instructed that the bed in the main room be the focus of their attention.

As she wandered around the flat, she noticed that the phones in the bedroom and the kitchen had been unplugged; however, the Trim phone in the front room was still plugged in.

Fetching her notebook and a pen from her handbag, she pressed the redial number on the phone and noted down the last number called, then dialled the number herself.

The phone was answered by the controller of a local taxi company.

"I'm Detective Inspector Irene Crichton of the Govan CID," she identified herself and asked to speak with a supervisor.

When the man came on the line Irene explained that she was in house in Burghead Drive and asked for details of when a taxi was ordered for the address and where the destination of the fare was.

"It might take ten or fifteen minutes by the time I get through the logs, hen," the man explained. "What number can I call you back on?"

She gave the number written on the Trim phone and hung up

just as the SOCO supervisor came into the room and beckoned her.

In the bedroom, the supervisor said, "Looks like bloodstaining on a sheet and on a quilt cover that we found in the laundry basket in the kitchen, Ma'am, and there are some droplets on both the bedroom carpet and the wall too as if the blood has spurted. Nothing on the bed sheet or quilt cover on the bed at the minute nor on the mattress, but I'm guessing that's because the sheet and quilt cover in the laundry basket soaked the blood up. We'll bag the the sheets and the quilt cover and cut out the droplets from the carpet and wallpaper then pass the lot to the Lab."

"Everything photographed?"

"All done," he nodded before asking, "Do you need the place fingerprinted at all?"

"No, that won't be necessary. We know who lives here and…" she stopped when she heard the sound of the Trim phone and hurried back through to the front room.

It was the taxi supervisor who said, "Quicker than I thought. One fare from Burghead Drive last night about ten-forty-eight, going to the Thistle Hotel in Cambridge Street. That what you're looking for, hen?"

"That's exactly what I'm looking for," she grinned.

****

Just over an hour later, Charlie Gallagher, hands cuffed to the back, found himself being frogmarched by the two arresting detectives through Govan police station to the CID suite on the first floor.

He hadn't made the arrest easy with one detective nursing a swollen cheek, but paid for his reluctance to come quietly with an eye that was slowly turning black and bruised testicles that throbbed with every step he took.

It wasn't the first time that Gallagher had enjoyed the hospitality of the Govan polis. Glancing around him he would have no interest in knowing that constructed in 1867, the Victorian building had initially functioned as the Govan Town

Hall when Govan itself was an independent Police Burgh and remained so until 1912 when it was incorporated into the City of Glasgow. While the building's exterior remained as it was built, it had through the years the occasional interior refurbishment, but unfortunately none of this renovation included dedicated rooms for interviewing suspects and so it was that Gallagher found himself being propelled to the DCI's room where behind his desk, Colin Morton impatiently awaited him.

To one side, her notebook in her hand, Irene Crichton sat ready to take notes while as a back-up, Tam Whelan stood with his arms folded in a corner in the event Gallagher decided to to start any nonsense.

Thrust down into a chair in front of Morton's desk, the DCI said, "I'll order the cuffs taken from you if you assure me you'll be on your best behaviour, Mister Gallagher. I should warn you that any funny business and DS Whelan stood behind you there," he nodded, "has my permission to take whatever action he needs to subdue you. Do you agree?"

Gallagher stared venomously at Morton, but remaining tight-lipped, nodded.

Once the cuffs were removed and the two detectives had left the room, Gallagher rubbed at his wrists then found his voice and growled, "What the *fuck* is this all about? I'm grabbed from my hotel room and brought to this shitehole for what!"

Morton resisted the opportunity to agree with him, that the building was in fact a shitehole, before calmly replying, "My name is Detective Chief Inspector Colin Morton, Mister Gallagher, and you're hear to be interviewed about the murder of your live in partner, Paula Menzies…"

He paused for he had seen a distinct narrowing of Gallagher's eyes and knew he had scored a hit, then with a knowing smile continued, "Of which you are of course aware. I'm informed that at the charge bar when you were booked in and were formally cautioned in common law terms, you refused the services of a lawyer. Is that correct?"

"I don't need a lawyer. I've done fuck all."

"Please, Mister Gallagher," Morton grimaced theatrically, "mind your language. There *is* a lady present."

"Where?" he sneered as he turned towards her, "all I see is a polis ride." Then to her surprise, he added, "It was you that left me the wee present, wasn't it?"

Morton quickly raised a hand to stop Whelan who with his hands bunched into fists, had taken a step forward towards the smirking Gallagher.

"Moving on," Morton frowned, "we already know that you killed Paula and have more than enough evidence to prove it, so I'll remind you that you have been cautioned. Now, tell me about killing Constable Lesley Rudd."

Gallagher's eyes flickered for the question took him by surprise. What confused him was that the detective hadn't asked any further questions about killing Paula and for one heart stopping instance he realised that Morton was telling the truth; they had evidence of the murder. He felt as though he'd been brutally punched in the chest and was trying to breath through a straw when he asked, "Who?"

Morton sighed as though he knew this was going to be a long process and said, "Constable Rudd. The woman that Paula was providing information to about your operation. Oh and by the way, would that be the one that went apeshit last night in the Waterloo Bar?"

His stomach churning, he thought he was going to throw up. The bastards knew about the handover and with a sickening feeling confirmed for him they also knew about what he did to Paula. But who the fuck was this woman cop they were talking about? That's when it hit him, when he remembered.

She was the cop Paula had mentioned and he involuntarily closed his eyes.

Watching him, Morton knew that he had scored another hit and quietly said, "We've arrested your friend Philip Smith, though I understand you know him as Smudger. You know, the pig farmer with the big mouth? That and the Forensic evidence that we recovered from your flat and we know about you and your pal Martin Boyle using the hatchet on Paula's body." He pretended to shudder before adding, "Oh, and did I mention that we also have the hatchet and the gloves you wore, too?" Morton let this sink in before he continued again, "Now, would you like to tell me about Constable Rudd, get it all off your chest? I mean, you start cooperating now and I'm obliged to mention it to the Crown Office when we charge you with the murders."

Smudger! The drunken bastard, thought Gallagher! He's given me up and, he stared malevolently at Morton, if he knows about me and Boyle using the hatchet that means only one thing, because the only other bugger there that night was Seamus!

But what does he mean murders, thought Gallagher?

He must mean the polis lassie!

"I didn't kill your cop," he hissed, "this polis woman you're talking about. I don't know anything about that."

"But you do know about Paula and the delivery of the heroin?" He swallowed with difficulty, trying to work out how to extricate himself from the situation he now found himself in. It seems obvious, he thought, they know about Paula and one of those two sods, Boyle or O'Brien, had also grassed on him too about the delivery.

His eyes narrowed.

No, not the wee guy.

O'Brien.

He's grassed me up for murdering Paula and buying the heroin! It *had* to be that red haired bastard!

The game was up. He'd been grassed up by that drunken bastard Smith and that backstabbing bastard, O'Brien!

His stomach fell because he knew for certain that he was well and truly fucked!

It wiped his brow with the back of his hand and it was then he realised with sudden clarity there wasn't a chance in hell that he was going to walk away from this.

The hard man in the movies or the tele would say something smart like, "Prove it," but this wasn't the movies or the tele. This was a wee shitty office in a wee shitty polis station in Govan and his balls were in a vice.

His mouth as dry as tinder, he stared at Morton before quietly asking, "Can we look at talking about some kind of deal here, pal?"

****

Sitting in his office nursing a coffee after charging Gallagher with Paula Menzies murder, Morton asked Irene Crichton, "What the hell do you think he meant when he said you'd left him a present and asked where we'd hidden the bug?"

"God knows," she sighed. "I'm no expert but I think that sick bastard is either off his head or heading that way. Tell me, Colin," she stared at him, "did you consider charging him with the drug offence?"

He didn't immediately respond, but then explained that as far as he and Mister Cruickshank were concerned that other than hearsay at the minute there was no direct evidence to link Gallagher with the delivery of the heroin. He told her, "The boss has agreed the Scottish Crime Squad should deal with the murder in the pub and the heroin inquiry so as far as I'm concerned, that's down to the team investigating the Waterloo Bar incident and whatever evidence they gather against him. Once Crown Office get the reports they will likely tie the two into the one indictment against him. For the minute we've done our bit so they can do their own investigation to tie him in to the delivery. After all," he grinned, "he'll not be hard to find for a few years, eh?"

"What do you think of his denial about murdering Lesley?"

"I hate to admit it," he drew a breath, "but I don't think he knows anything about it. I mean, even criminals sometimes tell the truth, don't they?"

"So where do we go from here?"

Morton shrugged and replied, "We keep plodding on. If I'm honest, I'm disappointed that it wasn't Gallagher for I believed he was our best bet for her murder. It seemed so straight forward; Paula wanting revenge for her sister and touting to Lesley, Gallagher finding out and doing them both in." He sighed and added, "Looks like we're starting from scratch, again."

"Oh, and there's more bad news," she frowned. "Iain Meikle phoned Tam from the Fingerprint Department who have finally confirmed that the print discovered in her toilet seat does *not* belong to her brother-in-law, Jacob McNeill."

"Well, that's another source of inquiry down the tube," he shook his head before adding, "at least we still have the print to work on. Course our only problem now is we don't have a suspect to compare it against," he slowly exhaled.

She finished her coffee and standing said, "You'll want to phone Mister Cruickshank to let him know about Gallagher, so I'll leave you to get on with that. In the meantime, what do you want me to tell the team?"

His brow knitted as he thought about it before he replied, "Get them together and I'll be out in about ten minutes. I want to thank them for what they've done so far and I don't want them to get disheartened because Gallagher isn't our man for Rudd." He smiled and said, "Digressing, how are things between you and Iain Meikle? I hear you arrived together this morning, so does that mean…?"

"Hanky-panky?" she grinned at him then saucily winked and added, "Absolutely."

****

Sitting slouched against the wall in the cold and forbidding cell with his legs drawn up, Charlie Gallagher touched gently at his swollen eye and with his hand, massaged his aching balls as he wondered how it all had so quickly gone so wrong.

Yet it had and all because he made the mistake of trusting those two bastards O'Brien and Boyle, though in his gut he could not believe the wee man had really given him up.

And as for that stupid drunken git, Smudger; well, he scowled, the Bar L Remand Wing was a dangerous place and all sorts of things could happen to a man in there. Fingers crossed he'd bump into the three of them and find out what the real story was and then, his eyes narrowed, have his own private chat. His thoughts turned to what the detective Morton had asked him about killing the policewoman.

Where the hell did the cops get that idea from?

Aye, he done in Paula and they had him fair and square by the short and curlies for her.

But why they thought he'd killed the polis bird God only knew, though now he was in no doubt that it was the same polis that Paula had spoken about and was touting to.

Sitting on this bloody concrete floor will give me piles, he scowled and began to whistle tunelessly as he imagined how he would get his revenge on those bastards that had screwed him and in particular, Seamus O'Brien.

****

Minutes after receiving Colin Morton's phone call, Alistair Cruickshank sat back in his chair and though it wasn't something he would himself condone, he was sick of dancing around with Martin Kerr and so made his decision. First checking his handwritten note, he called the Chief Constable's secretary and asked if he was available to speak with the DCS.

"He's just finished a call so I'll put you straight through, sir," the matronly woman told him.

Seconds later, the Chief said, "Alistair, I understand you're looking for me?"

"Yes, sir, I apologise for coming directly to you rather than Mister Kerr, but it seems the ACC is not immediately available."

"And why doesn't that surprise me?" the Chief dryly responded.

Cruickshank felt ashamed of his lie, but continued, "I believe because of your interest in DCI Morton's inquiry you should be informed straightaway," then during the course of the next five minutes related the circumstances of the arrest and interview of Charlie Gallagher.

"Pity you can't nail him for the lassie Rudd, but what about Gallagher's involvement in the Waterloo Bar incident? I understand from the Scottish Crime Squad they believe he was the purchaser of the heroin?"

"That's correct, sir, but DCI Morton does not have direct evidence at this time and suggests the drug investigation team treat that as a separate inquiry, but I'm certain he'll be held to account in due course."

"The Chief at Merseyside contacted me earlier today to inform me that the mother of the dead man, Derek Stokoe, has been informed. Seems that his murder has caused quite a ruckus down in Liverpool."

"At the risk of sounding hard hearted, as far as I'm concerned, sir, Stokoe is just another bad guy off the street. I can't imagine the misery and hurt that amount of heroin would have caused if it had hit the streets of Glasgow."

"Indeed," the Chief quietly agreed. "And good work by Morton's team in detecting that pig farmer who I also understand has provided our Serious Crime Squad with an interesting investigation regarding a number of missing persons from the criminal fraternity."

"Aye, that's correct, sir. I gather the Squad's investigation might take several months, but there's every possibility of putting away some top players from the West of Scotland."

"Good news indeed," the Chief agreed, "but how is Morton's inquiry into the murder of my young constable?"

He didn't miss Cruickshank's slight pause before the DCS replied, "That's not going so well, I'm afraid. It seems that Gallagher was the only real suspect and even that was based on assessment and suspicion rather than evidence. However, I'm confident that DCI Morton will continue the good work and God willing, he'll get a result."

"Well, I'm certain you'll apprise me of any positive result, so I'll leave you to pass on my congratulations and grateful thanks for a job well done."

"Thank you, sir, I'll see that DCI Morton and his team are

told."

He thought that was the end of the conversation, but the Chief suddenly said, "One more thing, Alistair, and please treat what I am about to tell you in the strictest confidence."

"Sir?"

"I have been informed just today by Mister Kerr that he had made application for the Deputy's job at North Yorkshire Police. It's not a large force and I hear he is in with a good chance of securing the post. If it does transpire that he is the successful candidate, I'll be looking to you to stand ready to replace him. I take it that you would be interested?"

He could feel a warm glow across his chest and with a smile, replied, "Of course, sir. Thank you."

"Nothing that shouldn't have happened a long time ago, Alistair," the Chief said and ended the call.

Though not completely stunned, Cruickshank was taken aback by this news and slowly smiling, reflected on what the Chief had disclosed. He was politically astute to realise that had the Deputy's job for Kerr at the English force not been a done deal and if the Chief had not already cleared it with Strathclyde Police Board, he would not even have hinted at the possibility of promoting Cruickshank to the post of ACC (Crime).

Smiling, any misgiving he had previously felt when lying about being unable to contact Kerr was now gone.

Buoyed by the good news, he dialled the number for Colin Morton.

CHAPTER TWENTY-FIVE

As far as Irene Crichton was concerned the day seemed to have flown and by five o'clock that afternoon, she ached for a hot bath and a glass of vino. Glancing across the room, she caught the eye of Iain Meikle who subtly raised an eyebrow as he sat at a desk completing a report.

The door opened to admit Colin Morton who carrying a cardboard box that he laid down onto Tam Whelan's desk, called the attention of the team and began by thanking them all for their hard work that resulted in the arrest of Charlie Gallagher, then passed on the thanks of the Chief Constable. A small cheer and some handclapping ensued, but calmed when Morton disclosed that regretfully Gallagher seemed no longer to be a suspect for the murder of Lesley Rudd.

"That said," he forced himself to sound cheerful, "we've still a long way to go to find the killer so what I'm doing is dismissing you guys for the evening, but before you go," he tapped at the cardboard box, "CID tradition requires that on the back of a successful murder detection, I give you all a can of your choice or a wee half. However," he grinned widely, "it doesn't mean you get pissed, so be careful on the way home, okay, because I want you all back here bright and bushy tailed to start first thing tomorrow morning. Any questions?"

"Any likelihood Gallagher will be definitely tied in to that incident at the Waterloo Bar, sir?" asked a young Detective constable.

"I've made the DCI at Stewart Street aware of his arrest so they're sending someone to interview him regarding that, but unless they can get his pal Marin Boyle to burst to the fact he was working on Gallagher's orders," he sighed, "I don't know that they will. Let's just celebrate the fact he's going away for Paula Menzies murder and perverting the course of justice for the dismemberment of her body and any other bloody thing we can hang on him. Anything else? No? Right then, guys, have a wee swally then get yourselves away home for the night and again, thanks for all your hard work to date."

As the team made their way to Whelan's desk for a can of beer or a small whisky, others declined and grabbing coats and jackets began to make their way from the room. Irene strolled across to where Iain sat and conscious it wasn't unnoticed by several of their colleagues, knew that it appeared to confirm to the doubters that the rumour was true; the DI and Iain Meikle seemed to be an item.

"Putting it right out there aren't you?" he quietly said.

"Are you embarrassed?"

"Me? Not at all," he sat back in the seat and shook his head, then with a smile, suggested, "On the way to your place why don't we get that takeaway we promised ourselves last night?"

"Seems like a plan," she replied and nodded that if he was ready, they leave.

****

Billy Madison was at his wits end.

By now the news was out in Liverpool, that Doughnut Stokoe had been murdered in a Glasgow pub.

Some who knew him thought it bad luck for the big guy, others raised a glass in his memory, some quoted the old adage that fly with the crows, get shot with the crows, but most were just glad to see the back of the bullying bastard.

Of course Madison didn't care about Stokoe getting himself killed. His concern was the money Stokoe was supposed to have collected for the heroin; the heroin that the Jamaican wanted payment for by Saturday.

He gulped and glancing nervously through the window to the street outside, wondered if news about his misfortune had yet reached London.

****

Though she would never admit to it, Annie Stokoe heaved a quiet sigh of relief when the rozzers informed her that Doughnut was dead. Fearful of his quick temper she would no longer have to walk on tiptoe when he was in the house.

Knocking back her second half bottle of vodka of the day, she reflected on that morning's visit by Jimmy Blackwell, the local undertaker who thinking he might get a bit of business, had called by to offer his assistance and solemnly inquired what arrangements she required be made for bringing her son Derek back to the family home.

"Where would I get money to do that and bury him?" she had wailed, a performance that any practised actress would have been proud of, for Annie thought it would seem curious had she not to have shown some emotion at the loss of her only child. Ten minutes later Blackwell had stumbled from the house, annoyed at a wasted visit and wondered what the Glasgow police might do with Derek's body for it was apparent even his mother didn't want him back.

****

On the way down the road to England he'd slung the Smith and Wesson into a river then dumped the hire car outside the rental agency's office in London before making his way to Heathrow Airport.

Now stood nervously in the passport queue at the Arrivals Gate in Alicante Airport, Seamus O'Brien glanced nervously at the uniformed police officer with the holstered sidearm. The holdall slung on O'Brien's back contained the money he'd stolen and again he cursed his decision not to buy a suitcase and try to hide it among the clothing. But too late now as he neared the female officer who glancing up, waved him forward to her desk.

Removing his sunglasses, he forced a smile and handed her his passport. It troubled him that he was arriving under his own name, but there hadn't been time to obtain a fake passport. Staring at the passport, the officer gave a sideways glance up at him and to his relief, smiled, stamped his passport and waved him through.

He resisted the urge to punch the air in joy as with a brisk step he stepped lively towards the exit to find a taxi.

****

Making their way downstairs to the front doors, Irene Crichton and Iain Meikle were discussing whether to order Indian or Chinese when he saw Ian Harris, the probationary cop on his shift, standing behind the uniform bar. Waving a greeting towards Harris, his eyes narrowed as though something was bothering him, however he couldn't think what it was.

"I said I favour a Chinese. Are you listening?" she asked him.

"Sorry," he smiled apologetically, "I was miles away."

She glanced curiously at him as he pushed open the heavy wooden door and asked, "Is it still bothering you?"

"What?"

"That thing you can't remember?"

"Yeah, it is," he sheepishly admitted.

"I told you," she chided him as they walked towards her car, "Don't force it. It'll come when it's ready, particularly if it's important." She stopped and stared at him. "You think it *is* important, don't you?"

"I really don't know, but it's certainly bugging me," he smiled. It was then he heard his name being called and turning, his face fell.

Striding towards him was his ex-wife Carol.

Irene had also turned when Iain's name was loudly shouted and saw the attractive woman with short, brunette and fashionably styled hair, wearing an expensive light yellow coloured jacket, black trousers and literally dragging a young teenage boy by the arm with her.

She quickly realised from the photos in Iain's house the lad, who was as tall as his mother and wore a white shirt, striped tie and a school blazer, was James and who looked uncannily like a younger Iain.

"Bloody hell," she heard Iain mutter.

The woman came to a halt and as the boy said, "Hello, dad," the woman who Irene now realised must be Carol, snapped, "I tried your house, but of course you were at work as usual."

"Hello, son," he smiled at James then turning to her, calmly continued, "Yes, I was out working on the job that pays for your fancy clothes and your lifestyle, Carol. Now, what are you doing here?"

"I want you to take him for a couple of days," she folded her arms defensively. "I'm going for a short break with a friend."

Turning she stared coldly at Irene than asked, "And who is this? One of your fancy women?"

Irene nearly choked and was about to angrily retort when she caught Iain's eye, who quickly said, "This is Detective Inspector Crichton, my boss. Now, I'm not prepared to have an argument standing here in the middle of the street, Carol, so yes, of course I'll be delighted to take my son for a couple of days. Where's his bag?"

"His bag," she frowned.

"You did think to bring him a change of clothes?"

She hesitated, then dismissively waving a hand replied, "You can just buy him something to wear, can't you?"

"With what? You take all my spare money."

"Well, if you can't afford to buy your own son…"

He raised a hand to interrupt her and calmly said, "I don't need a lecture on how to look after my son. When will you be back?"

"Why, are you keen to hand him back already?"

He reached across to lay a hand on his son's shoulder and smiling at him, said, "If you would consider signing the papers, Carol, I'll keep James for as long as he wants to stay with me."

Watching the exchange, Irene saw a look of relief pass across the teenagers face as Carol snorted, "Yes, that would suit you, wouldn't it? Then you wouldn't have to pay me the pittance of an alimony that you do."

"Aye, I see what you mean," he thoughtfully nodded, then said, "If I didn't pay the alimony you'd need to get off your arse and find a job, wouldn't you?"

Carol's face turned so brightly red Irene thought her head might explode, then with a sneer she turned on her heel and stamped off towards a black coloured Mercedes car parked fifty yards away with a man seated in the drivers seat.

Watching her get into the passenger seat, Iain murmured, "No cheerio, then?"

As the car raced past them, neither Carol nor the driver glanced their way.

"That'll be mum's friend?" Iain turned to James who blushed as he nodded.

Turning to Irene, he said, "I'm sorry you had to witness that and sorry about tonight, too."

She knew she had a decision to make, a decision that if she got it wrong might affect any hope she would have of a future with Iain and so she brightly smiled then turning to James, said, "Hello, James, I'm Irene. Do you like Chinese food?"

****

So as not to confuse the lad they made the decision they'd eat at Iain's house and stopping on Paisley Road West at a takeaway, bought their evening meal.

Arriving at the house Iain suggested that James might want to watch some TV while he and Irene prepared the food in the cramped kitchen which gave them the opportunity to have a quiet conversation.

"Is she always like that?" she faced him, her back to the window and her arms folded.

"Carol? Also was and likely always will be and yes," he raised a hand, "I must have been out of my mind when I married her." Irene stifled a grin as he continued, "Acerbic, I think is the word I would use to describe her and even then I'm being kind. Couldn't then and still don't understand why the bloody court gave her custody of James though," he bitterly complained.

"If you don't mind me saying so, he doesn't seem to be a happy young lad."

Reaching up into a cupboard, he brought out three plates and laid them on the worktop before he answered, then quietly said, "Carol has a pecking order, Irene, and she always comes first. I don't kid myself when I say James is a bargaining chip, nothing more. I wasn't kidding when I said that she dreads the day alimony stops for she'll need to get out and find herself a job. Or a man with plenty of money." He stood with his back to the sink and sighing, said, "I'll share this with you, something I've never told another soul. Her pregnancy, as far as she is concerned, was a complete mistake. She even tried to persuade me to help her abort the baby."

Shocked, Irene reached across to sympathetically rub at his arm.

"What she said about the alimony. I take it she's financially screwing you into the ground?"

"It's difficult some months, yes," he exhaled, "but James is a growing lad and it seems like every couple of weeks he's needing new shirts or shoes or trousers or whatever. The problem is," he frowned, "I can't say for certain that the money I'm handing across is actually going to pay for what he supposedly needs. You saw the way she's dressed. Always likes the best of the best, does Carol."

"The man in the car that drove her away. Do you know who that is?"

"Likely just the latest in a long line of boyfriends, though judging by the newness and the model of the Mercedes it looks like this time she's landed herself someone with a couple of bob." He shrugged and continued, "I don't like asking James about the new men in Carol's life because it puts him on the spot, but occasionally he'll mention a name or someone his mother is going out with or where she's been with a man. It seems to me that she's trying to find someone to take care of her and her lifestyle and when that happens…" he suddenly grinned, "I have absolutely no doubt that she'll hand James over without a fight."

Irene was aghast. "You mean, James will just be a burden to her?"

"It sounds like I'm boasting here, but when we lived together as a family…no, that's not quite right." Holding up his forefingers like quotation marks, he said, "We weren't ever a family *per se* because Carol never settled into the role of a wife and mother. If it hadn't been for my mother-in-law Jill who fortunately is a really good woman and nothing like Carol, I don't know how I'd have managed to get to work because it was Jill and I who raised James through the early years. As far as I know and from what James says," he huffed, "Jill still does more than her fare share of caring for him."

"Are you still in contact with her?"

"I get the occasional phone call to find out how I'm doing and she keeps me informed how James is getting on."

"She sounds like a star," Irene mused.

"Oh, she is. I'd have fared better if I'd married her," he grinned.

"So, what's your plan for the lad over the weekend?"

"Play it by ear," he shook his head, "but the only problem I have is now that you've heard my tale of woe is, are you still interested in me?"

She wrapped her arms around his neck and replied, "Oh, I think I can live with you having a son, Mister Meikle."

"I have to be completely honest with you," he pulled her close, "he's first on the list in *my* pecking order." Staring at her, he frowned and asked, "Does that upset you?"

She slowly smiled and replied, "No, it doesn't upset me and I'd be surprised if you thought it did."

"Thanks," he smiled and added, "for listening. Now, maybe we'd better get that grub onto the table."

Her eyes narrowed and he could see she was thinking about something when she said, "Did I ever mention that I have a good friend who is a lawyer that specialises in family law?"

****

In the short time he had been banged up in the Remand Wing, Marty Boyle had already been involved in two fights and for his own protection was now locked in solitary for no fewer than a dozen cons recognised him as the bastard who had been putting the squeeze on family members or friends on the outside who were involved in the drug scene. Outside the prison walls Boyle might have been a force to reckon with when he was a free man, but among his violent peers the hard man reputation he had so craved now hung about his neck like a bull's-eye.

However, as it happened the cons in the Remand Wing was the last thing Boyle had to worry about.

The Remand Wing was separated from the wings holding the convicted inmates, but it wasn't that far from the prison exercise yard and no matter that they tried, the warders could not prevent the shouted communication between the two areas of the prison.

One shout in particular still rang out in his ears, a shout from a voice that he had not heard in a number of years.

"Boyle, ya wee bastard! Heard you're in Remand! Wait till you get in here with me! I'm having you, ya fucking dwarf! I'm going to carve you a new hole, ya wee shite ya!"

It was Boyle's proud boast that nothing scared him, that he was frightened of nobody and that included the polis, but that wasn't strictly true. He would never admit it even to himself, but Boyle *was* afraid of two men.

Both men were serving life sentences for murder with one locked up in HMP Peterhead. The other was Angus 'Slasher' McKenna, the younger, heavily tattooed and vicious brother of Maggie McKenna, the drug dealing woman that Boyle had so recently beaten and humiliated in her flat in Easterhouse.

And it was McKenna who received regular visits from his sister Maggie, who learned of the humiliating beating she had received at the hands of Boyle and who now patiently waited for a reunion with the small man.

Cowering in his cell, Marty Boyle experienced an emotion he had not felt since he had been a small child.

He felt fearful.

****

Seated in his favourite armchair, listening to the regular clicking of the needles and nursing a glass of Laphroaig, Colin Morton glanced across at Alice seated in the opposite chair and asked, "Who are you knitting for now?"

"One of the lassies at work. Her daughter's due in a couple of weeks. Bugger that got her pregnant left as soon as she broke the news of the pregnancy."

"Bastard," Morton quietly mouthed.

"How was your day?" his wife asked.

"My day? I feel as though I lost a shilling and found a tanner," he replied.

"No progress on that young woman's murder, then?"

"No, not yet, but I'm trying to remain optimistic."

She stopped knitting and laying the needles and ball of wool down onto her lap, reached for her own glass and took a sip. "Nothing else happening, then?"

"Well," he smiled, "Irene Crichton's got herself a man."

"Really," his wife smiled too. "Do you know who it is?"

"Aye, one of the cops on the shift. He's working on my murder team at the minute. A nice guy, Iain Meikle."

"A shift cop? He's a constable?" her voice expressed her surprise.

"Aye, but so what? Like I said, he's a good man, from what I know of him."

"Oh, I didn't mean anything by it, I just thought…" she frowned. "No, forget what I'm thinking. If Irene is happy with him, that's all that matters."

Colin Morton knew exactly what his wife had thought, that as a Detective Inspector and two ranks above Meikle the police management might not take kindly to Irene fraternising with a junior rank, but wisely decided to finish the discussion there.
****

They'd agreed that it made sense for Irene to return home that night, that her staying over would only confuse the young lad and walking her along the path to her car, he said, "This only defers my visit to your place, you know."

She smiled and nodding, replied, "It's Friday tomorrow so I don't see Colin Morton running the incident room any later than six, so why don't you bring James for dinner."

"You'd be okay with that?"

"Course I would," she frowned and pretended to punch him on the shoulder. "I don't know him, but he comes across as a really nice young lad and," she moved closer to him, "if we're going to make a go of this thing between us, I'll need to get to know him, won't I?"

He could feel himself become aroused and taking a step back, raised both hands and said, "You'd better go before I embarrass myself and lay you down right here on the path."

She giggled and pulling him close again kissed him, then turned away and got into her car.

He watched her drive off till the car was out of sight and turning, saw the front room curtain move.

With a smile he returned to the house where he saw James was staring fixedly at the television, watching a game show.'

"Nothing else on?" Iain asked, but James just stared at the television and shrugged.

He didn't say anything, just sat down and waited for the question.

A couple of minutes passed before James asked, "Is she your girlfriend?"

"She's someone I really like, yes, but my girlfriend? I thought somebody my age was too old to have a girlfriend?"

James shrugged then said, "I like her. She's cool."

"Cool?" he smiled and slowly nodded his agreement that Irene was indeed cool.

****

Iain Meikle's eyes snapped open and he suddenly sat up in the darkness of the room.

That was it, what had been bothering him.

He wheezed and turning, reached for his wristwatch on the bedside cabinet and saw it was just three-thirty-eight in the morning.

Rolling his head to ease the stiffness in his neck, he briefly considered phoning Irene to tell her what he thought, but grinned for he knew she'd only tell him to bugger off, that she'd see him at the office in the morning.

He drew his knees up and resting his arms on them, squeezed his eyes tightly shut and tried to recall exactly what it was that had been said.

No, he couldn't recall, but that didn't mean he couldn't ask again.

Deciding that he'd not get back to sleep immediately, he climbed out of bed and conscious that James was sleeping in the other bedroom, quietly made his way through the house to the kitchen to brew a pot of tea.

CHAPTER TWENTY-SIX

Irene Crichton, showered and dressed, reflected on Iain Meikle's early morning phone call, that she return to his house for some breakfast because he needed to speak to her.

"Can't I just meet you at the office?" she had asked.

"I'd rather speak with you before we get to the office. I need some advice in case I'm making a mountain out of a molehill," he had said then added, "Besides, I like seeing you."

"Well, what my man wants, my man gets," she had cheerily replied then hanging up, blushed then relaxed, curiously comfortable in calling Iain her man.

Ten minutes later she finds herself driving from her home in Newlands Quadrant Drive through light morning traffic to Iain's home in Tealing Avenue. During the working week, the five and a half mile trip normally takes a little over thirty minutes, but today she is there in twenty minutes to find Iain has prepared a light breakfast of bacon and eggs.

James opens the door and shyly says, "Hello."

She couldn't later explain it, but impulsively gives the lad a quick hug and is surprised when he hugs her back.

"Dad's in the kitchen, he says you've to go straight through," James beams as he tells her then returns to his room to finish getting himself ready for school.

"Hi," his shirt sleeves rolled up to his forearms, he's wearing an apron and gives her a kiss on the cheek, then turns back to flip the sausages. She sees three plates set out with buttered rolls and guesses he's been out earlier and walked to the shop on Mosspark Boulevard for the breakfast.

Irene squeezes into one of the chairs at the folding table and asks, "Will James need a lift to school?"

"No, he'll be fine. He can get a bus on Paisley Road West that will take him over to the south side and it's a short walk to Holyrood when he gets off the bus. But thanks for asking," he smiles at her.

"Okay," she nods then asks, "So, what's this all about?"

As he serves her breakfast, he tells her, then asks, "Am I being too suspicious? I mean…"

But she cuts him short and eyes narrowing, chews at a roll as she replies, "No, it's a possibility, but we'll need to interview this lad Ian Harris, won't we?"

****

Constable Ian Harris was delegated first break that morning and walking towards the Portacabin located on Paisley Road beneath the Kingston Bridge that served as a temporary office, heard his call sign on the radio.

"Three-six-zero, go ahead," he stopped and replied.

'Hammy' Hammond, the controller, asked, "What's your position? You're wanted at Govan office pronto, Ian. Eric Little will pick you up in the Pollokshields panda and bring you down, over."

Harris sighed at the two hot, scrambled egg rolls in the paper bag and replied, "Commerce Street towards the Portacabin, Hammy. I'll see him there in five minutes, over."

"Roger, three-six-zero, out."

Now what the hell have I done he wondered as he plodded along.

****

Tam Whelan had just sat down at his desk when Irene Crichton appeared at his elbow and handed him a piece of paper.

"The boss wants you to phone the Fingerprint Department right away and have them as a matter of urgency compare the fingerprint lifted from Lesley Rudd's flat with him."

Whelan took the paper from her and glancing at it, turned sharply to her and said, "You're shitting me!"

"Afraid not. If anyone tries to bullshit you that it can't be done right away, you're to say that DCS Cruickshank has personally authorised the request and again, tell whoever you speak with that we need the information within the next twenty to thirty minutes."

"I'm on it," he reached for the phone, but almost unbelievingly again stares at the written name he is about to quote.

****

Grim faced, Colin Morton glanced from Irene Crichton towards Iain Meikle and asked, "Tell me you're sure about this."

"I can't, sir, because I'm not certain," he honestly shook his head, "but I know there's been talk in the past. Nothing definite, just a bit of craic on the shift. I've never actually spoken to anyone about it mainly because I thought it was just office gossip and I'm aware that bandying something like that about could cause a guy all sorts of trouble and particularly if it's not true. When the gossip was," he hunched his shoulders, "I can't really remember, but it stuck in my mind, along with the other thing that just came to me…"

"Aye, through the night, you said," Morton nodded. "For what it's worth, Iain, I've had a few wake-up calls like that when something has been playing on my mind too." He turned to Irene and shrugging, said, "Let's have him in."

She opened the door and beckoned Ian Harris to come into the room, then pointed to the chair in front of the DCI's desk. His head twisted back and forth, seeing Iain stood solemn faced in the corner and nervously smiled at him.

"Have I done something wrong, sir?" he turned and addressed Colin Morton whose face like Iain's, was grim set.

Morton recognised the worry in the young cops face and shaking his head, quietly replied, "No, Ian. We just want to have a little chat with you about something you told Iain Meikle, okay?"

****

Downstairs in the uniform refreshment room, Shona Murtagh excitedly broke the news to her four colleagues who were also having their break that Ian Harris had been taken upstairs to the DCI's room and was being interviewed.

"What's that you're saying?"

The constables turned to see Sergeant Jimmy Cole stood in the doorway with a sheaf of papers in his hand.

"Eh, it's Ian Harris, Sarge," she gulped. "He's being interviewed by the DCI," she repeated.

"About what?"

"Eh, I don't really know, but when I passed him and DI Crichton on the corridor upstairs when I was coming back from the typists, I heard her say that Mister Morton wanted to speak with him."

Cole frowned and snapped, "Well, whatever else you hear, Constable Murtagh, you refrain from gossiping. Either come and speak with me or the Inspector, okay?"

"Yes, Sarge," she quietly replied.

****

Tam Whelan was getting angry now and snapped to the cantankerous woman on the other end of the line, "Listen ya muppet, I don't really give two shits about protocol. Get me a supervisor on the line or your arse is going to hang out to dry, savvy?"

A full minute passed when a pompous voice announced, "This is Inspector Greig. DS Whelan, is it?"

"That's right, sir."

"And exactly who do you think you are to demand preferential treatment for a comparison, threaten one of my staff and use such language like that!"

Whelan was old school and with a grim smile, replied, "I'll tell you who I am, Inspector. I'm the Detective Sergeant running the incident room for a murdered *colleague* and I've personally been instructed by Detective Chief Superintendent Alistair Cruickshank, head of the Southside CID to get an immediate comparison done with the fingerprint lifted from our murdered colleagues home against the name of the individual I just gave to your member of staff!"

He took a breath then calmly continued, "So, Inspector Greig, let me just take a note of your own details so when Mister Cruickshank asks *me* how I got on, I can truthfully tell him *you* and your staff are too fucking *busy* to assist with the investigation into the murder of *our colleague*!"

Silence followed his outburst and glancing about the incident room, Whelan saw that everyone had stopped what they were doing and were watching him…or so he believed. For a few seconds he thought the Inspector had hung up, but then a quiet voice irritably said, "You'll have the result within ten minutes."

"Thank you, Inspector," he politely replied and ended the call. Turning, Whelan got the shock of his life for behind him stood Alistair Cruickshank who slowly shaking his head, smiled and said, "Same old Tam Whelan. Now tell me, Tam. What's this comparison I've apparently authorised?"

****

Iain Meikle knocked on the door of the Sergeants Room and said to Jimmy Cole, "Any chance you can pop up to see the DCI, Sarge? He's wanting a wee word."

"This about Ian Harris being interviewed?"

"You know about that," Iain's face expressed his surprised.

"Word gets out," Cole smirked them slipping on his tunic, added, "Let's go."

Iain followed Cole through the muster room and up the winding wrought iron stairs that led to the CID suite.

"The DCI says to just go in," Iain said from behind him, but as Cole reached for the door handle it was opened by DS Tam Whelan who ignored Cole, but nodded to Iain as he passed them by.

Iain remained in the corridor as Cole entered the room where Colin Morton sat reading a sheet of paper and indicated that Cole take a seat.

Cole was confused for Harris was not present and apart from the DCI, the only other individual in the room was DI Irene Crichton who was seated in a corner.

"Can I ask what this is about, sir?" he directed his question to Morton before adding, "Is it about Ian Harris?"

Morton very deliberately placed the sheet of paper down onto his desk before he replied, "No, it's a separate issue, Sergeant Cole. Now, I understand your shift Inspector Mickey Kane is currently conducting a personnel review for the Divisional Commander that takes up a lot of his time causing him to work dayshift and so quite often the running of the shift is left to you? Is that correct?"

"Yes, sir," Cole's face flushed, a little uncertain where this was going, but saw an opportunity to project himself. "I'm happy to assume the responsibility and if I dare say, I do quite a good job."

"Indeed," Morton stared at him and arched his fingers. "Tell me, Sergeant Cole, are you aware of the Force Regulations prohibiting the use of a private vehicle for police purpose?"

Cole gulped and nodding, replied, "Yes, of course sir."

"And do *you* use your private vehicle for such police purposes?"

"No," he vigorously shook his head, "of course not, sir."

"So, if I were to suggest that you are not being truthful…"

"Look, sir, I don't know what Harris told you," he burst out, then stopped and trying to recover his composure, continued through gritted teeth, "I do not use my own vehicle for private purpose when I am on duty, *sir*!"

"Why would you think Constable Harris told me that?"

"Eh, well, he was up here and you spoke with him and he has a personal grudge against me because…" he stopped, realising that Morton was staring curiously at him, that he was running off at the mouth.

"So, you believe Constable Harris has disclosed something about you?"

His mind was working overtime as he thought fast, for this

definitely was not what he expected; being grilled by this old bastard about using his car.

"I can't think who might have told you that lie," he said, his mouth so dry he almost choked trying to swallow.

"Yet on the night that Constable Rudd was killed, you were out in your car that night too, were you not?"

So this is what it was about! Morton was trying to trick him, but before he could respond, Morton quickly said, "Tell me about your relationship with Lesley Rudd?"

In the corner, Irene sat perfectly still, hardly daring to breathe for she was aware that Coles response to that one and extremely important question would now determine how the interview would proceed.

"Relationship? What *fucking* relationship?" he snapped back and rose to his feet.

It was the answer they hoped for and Irene could feel her body tense.

"Sit down!" Morton barked at him, then again, calmer, "Sit…down, Sergeant Cole!"

Slowly, very slowly, Cole sat back down, his eyes boring into those of Morton's as the DCI calmly told him, "This is your one chance to tell me everything, Sergeant Cole."

His legs were shaking and he suddenly needed to piss, but could not avert his eyes from Morton's stare. His voice shaking, he said again, "I did *not* have a relationship with Lesley Rudd."

"You say you did not have a relationship with Lesley Rudd, but you visited her flat, didn't you?"

He could feel himself begin to grin for now he was on safe ground and shaking his head, slowly hissed, "With respect, Mister Morton, I know you're lying because I have never been *in* her fucking flat!"

Morton slowly smiled for he recognised in Cole's eyes that he was lying, then lifting the sheet of paper from his desk waved it like a trophy before he replied, "The fingerprint evidence says otherwise."

He stared at the paper held in Morton's hand and then slowly lowering his head, his shoulders slumped for he knew it was not a bluff and said in a voice that was almost a whisper, "I want a lawyer."
****

Just under two hours later, Sergeant James Cole was taken from Detective Chief Inspector Colin Morton's office to the uniform charge bar where in the presence of his lawyer and Detective Inspector Irene Crichton, Morton again formally cautioned Cole then charged him with the murder of Constable Lesley Rudd. An additional charge was libelled that on the same night he broke into the flat occupied by Constable Rudd for the purpose of stealing what he believed to be a written document of complaint against him.

The duty officer, Inspector Willie McCrae who was at that time completely sober, instructed that Cole be detained for appearance at the city's Sheriff Court the following Monday. While this was going on Detective Sergeant Jack Fleming and a corroborating detective officer attended at Cole's locker where Fleming, wearing Forensic gloves, removed Cole's aluminium bodied Kel-Lite torch that he placed into a paper bag. However, though Fleming was no Forensic expert he took the opportunity to closely examine the torch and grinned for he could see what looked like crusted blood on the exposed metal body of the torch where the black paint had worn away.

"Got ya, ya bastard," he muttered.
****

Colin Munro called the inquiry team together and after informing them of the arrest of Jimmy Cole, told them, "It's been a bit of a hectic morning, guys, and I know that during the course of the last week, you have all put in a lot of hours. Not that any of you intend claiming overtime of course," he added to good natured jeers, "but as it's Friday, I'm calling a halt to the inquiry for the day. So, get yourselves up the road and I'll see you all tomorrow at nine when I'll give you a full briefing of the events. However," his face was stern, "I trust that in the meantime none of you will discuss or disclose to any person outside the inquiry that we've locked up Cole for Lesley's murder."

He knew that was a faint hope for nobody gossiped like the polis and so with a wave, dismissed them. That done he raised a hand to beckon both Tam Whelan and Iain Meikle to him and said, "Don't be rushing away. I want you both to join us in my room. Irene and Mister Cruickshank are there and I think it's only fair you listen in when I give the boss the story about what happened."

Two more chairs were brought in and when everyone was seated, Colin Morton begun.

"First, before I begin, let me say that the interview with James Cole went a whole lot easier than I expected.' He glanced at Irene who nodding, added, "Cole desperately wanted to give us his side of the story so Colin and I believe that's why he was so keen to cooperate. Colin?"

"Thanks, Irene. Obviously what I'm about to relate is what Cole has admitted to, so added to what we know, Cole's story," he paused then raising his hands, said, "let me remind you, it's what *he's* saying, not what we believe to be true. According to him it seems that Constable Rudd had an infatuation with Cole and, he initially responded to her advances…"

He stopped when he saw Iain Meikle shaking his head and raising a hand, said, "I know what you're thinking, but remember, Iain, this is what Cole is telling *us*. Anyway, to continue. He alleges that Lesley demanded he leave his wife and children for her and when he refused she threatened to go public with their affair, told him that she would make an official complaint about his conduct and that she had already composed a letter to the ACC at Personnel. Last Saturday night, he deliberately put her out on a beat on her own because he intended speaking to her while she was alone to confront her about her intention to complain against him, but before he did so he used his own car to travel to her flat, broke in and searched for the letter that he claims he did not find. He used gloves while he was in the flat and that's why he was so confident that when I challenged him about being in the flat, he thought I was bluffing. However, you'll recall we know while he was there he removed a glove in the toilet to pee and of course that's where his fingerprint was discovered." He paused and glanced down at his notes before continuing. "Upset at being unable to find the supposed letter, he decided to meet with Rudd and used a phone box to make the anonymous call about a drunk lying in Middlesex Street and got there before Lesley arrived. He says he persuaded her that they need to talk and drove her to Mavisbank Quay where he knew there would be nobody about. Did he force her into the car? That he'll never admit to and we'll never really know. He says when they were at the Quay she got angry and got out of the car and then attacked him, but when he lifted his torch to defend himself he accidentally hit her on the head and she fell into the water. He said he panicked, dumped his car in Lorne Street and went walkabout to clear his head before he met with you, Iain," he turned towards him, "and your neighbour in Paisley Road West."

Tight-lipped, Iain's nod confirmed at least that part of Cole's story was true.

"What's your take on his story, Colin?" Cruickshank asked.

"Mostly baloney, sir. Cole thinks that by making Constable Rudd out to be some sort of scheming woman he'll justify what he did, but I believe the truth of the matter is that he is a sexual predator for if what Iain here tells us is true," he raised a had to forestall any protest, "and I have no reason to doubt it, Cole has made advances to other young women in the station so it's my intention to have Irene speak to all our female officers and obtain statements about Cole's previous conduct. I believe we will be able to obtain enough statements that grouped together will demonstrate a pattern of behaviour that we can show a court will refute his allegation that Rudd was the primary mover in the alleged relationship."

"You're talking about the Moorov Doctrine," Cruickshank said.

"Yes, sir, exactly." He drew a deep breath, then said, "Having discussed with Irene what Cole told us about Rudd's alleged letter, we are both of the opinion that the letter likely does not exist." Almost apologetically, he continued, "It's no great secret that we in the police view with suspicion or don't take kindly to any officer who makes an allegation against a brother officer and so we think rather than make an official complaint and thus be tarred as a…a…" he struggled for the word, but then Cruickshank suggested, "Bosses tout?"

"Maybe," Morton agreed. "We know that Rudd was very ambitious and probably thought that a complaint against a supervisory officer might blacken her career and figured threatening Cole with this fictitious letter might scare him off from harassing her without having to resort to an official complaint."

"And when he didn't find the letter, also decided it probably didn't exist and decided the only way to shut her up was to kill her?" Cruickshank suggested.

"Perhaps," Morton nodded, but his face reflected his doubt. "Perhaps?"

Morton turned to Irene who said, "When he took Lesley to Mavisbank Quay and contrary to what he told us, what we believe happened is he tried to dissuade her from making her complaint about his behaviour, but it's no secret that Lesley was a feisty young woman and probably wouldn't cooperate. We think an argument occurred and he lost his temper and struck her on the head with his metal handled torch. Did he intend to murder her? Did he intend that she fall into the water?" She pursed her lips and shook her head. "We'll never know, but having knocked her down did he decide to take the opportunity and *push* her body into the water? Again, we really don't know," she shrugged, "but hopefully the Laboratory will find her blood on his torch and if nothing else we can then prove that he is responsible for the wound on her head that in all probability caused her to *be* in the water where she drowned. I don't think Cole realises that when he admits he was there when she went into the water and that his conduct after the incident by making no attempt to save her or call for assistance, in itself indicates his complete disdain for her life. That conduct continued when having full knowledge of the circumstances regarding her disappearance, he continually to fail to notify us of her whereabouts and thus perverted the course of justice. Any jury hearing that must rightly assume it suited his purpose that she had to die."

"And all good evidence against him," muttered Cruickshank.

"The fingerprint evidence is of course irrefutable, so no problem there too," Morton reminded them.

"Well, Colin," Cruickshank rose to his feet, "you and Irene seem to have wrapped this up nicely, so if you excuse me Irene," he courteously nodded to her, "and gentlemen, I'll give the Chief Constable a phone and break the good news. Again," he nodded to them in turn, "well done to you all."

When he'd left the room, Colin Morton opened a bottom drawer in his desk and lifting out four glasses and a bottle of Glenfiddich, poured two fingers into each glass as he said, "Let's have a quiet toast to Lesley Rudd."

EPILOGUE

The media frenzy that erupted when an anonymous tip to the 'Glasgow News' crime desk that the murderer of Constable Lesley Rudd was in fact her colleague and fellow officer, Sergeant James Cole, lasted a full three days. While it was suspected the tip-off came from someone within Govan police office, the source was never discovered.

****

At his trial, James Cole's defence team tendered a plea of Culpable Homicide admitting that though Cole did assault Lesley Rudd, he did not intend for her to fall into the River Clyde whereby she drowned.

However, the Crown rejected Cole's plea and argued that whether or not Cole intended killing Rudd, he did admit to assaulting her. That and his later actions of ignoring her predicament and failing to render or call for assistance indicated a clear disregard for her safety and wellbeing and thus was convicted of her murder.

Sentenced to life imprisonment, Cole was told he must serve at least twenty years before being considered for release.

****

Contrary to the threat made to Billy Madison's wife by the London based gangster known as The Jamaican, no harm befell Sheila Madison. However, early on Sunday morning, the day after payment was due for the shipment of heroin, Madison was abducted from his home by three large and balaclava masked men who despite his screaming wife's protests, bundled the struggling and terrified Madison into a van parked outside the house.

Upon the arrival twenty minutes later of a posse of Merseyside's finest, the distraught and hysterical Sheila was unable to describe the men and could only tell the officers that the van was white in colour.

To date, no trace of Madison has been discovered and it is widely assumed by both the police and customers of the drug dealer known as the Jamaican, that Madison was murdered and his body disposed of.

****

The body of Derek Stokoe, widely known in his native Liverpool as Doughnut, was finally released by the Crown Office to the City of Glasgow Bereavement Services who arranged for the remains to be cremated at the city's Linn Crematorium.

There were no mourners at the five-minute ceremony.

Stokoe's killer, Martin Boyle, pled not guilty but following a three-day trial was convicted of his murder and sentenced to life imprisonment.

During his trial, Boyle repeatedly refused to give evidence on his own behalf and steadfastly refused to admit any knowledge of the seized heroin. However, on this occasion, silence is not golden and he was duly convicted on all the drug related charges and sentenced to six years to run concurrently with the life imprisonment.

After sentencing and to his dismay, Boyle was escorted from the High Court at the Saltmarket to his new home at HMP Barlinnie where his nemesis, Angus 'Slasher' McKenna, eagerly awaited his arrival.

****

Assistant Chief Constable (Crime) Martin Kerr was the successful candidate for the position of Deputy Chief Constable of the North Yorkshire Police. His promoted replacement, Detective Chief Superintendent Alistair Cruickshank, was a popular appointment.

****

Charles Gallagher denied any knowledge of the seized heroin and due to the lack of evidence implicating him in the procurement, Crown Office decided not to proceed with any drug related charges.

However, the anonymous letter that was later proved to have upon it the fingerprints of the convicted felon Seamus O'Neill, Forensic evidence from the flat and the witness evidence given by the former pig farm owner, Philip Smith, was deemed by Gallagher's defence team sufficient to convict him of the murder of Paula Menzies.

Acting on their advice, he pled guilty and was sentenced to life imprisonment in the cold and bleak HMP Peterhead.

His former associate Philip 'Smudger' Smith was convicted of a number of charges relating to the disposal of human remains and during several subsequent trials provided evidence against a number of notable gangsters. For his own safety, Smith was placed in solitary confinement; however, his addiction to alcohol proved to be his undoing for seven months into his six-year sentence, Smith succumbed to liver failure and died.

****

Though still sought for interview by Strathclyde Police, Seamus O'Neill, now known as Patrick Daly, continues to evade arrest on the island of Majorca where he is the successful owner of a small bar in the seaside town of Cala Bona. The bar is much frequented by local officers of the Policía Local de Son Servera who are friendly with the likeable and very generous Scotsman and unwittingly keep him informed of any contact they occasionally have with the Scottish police.

****

The week following the breakup of the relationship between Paul 'Sharkie' Fisher and his former girlfriend, Constable Janie Wallace, Fisher was transferred from Partick Thistle to Nottingham Forest for six-hundred-thousand pounds. However, within three months of signing for Forest and following several side-lining injuries, Fisher's form deteriorated and after being dropped to the reserve team, was released seven months later without contract.

Janie Wallace was appointed to the Giffnock CID where she continues to serve as a Detective Constable.

****

DCI Colin Morton recognised that Iain Meikle would be a valuable asset to the CID and invited him to make a formal application to join the Department. After much thought, Iain decided he enjoyed life as a beat constable and declining, returned to his uniform shift.

Irene Crichton was much more ambitious and three months after the conviction of the former police Sergeant James Cole for the murder of Constable Lesley Rudd, Irene was promoted to uniform Chief Inspector at Shettleston Police Office; however, she has made it known that she is keen to re-join the CID and eagerly awaits a DCI vacancy.

The relationship between Irene and Iain continued to flourish and six months after their initial date at the Paisley Road West curry restaurant, Iain put his house up for sale and moved in with Irene.

True to her promise Irene introduced her new fiancé to Irene's lawyer friend and with the full support and evidence provided by his former mother-in-law Jill, negotiations are ongoing to award full custody of James Meikle to his father.
****

The funeral service of Constable Lesley Rudd was held within St Brides Roman Catholic Church in East Kilbride and attended by a record number of officers with representatives from all of the Scottish Police Forces and several of the major English Forces too.

Members of her shift were a little startled to see Lesley's identical twin sister Ellen who attended the ceremony with her husband Jacob and their children and who were greeted at the entrance doors by the Strathclyde Police Chief Constable and a large number of senior officers.

The eulogy was delivered by her shift Inspector, Michal Kane, and her coffin borne by six of her colleagues that included Iain Meikle and Eric Little. Following the moving ceremony, Lesley was laid her to rest beside her parents in the Philipshill Cemetery in East Kilbride.
****

On a bright and sunny August morning and almost full year after she struck old Sam Fullerton on the head with a bottle, the naked body of Elsie McClure, who had been prostituting herself the previous evening, was discovered in a garbage littered St Vincent Lane. Like two young female prostitutes in the preceding month, McClure had been beaten, raped then strangled.

The hunt for the women's killer continues.

****

Thank you for your support in reading this book.

Needless to say, this story is a work of fiction and none of the characters represent any living or deceased individual.

As readers of my previous books may already know, I am an amateur writer and self-publish on Amazon as well as also self-editing, therefore I apologise for and accept that all grammar and punctuation errors are mine alone.

I hope that any such errors do not detract from the story.

If you have enjoyed the story, you may wish to visit my website at:

www.glasgowcrimefiction.co.uk

I also welcome feedback and can be contacted at:

george.donald.books@hotmail.co.uk

Kind regards,

George Donald

33147373R00241

Printed in Great Britain
by Amazon